nce

Written by **Minh Lê**

Drawn by **Andie Tong**

Colored by **Sarah Stern** (pages 1-46, 48-59)

and **Carrie Strachan** (pages 47, 60-119)

Lettered by **Saida Temofonte**

JIM CHADWICK	Editor
COURTNEY JORDAN	Associate Editor
STEVE COOK	Design Director – Books
AMIE BROCKWAY-METCALF	Publication Design
TIFFANY HUANG	Publication Production
MARIE JAVINS	Editor-in-Chief, DC Comics
ANNE DePIES	Senior VP – General Manager
JIM LEE	Publisher & Chief Creative Officer
DON FALLETTI	VP – Manufacturing Operations & Workflow Management
LAWRENCE GANEM	VP – Talent Services
ALISON GILL	Senior VP – Manufacturing & Operations
JEFFREY KAUFMAN	VP – Editorial Strategy & Programming
NICK J. NAPOLITANO	VP – Manufacturing Administration & Design
NANCY SPEARS	VP – Revenue

GREEN LANTERN: ALLIANCE

DC Comics, 100 S. California Street, Burbank, CA 91505
Printed by Worzalla, Stevens Point, WI, USA. 9/9/22.
First Printing.
ISBN: 978-1-77950-380-0

Library of Congress Cataloging-in-Publication Data

Names: Lê, Minh, 1979- author. | Tong, Andie, illustrator. | Stern, Sarah (Colorist), colorist. | Strachan, Carrie, colorist. | Temofonte, Saida, letterer.
Title: Green Lantern : alliance / written by Minh Le ; drawn by Andie Tong ; colored by Sarah Stern and Carrie Strachan ; lettered by Saida Temofonte.
Other titles: Alliance
Description: Burbank, CA : DC Comics, [2022] | Audience: Ages 8-12 | Audience: Grades 4-6 | Summary: Tai Pham struggles with balancing school, his work in the family business, his friendships, and his new Green Lantern responsibilities, but Kid Flash arrives on the scene to become the super-hero partner Tai just might need.
Identifiers: LCCN 2022031069 | ISBN 9781779503800 (trade paperback)
Subjects: CYAC: Graphic novels. | Superheroes--Fiction. | Ability--Fiction. | Friendship--Fiction. | LCGFT: Superhero comics. | Graphic novels.
Classification: LCC PZ7.7.L398 Gn 2022 | DDC 741.5/973--dc23/eng/20220711
LC record available at https://lccn.loc.gov/2022031069

FSC www.fsc.org MIX Paper from responsible sources FSC® C002589

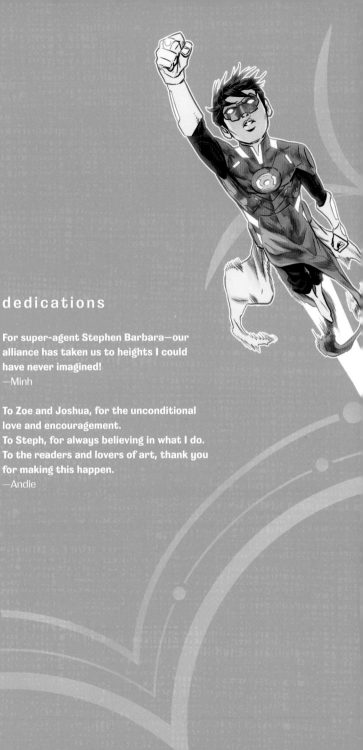

dedications

For super-agent Stephen Barbara—our
alliance has taken us to heights I could
have never imagined!
—Minh

To Zoe and Joshua, for the unconditional
love and encouragement.
To Steph, for always believing in what I do.
To the readers and lovers of art, thank you
for making this happen.
—Andie

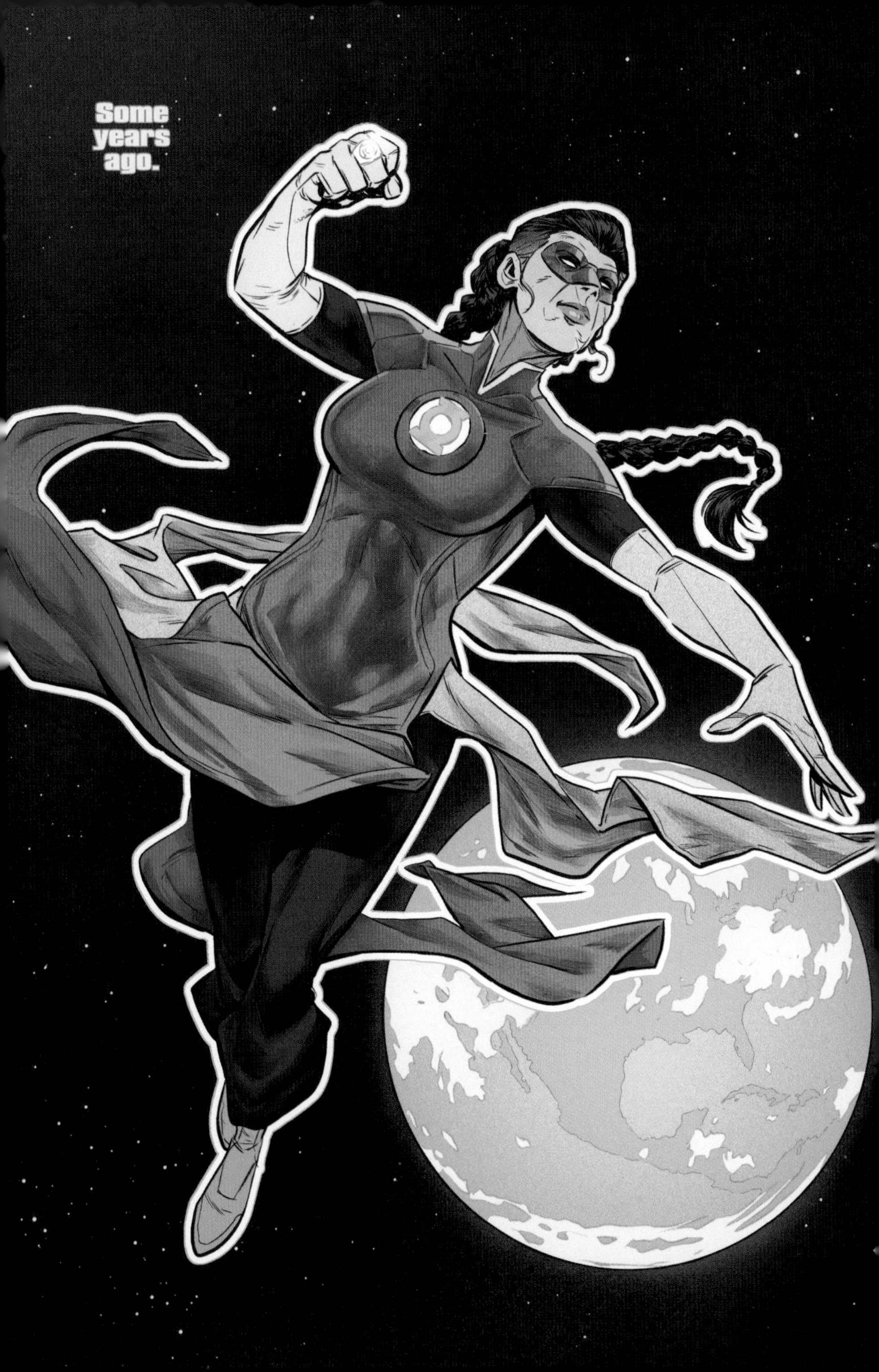
Some years ago.

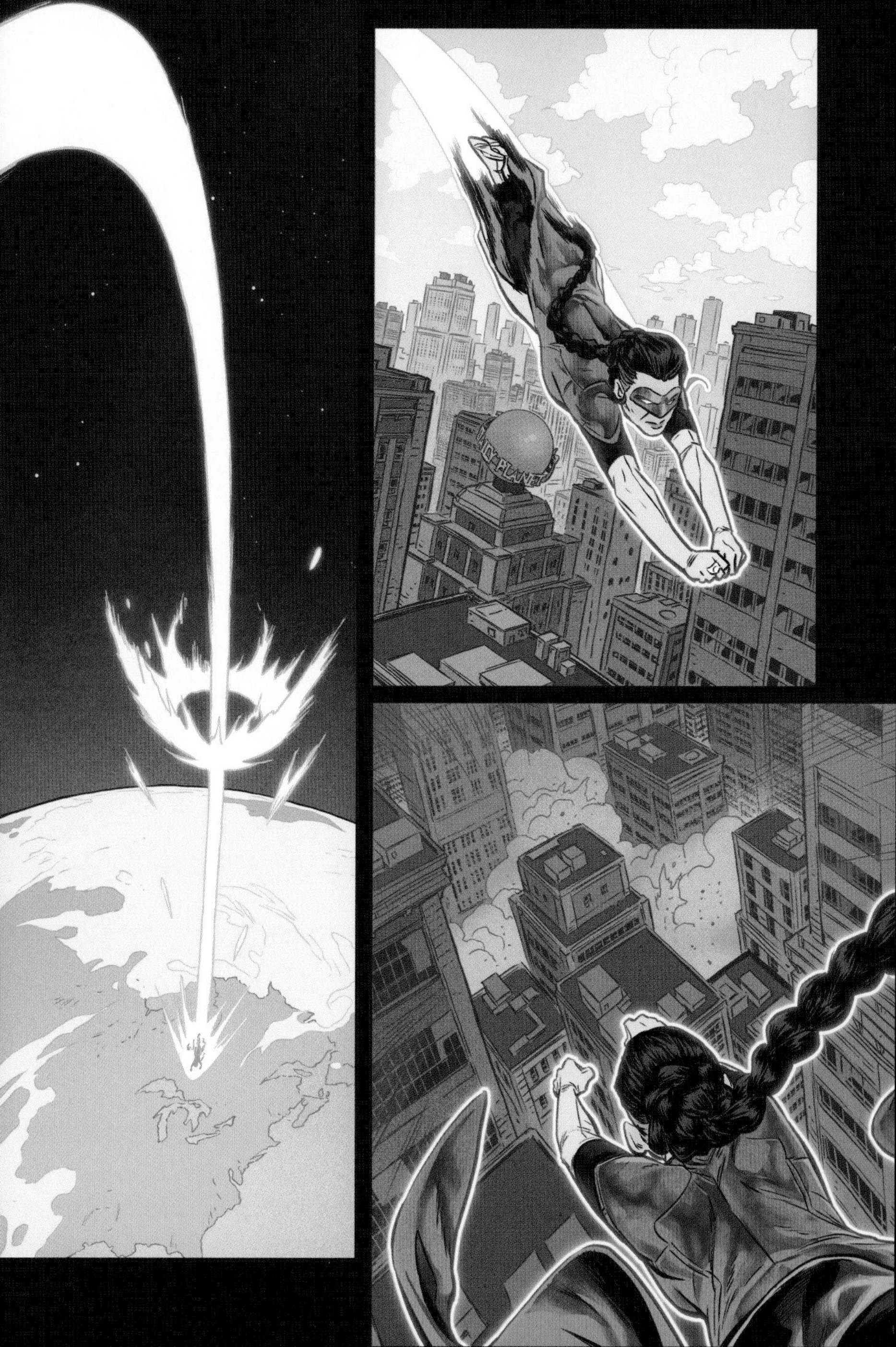
PLANET

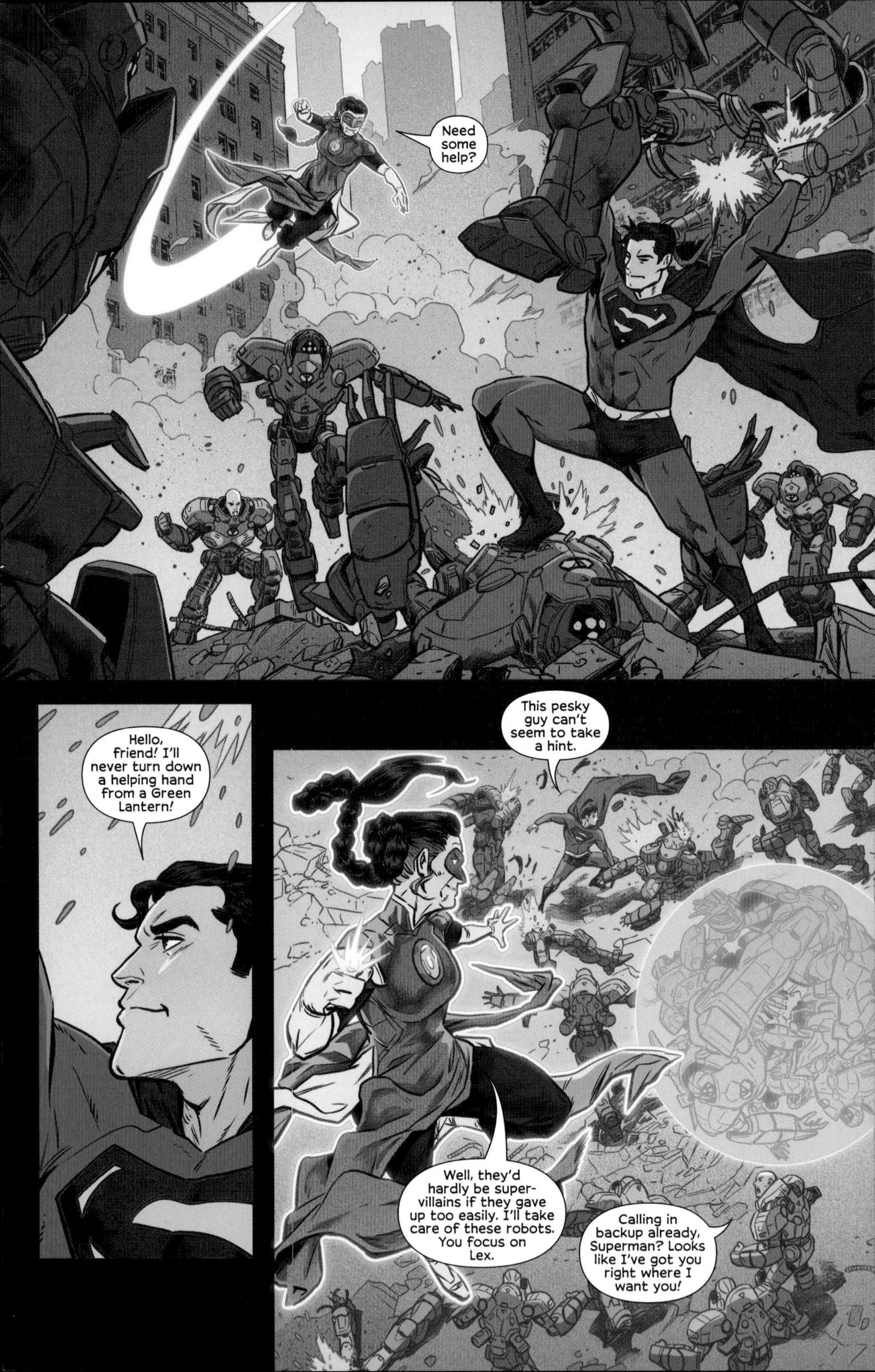
Need some help?
Hello, friend! I'll never turn down a helping hand from a Green Lantern!
This pesky guy can't seem to take a hint.
Well, they'd hardly be super-villains if they gave up too easily. I'll take care of these robots. You focus on Lex.
Calling in backup already, Superman? Looks like I've got you right where I want you!

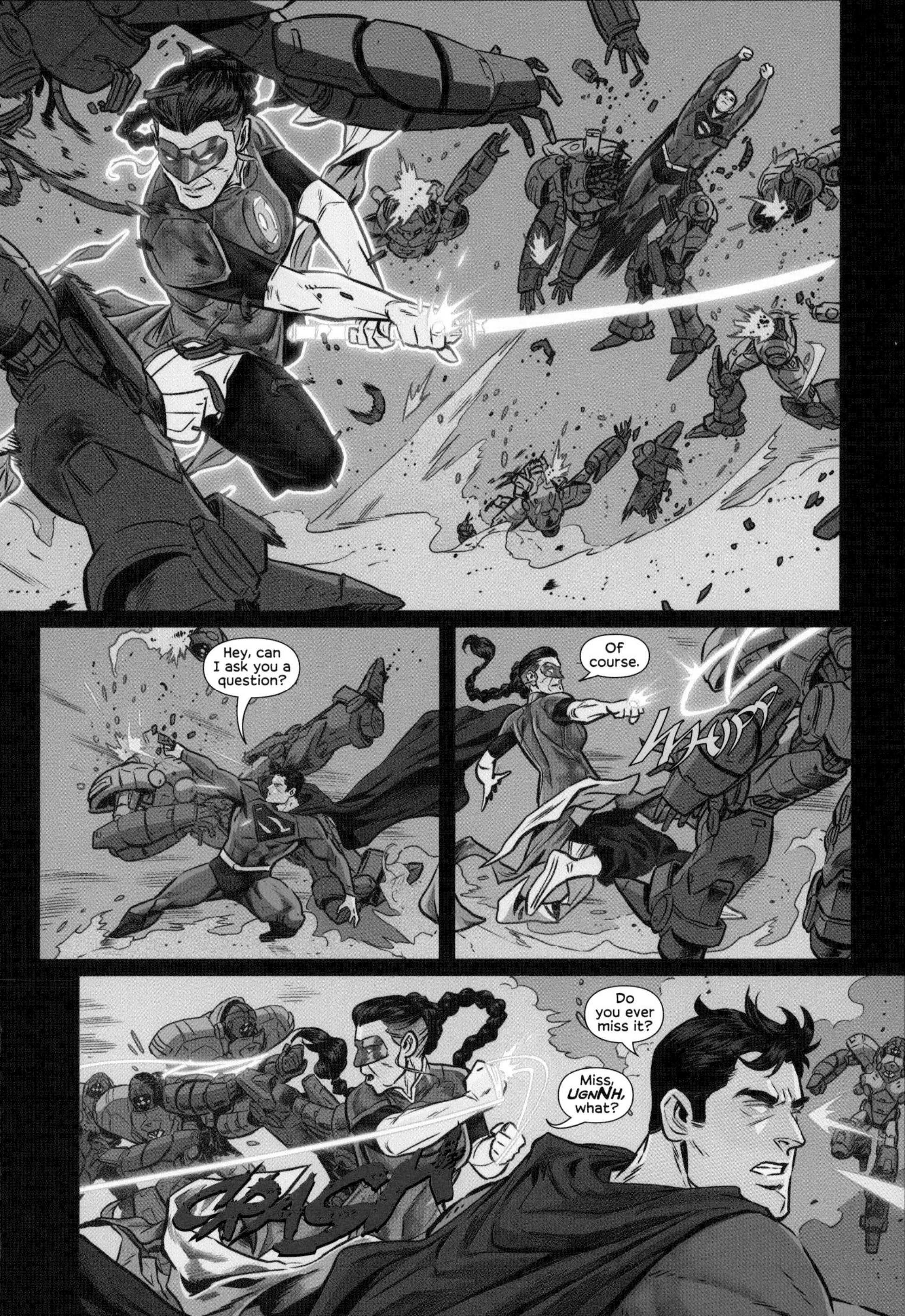
Hey, can I ask you a question?
Of course.
Do you ever miss it?
Miss, UGNNH, what?

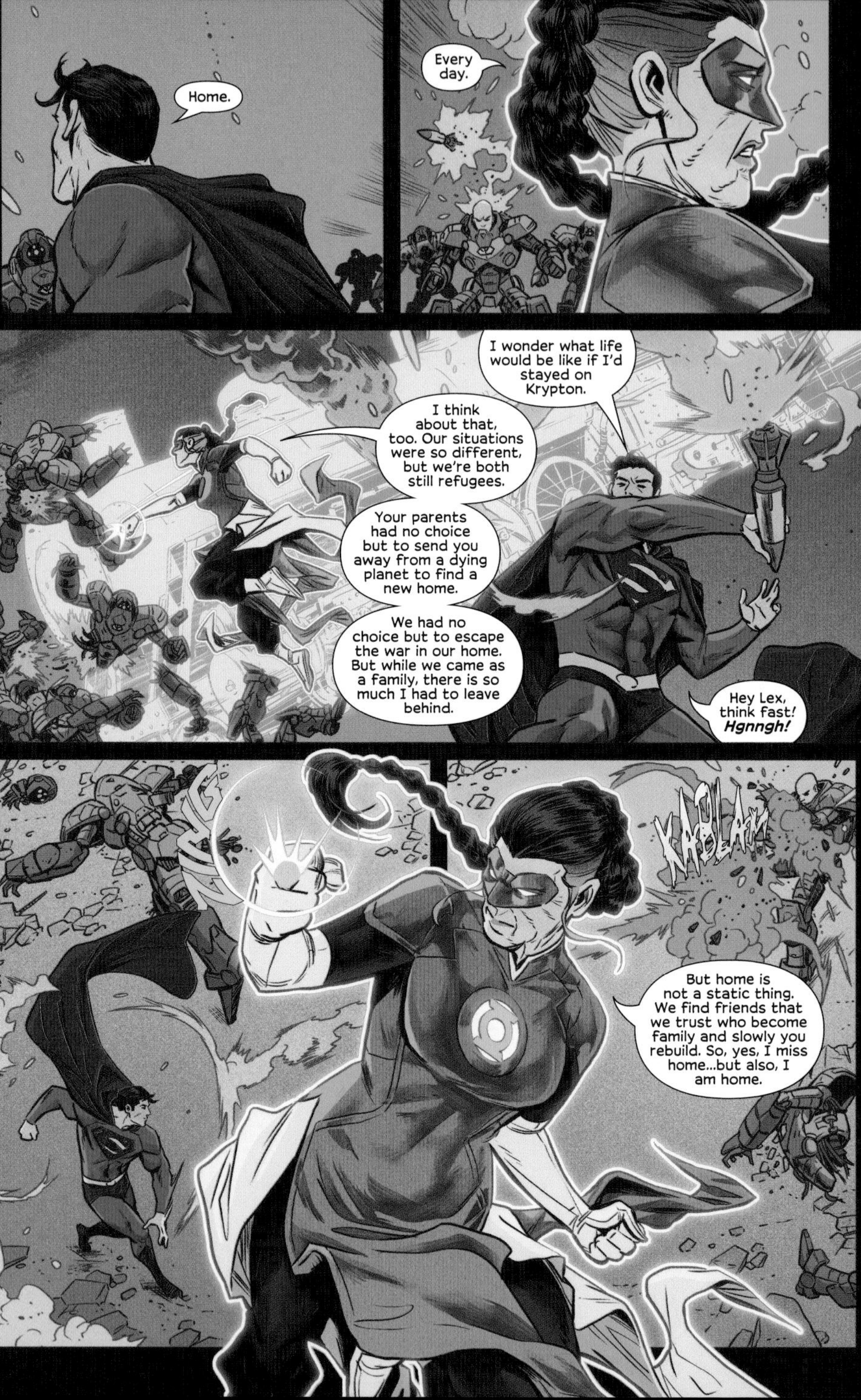
Home.
Every day.
I wonder what life would be like if I'd stayed on Krypton.
I think about that, too. Our situations were so different, but we're both still refugees.
Your parents had no choice but to send you away from a dying planet to find a new home.
We had no choice but to escape the war in our home. But while we came as a family, there is so much I had to leave behind.
Hey Lex, think fast! ***Hgnngh!***
KABLAM
But home is not a static thing. We find friends that we trust who become family and slowly you rebuild. So, yes, I miss home...but also, I am home.

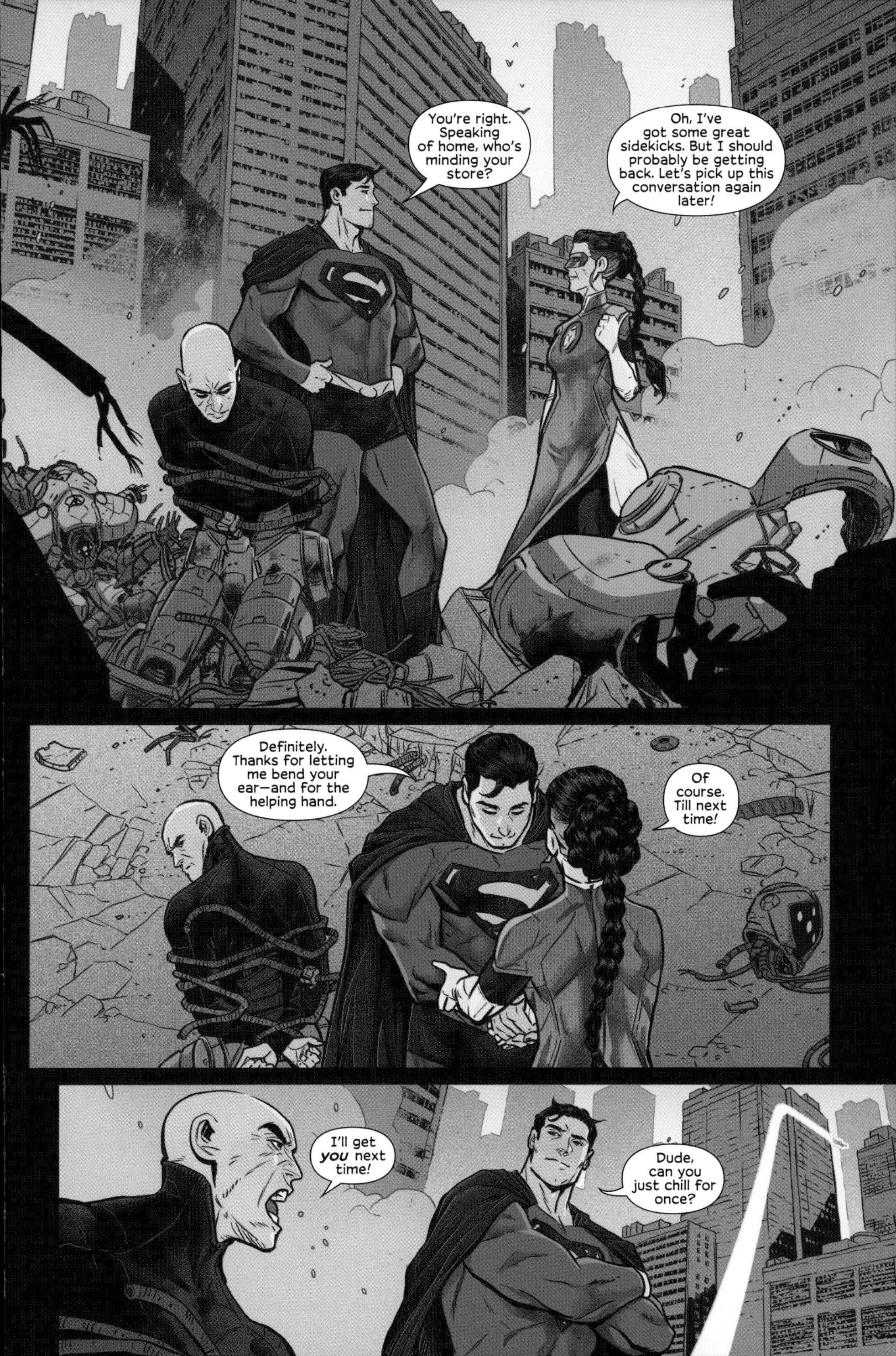
You're right. Speaking of home, who's minding your store?
Oh, I've got some great sidekicks. But I should probably be getting back. Let's pick up this conversation again later!
Definitely. Thanks for letting me bend your ear—and for the helping hand.
Of course. Till next time!
I'll get *you* next time!
Dude, can you just chill for once?

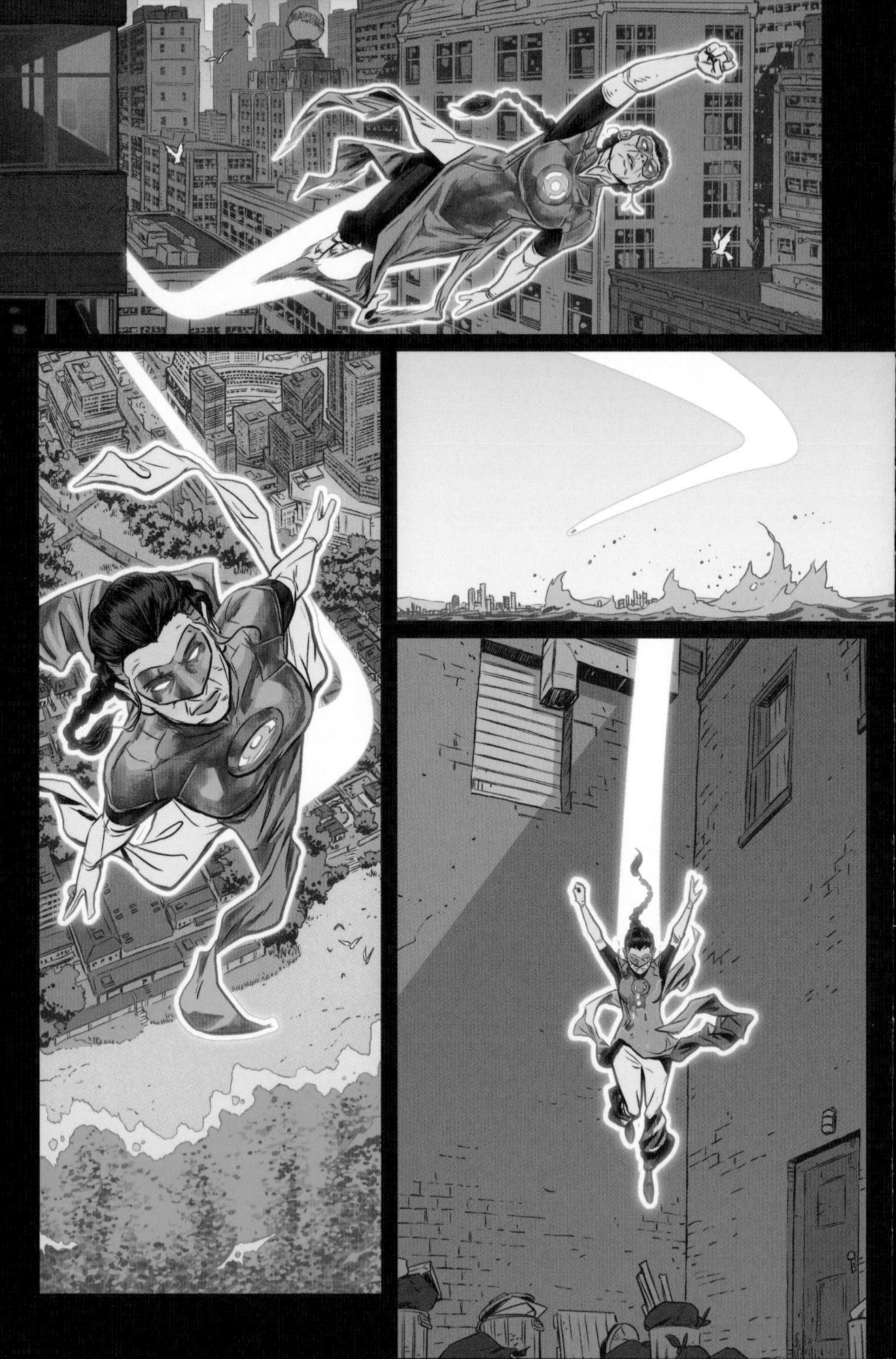

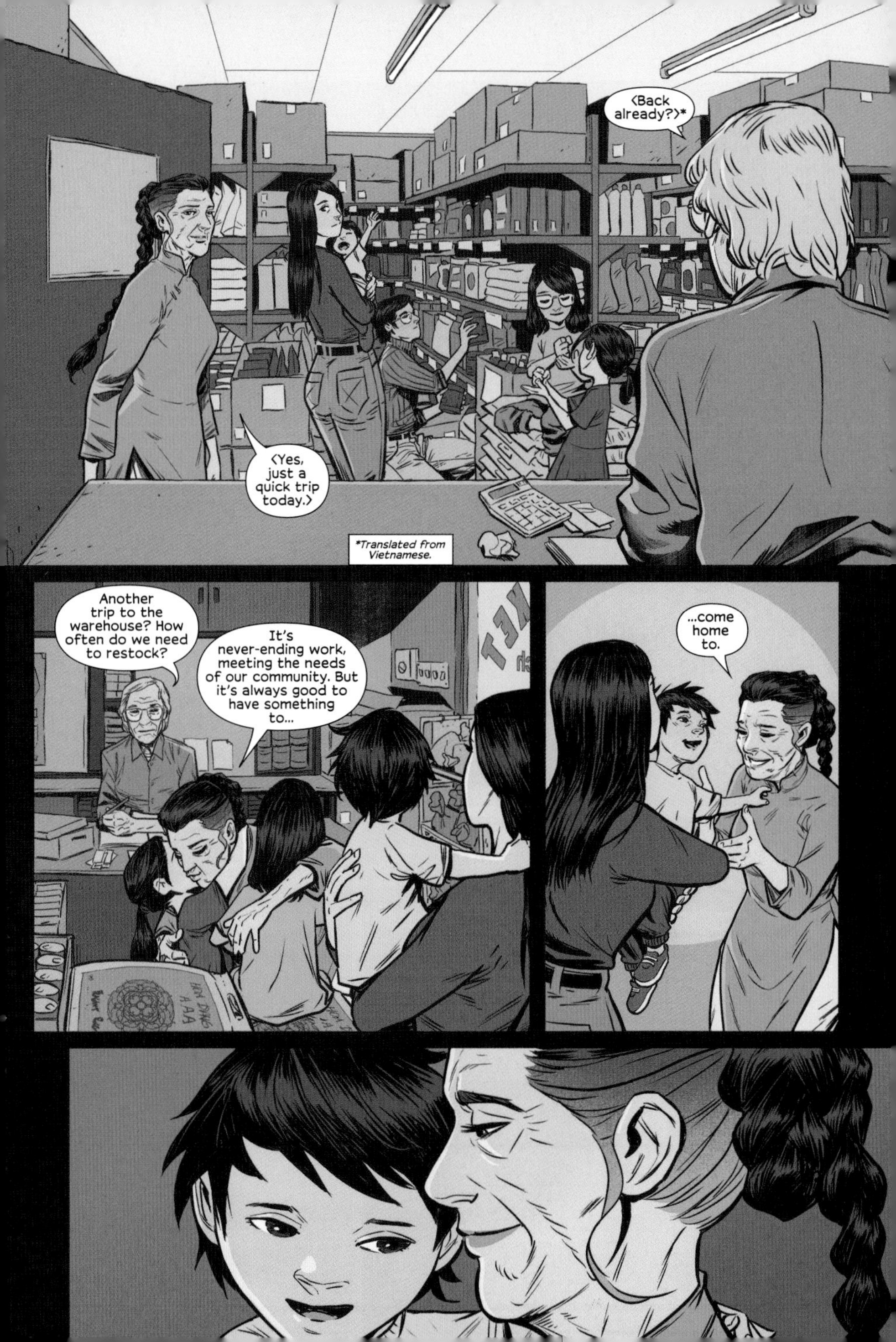
⟨Back already?⟩*
⟨Yes, just a quick trip today.⟩
*Translated from Vietnamese.
Another trip to the warehouse? How often do we need to restock?
It's never-ending work, meeting the needs of our community. But it's always good to have something to...
...come home to.

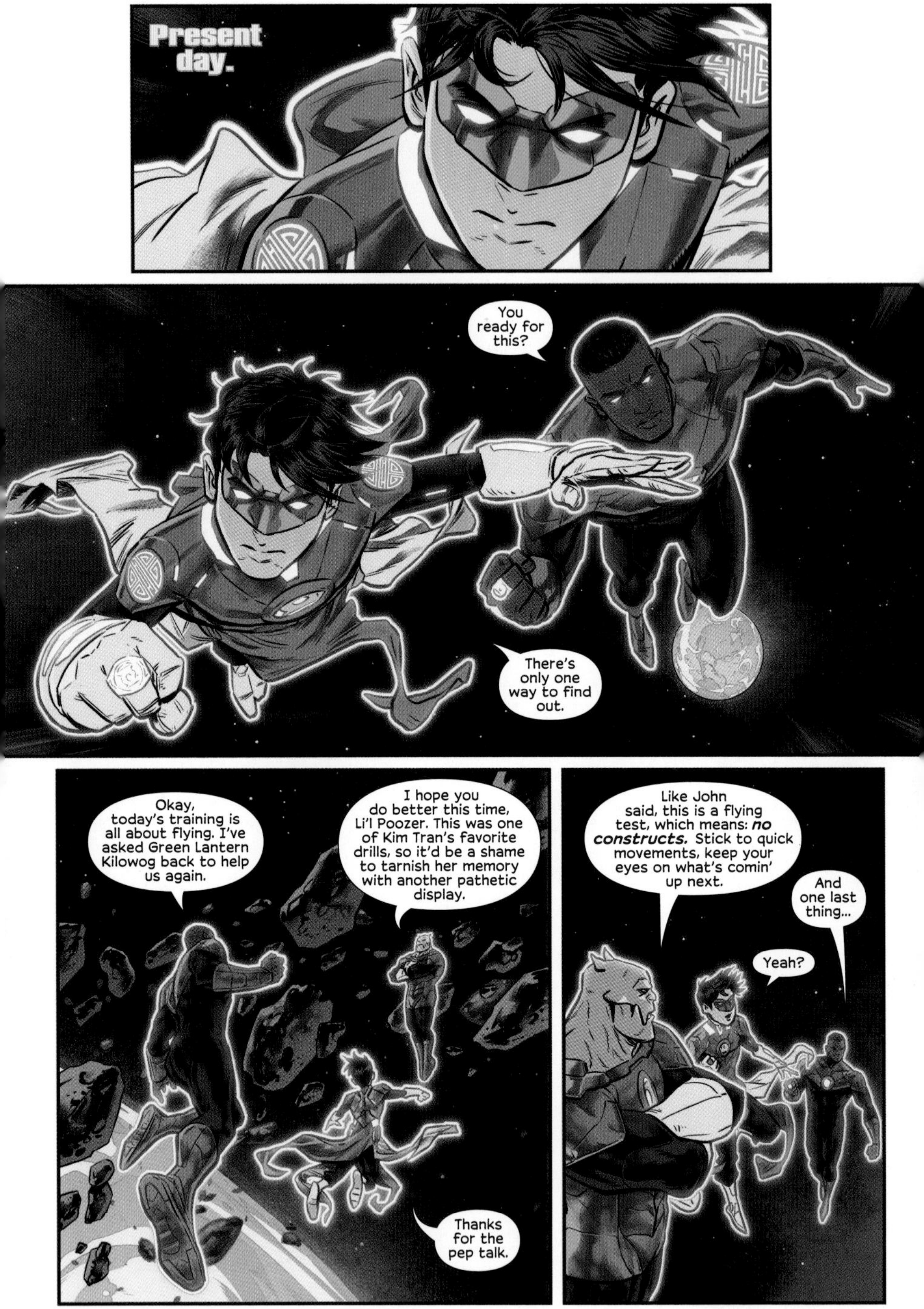
Present day.
You ready for this?
There's only one way to find out.
Okay, today's training is all about flying. I've asked Green Lantern Kilowog back to help us again.
I hope you do better this time, Li'l Poozer. This was one of Kim Tran's favorite drills, so it'd be a shame to tarnish her memory with another pathetic display.
Thanks for the pep talk.
Like John said, this is a flying test, which means: ***no constructs.*** Stick to quick movements, keep your eyes on what's comin' up next.
And one last thing...
Yeah?

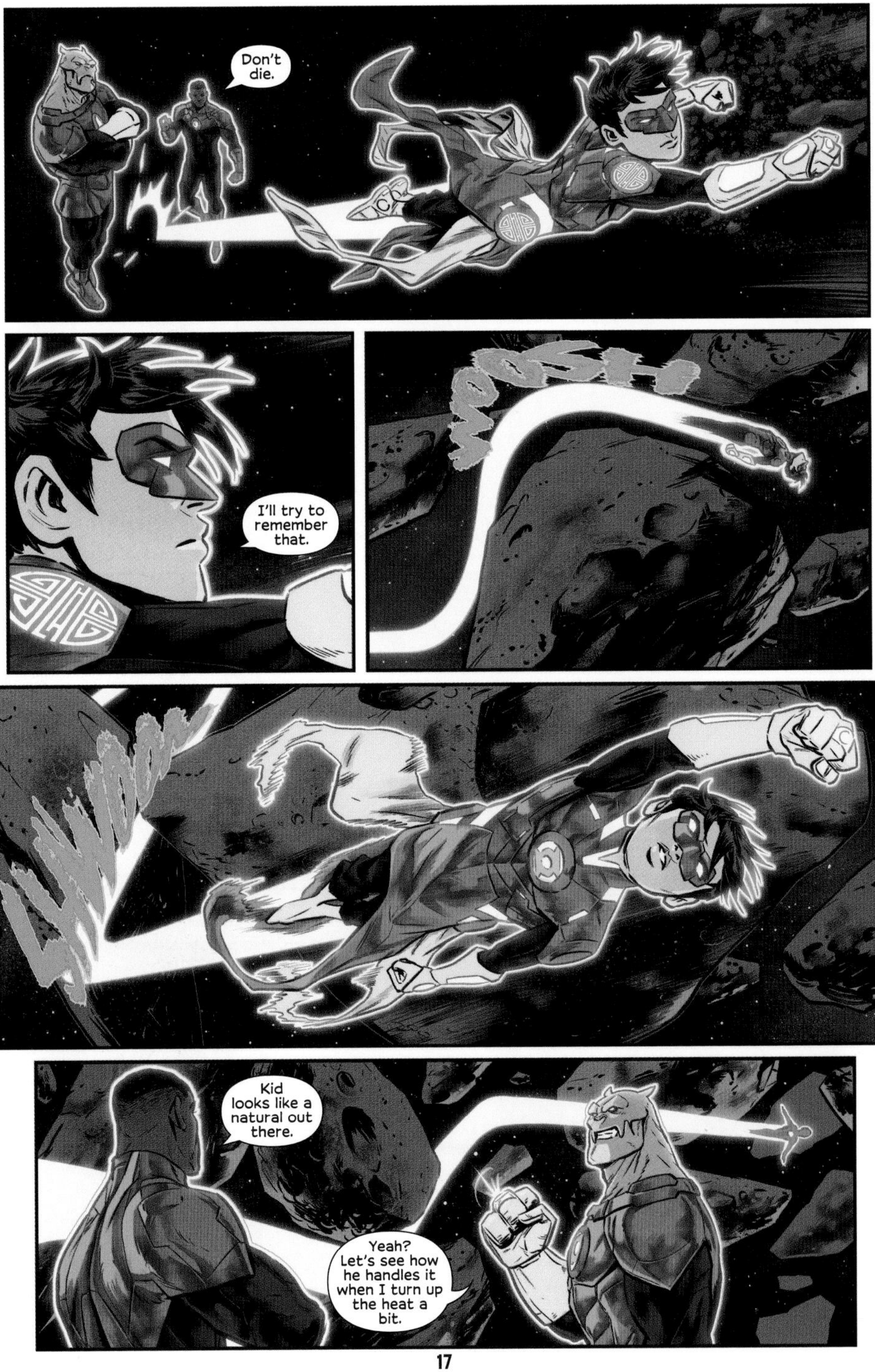
Don't die.
I'll try to remember that.
Kid looks like a natural out there.
Yeah? Let's see how he handles it when I turn up the heat a bit.

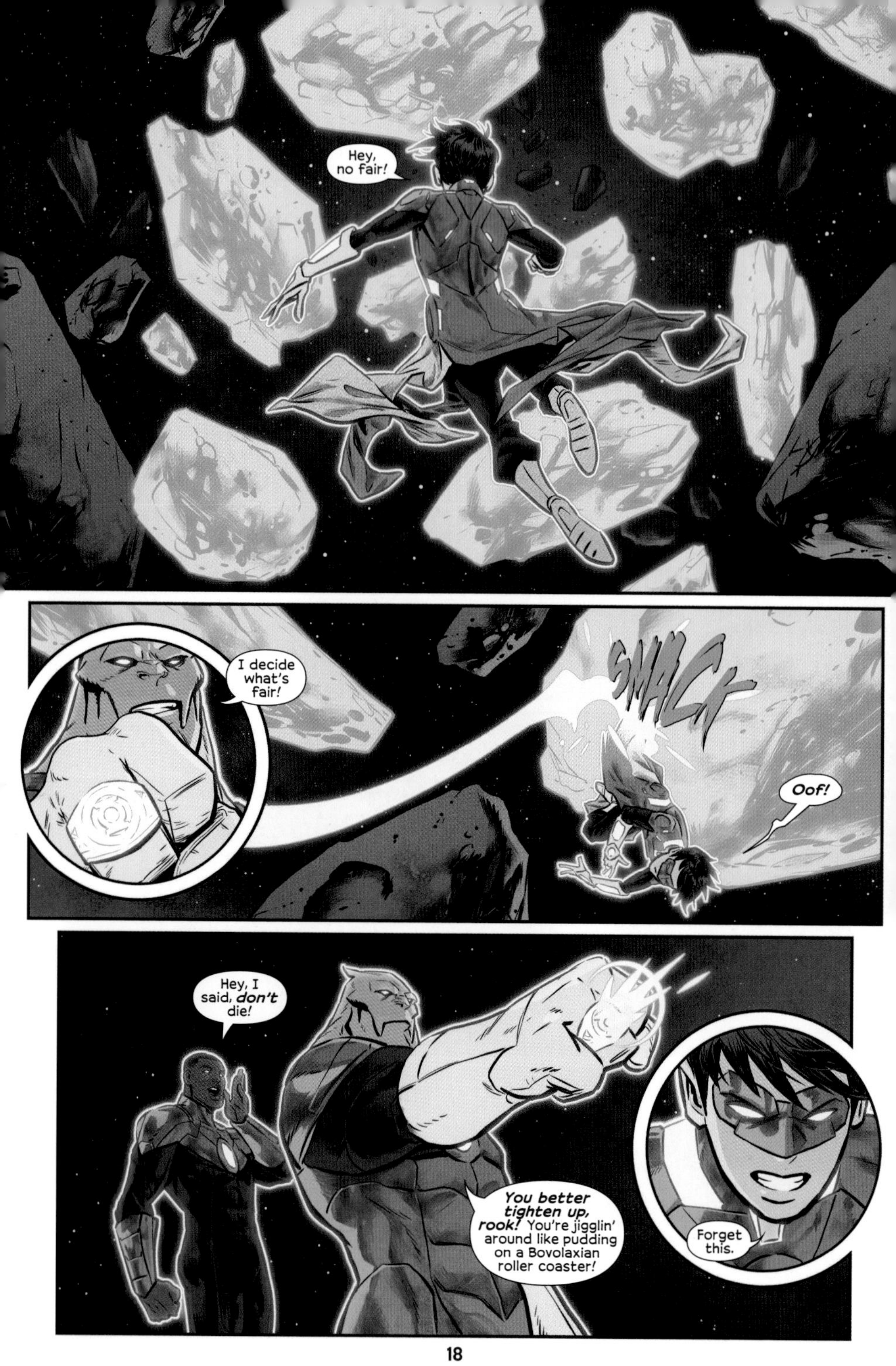
Hey, no fair!
I decide what's fair!
SMACK
Oof!
Hey, I said, ***don't*** die!
You better tighten up, rook! You're jigglin' around like pudding on a Bovolaxian roller coaster!
Forget this.

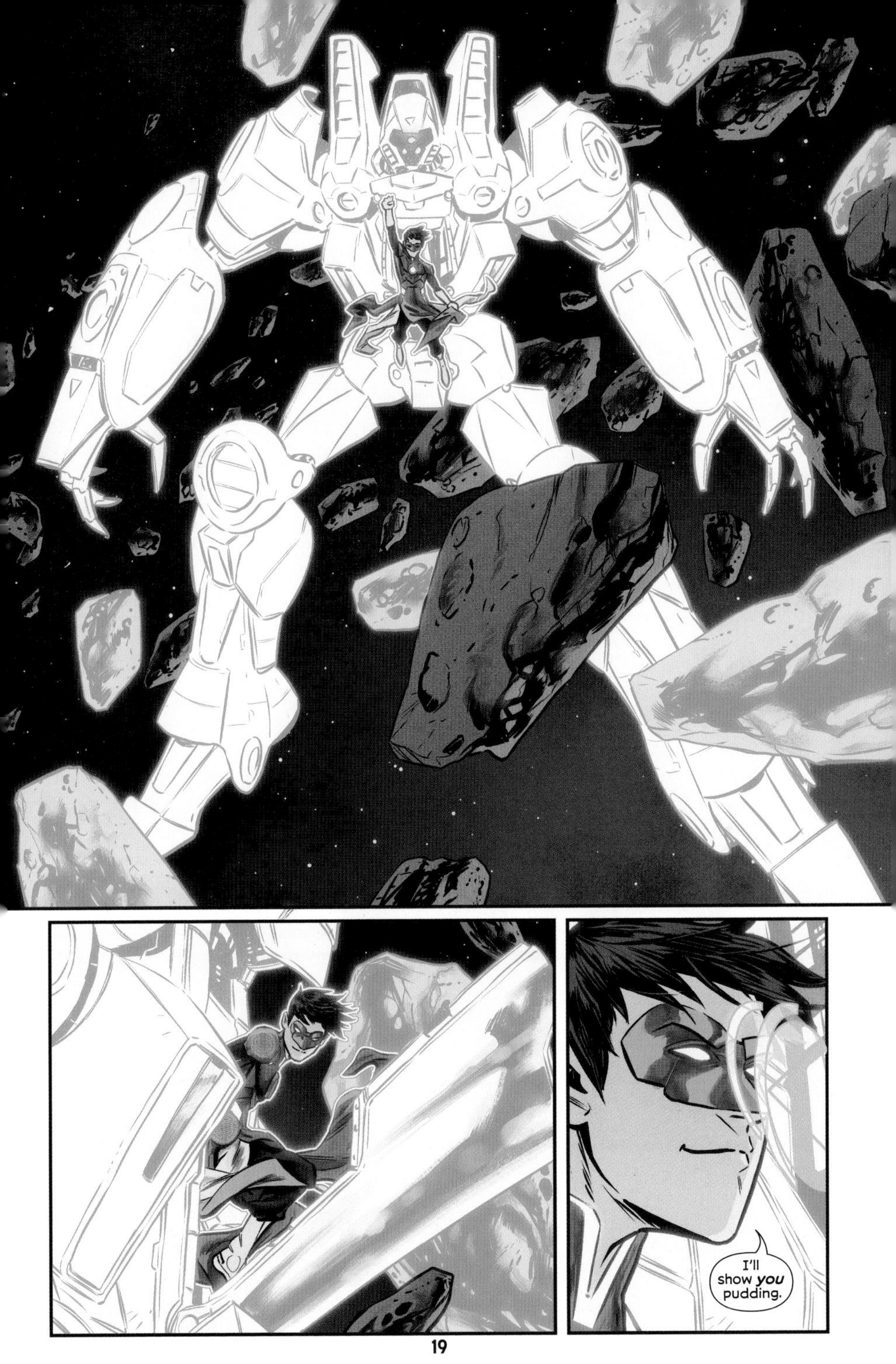
I'll show *you* pudding.

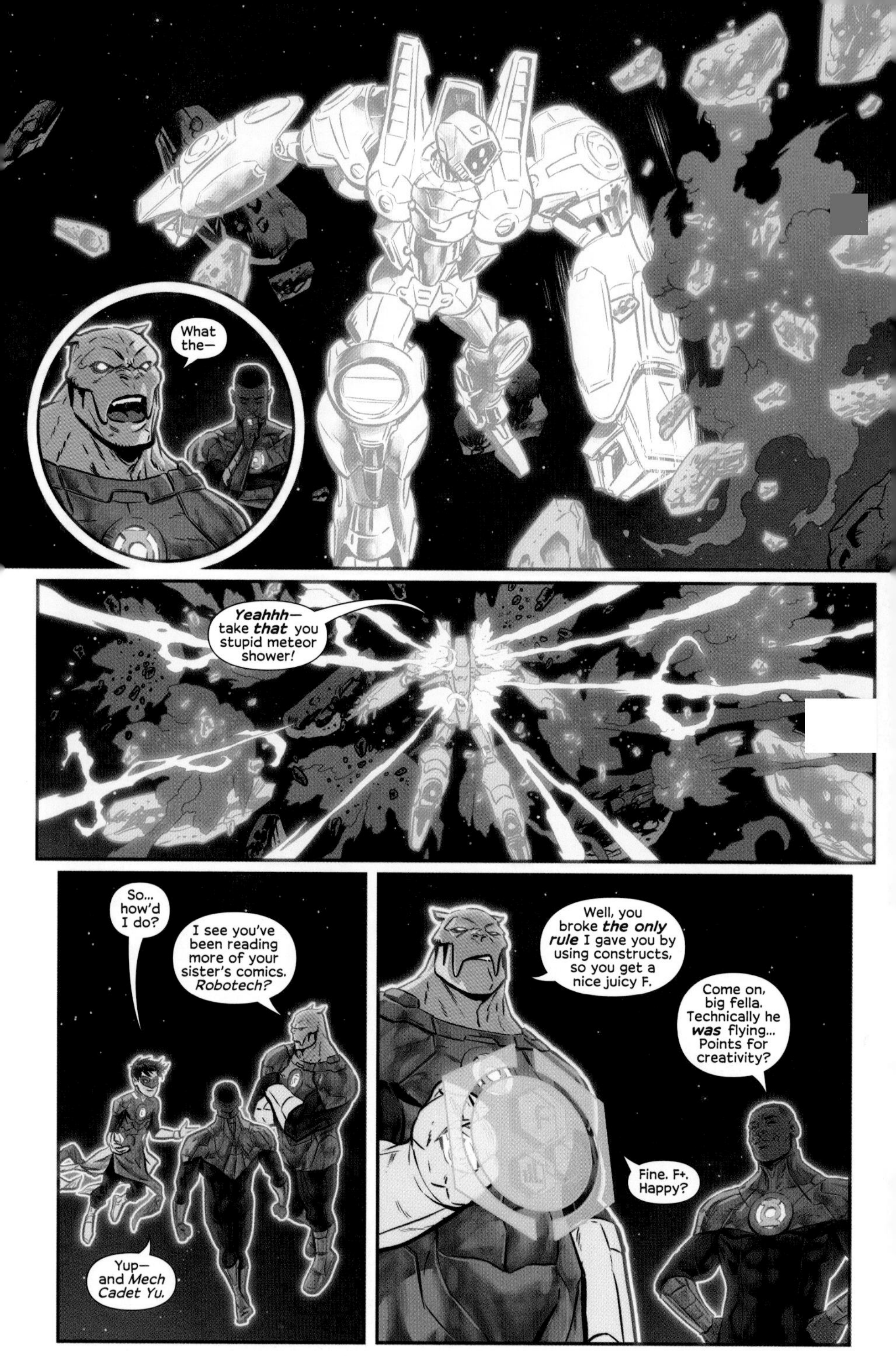
What the—
Yeahhh— take ***that*** you stupid meteor shower!
So... how'd I do?
I see you've been reading more of your sister's comics. *Robotech?*
Yup— and *Mech Cadet Yu.*
Well, you broke ***the only rule*** I gave you by using constructs, so you get a nice juicy F.
Come on, big fella. Technically he ***was*** flying... Points for creativity?
Fine. F+. Happy?

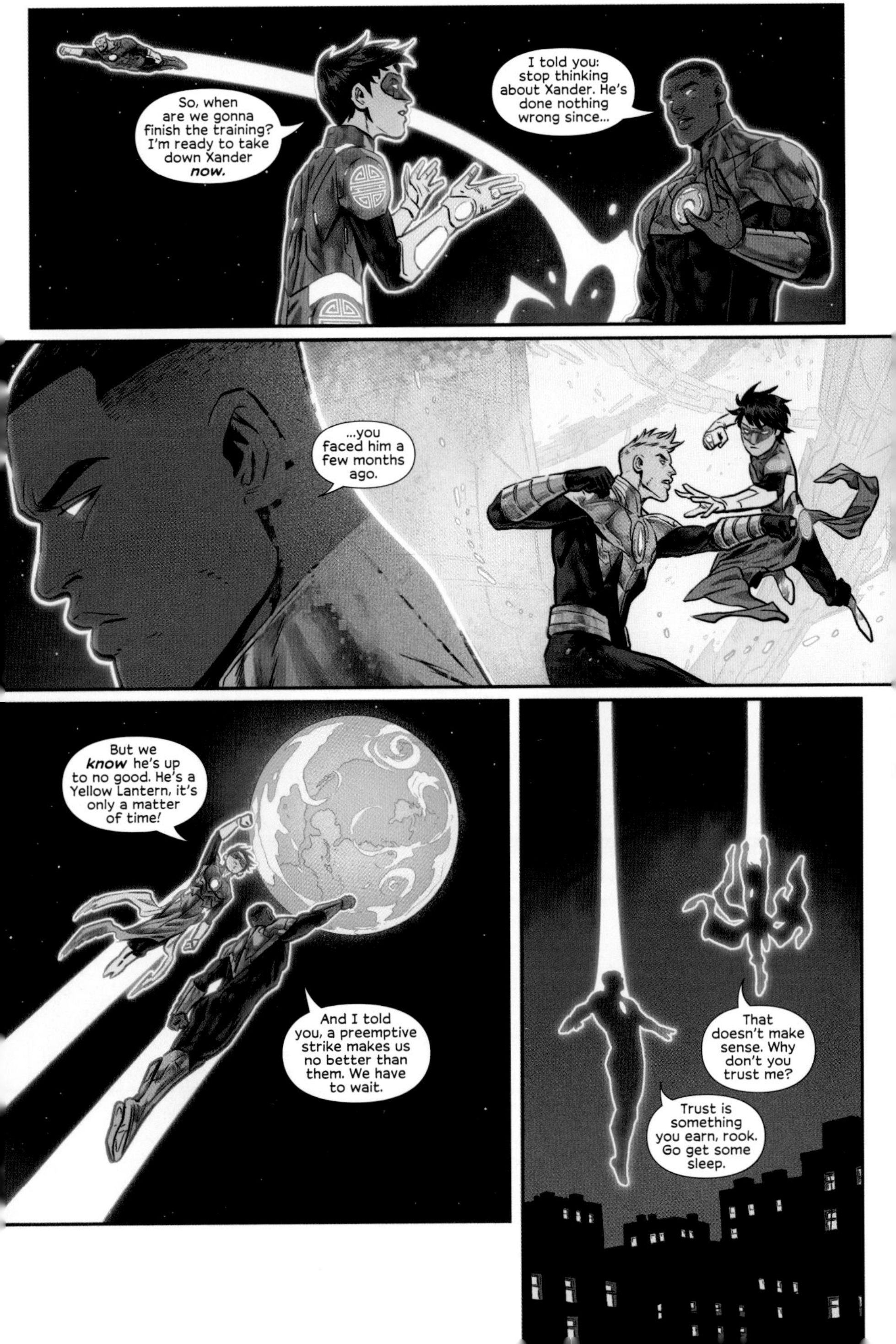
So, when are we gonna finish the training? I'm ready to take down Xander *now.*
I told you: stop thinking about Xander. He's done nothing wrong since...
...you faced him a few months ago.
But we *know* he's up to no good. He's a Yellow Lantern, it's only a matter of time!
And I told you, a preemptive strike makes us no better than them. We have to wait.
That doesn't make sense. Why don't you trust me?
Trust is something you earn, rook. Go get some sleep.

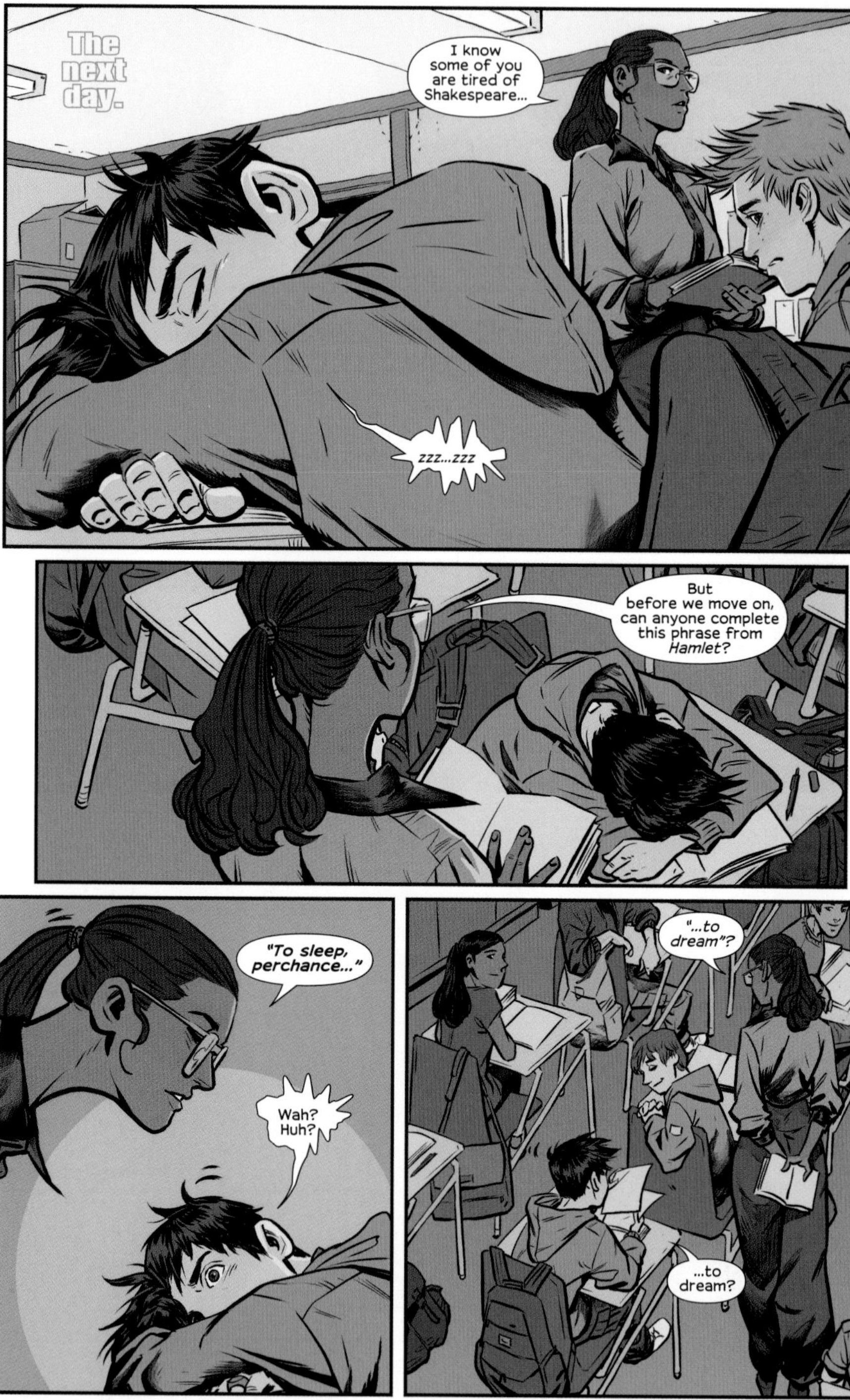
The next day.
I know some of you are tired of Shakespeare...
zzz...zzz
But before we move on, can anyone complete this phrase from *Hamlet*?
"To sleep, perchance..."
Wah? Huh?
"...to dream"?
...to dream?

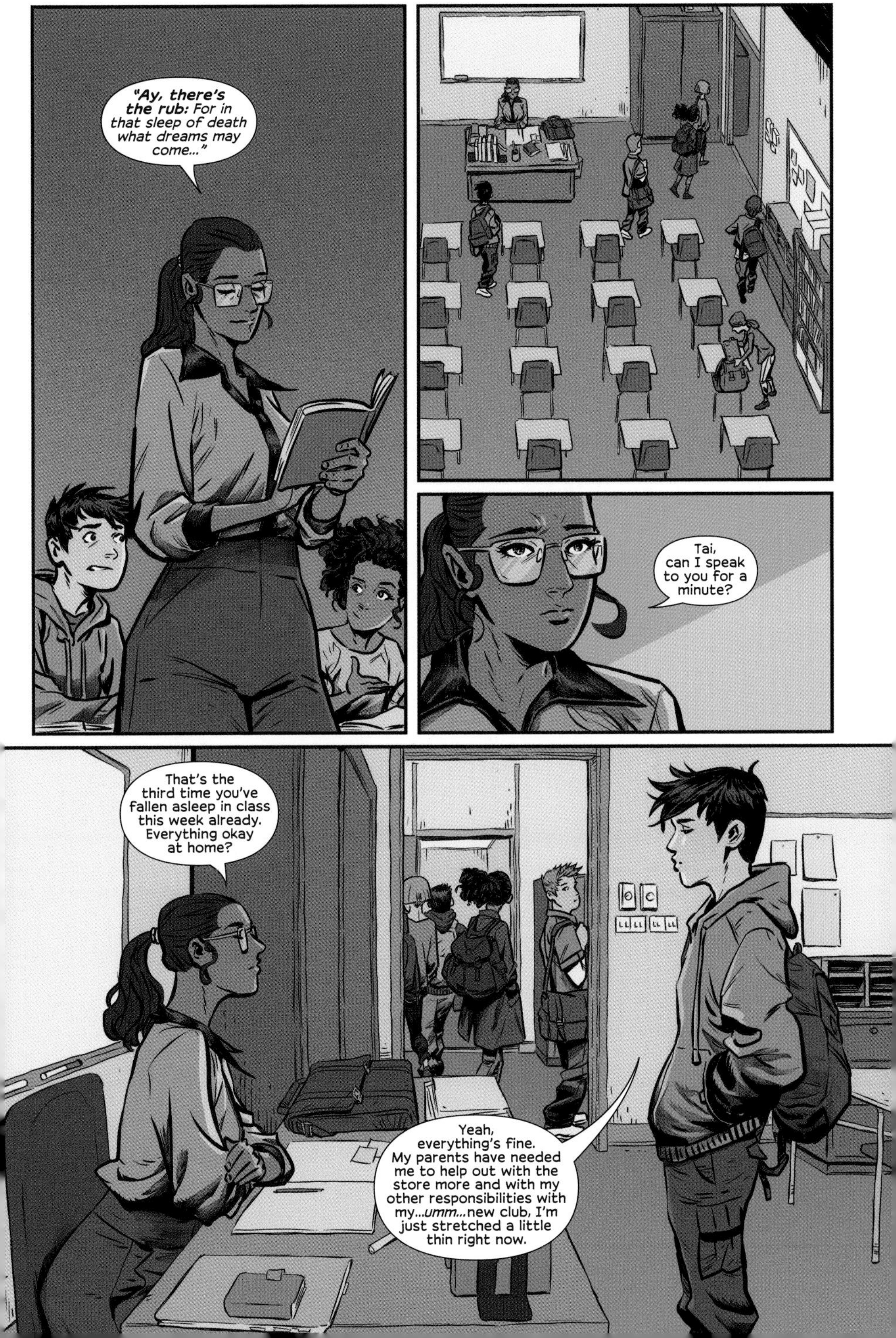
"Ay, there's the rub: For in that sleep of death what dreams may come..."
Tai, can I speak to you for a minute?
That's the third time you've fallen asleep in class this week already. Everything okay at home?
Yeah, everything's fine. My parents have needed me to help out with the store more and with my other responsibilities with my...umm...new club, I'm just stretched a little thin right now.

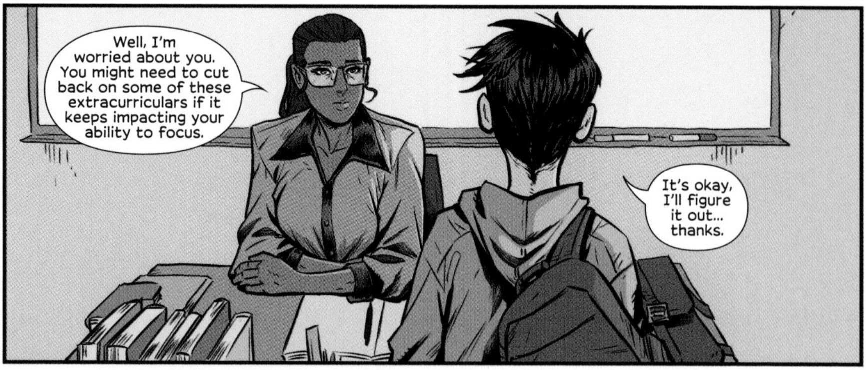
Well, I'm worried about you. You might need to cut back on some of these extracurriculars if it keeps impacting your ability to focus.
It's okay, I'll figure it out... thanks.

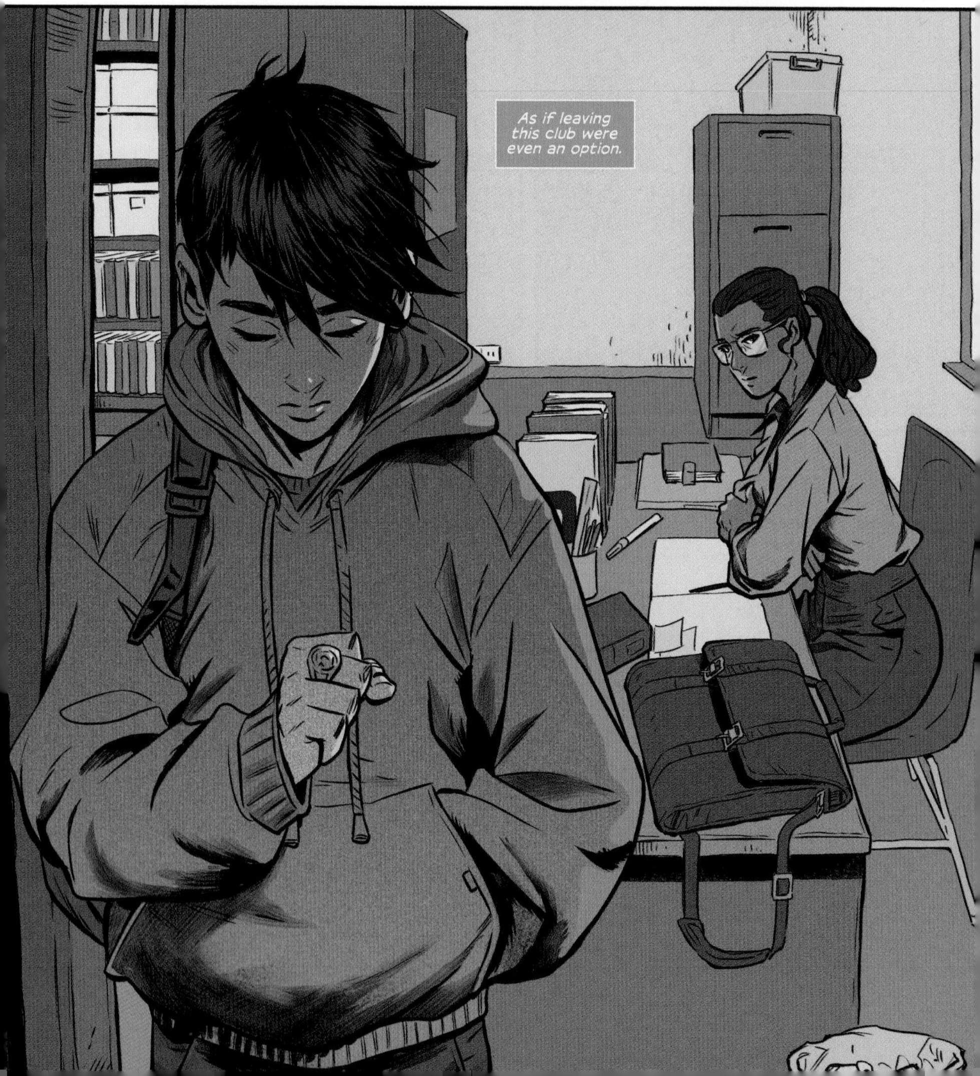
As if leaving this club were even an option.

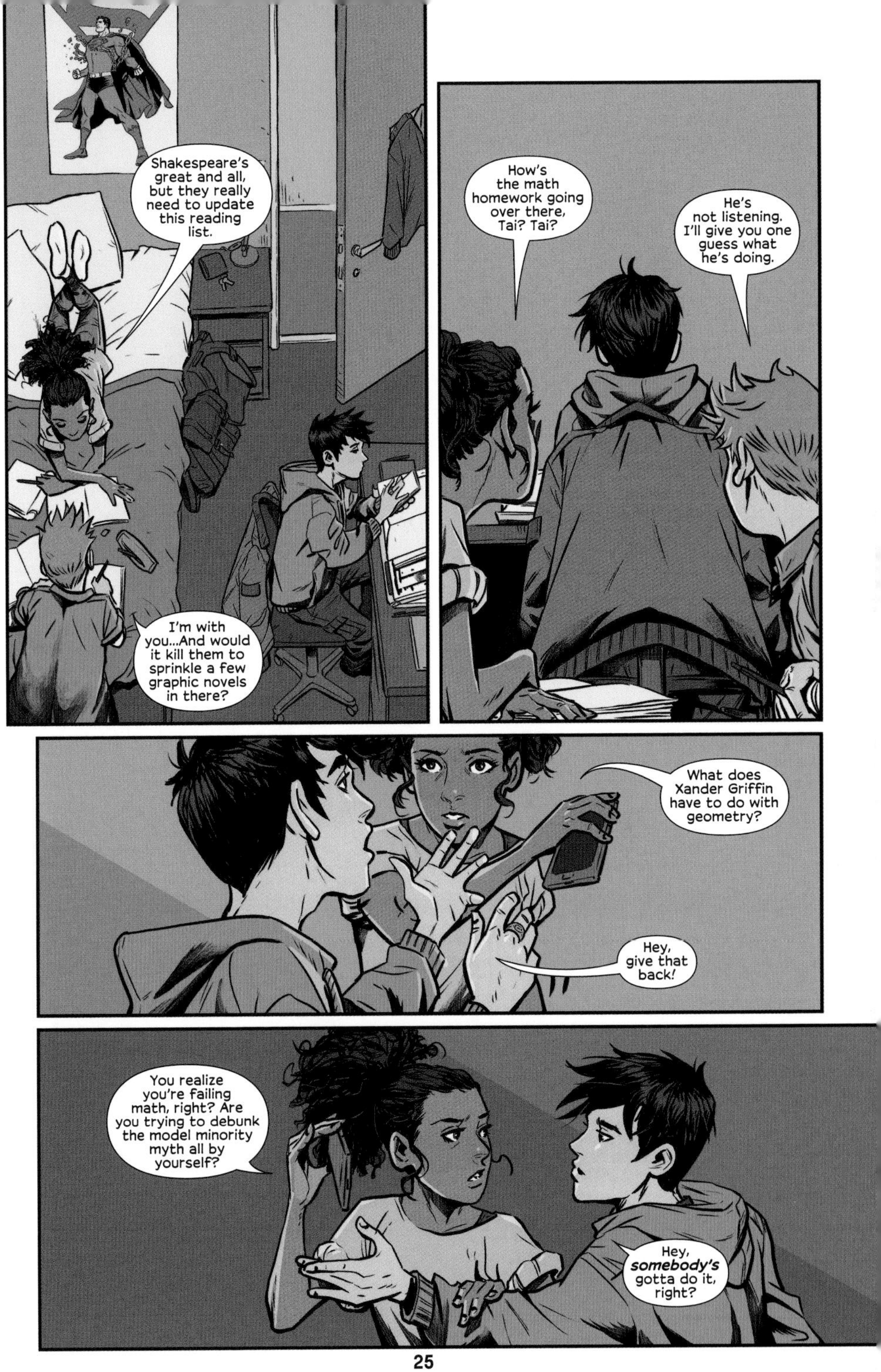
Shakespeare's great and all, but they really need to update this reading list.
I'm with you...And would it kill them to sprinkle a few graphic novels in there?
How's the math homework going over there, Tai? Tai?
He's not listening. I'll give you one guess what he's doing.
What does Xander Griffin have to do with geometry?
Hey, give that back!
You realize you're failing math, right? Are you trying to debunk the model minority myth all by yourself?
Hey, *somebody's* gotta do it, right?

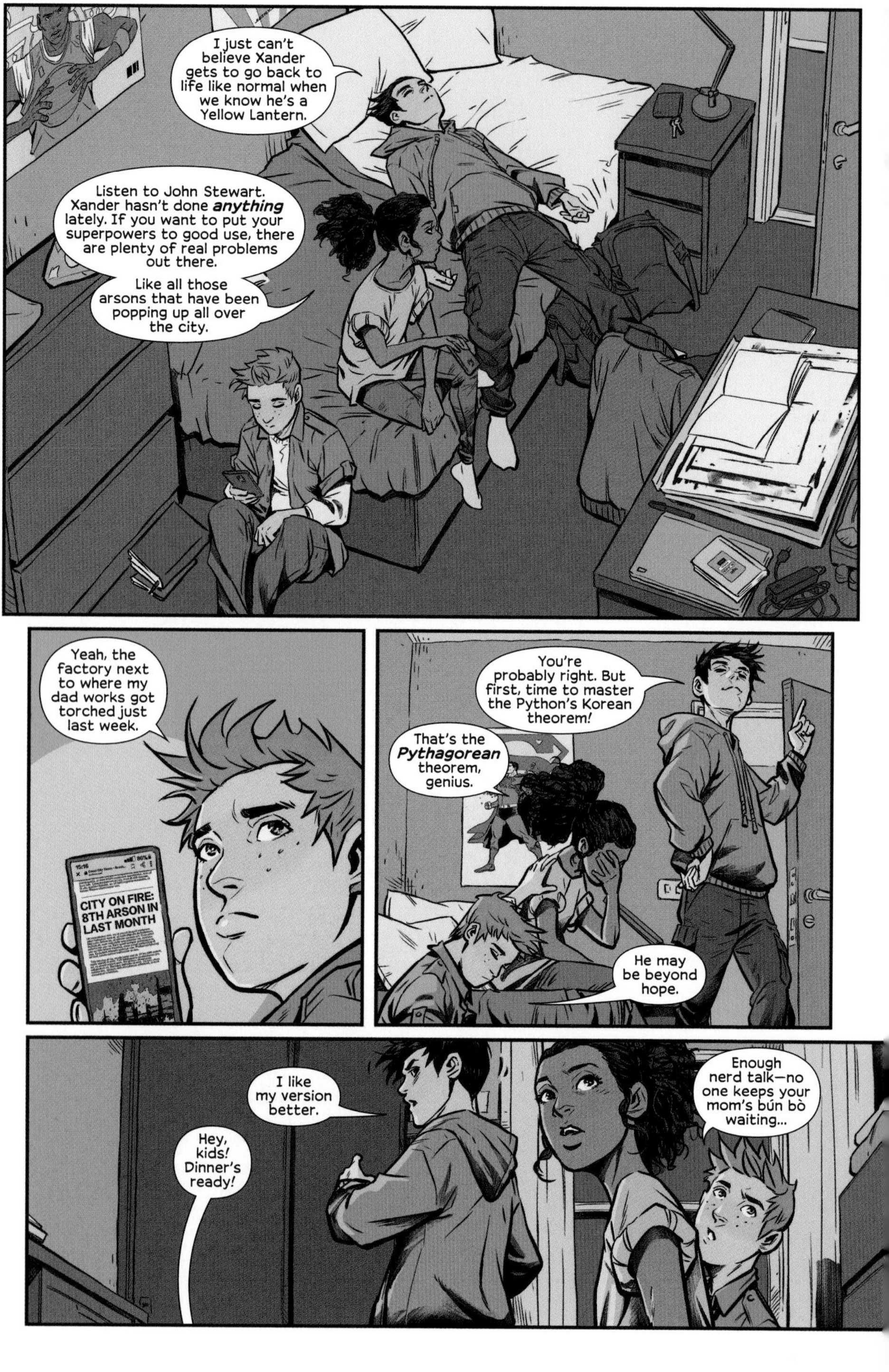
I just can't believe Xander gets to go back to life like normal when we know he's a Yellow Lantern.
Listen to John Stewart. Xander hasn't done ***anything*** lately. If you want to put your superpowers to good use, there are plenty of real problems out there.
Like all those arsons that have been popping up all over the city.
Yeah, the factory next to where my dad works got torched just last week.
CITY ON FIRE: 8TH ARSON IN LAST MONTH
You're probably right. But first, time to master the Python's Korean theorem!
That's the ***Pythagorean*** theorem, genius.
He may be beyond hope.
I like my version better.
Hey, kids! Dinner's ready!
Enough nerd talk—no one keeps your mom's bún bò waiting...

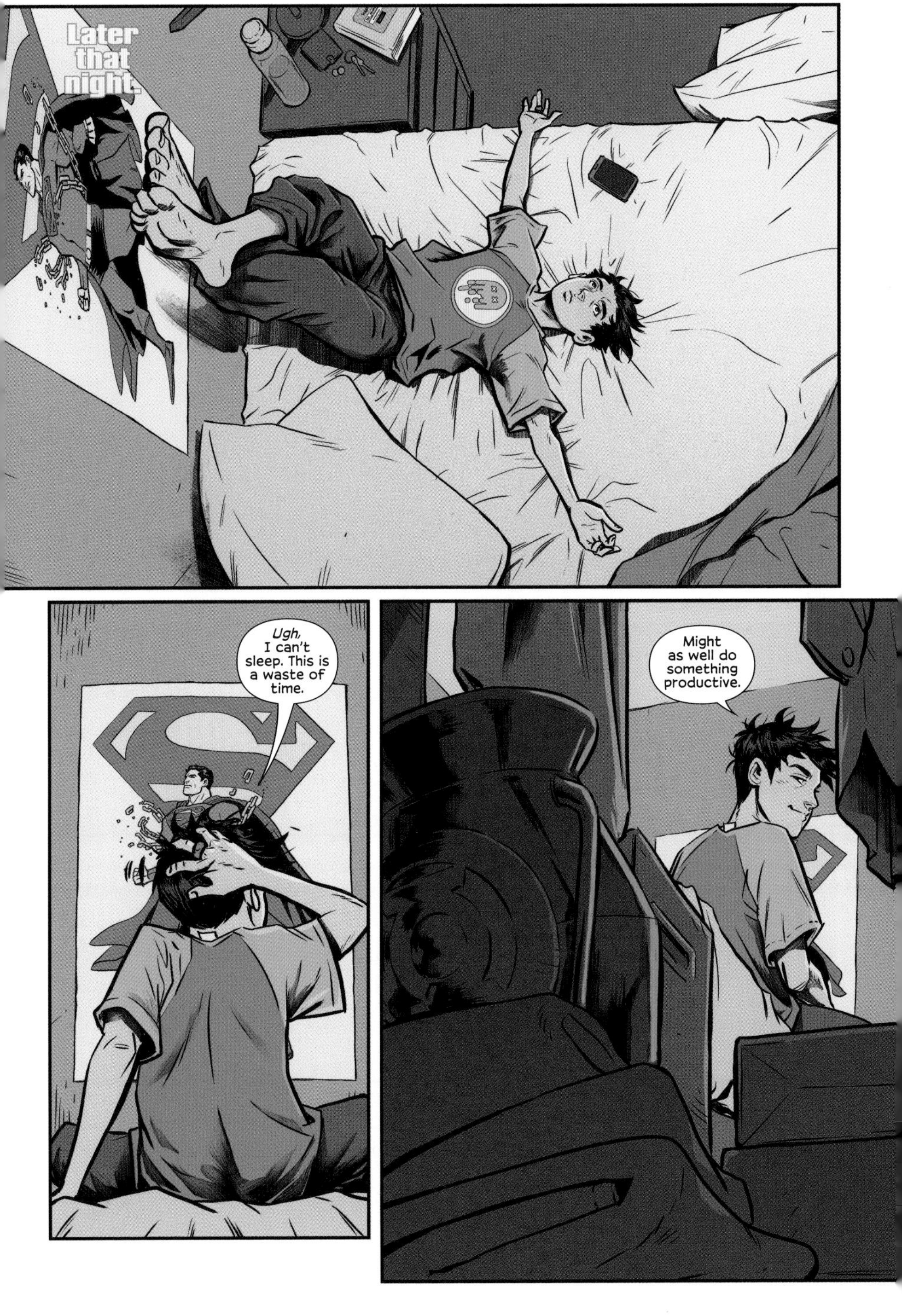
Later that night.
Ugh, I can't sleep. This is a waste of time.
Might as well do something productive.

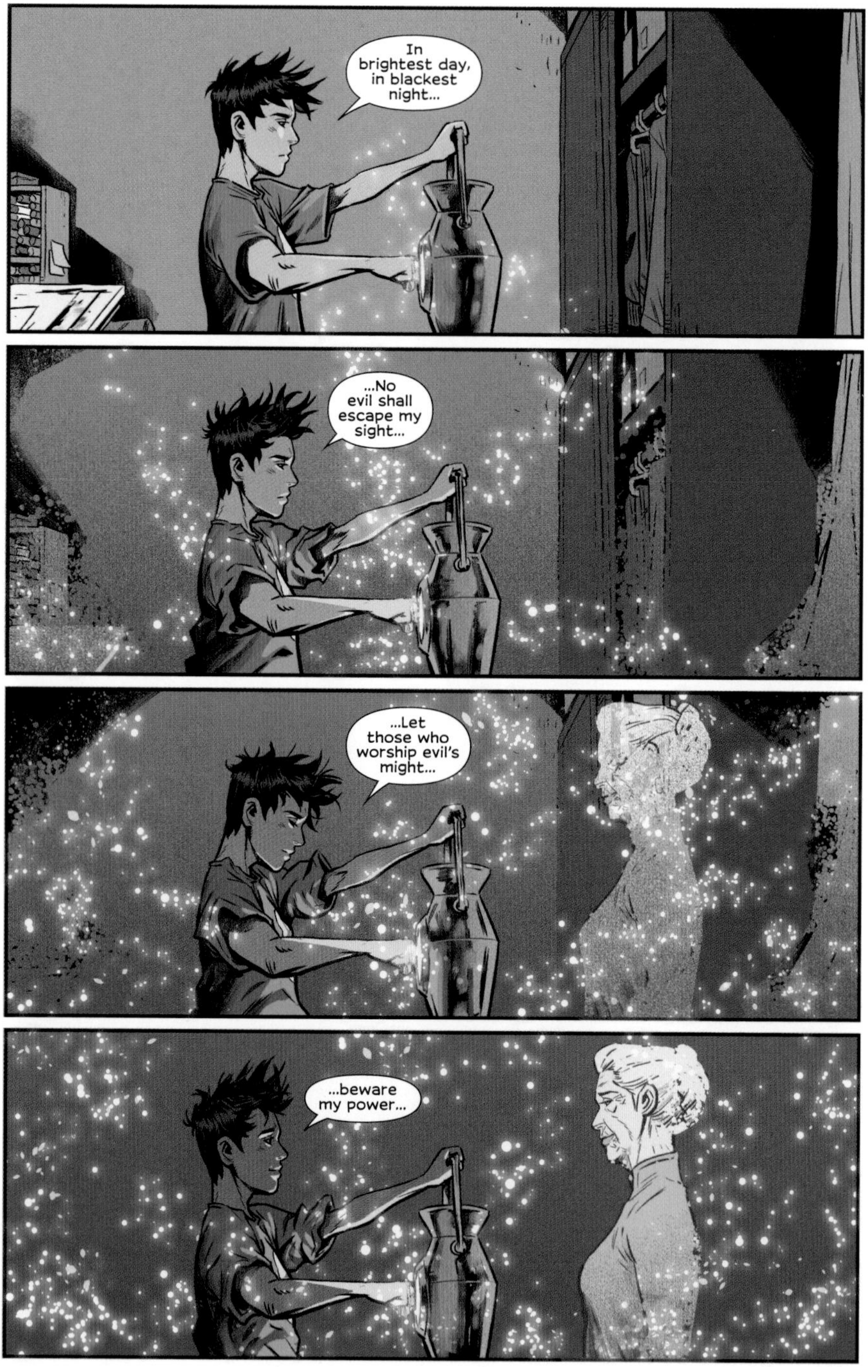
In brightest day, in blackest night...
...No evil shall escape my sight...
...Let those who worship evil's might...
...beware my power...

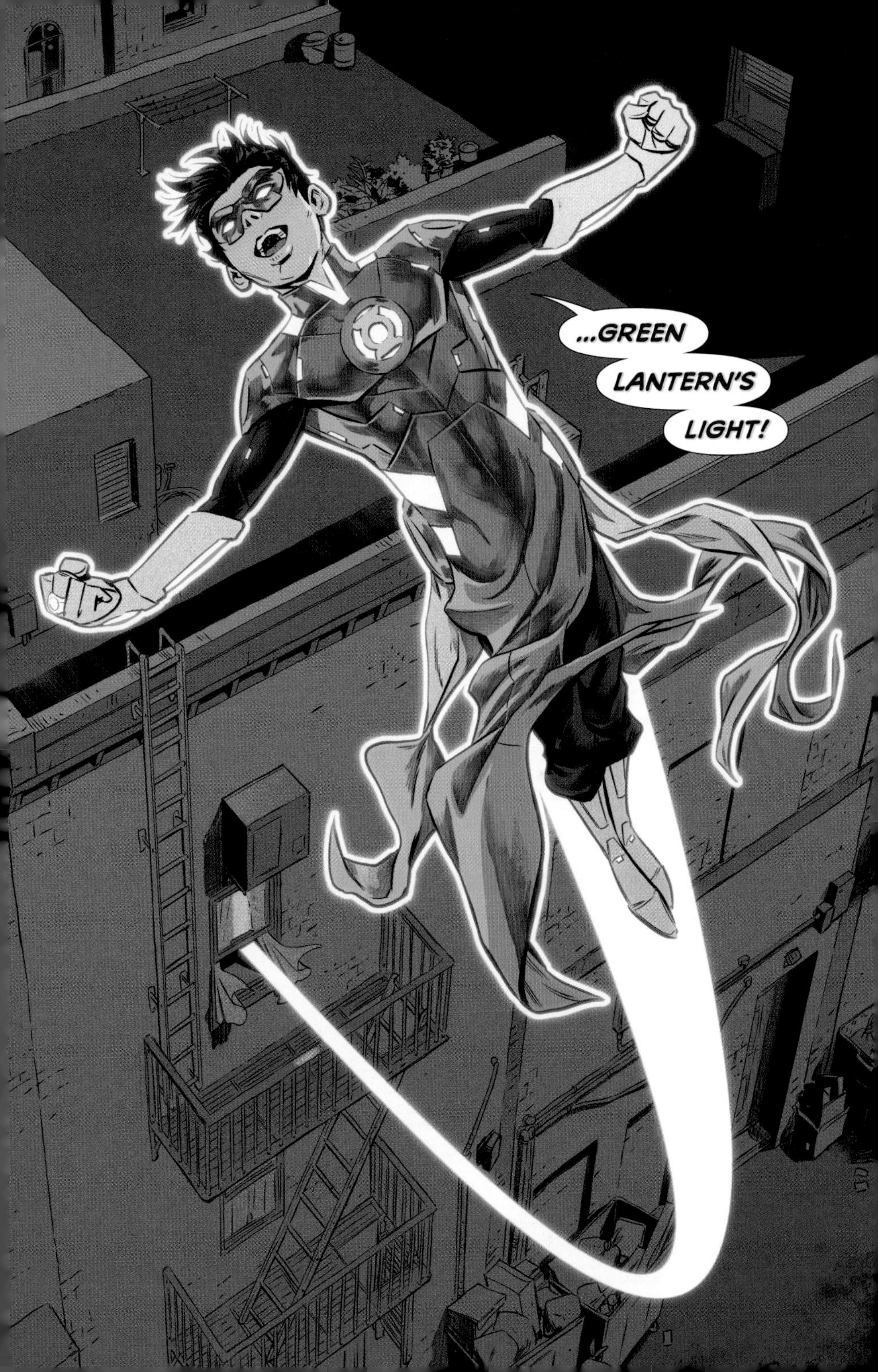
...GREEN LANTERN'S LIGHT!

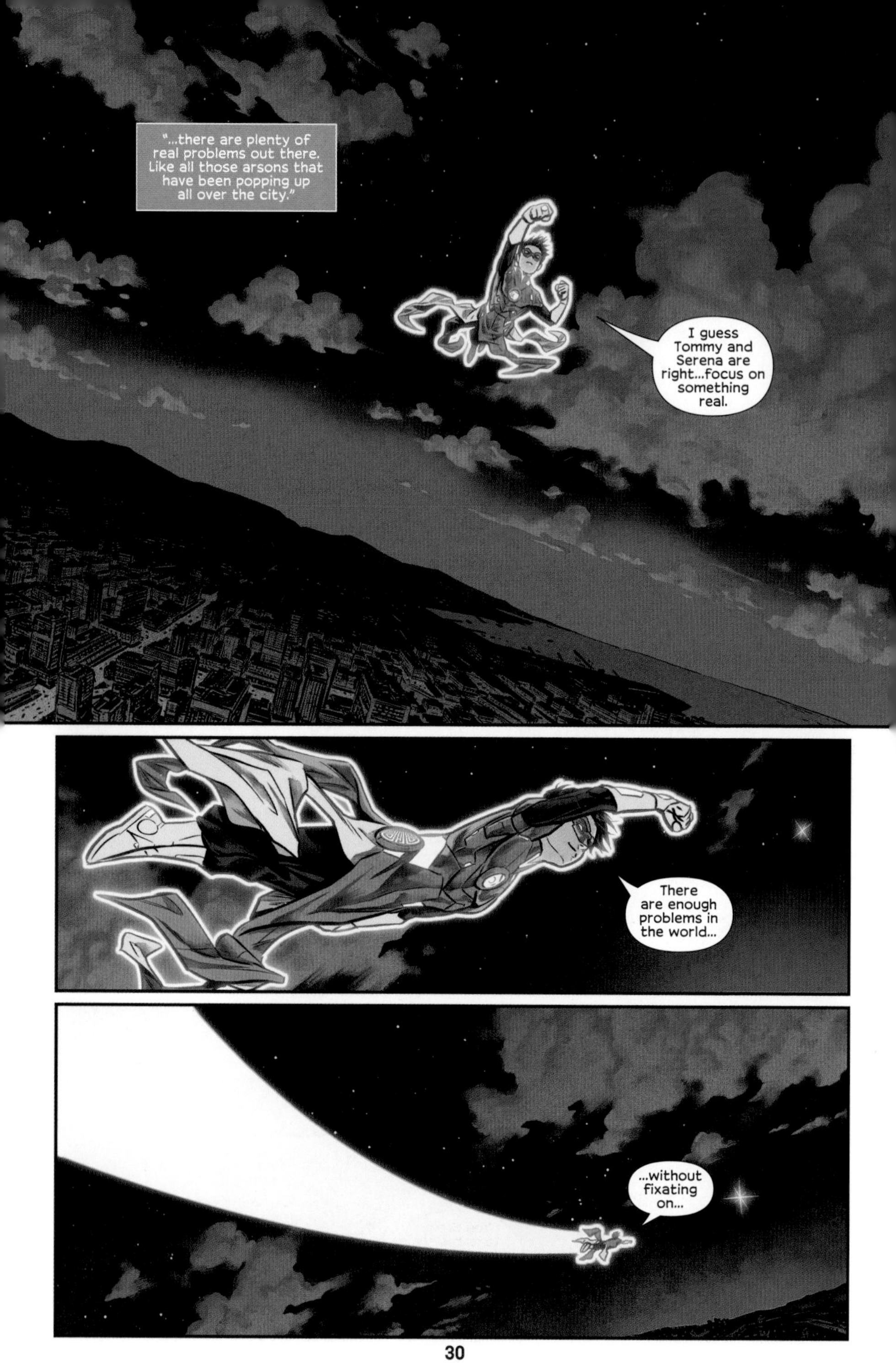
"...there are plenty of real problems out there. Like all those arsons that have been popping up all over the city."
I guess Tommy and Serena are right...focus on something real.
There are enough problems in the world...
...without fixating on...

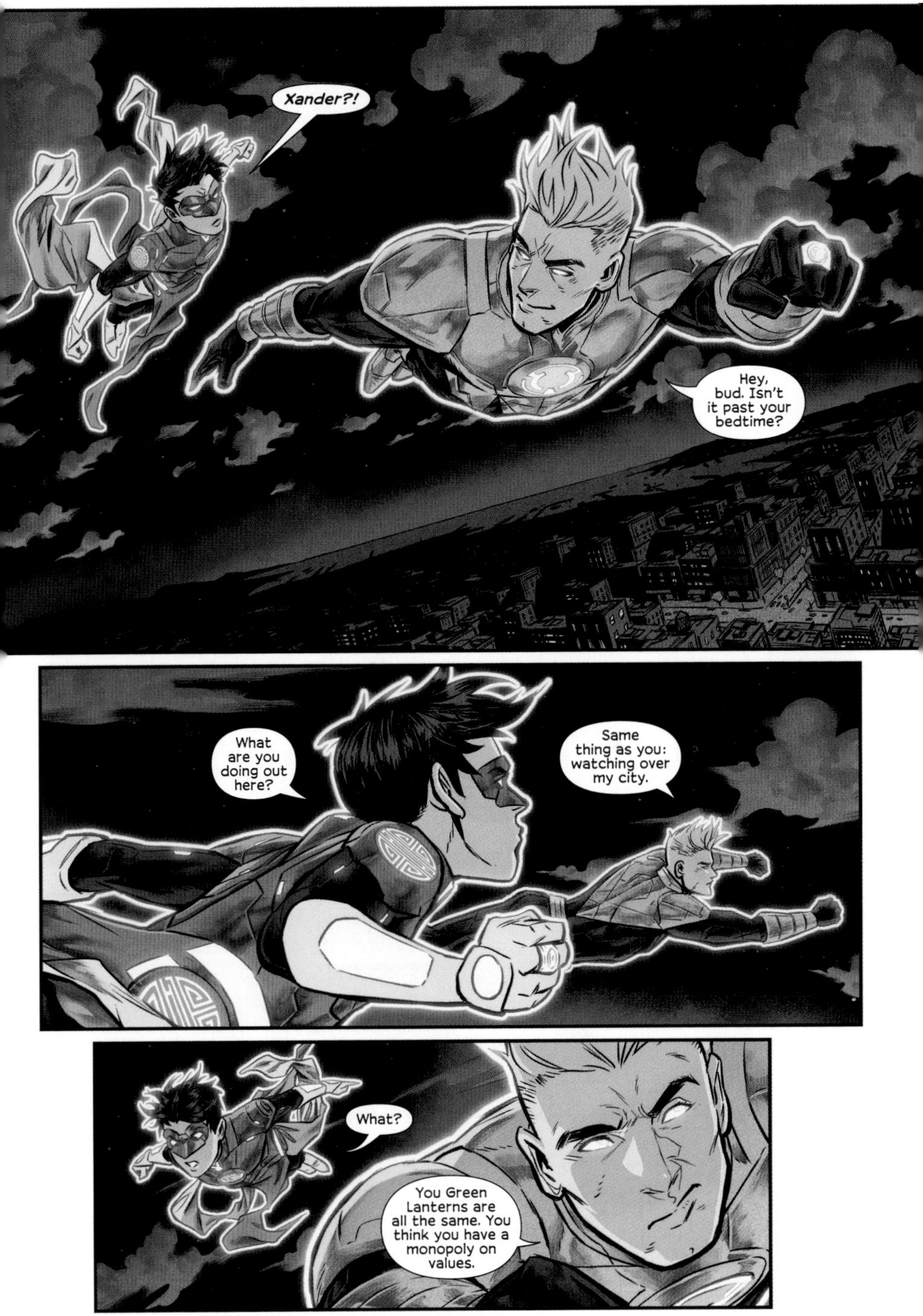
Xander?!
Hey, bud. Isn't it past your bedtime?
What are you doing out here?
Same thing as you: watching over my city.
What?
You Green Lanterns are all the same. You think you have a monopoly on values.

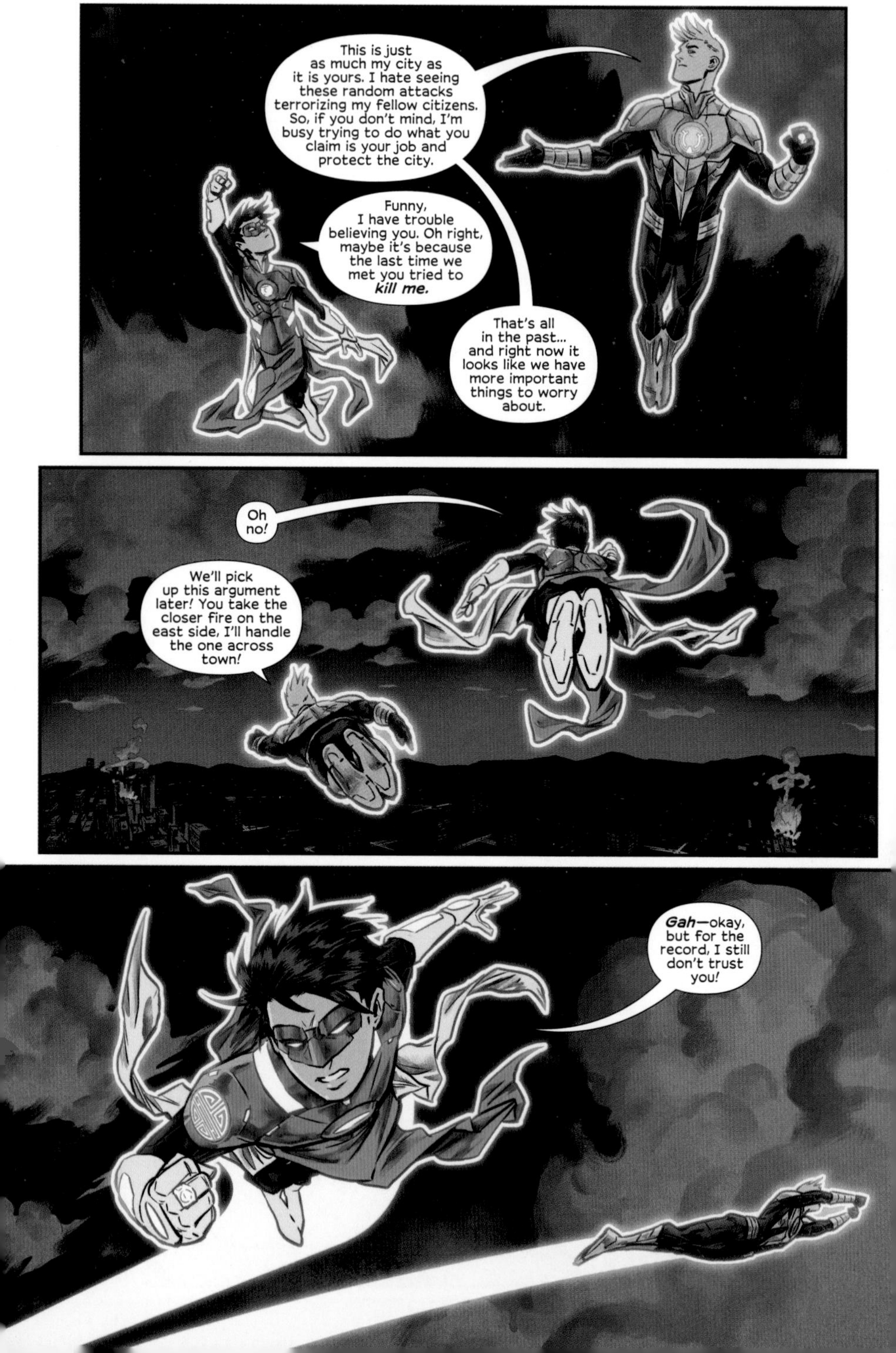
This is just as much my city as it is yours. I hate seeing these random attacks terrorizing my fellow citizens. So, if you don't mind, I'm busy trying to do what you claim is your job and protect the city.
Funny, I have trouble believing you. Oh right, maybe it's because the last time we met you tried to *kill me.*
That's all in the past... and right now it looks like we have more important things to worry about.
Oh no!
We'll pick up this argument later! You take the closer fire on the east side, I'll handle the one across town!
Gah—okay, but for the record, I still don't trust you!

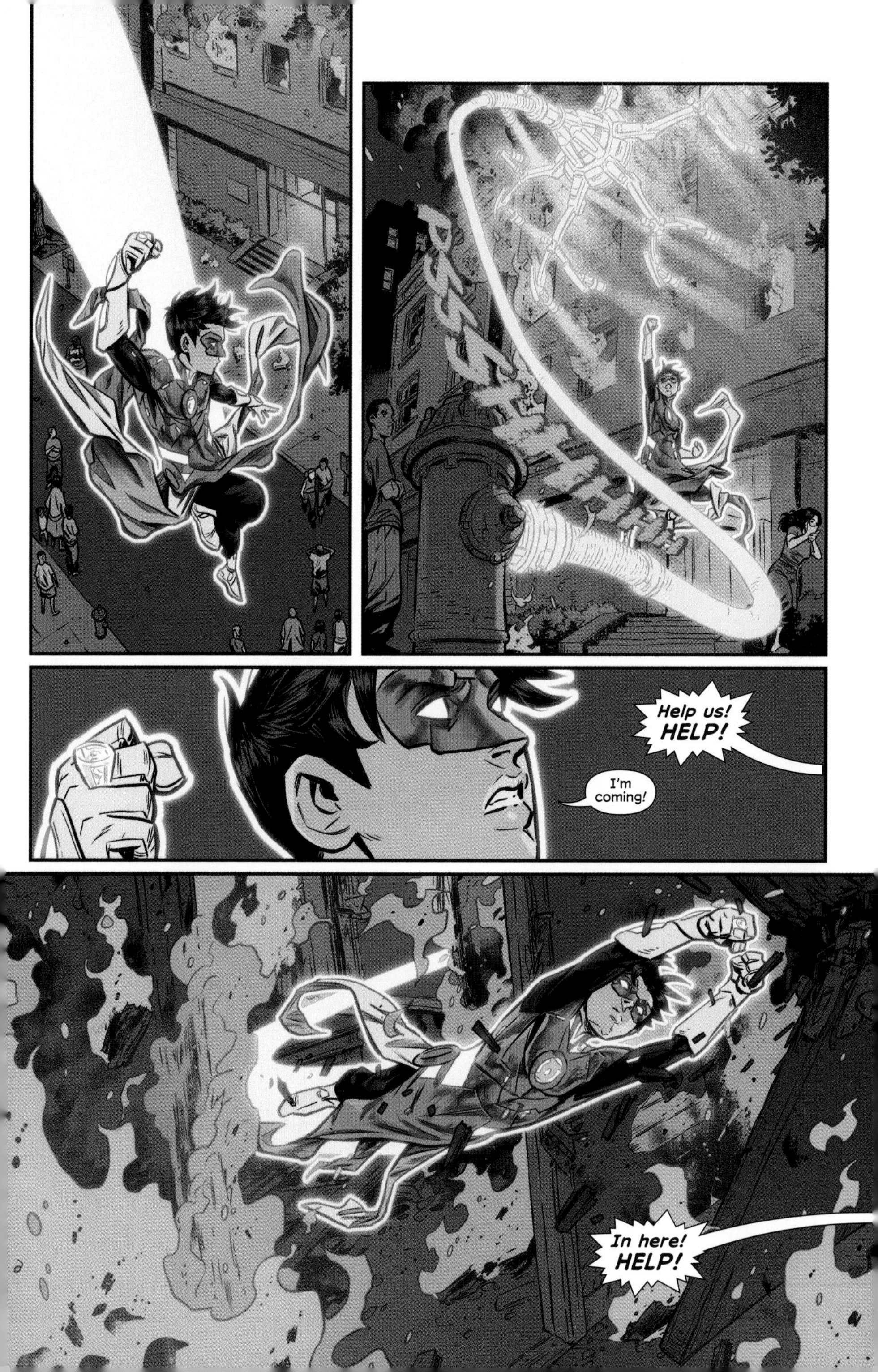
Help us! HELP!
I'm coming!
In here! HELP!

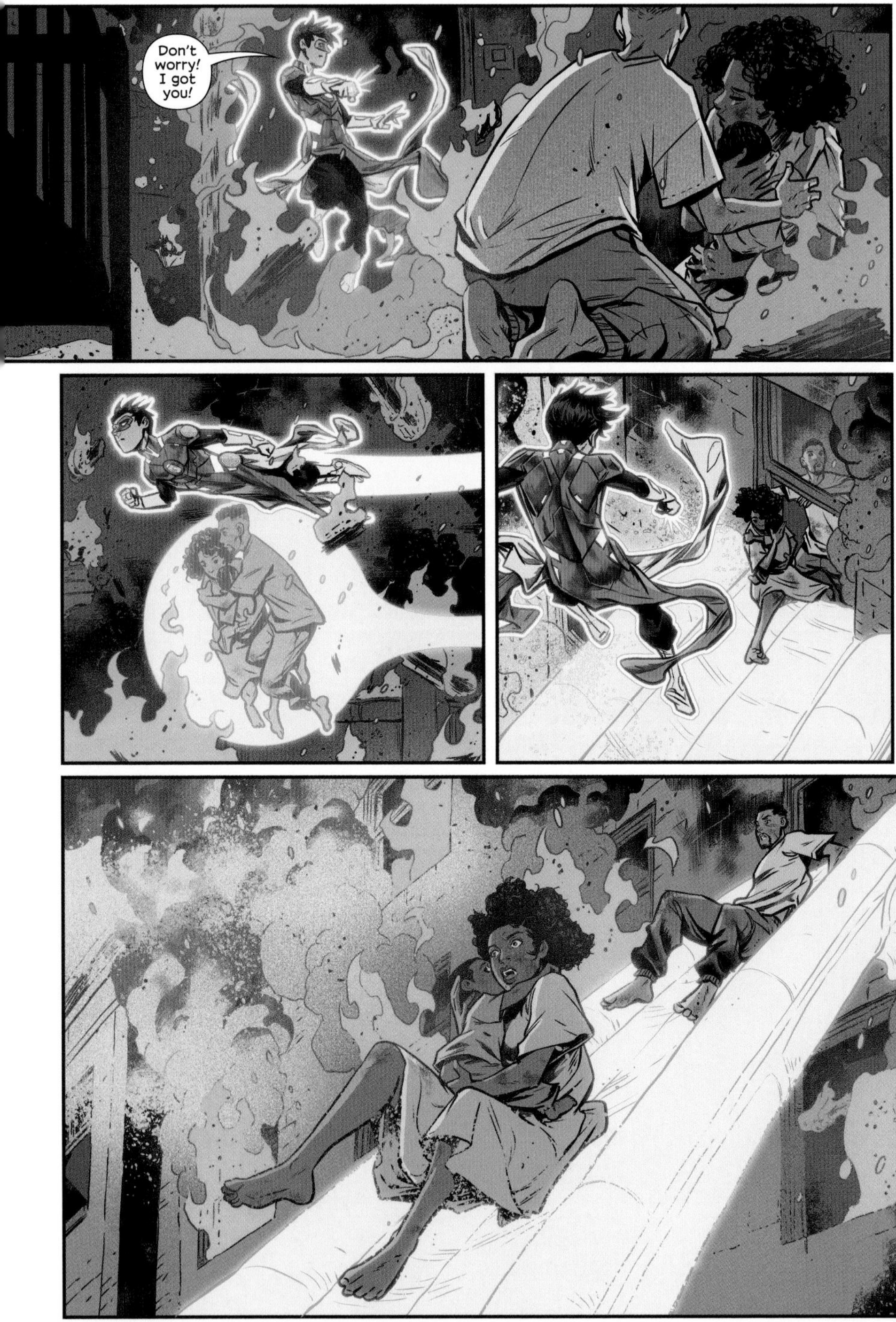
Don't worry! I got you!

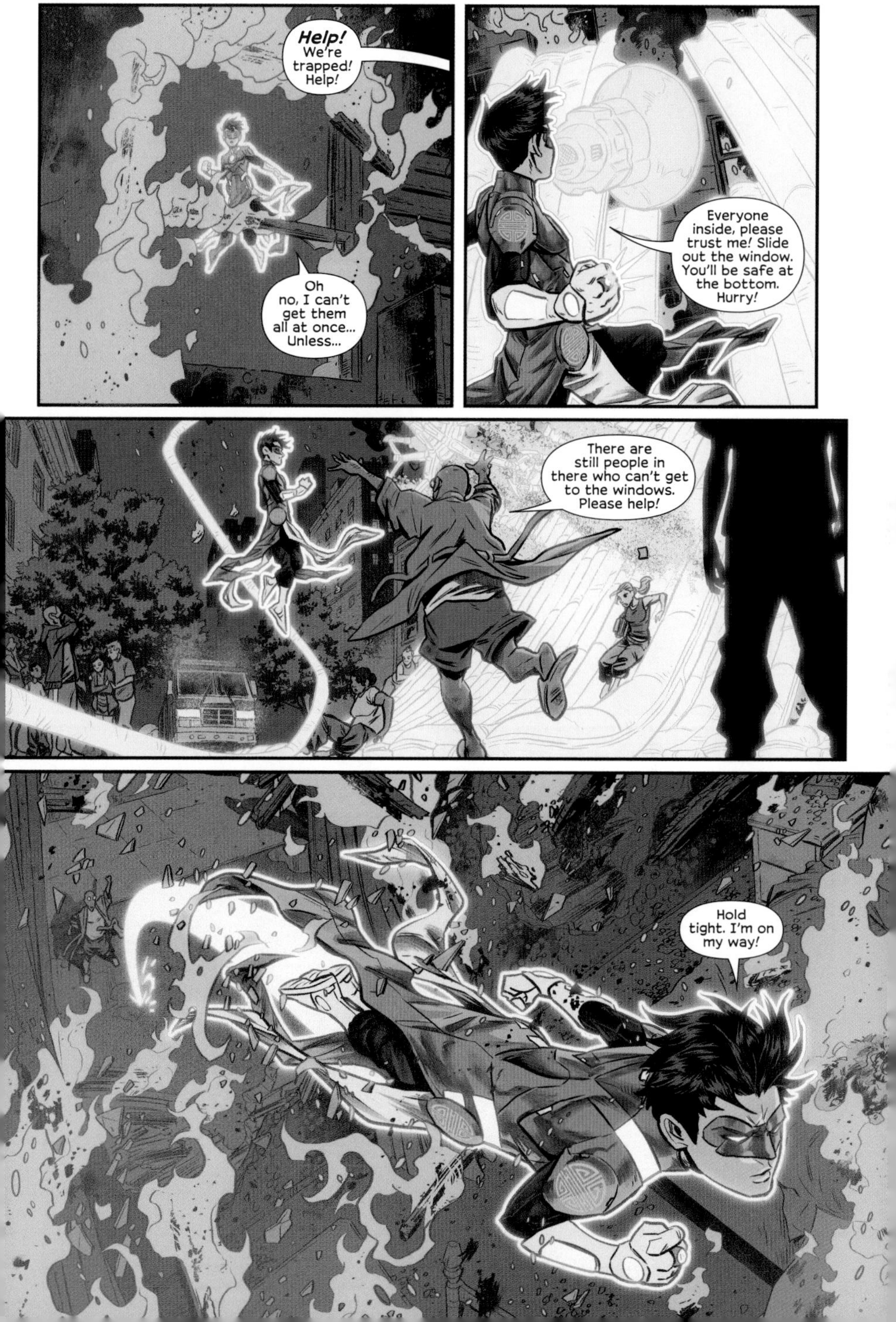

Help! We're trapped! Help!
Oh no, I can't get them all at once... Unless...
Everyone inside, please trust me! Slide out the window. You'll be safe at the bottom. Hurry!
There are still people in there who can't get to the windows. Please help!
Hold tight. I'm on my way!

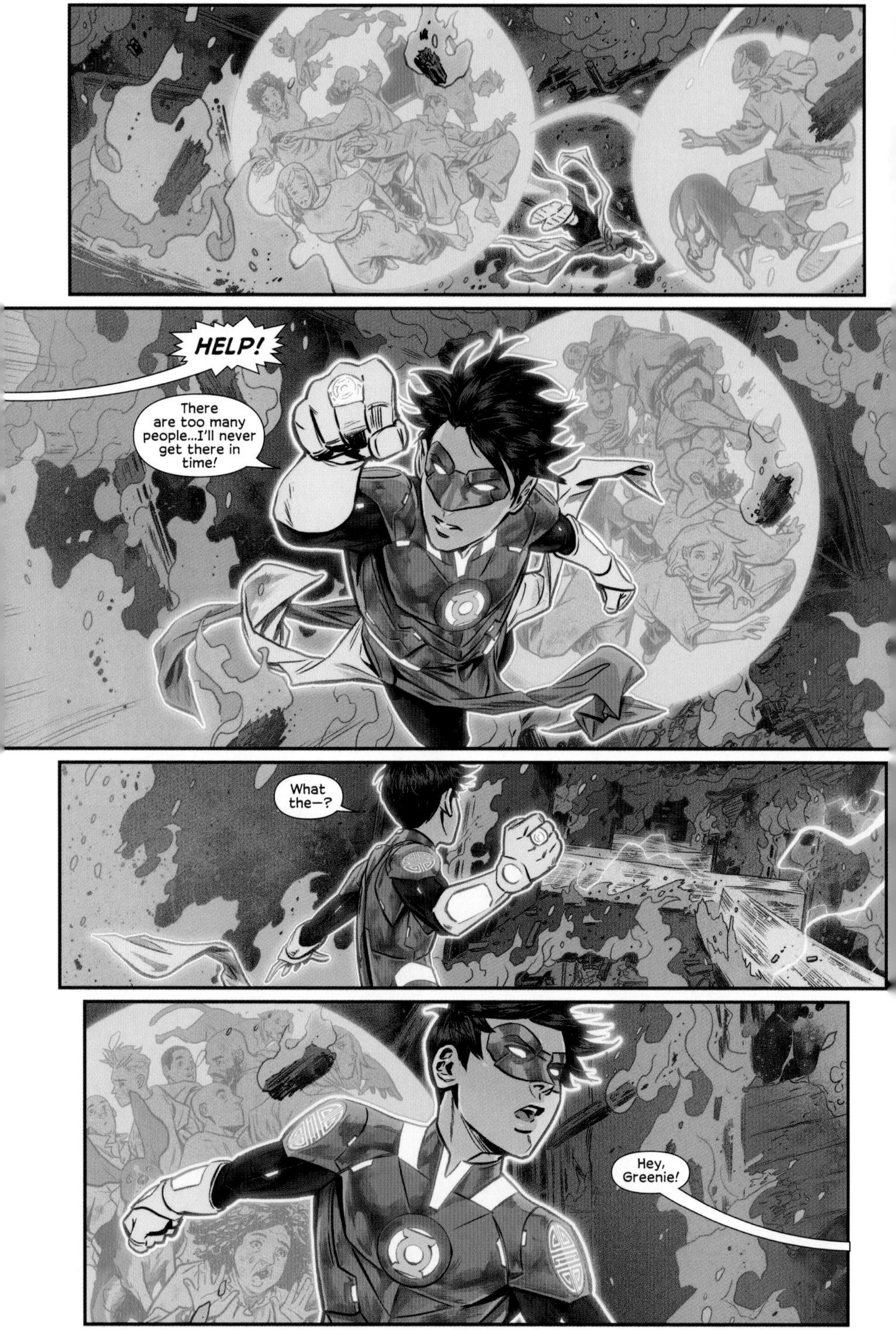
HELP!
There are too many people...I'll never get there in time!
What the—?
Hey, Greenie!

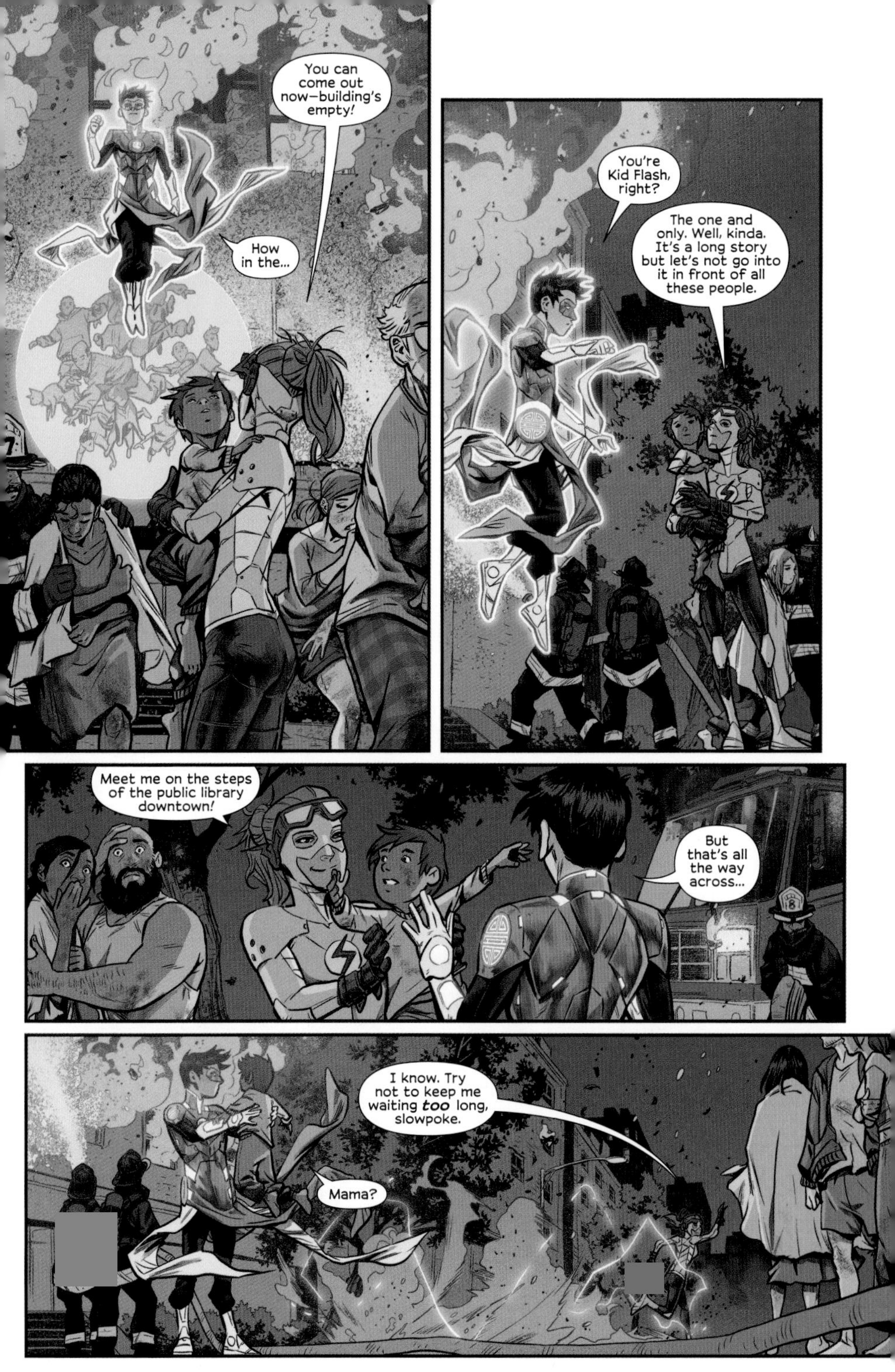
You can come out now—building's empty!
How in the...
You're Kid Flash, right?
The one and only. Well, kinda. It's a long story but let's not go into it in front of all these people.
Meet me on the steps of the public library downtown!
But that's all the way across...
I know. Try not to keep me waiting *too* long, slowpoke.
Mama?

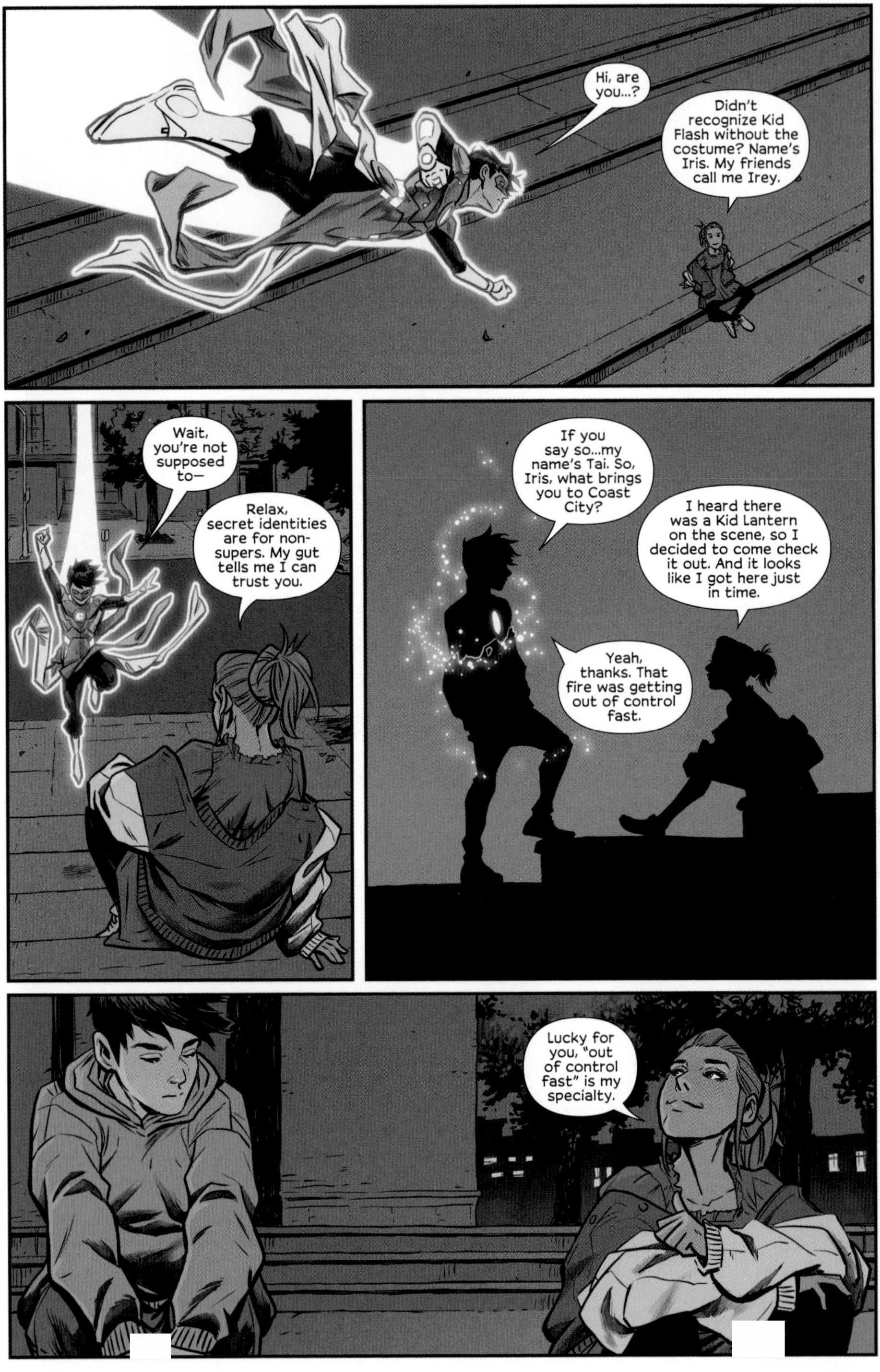
Hi, are you...?
Didn't recognize Kid Flash without the costume? Name's Iris. My friends call me Irey.
Wait, you're not supposed to—
Relax, secret identities are for non-supers. My gut tells me I can trust you.
If you say so...my name's Tai. So, Iris, what brings you to Coast City?
I heard there was a Kid Lantern on the scene, so I decided to come check it out. And it looks like I got here just in time.
Yeah, thanks. That fire was getting out of control fast.
Lucky for you, "out of control fast" is my specialty.

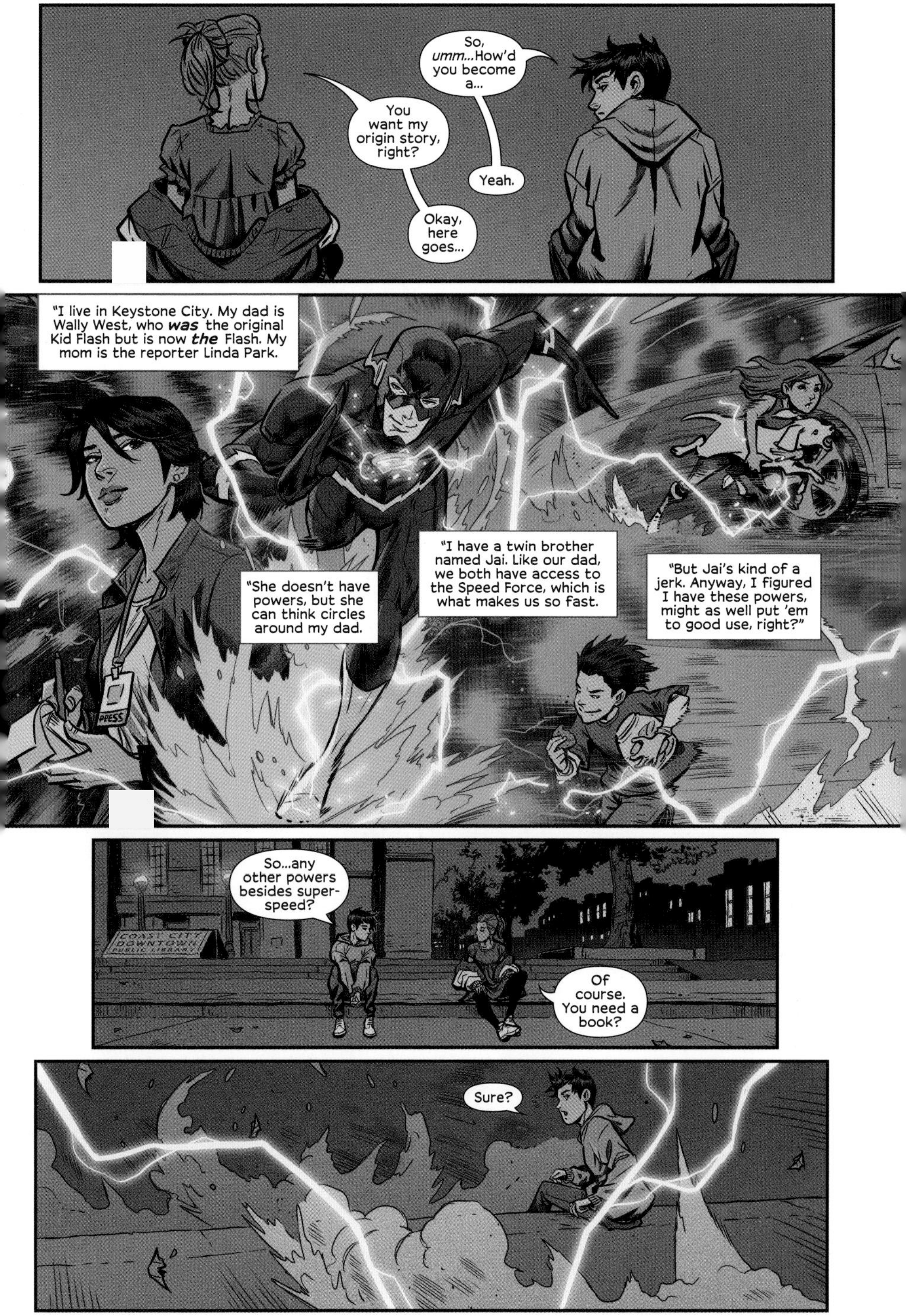

So, *umm*...How'd you become a...
You want my origin story, right?
Yeah.
Okay, here goes...
"I live in Keystone City. My dad is Wally West, who ***was*** the original Kid Flash but is now ***the*** Flash. My mom is the reporter Linda Park.
"She doesn't have powers, but she can think circles around my dad.
"I have a twin brother named Jai. Like our dad, we both have access to the Speed Force, which is what makes us so fast.
"But Jai's kind of a jerk. Anyway, I figured I have these powers, might as well put 'em to good use, right?"
PRESS
So...any other powers besides super-speed?
COAST CITY DOWNTOWN PUBLIC LIBRARY
Of course. You need a book?
Sure?

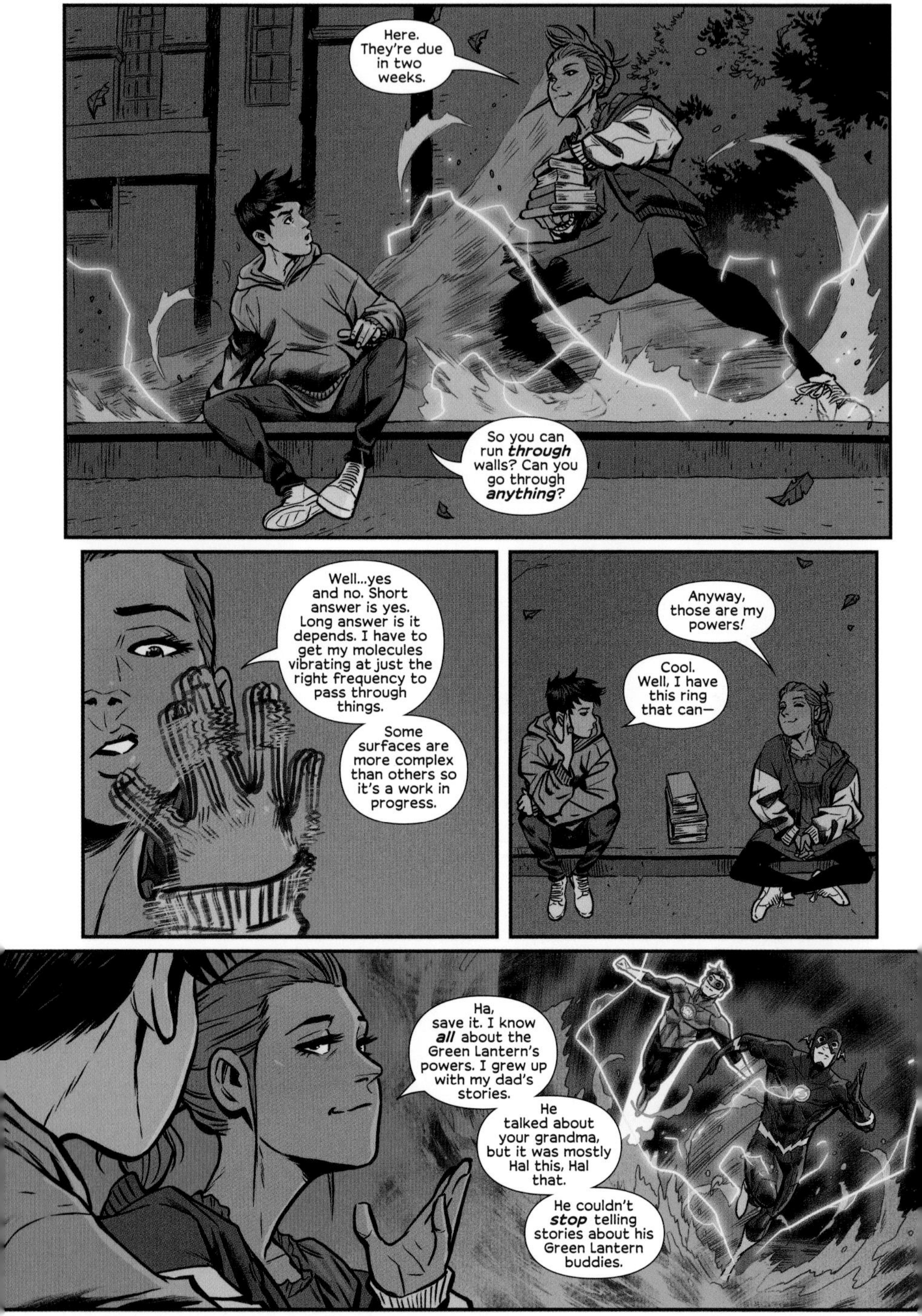

Here. They're due in two weeks.
So you can run *through* walls? Can you go through *anything*?
Well...yes and no. Short answer is yes. Long answer is it depends. I have to get my molecules vibrating at just the right frequency to pass through things.
Some surfaces are more complex than others so it's a work in progress.
Anyway, those are my powers!
Cool. Well, I have this ring that can—
Ha, save it. I know *all* about the Green Lantern's powers. I grew up with my dad's stories.
He talked about your grandma, but it was mostly Hal this, Hal that.
He couldn't *stop* telling stories about his Green Lantern buddies.

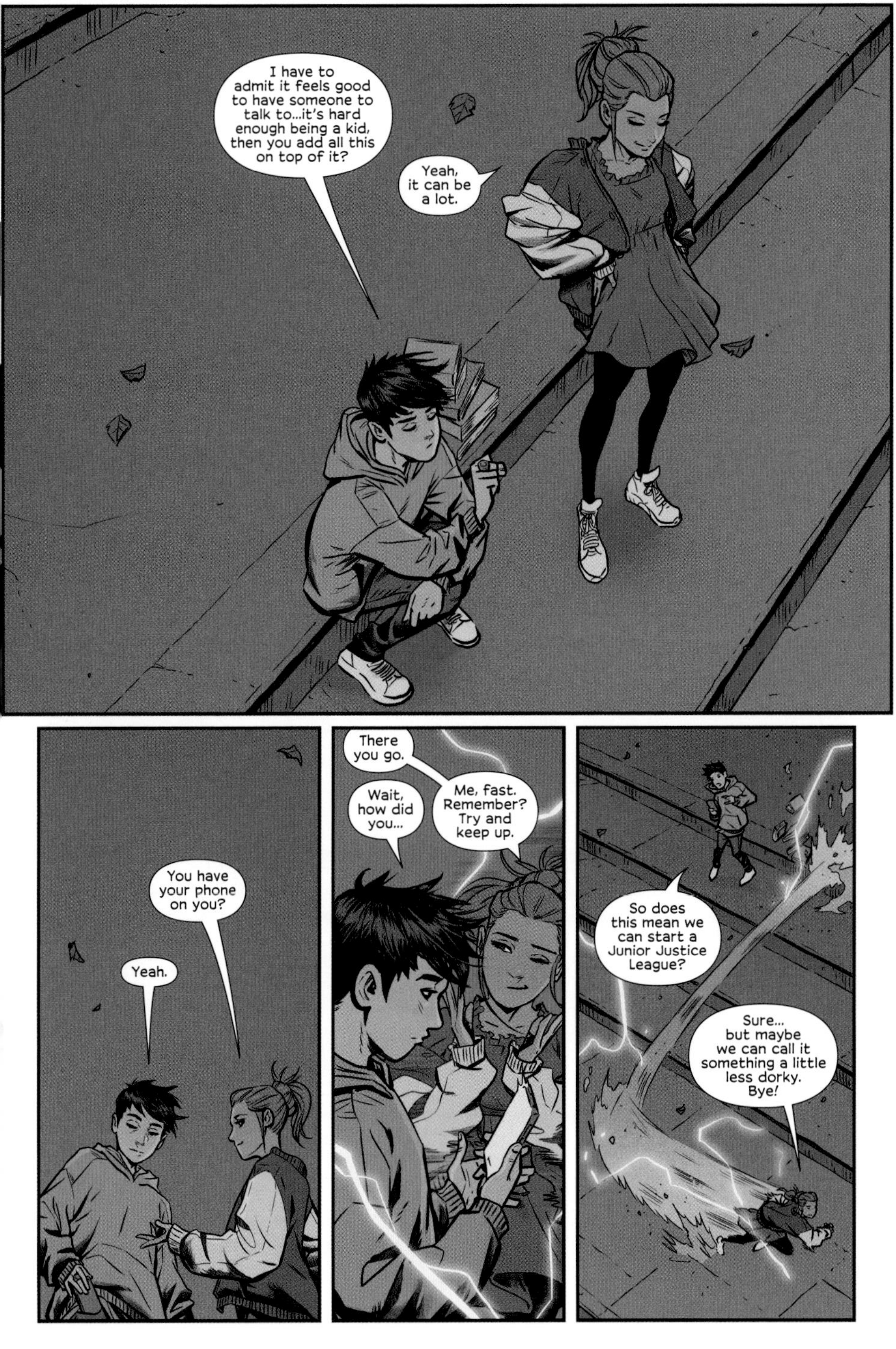

I have to admit it feels good to have someone to talk to...it's hard enough being a kid, then you add all this on top of it?
Yeah, it can be a lot.
You have your phone on you?
Yeah.
There you go.
Wait, how did you...
Me, fast. Remember? Try and keep up.
So does this mean we can start a Junior Justice League?
Sure... but maybe we can call it something a little less dorky. Bye!

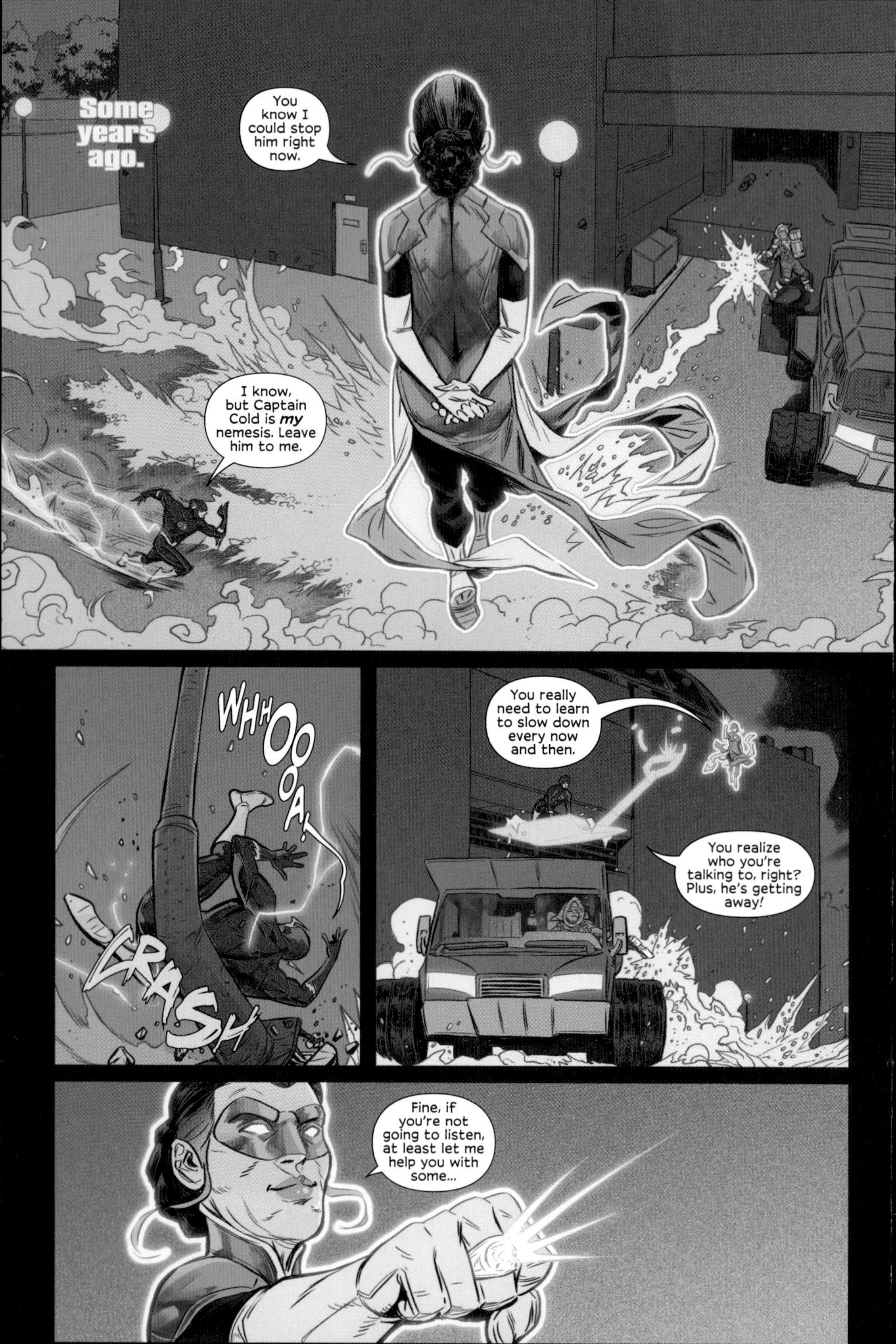
Some years ago.
You know I could stop him right now.
I know, but Captain Cold is *my* nemesis. Leave him to me.
WHHOOOA!
CRASH
You really need to learn to slow down every now and then.
You realize who you're talking to, right? Plus, he's getting away!
Fine, if you're not going to listen, at least let me help you with some...

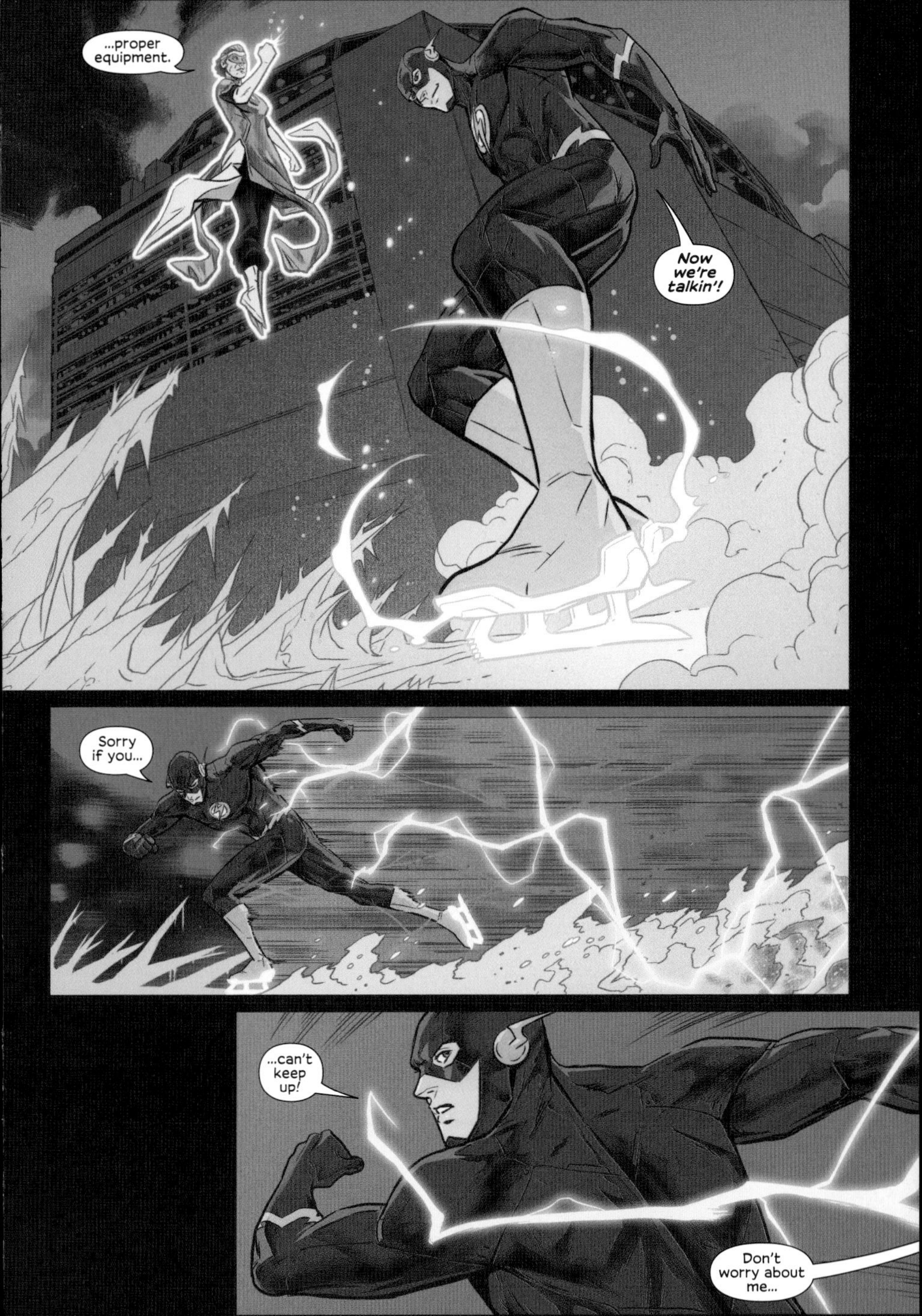
...proper equipment.
Now we're talkin'!
Sorry if you...
...can't keep up!
Don't worry about me...

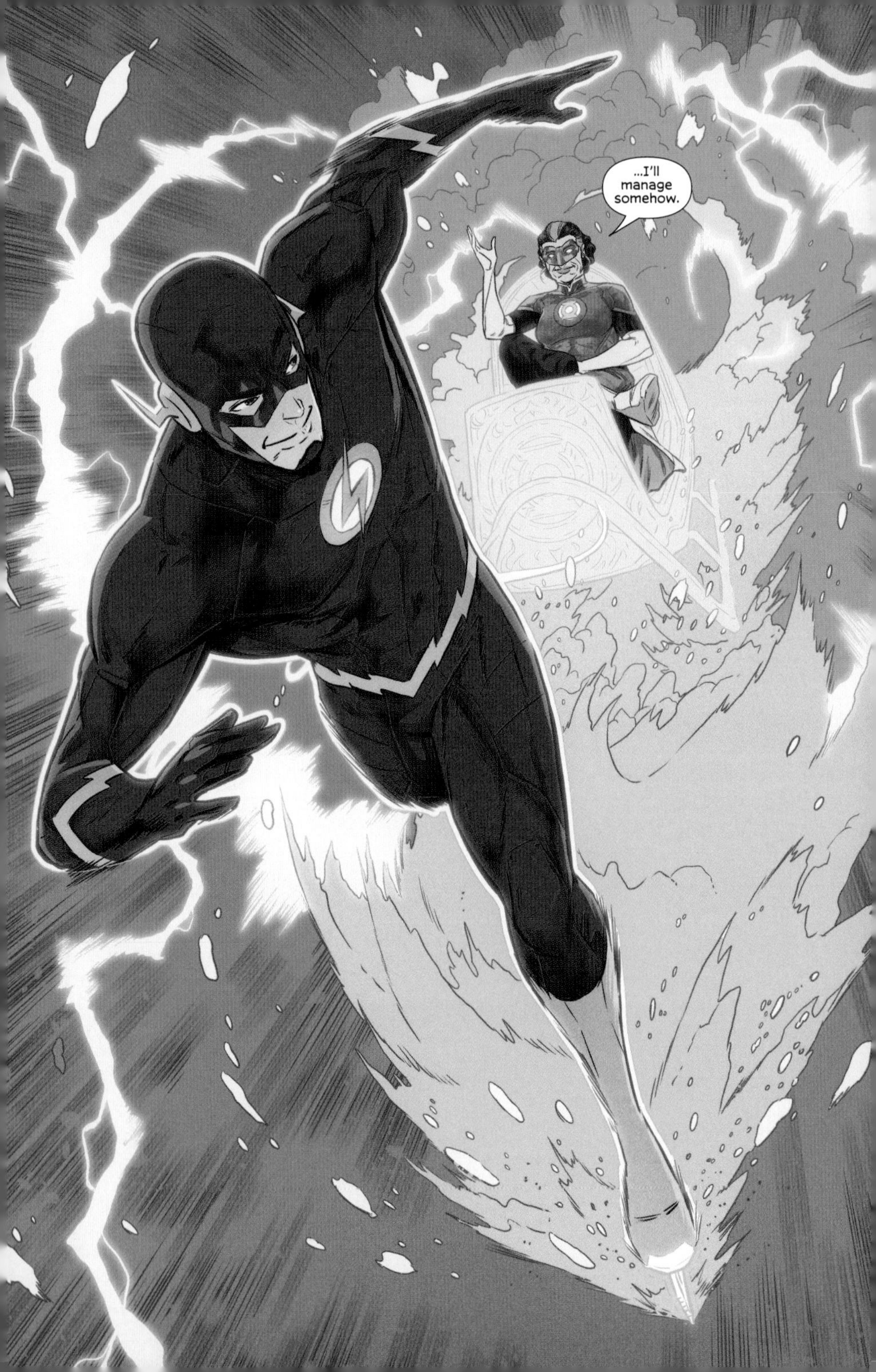
...I'll manage somehow.

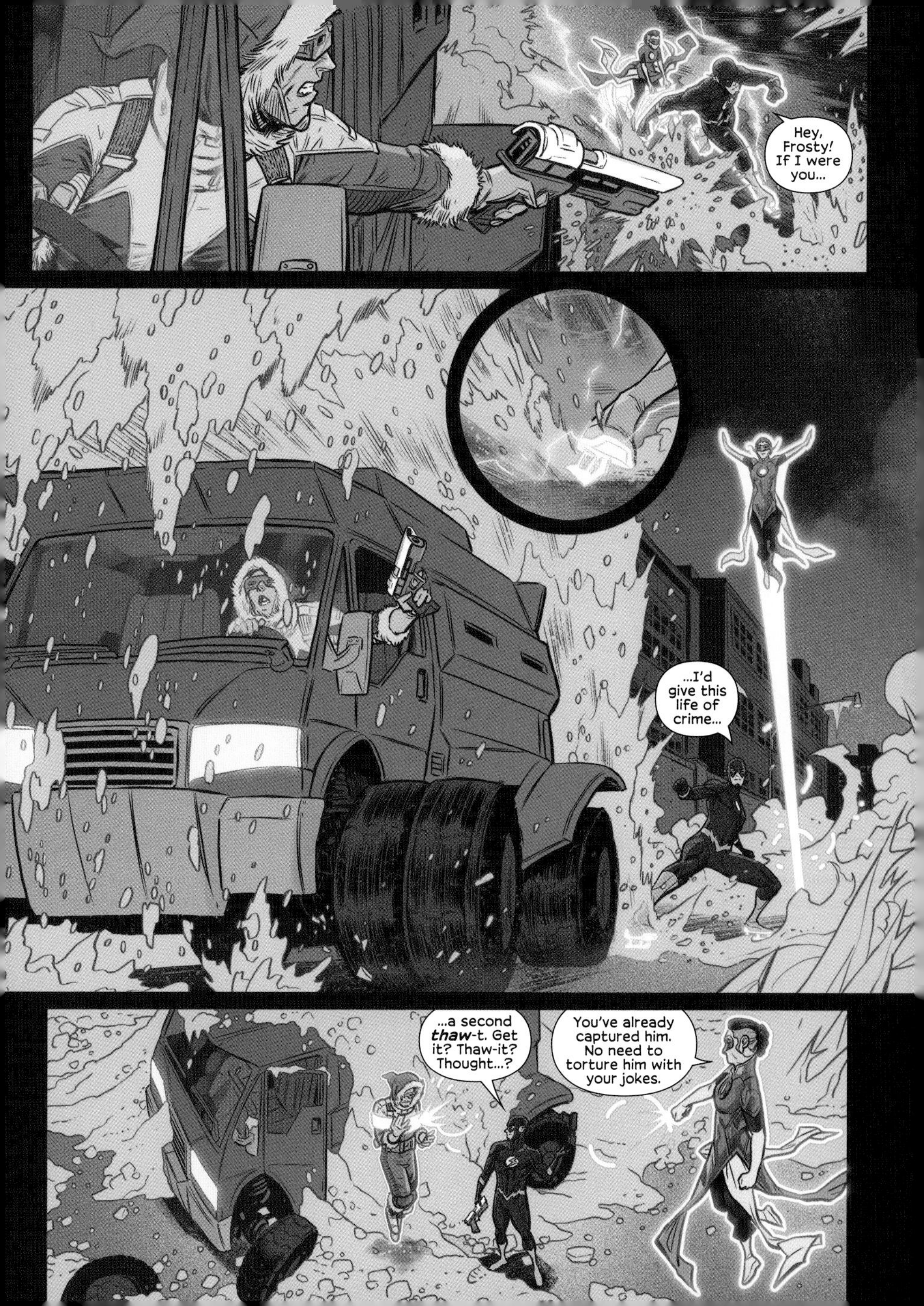

Hey, Frosty! If I were you...
...I'd give this life of crime...
...a second *thaw*-t. Get it? Thaw-it? Thought...?
You've already captured him. No need to torture him with your jokes.

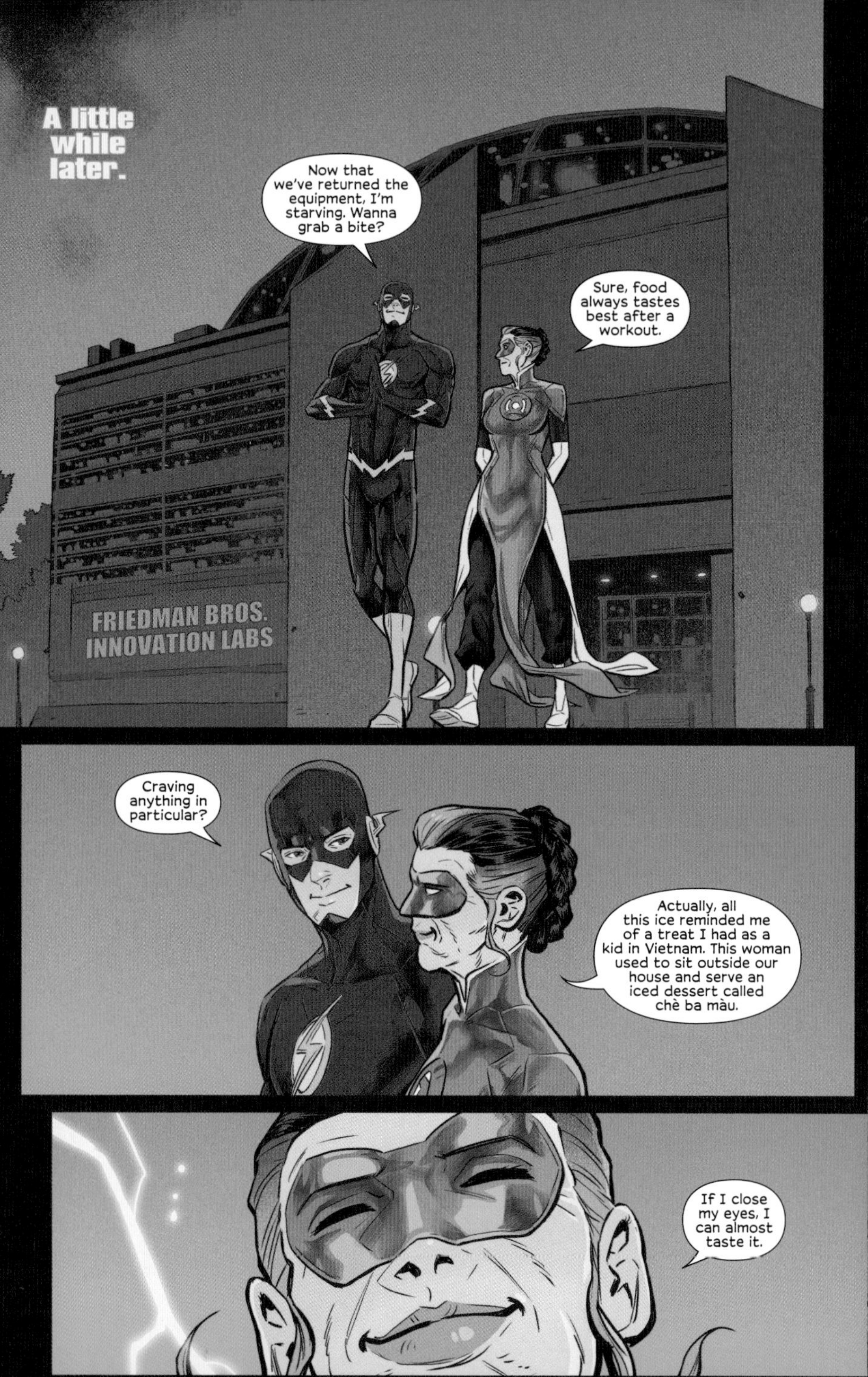
A little while later.
Now that we've returned the equipment, I'm starving. Wanna grab a bite?
Sure, food always tastes best after a workout.
FRIEDMAN BROS. INNOVATION LABS
Craving anything in particular?
Actually, all this ice reminded me of a treat I had as a kid in Vietnam. This woman used to sit outside our house and serve an iced dessert called chè ba màu.
If I close my eyes, I can almost taste it.

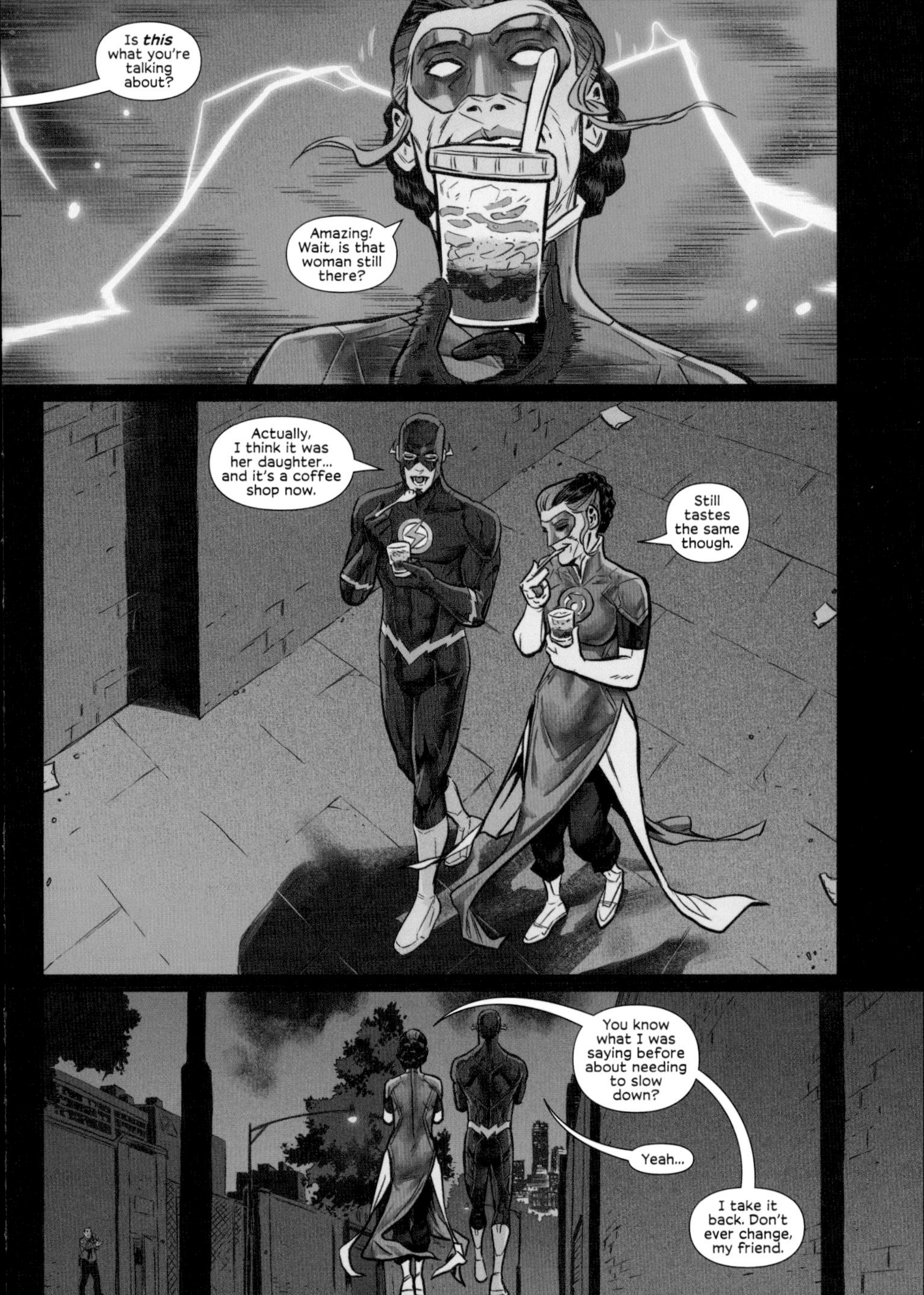
Is *this* what you're talking about?
Amazing! Wait, is that woman still there?
Actually, I think it was her daughter... and it's a coffee shop now.
Still tastes the same though.
You know what I was saying before about needing to slow down?
Yeah...
I take it back. Don't ever change, my friend.

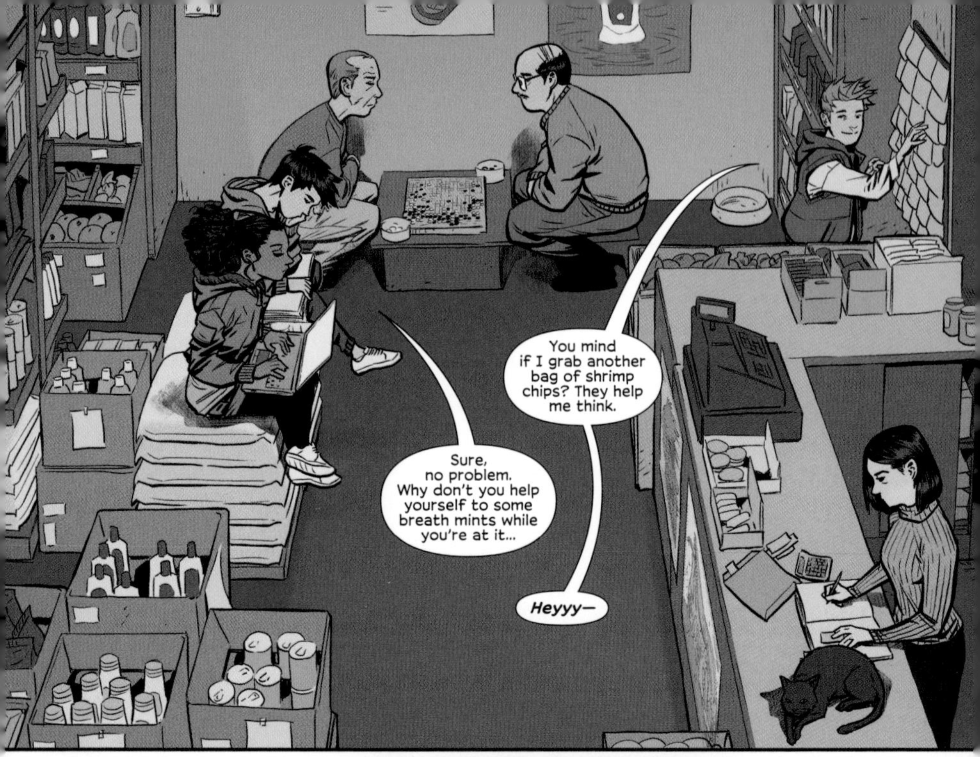
You mind if I grab another bag of shrimp chips? They help me think.
Sure, no problem. Why don't you help yourself to some breath mints while you're at it...
Heyyy—

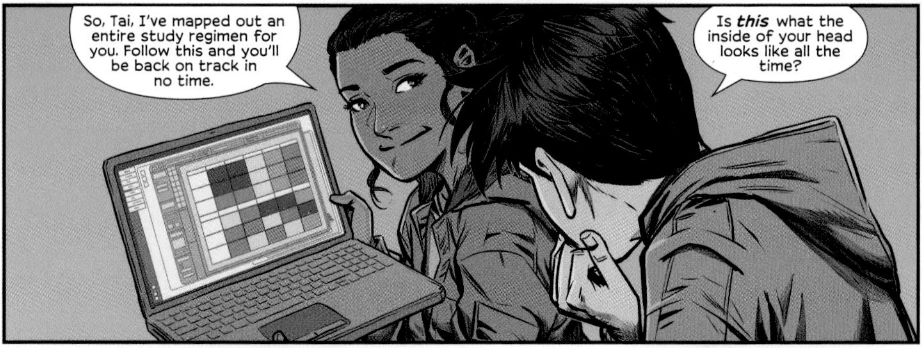
So, Tai, I've mapped out an entire study regimen for you. Follow this and you'll be back on track in no time.
Is *this* what the inside of your head looks like all the time?

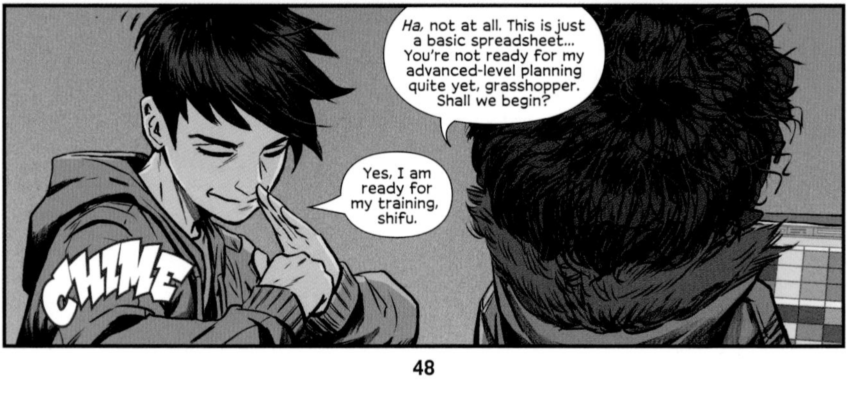
Ha, not at all. This is just a basic spreadsheet... You're not ready for my advanced-level planning quite yet, grasshopper. Shall we begin?
Yes, I am ready for my training, shifu.
CHIME

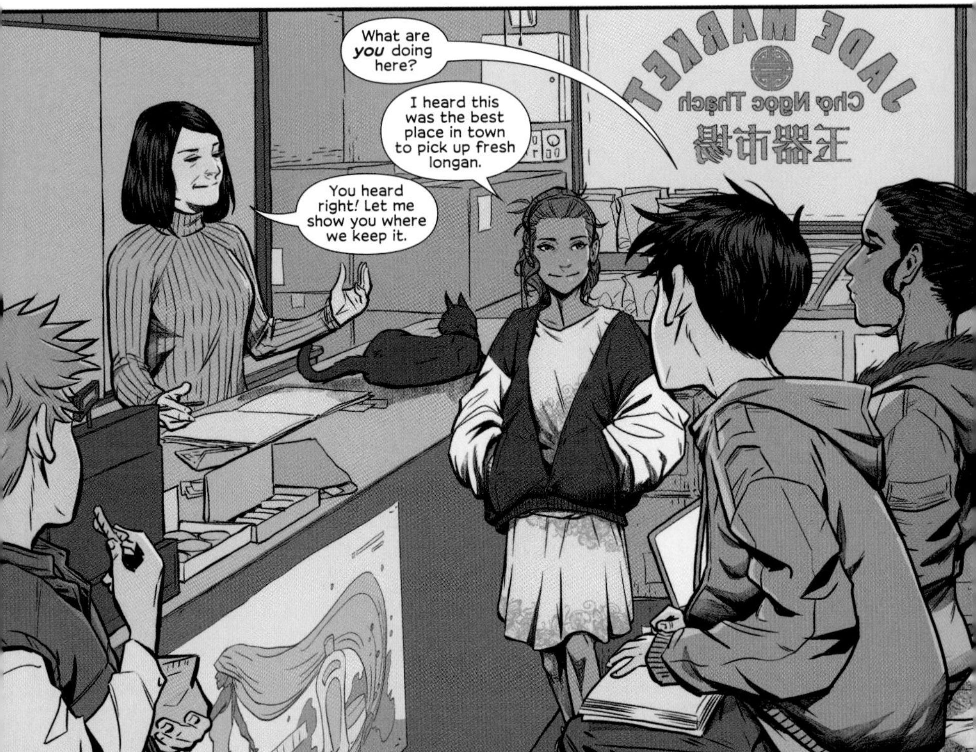
JADE MARKET
Chợ Ngọc Thạch
What are *you* doing here?
I heard this was the best place in town to pick up fresh longan.
You heard right! Let me show you where we keep it.

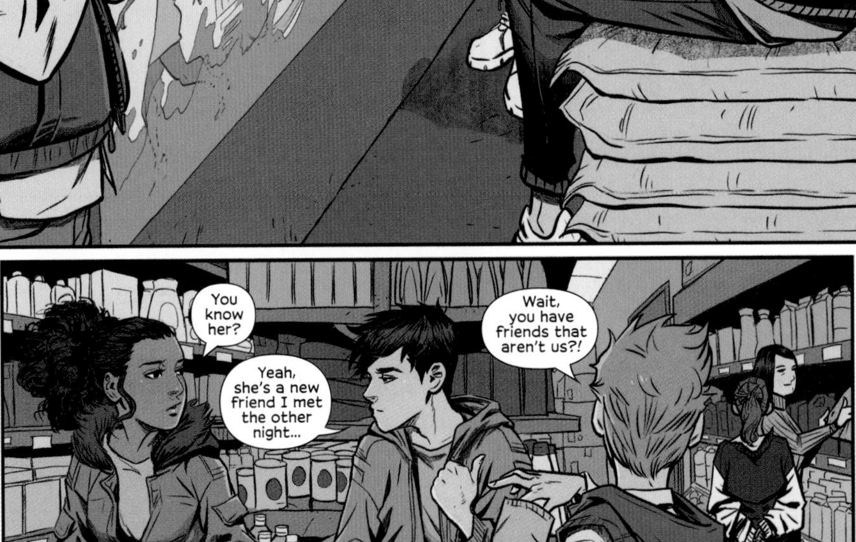
You know her?
Yeah, she's a new friend I met the other night...
Wait, you have friends that aren't us?!

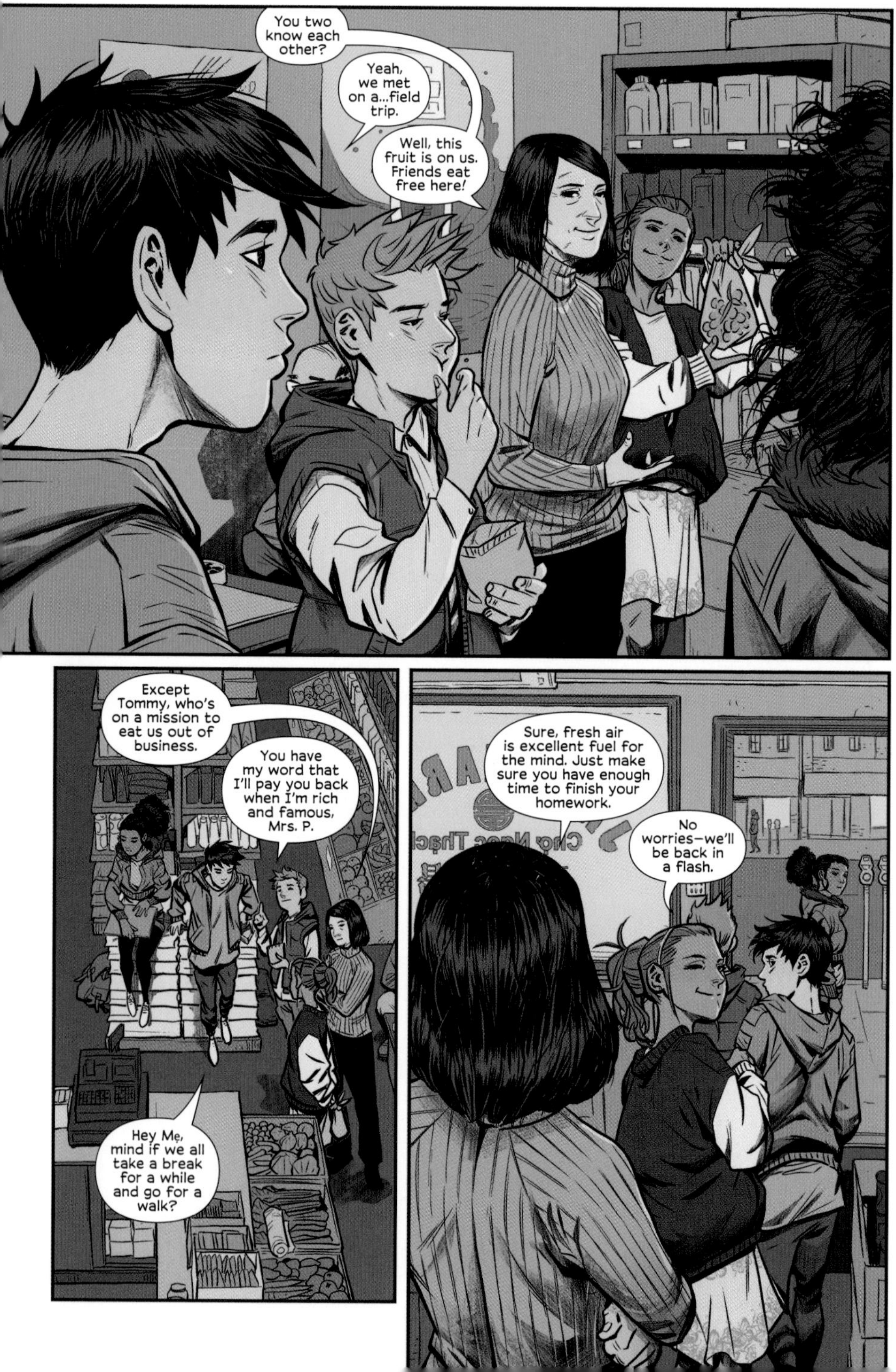
You two know each other?
Yeah, we met on a...field trip.
Well, this fruit is on us. Friends eat free here!
Except Tommy, who's on a mission to eat us out of business.
You have my word that I'll pay you back when I'm rich and famous, Mrs. P.
Hey Mẹ, mind if we all take a break for a while and go for a walk?
Sure, fresh air is excellent fuel for the mind. Just make sure you have enough time to finish your homework.
No worries—we'll be back in a flash.

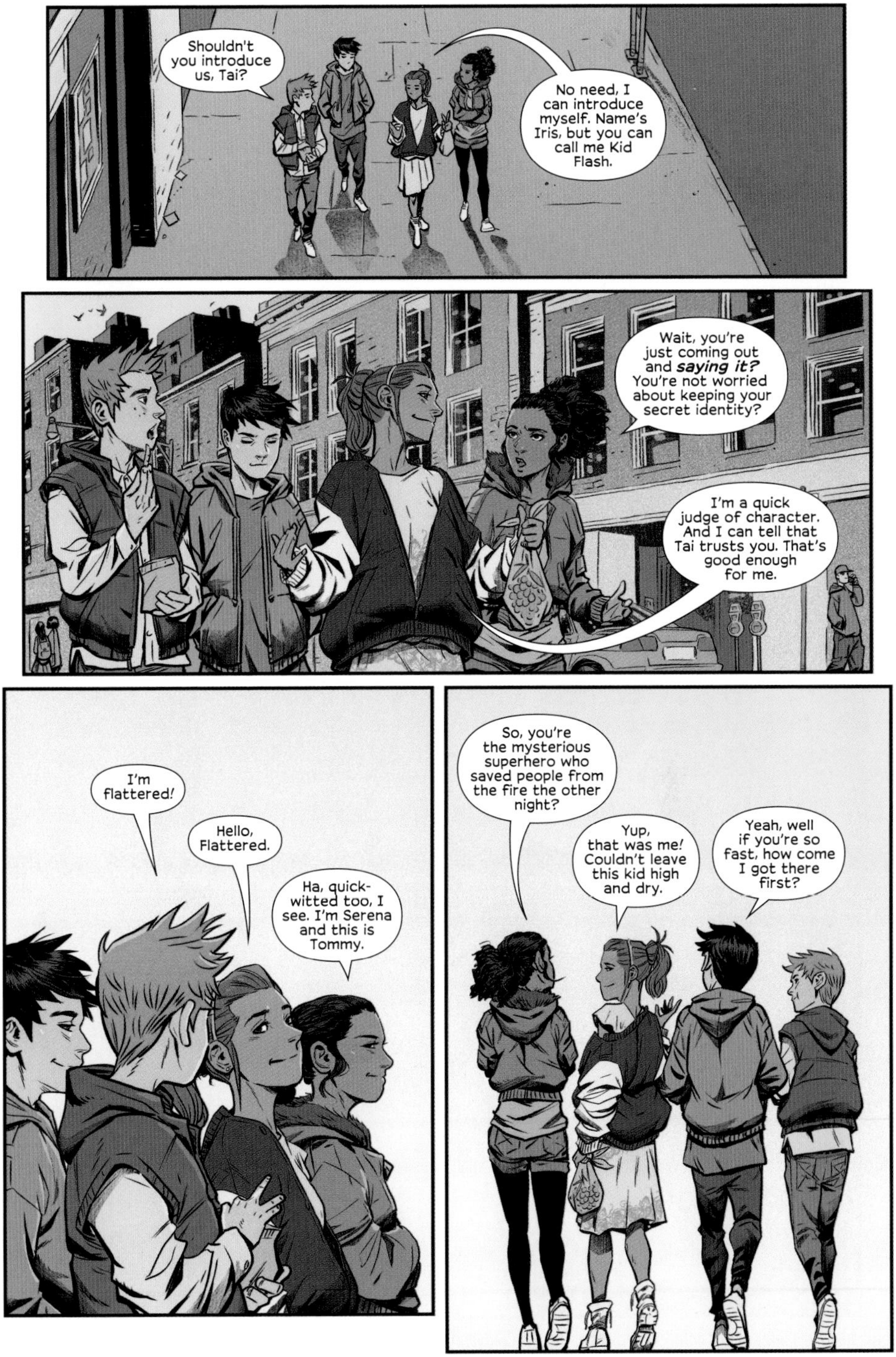
Shouldn't you introduce us, Tai?
No need, I can introduce myself. Name's Iris, but you can call me Kid Flash.
Wait, you're just coming out and *saying it?* You're not worried about keeping your secret identity?
I'm a quick judge of character. And I can tell that Tai trusts you. That's good enough for me.
I'm flattered!
Hello, Flattered.
Ha, quick-witted too, I see. I'm Serena and this is Tommy.
So, you're the mysterious superhero who saved people from the fire the other night?
Yup, that was me! Couldn't leave this kid high and dry.
Yeah, well if you're so fast, how come I got there first?

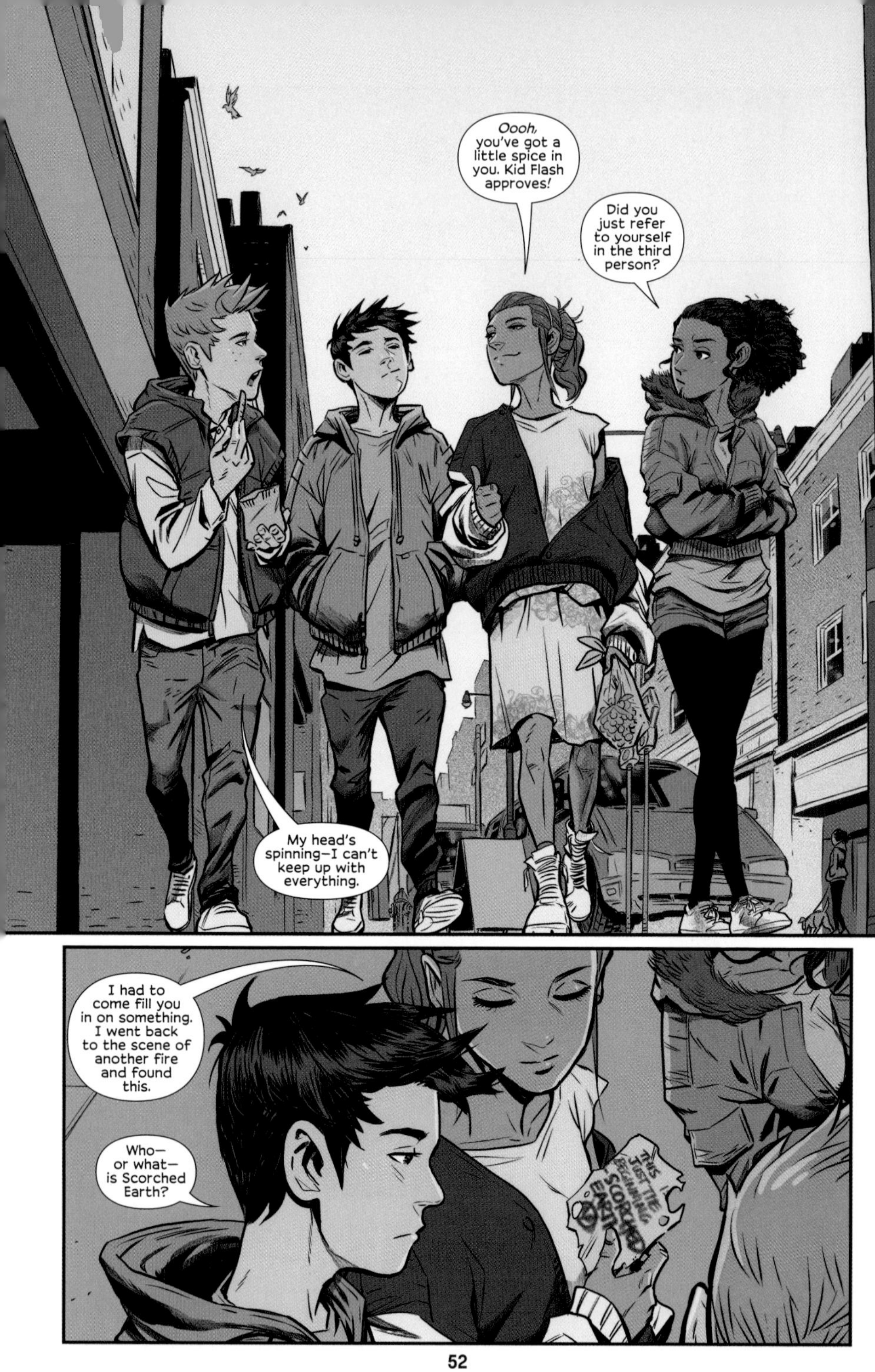
Oooh, you've got a little spice in you. Kid Flash approves!
Did you just refer to yourself in the third person?
My head's spinning—I can't keep up with everything.
I had to come fill you in on something. I went back to the scene of another fire and found this.
Who—or what—is Scorched Earth?
THIS JUST THE BEGINNING
SCORCHED EARTH

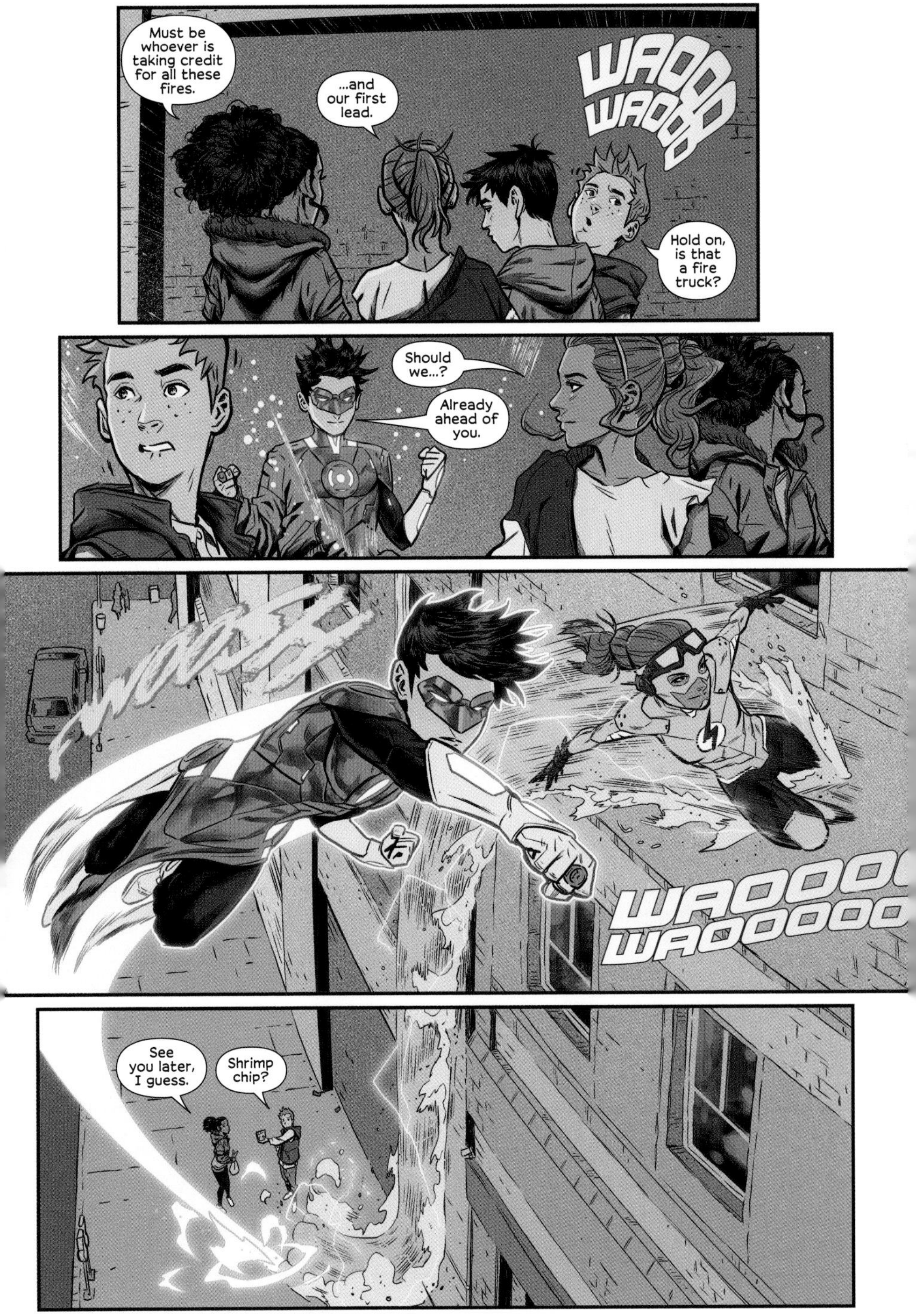
Must be whoever is taking credit for all these fires.
...and our first lead.
WAOOO WAOOO
Hold on, is that a fire truck?
Should we...?
Already ahead of you.
WOOSH
WAOOOOO WAOOOOOO
See you later, I guess.
Shrimp chip?

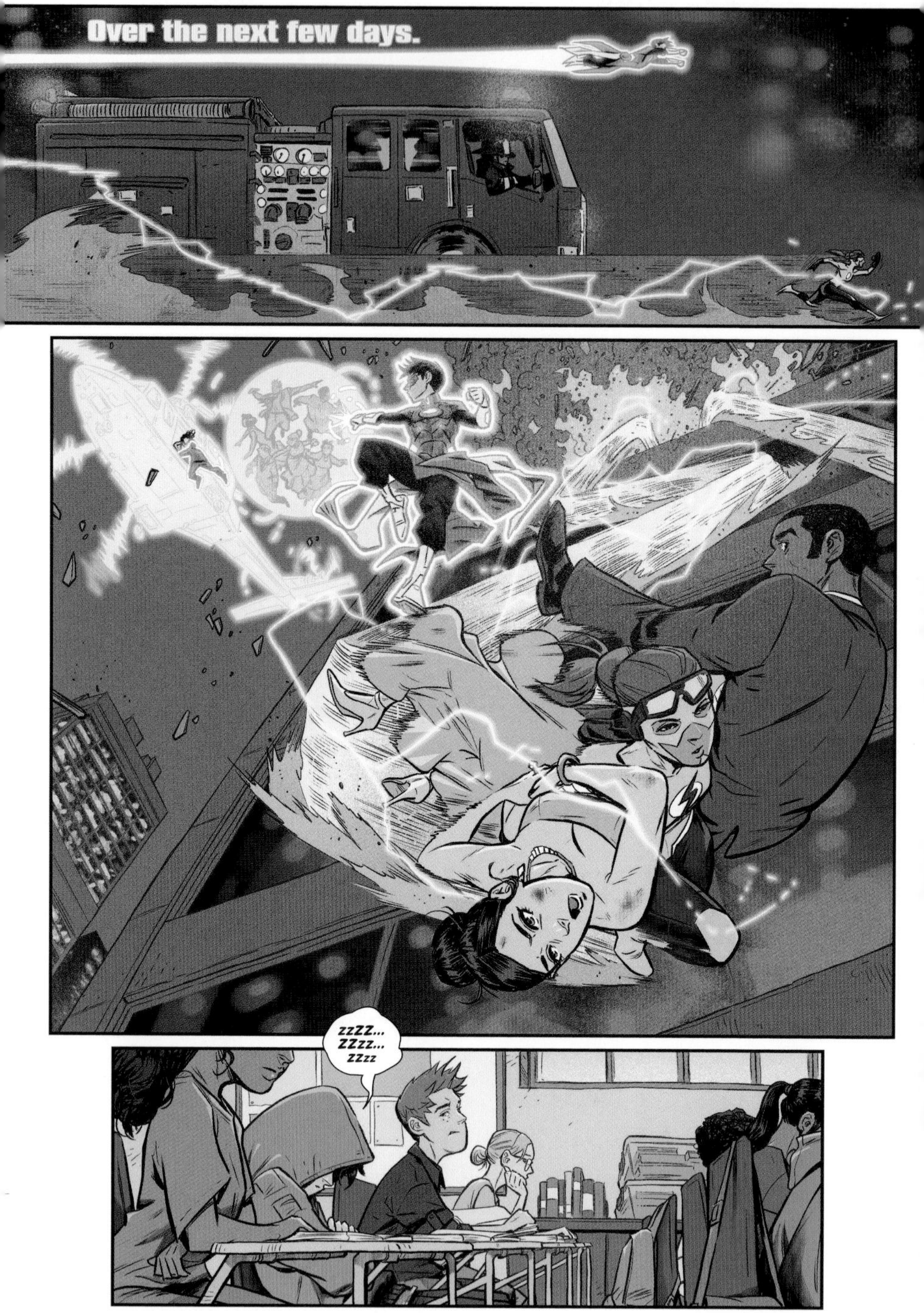
Over the next few days.
zzZZ... ZZzz... ZZzz

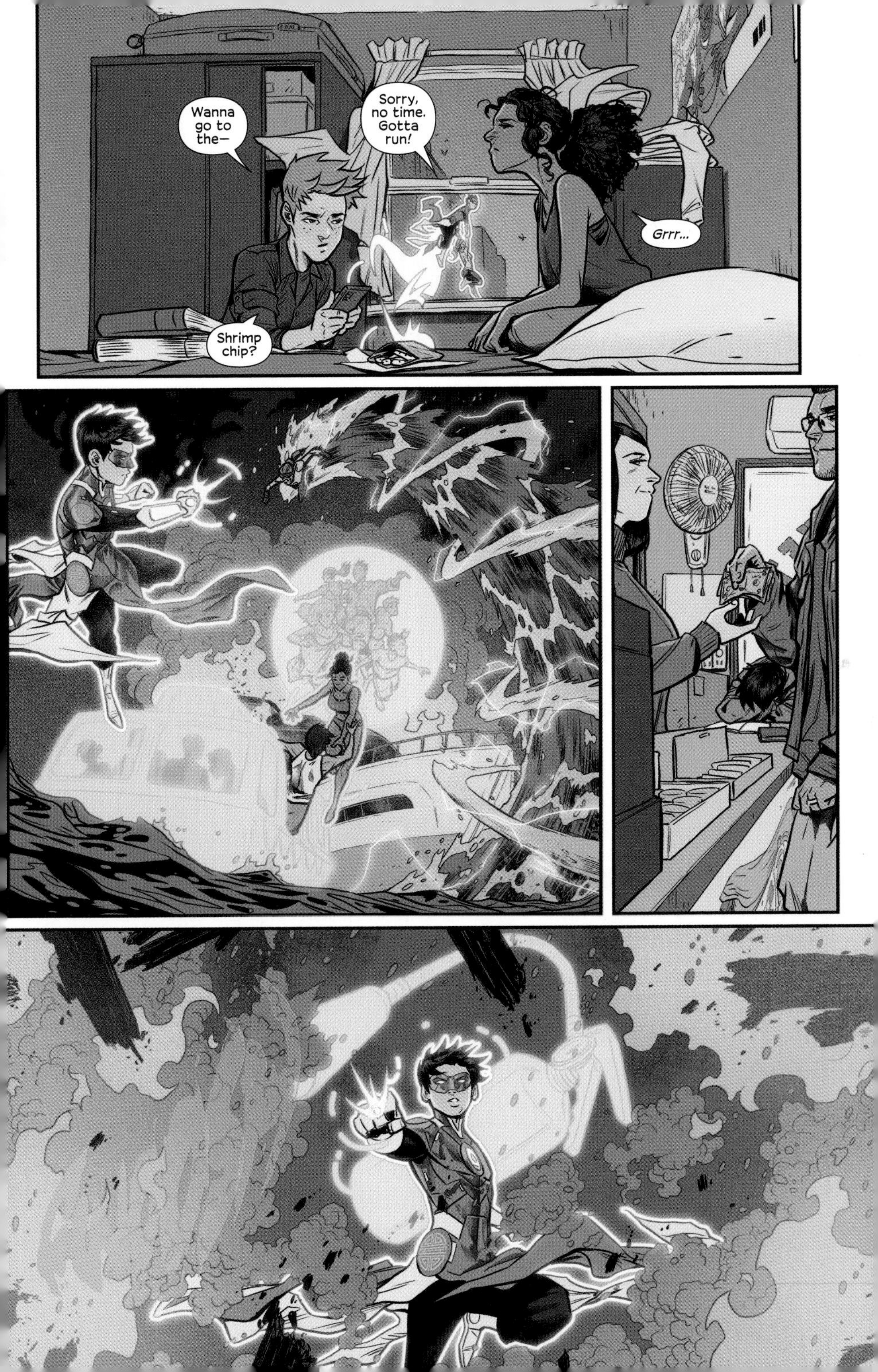
Wanna go to the—
Sorry, no time. Gotta run!
Grrr...
Shrimp chip?

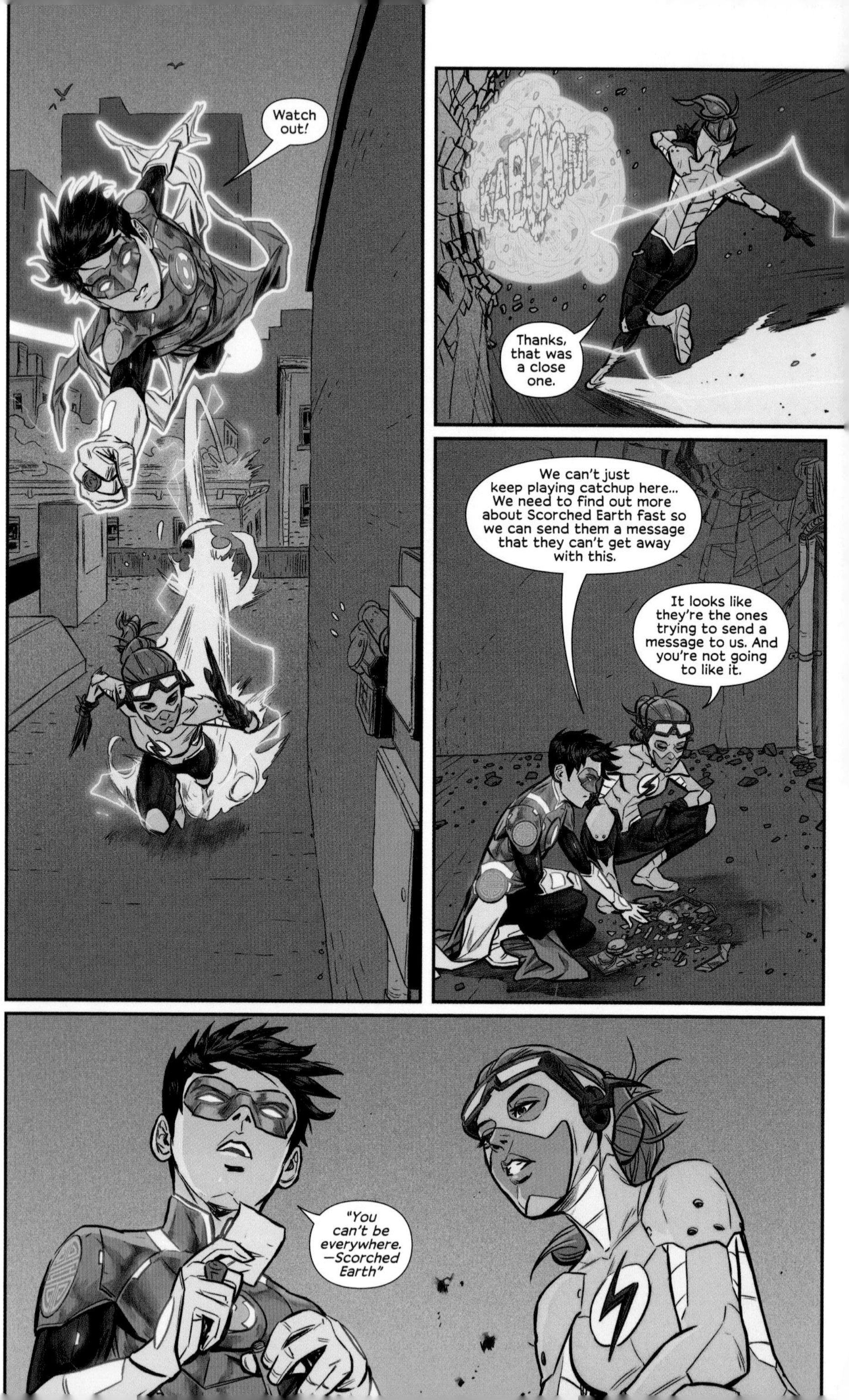

Watch out!
KABLOOM
Thanks, that was a close one.
We can't just keep playing catchup here... We need to find out more about Scorched Earth fast so we can send them a message that they can't get away with this.
It looks like they're the ones trying to send a message to us. And you're not going to like it.
"You can't be everywhere. —Scorched Earth"

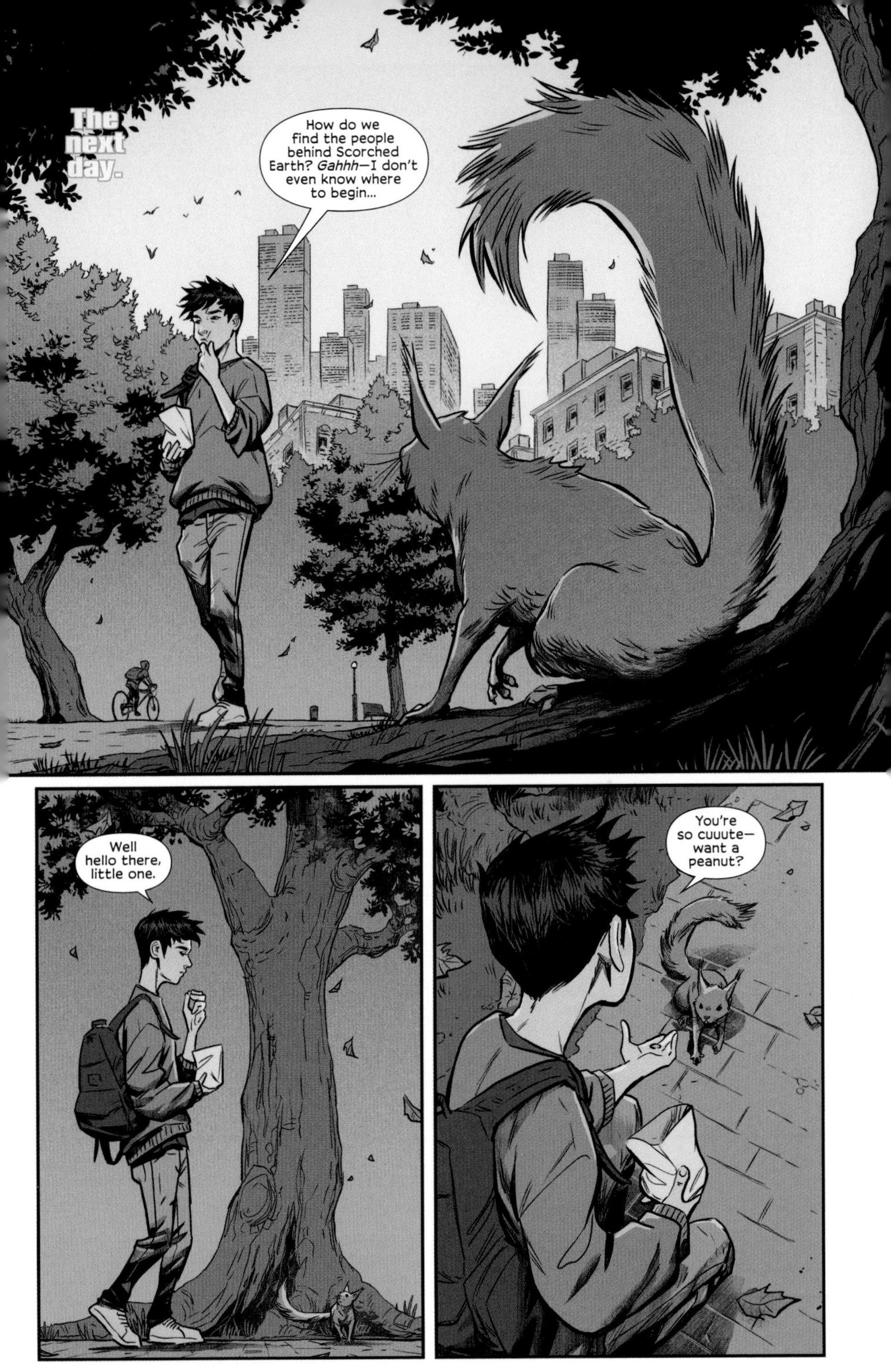
The next day.
How do we find the people behind Scorched Earth? *Gahhh*—I don't even know where to begin...
Well hello there, little one.
You're so cuuute—want a peanut?

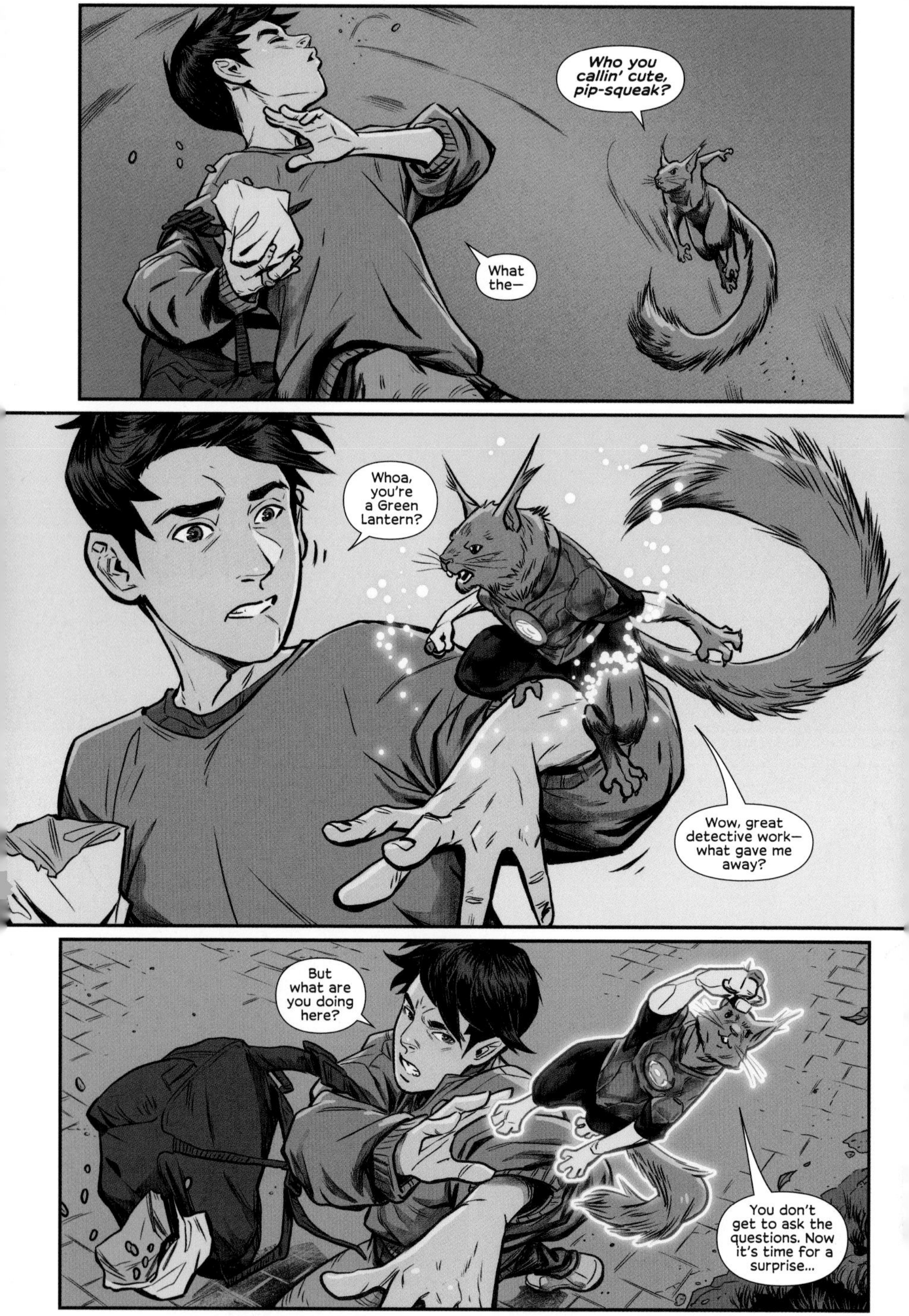
Who you callin' cute, pip-squeak?
What the—
Whoa, you're a Green Lantern?
Wow, great detective work—what gave me away?
But what are you doing here?
You don't get to ask the questions. Now it's time for a surprise...

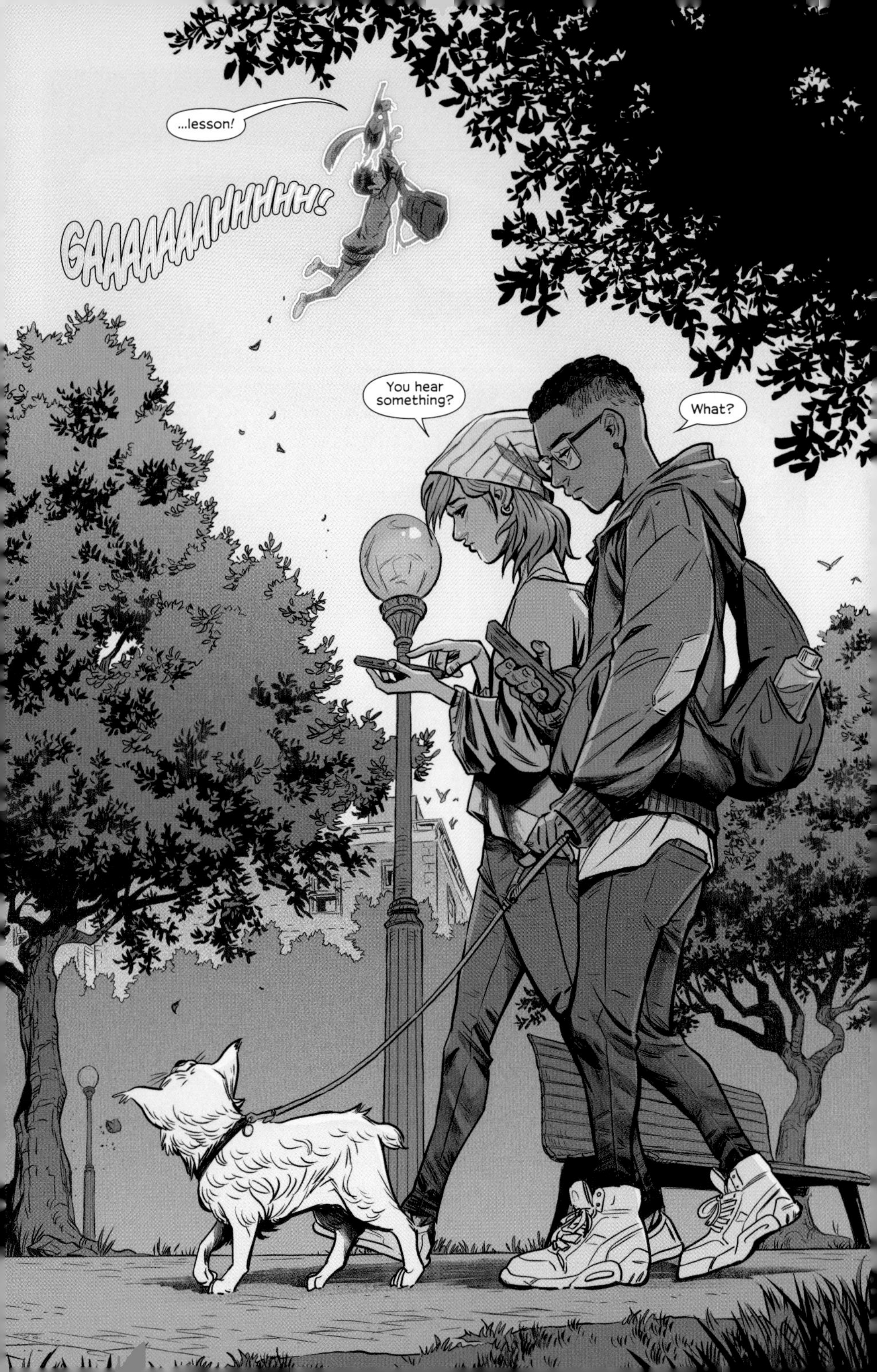
...lesson!
GAAAAAAAHHHHH!
You hear something?
What?

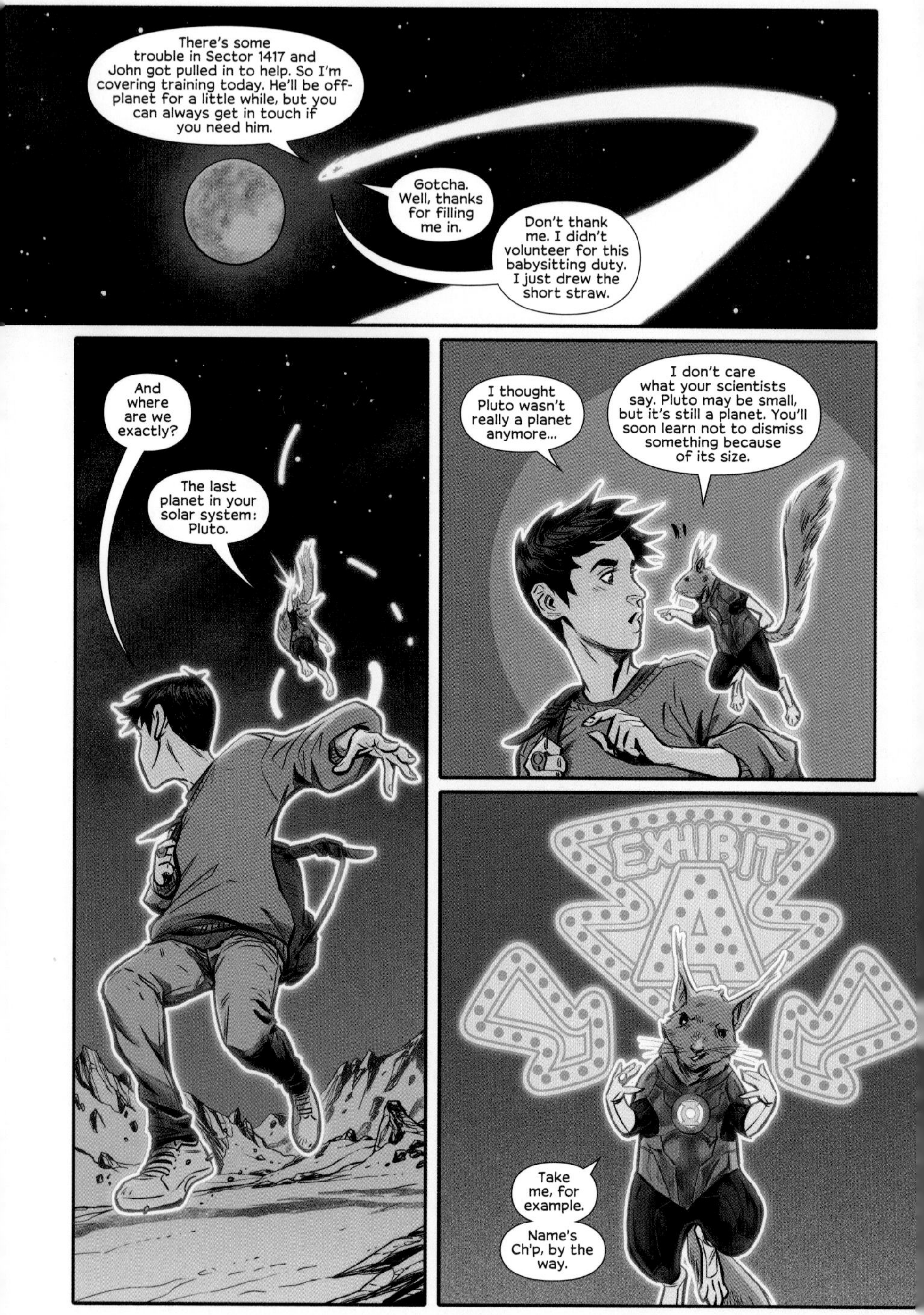
There's some trouble in Sector 1417 and John got pulled in to help. So I'm covering training today. He'll be off-planet for a little while, but you can always get in touch if you need him.
Gotcha. Well, thanks for filling me in.
Don't thank me. I didn't volunteer for this babysitting duty. I just drew the short straw.
And where are we exactly?
The last planet in your solar system: Pluto.
I thought Pluto wasn't really a planet anymore...
I don't care what your scientists say. Pluto may be small, but it's still a planet. You'll soon learn not to dismiss something because of its size.
EXHIBIT
A
Take me, for example.
Name's Ch'p, by the way.

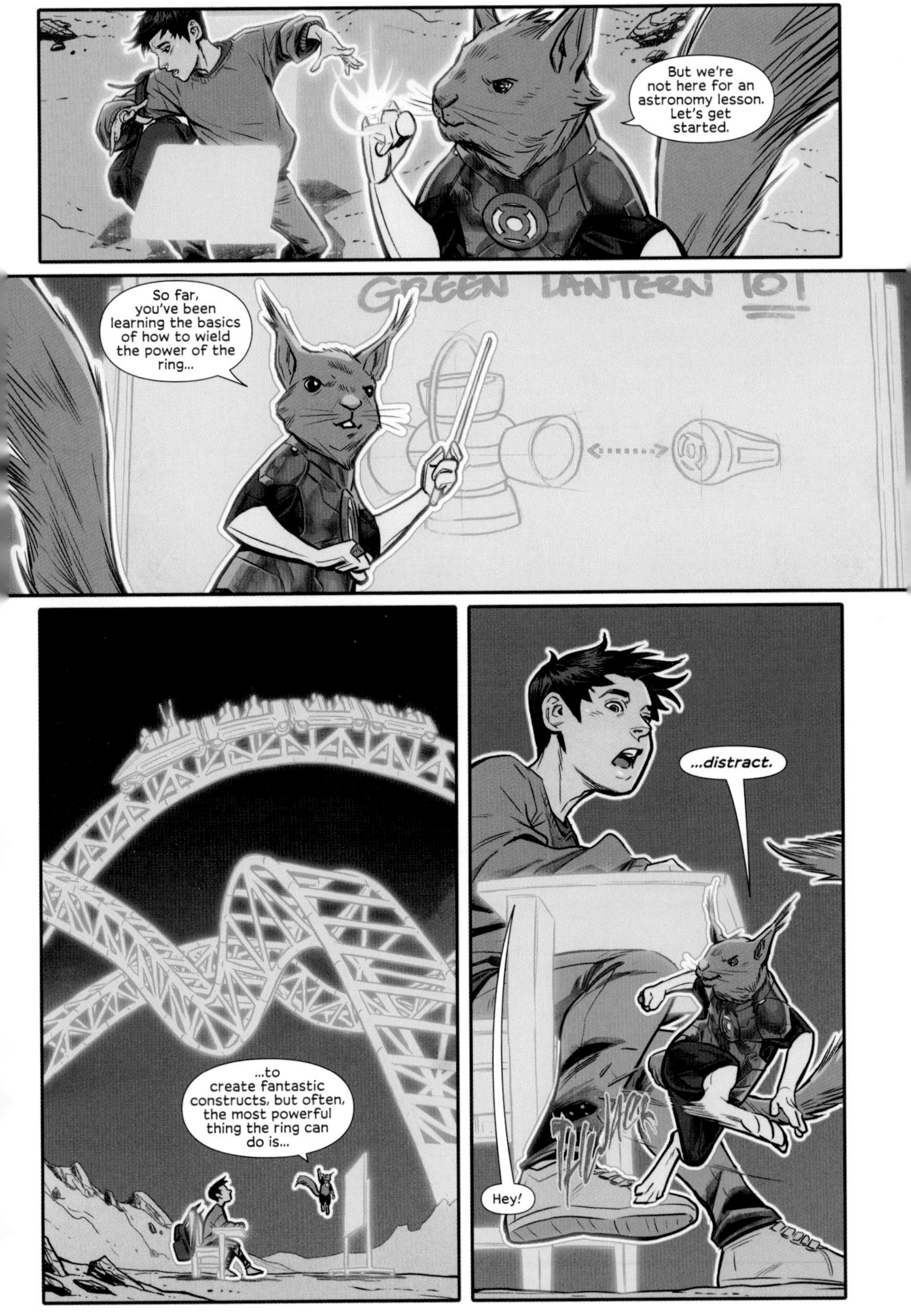
But we're not here for an astronomy lesson. Let's get started.
GREEN LANTERN 101
So far, you've been learning the basics of how to wield the power of the ring...
...to create fantastic constructs, but often, the most powerful thing the ring can do is...
...distract.
THWACK
Hey!

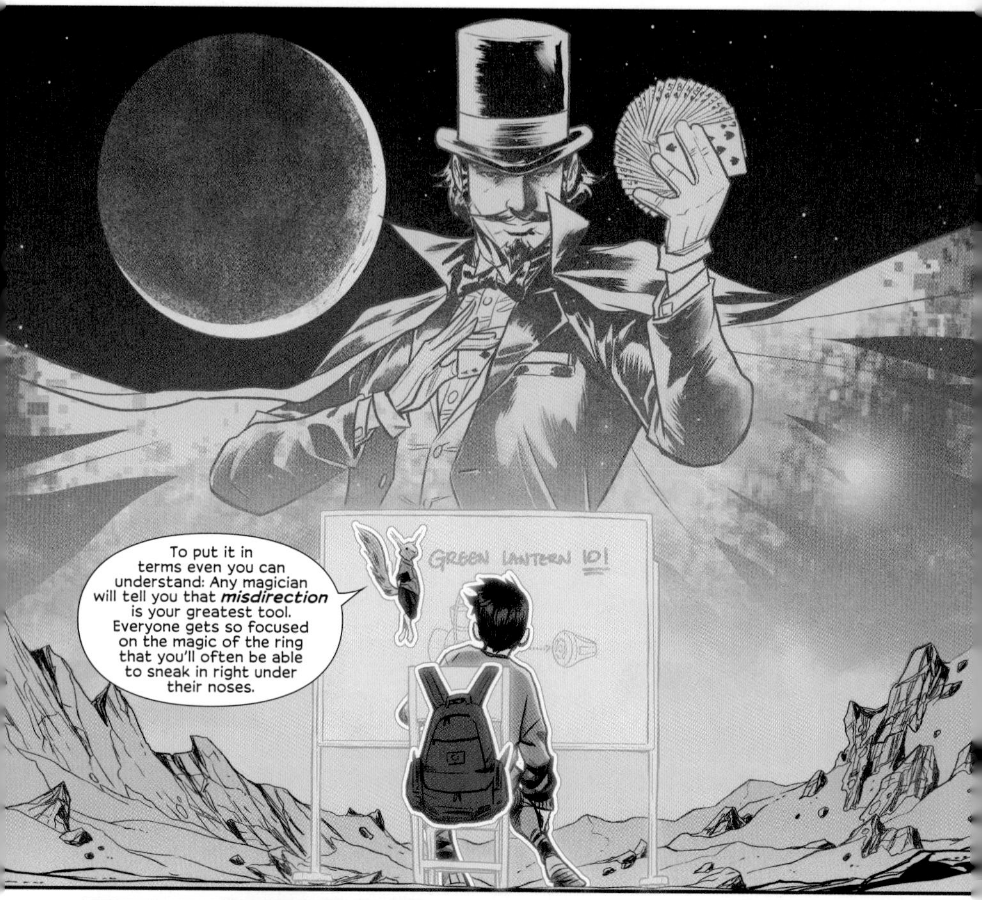
GREEN LANTERN 101
To put it in terms even you can understand: Any magician will tell you that ***misdirection*** is your greatest tool. Everyone gets so focused on the magic of the ring that you'll often be able to sneak in right under their noses.

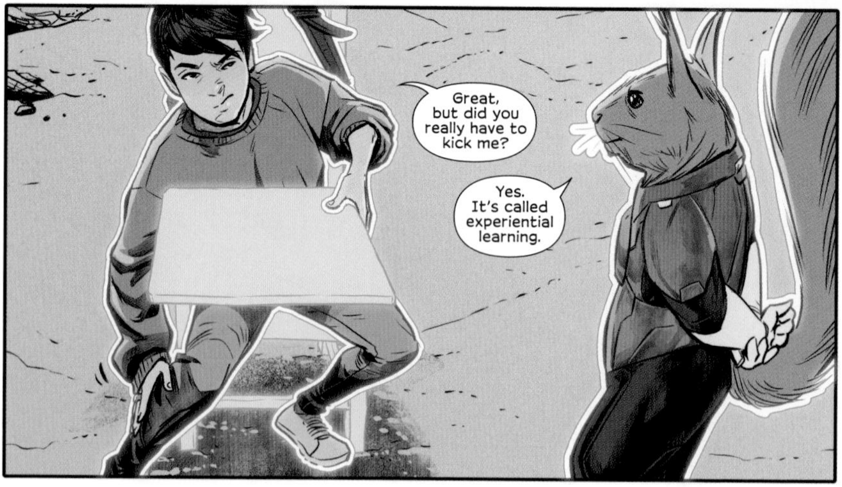
Great, but did you really have to kick me?
Yes. It's called experiential learning.

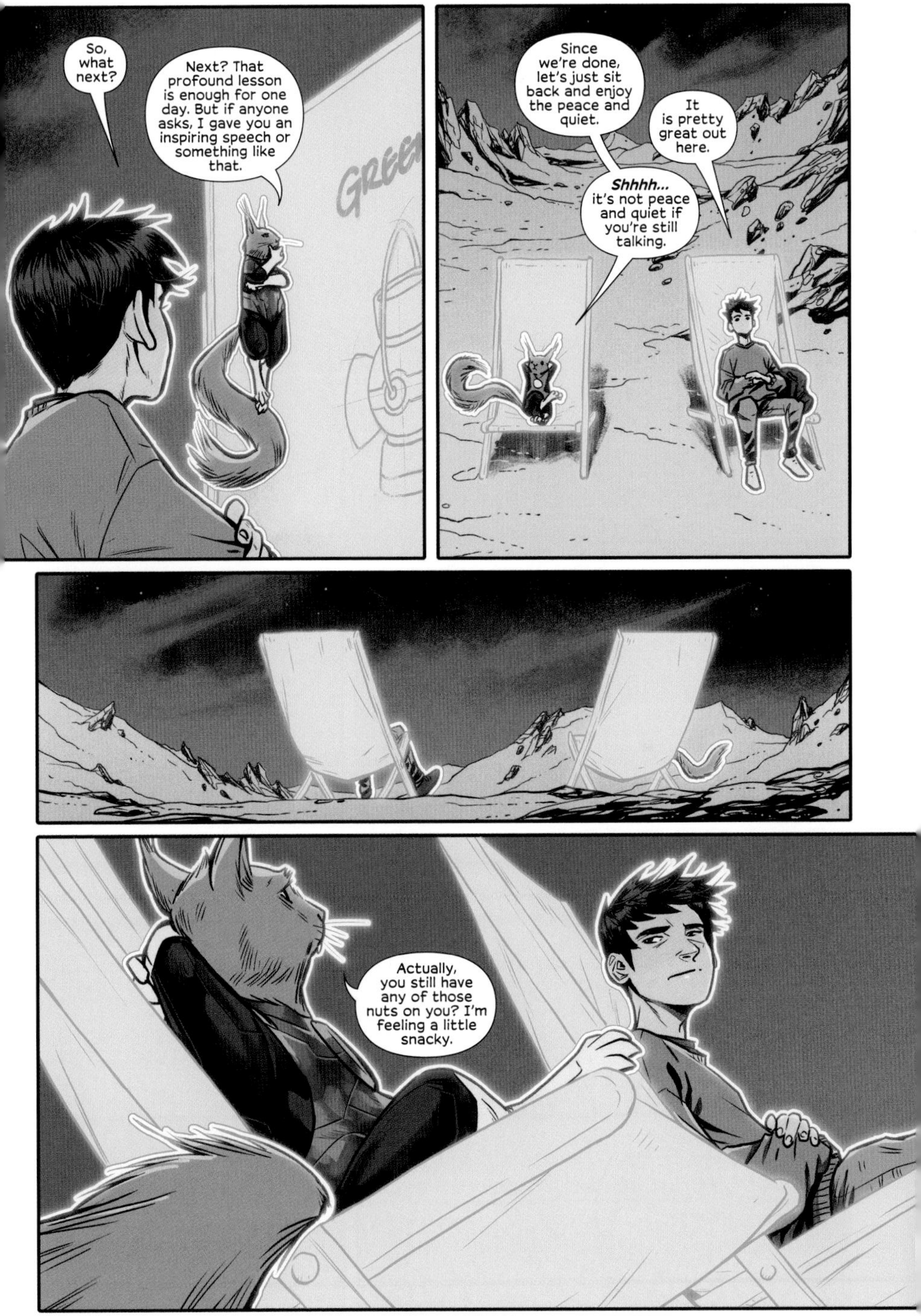

So, what next?
Next? That profound lesson is enough for one day. But if anyone asks, I gave you an inspiring speech or something like that.
GREE
Since we're done, let's just sit back and enjoy the peace and quiet.
It is pretty great out here.
Shhhh... it's not peace and quiet if you're still talking.
Actually, you still have any of those nuts on you? I'm feeling a little snacky.

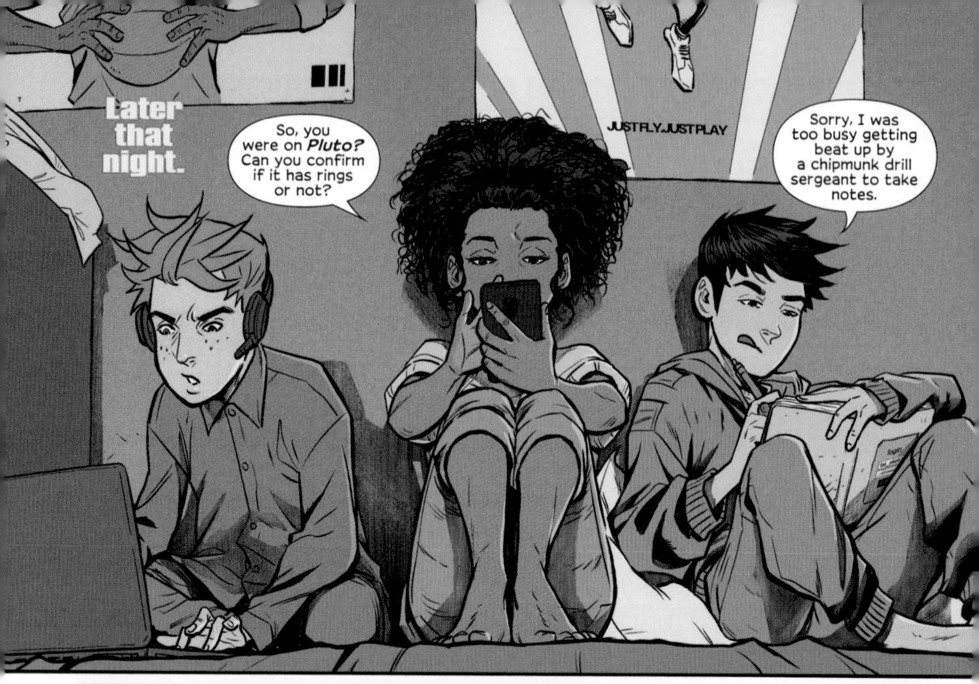
Later that night.
So, you were on *Pluto?* Can you confirm if it has rings or not?
JUSTFLY.JUSTPLAY
Sorry, I was too busy getting beat up by a chipmunk drill sergeant to take notes.

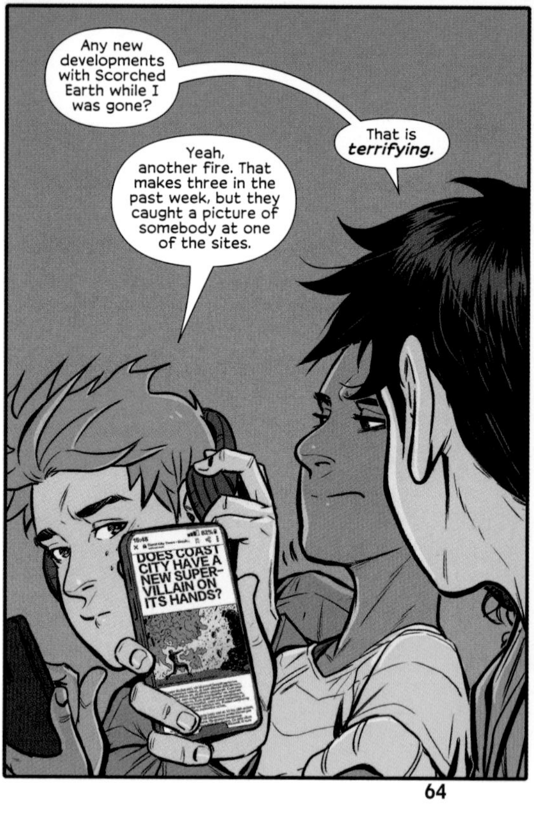
Any new developments with Scorched Earth while I was gone?
That is *terrifying.*
Yeah, another fire. That makes three in the past week, but they caught a picture of somebody at one of the sites.
DOES COAST CITY HAVE A NEW SUPER-VILLAIN ON ITS HANDS?

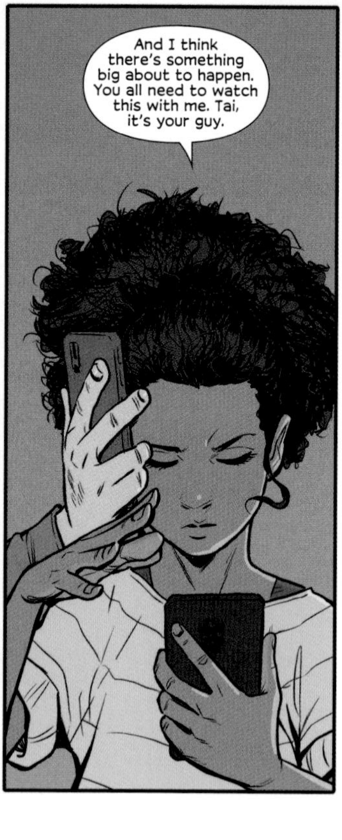
And I think there's something big about to happen. You all need to watch this with me. Tai, it's your guy.

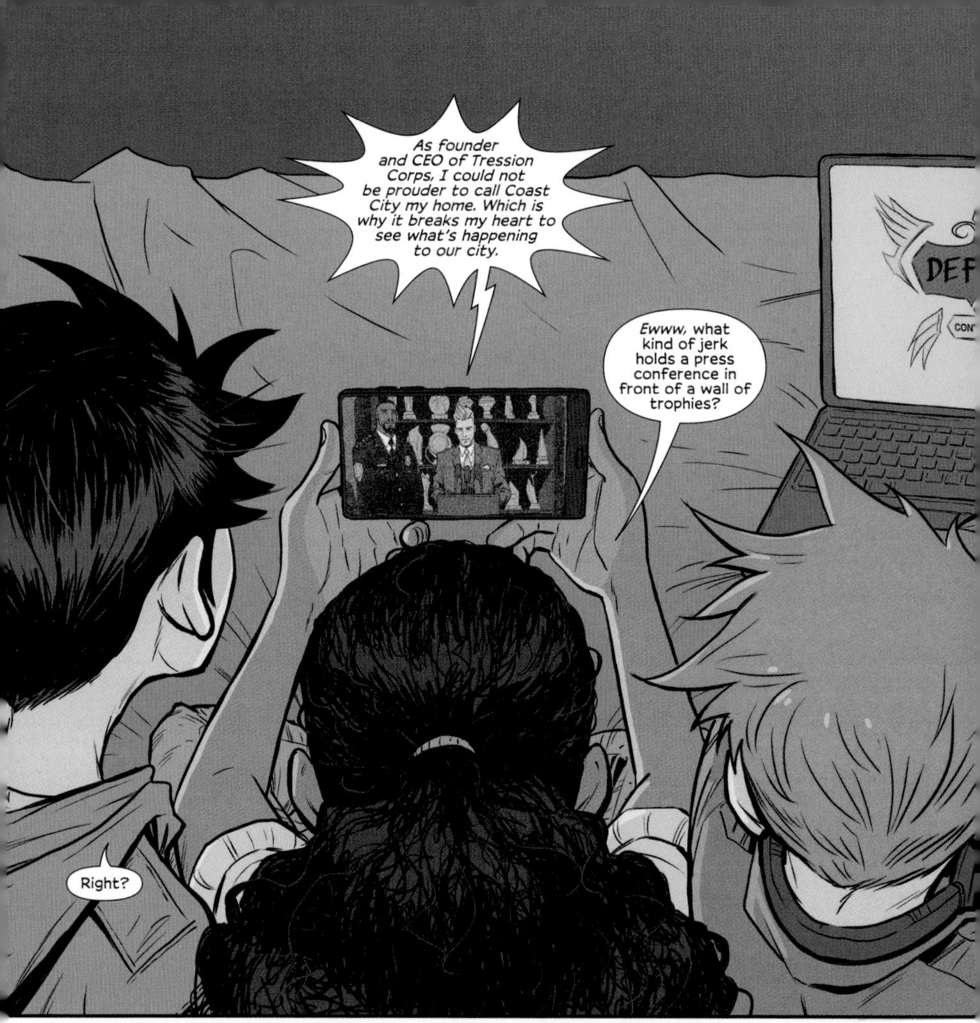

As founder and CEO of Tression Corps, I could not be prouder to call Coast City my home. Which is why it breaks my heart to see what's happening to our city.
Ewww, what kind of jerk holds a press conference in front of a wall of trophies?
Right?

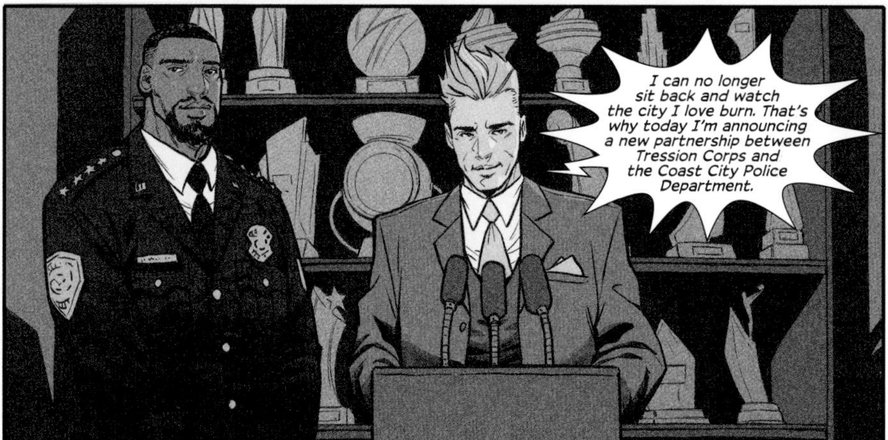

I can no longer sit back and watch the city I love burn. That's why today I'm announcing a new partnership between Tression Corps and the Coast City Police Department.

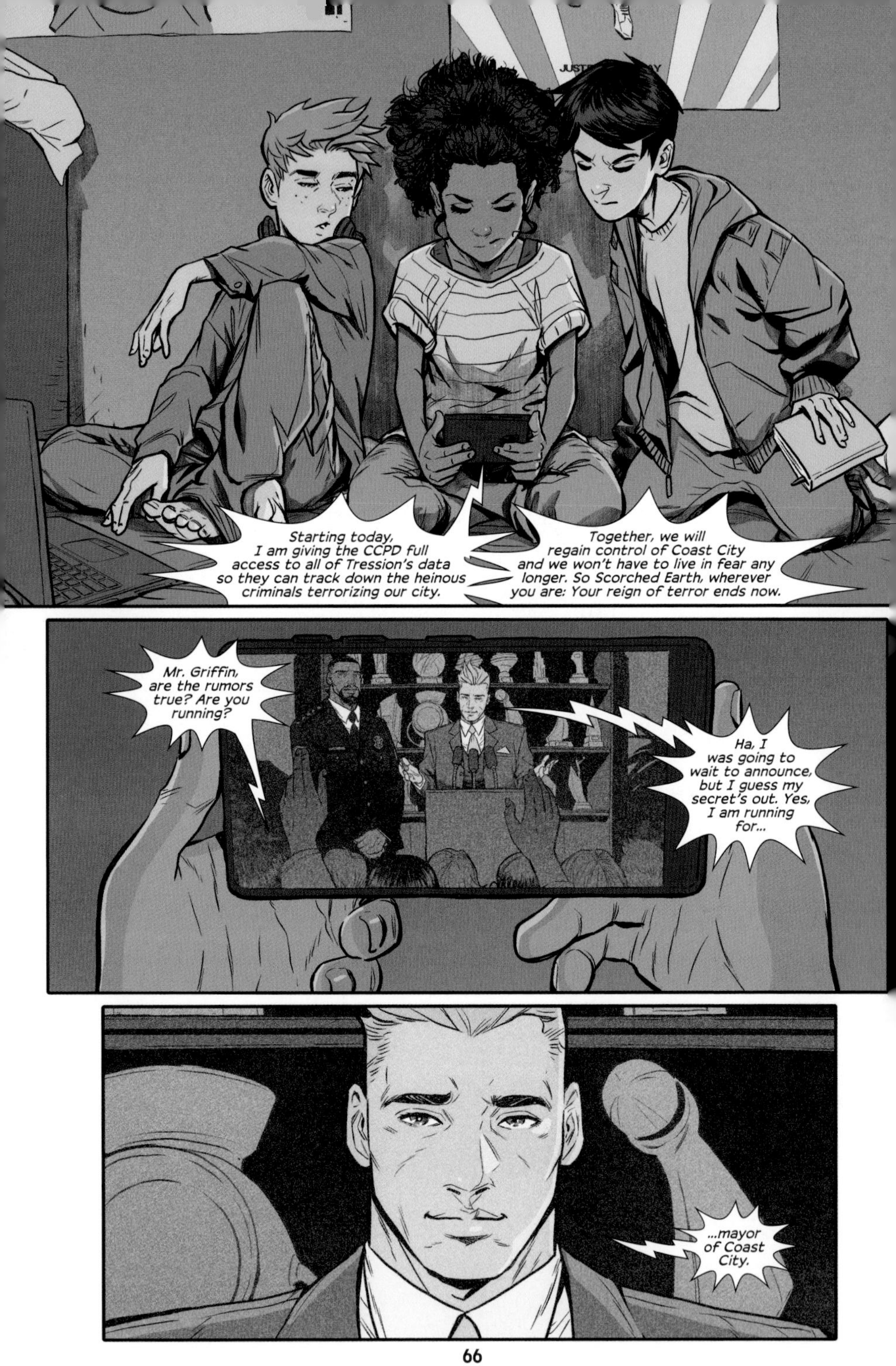

Starting today, I am giving the CCPD full access to all of Tression's data so they can track down the heinous criminals terrorizing our city.
Together, we will regain control of Coast City and we won't have to live in fear any longer. So Scorched Earth, wherever you are: Your reign of terror ends now.
Mr. Griffin, are the rumors true? Are you running?
Ha, I was going to wait to announce, but I guess my secret's out. Yes, I am running for...
...mayor of Coast City.

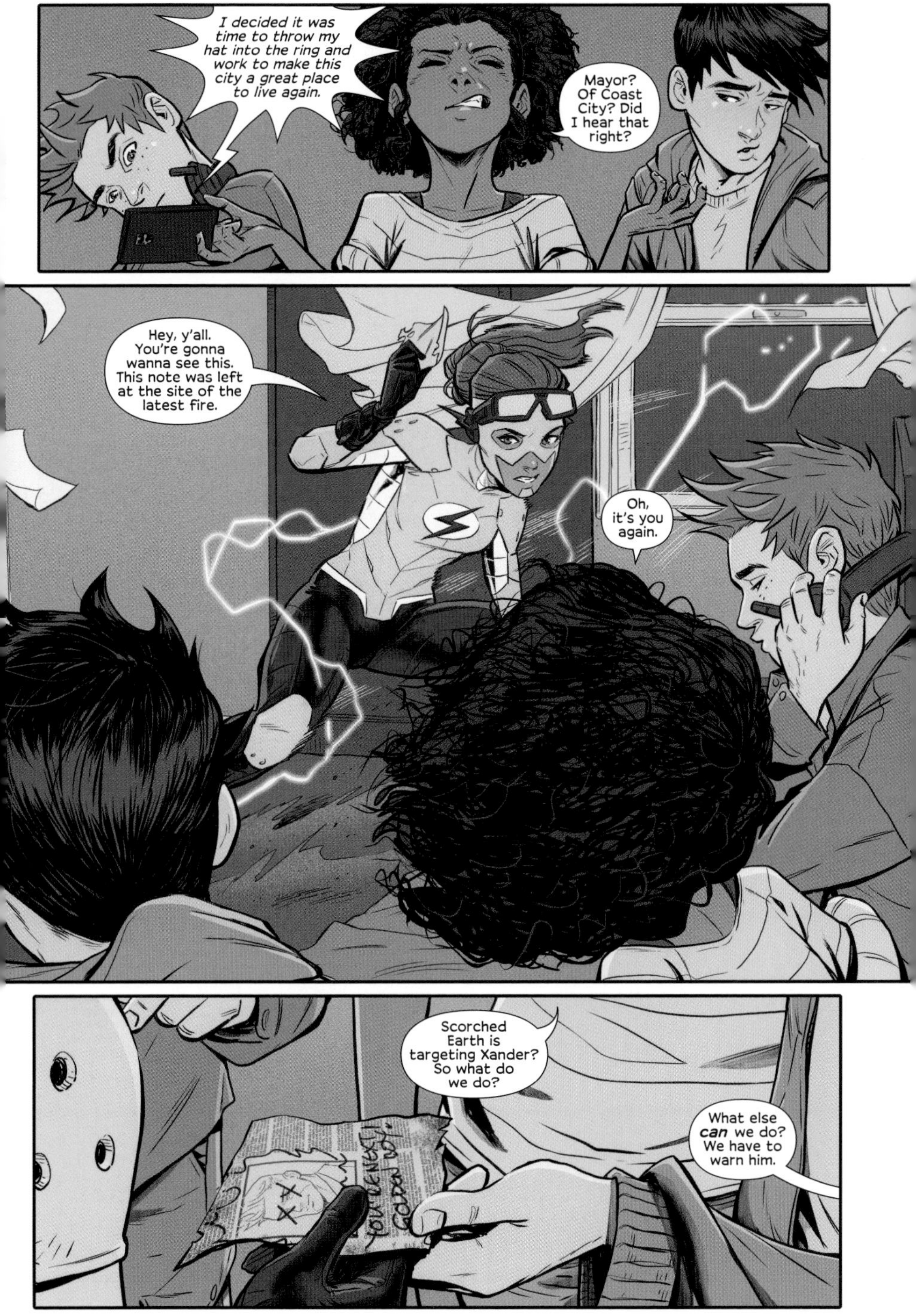
I decided it was time to throw my hat into the ring and work to make this city a great place to live again.
Mayor? Of Coast City? Did I hear that right?
Hey, y'all. You're gonna wanna see this. This note was left at the site of the latest fire.
Oh, it's you again.
Scorched Earth is targeting Xander? So what do we do?
What else *can* we do? We have to warn him.

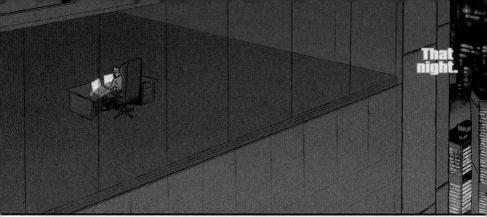

That night.

You know it's rude to hover, right?

I would have knocked on the front door, but your security is pretty tight.

Can't be too careful these days.

Speaking of being careful, I have to talk to you—

I'm not in the mood for another sanctimonious Green Lantern lecture from you. I've got important work to do.

68

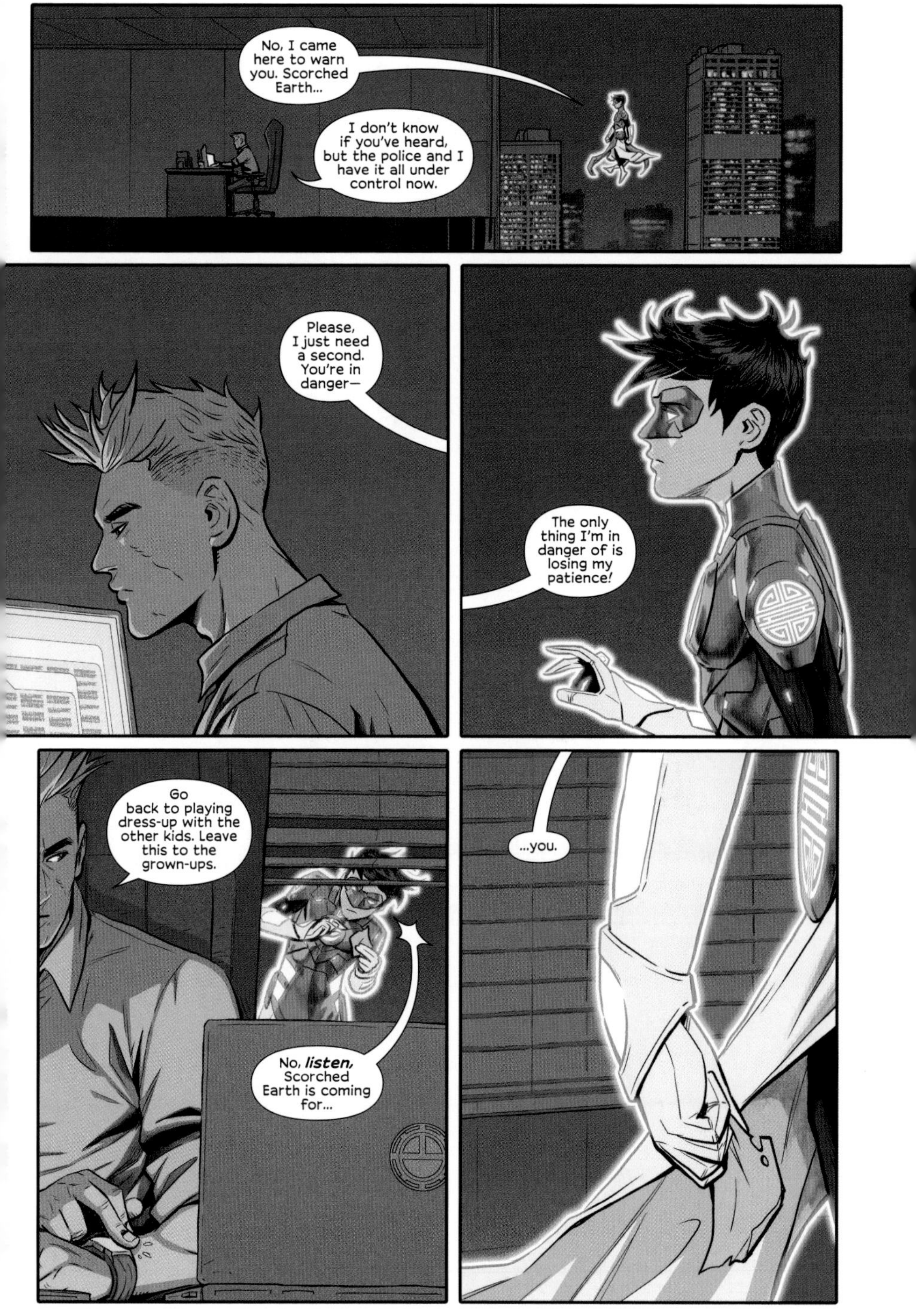
No, I came here to warn you. Scorched Earth...
I don't know if you've heard, but the police and I have it all under control now.
Please, I just need a second. You're in danger—
The only thing I'm in danger of is losing my patience!
Go back to playing dress-up with the other kids. Leave this to the grown-ups.
No, ***listen,*** Scorched Earth is coming for...
...you.

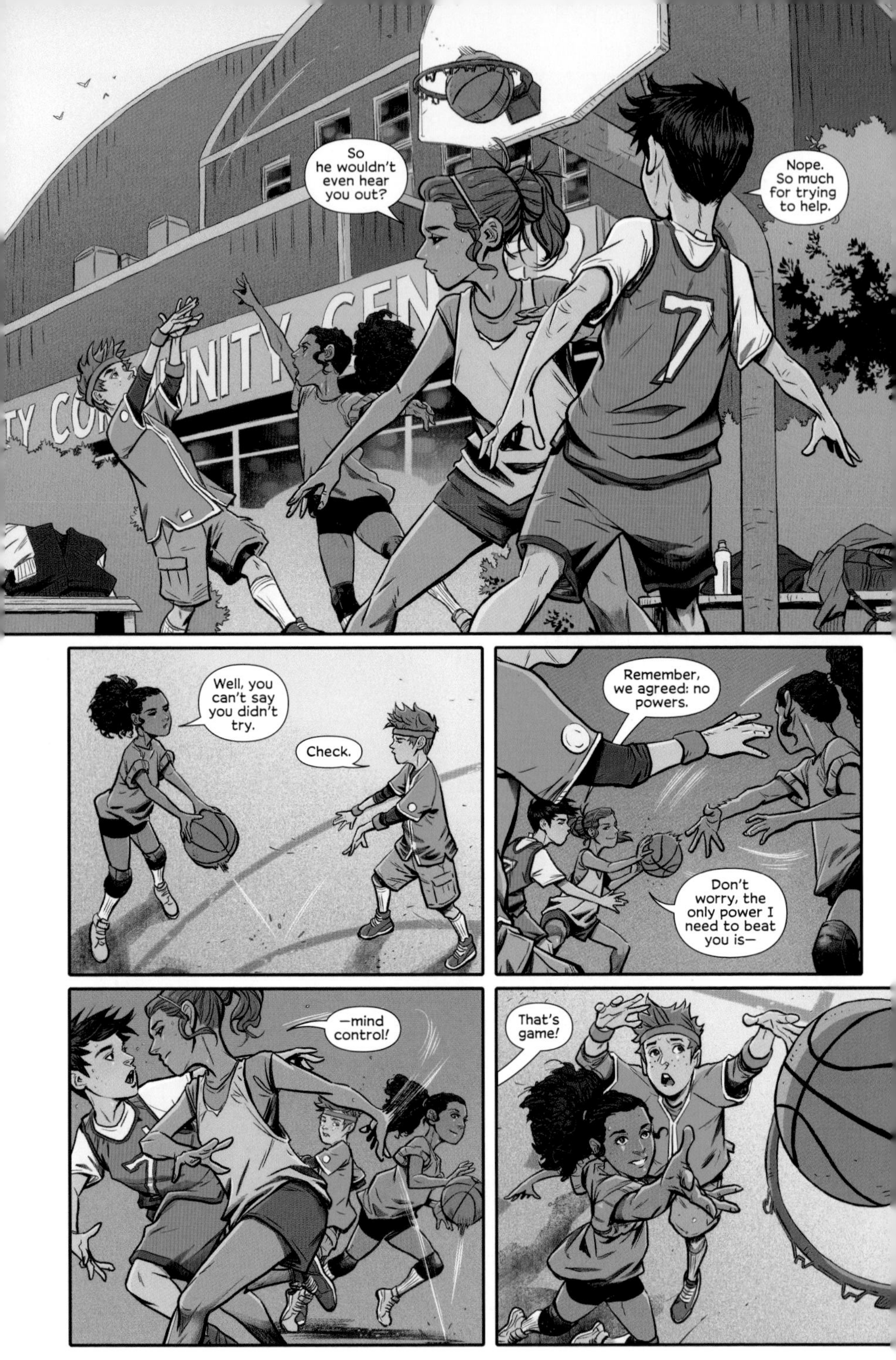
So he wouldn't even hear you out?
Nope. So much for trying to help.
Well, you can't say you didn't try.
Check.
Remember, we agreed: no powers.
Don't worry, the only power I need to beat you is—
—mind control!
That's game!

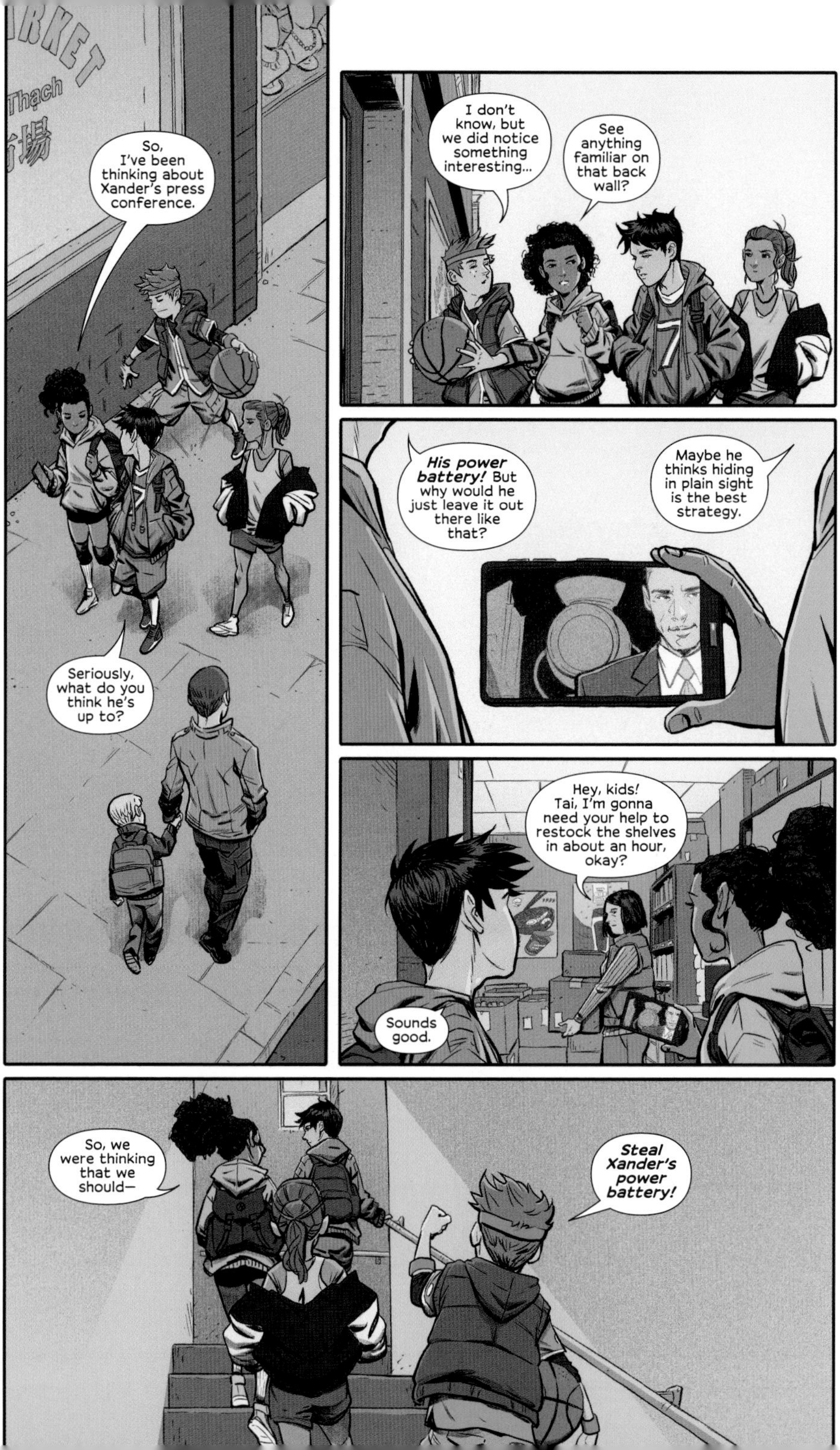

Thạch
So, I've been thinking about Xander's press conference.
Seriously, what do you think he's up to?
I don't know, but we did notice something interesting...
See anything familiar on that back wall?
His power battery! But why would he just leave it out there like that?
Maybe he thinks hiding in plain sight is the best strategy.
Hey, kids! Tai, I'm gonna need your help to restock the shelves in about an hour, okay?
Sounds good.
So, we were thinking that we should—
Steal Xander's power battery!

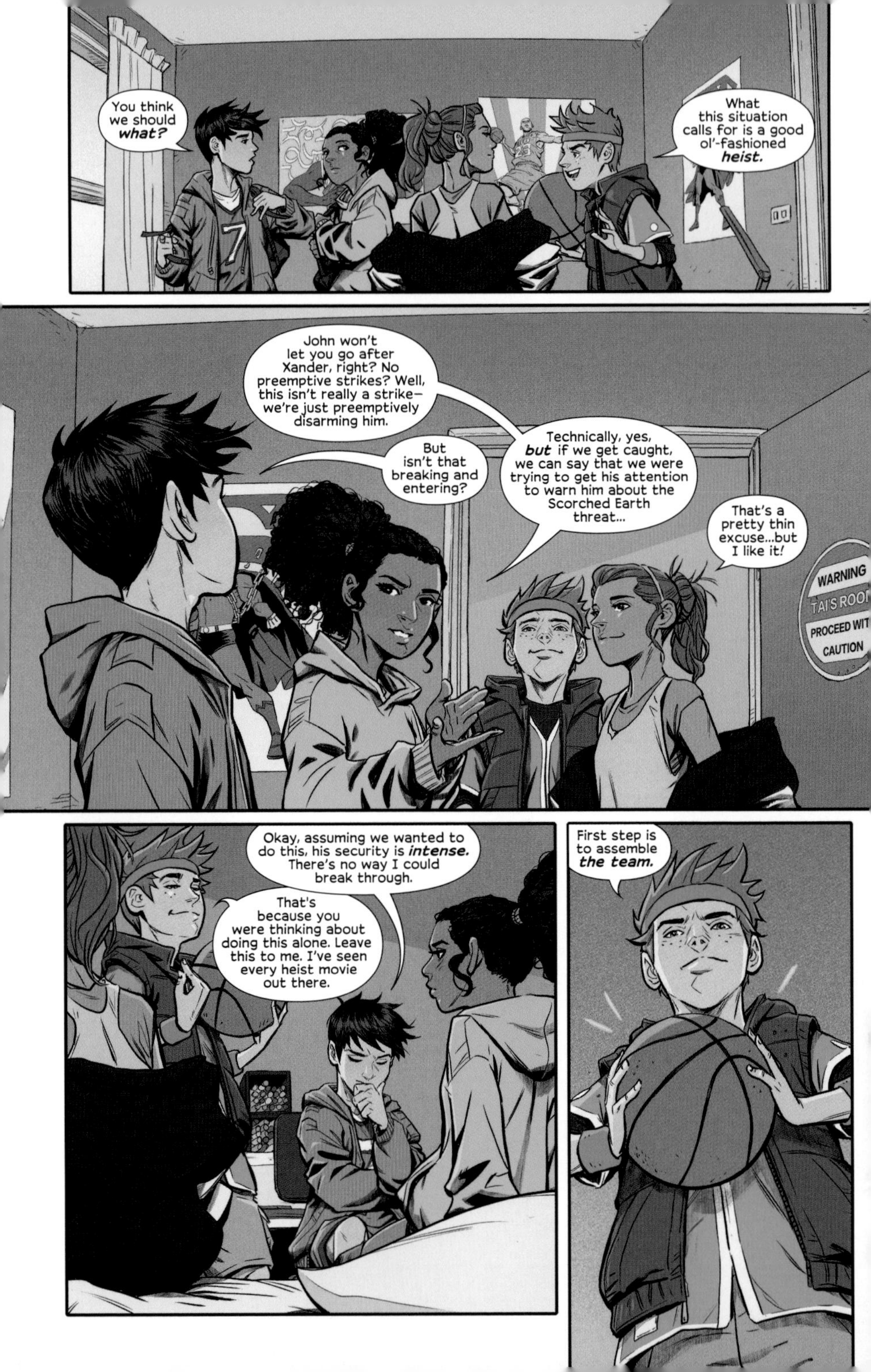

You think we should *what?*
What this situation calls for is a good ol'-fashioned ***heist.***
John won't let you go after Xander, right? No preemptive strikes? Well, this isn't really a strike— we're just preemptively disarming him.
But isn't that breaking and entering?
Technically, yes, ***but*** if we get caught, we can say that we were trying to get his attention to warn him about the Scorched Earth threat...
That's a pretty thin excuse...but I like it*!*
WARNING
TAI'S ROO
PROCEED WIT
CAUTION
Okay, assuming we wanted to do this, his security is ***intense.*** There's no way I could break through.
That's because you were thinking about doing this alone. Leave this to me. I've seen every heist movie out there.
First step is to assemble ***the team.***

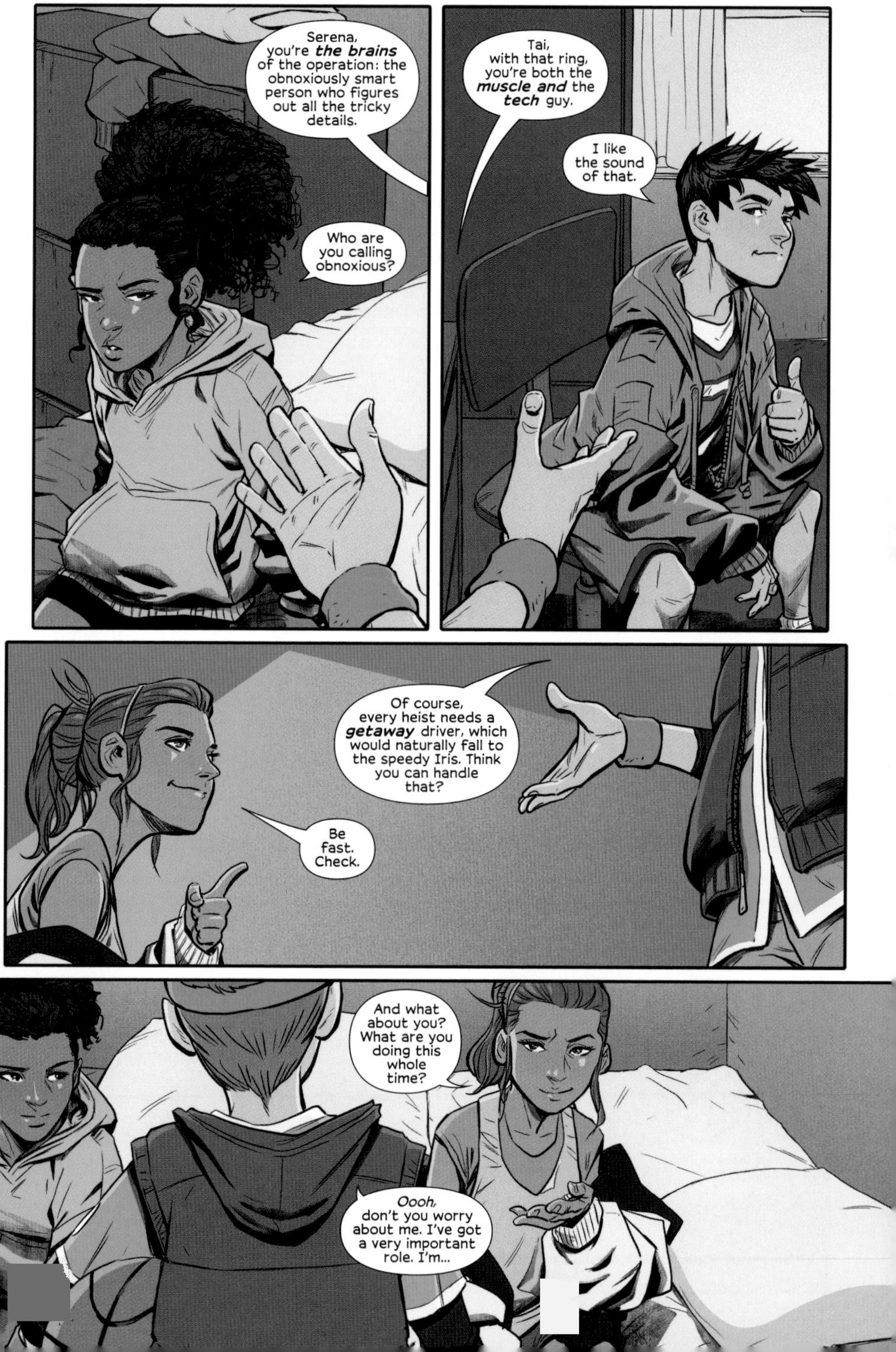
Serena, you're the brains of the operation: the obnoxiously smart person who figures out all the tricky details.
Who are you calling obnoxious?
Tai, with that ring, you're both the muscle and the tech guy.
I like the sound of that.
Of course, every heist needs a getaway driver, which would naturally fall to the speedy Iris. Think you can handle that?
Be fast. Check.
And what about you? What are you doing this whole time?
Oooh, don't you worry about me. I've got a very important role. I'm...

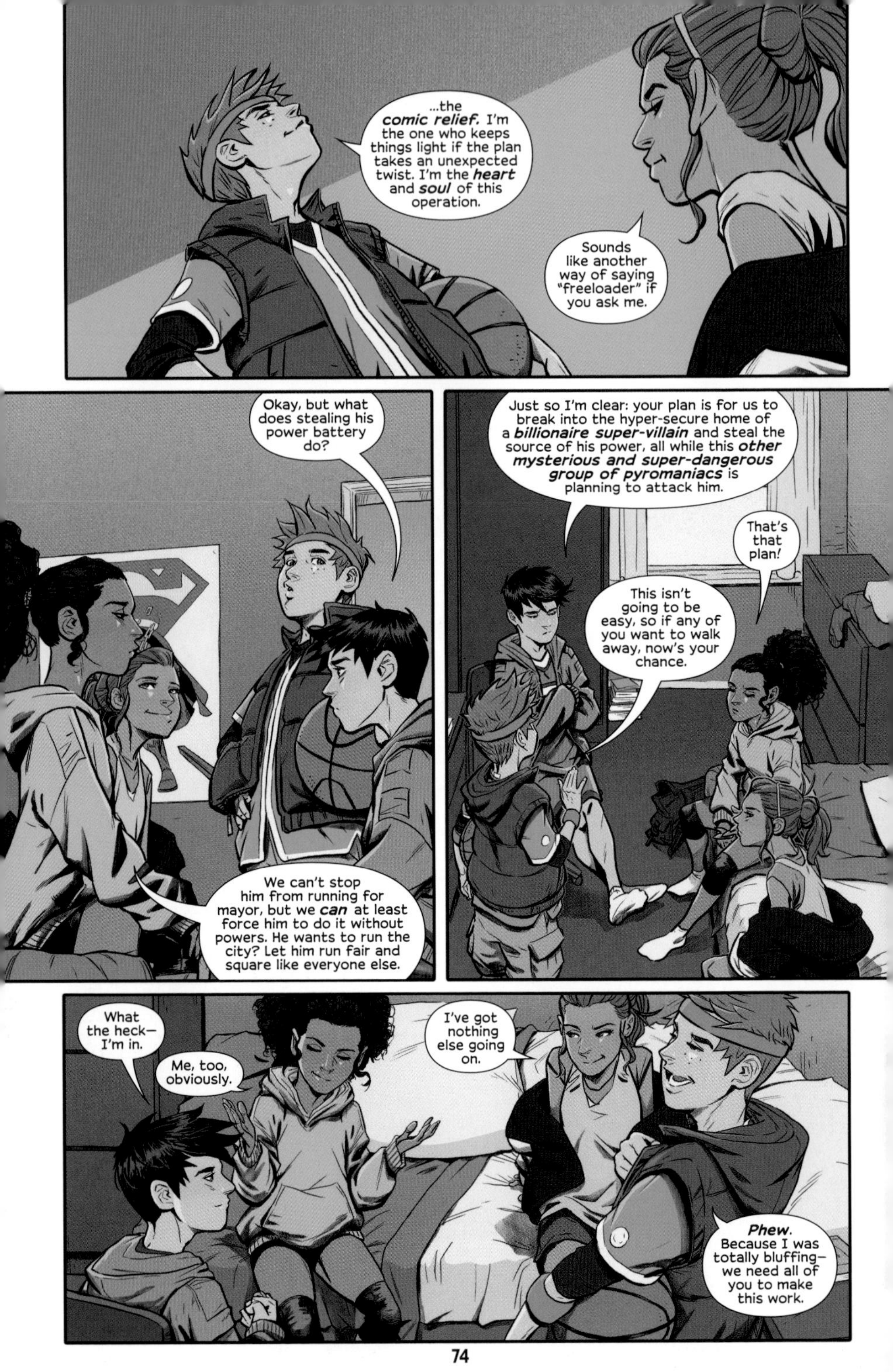

...the *comic relief.* I'm the one who keeps things light if the plan takes an unexpected twist. I'm the *heart* and *soul* of this operation.
Sounds like another way of saying "freeloader" if you ask me.
Okay, but what does stealing his power battery do?
We can't stop him from running for mayor, but we *can* at least force him to do it without powers. He wants to run the city? Let him run fair and square like everyone else.
Just so I'm clear: your plan is for us to break into the hyper-secure home of a *billionaire super-villain* and steal the source of his power, all while this *other mysterious and super-dangerous group of pyromaniacs* is planning to attack him.
That's that plan!
This isn't going to be easy, so if any of you want to walk away, now's your chance.
What the heck— I'm in.
Me, too, obviously.
I've got nothing else going on.
Phew. Because I was totally bluffing— we need all of you to make this work.

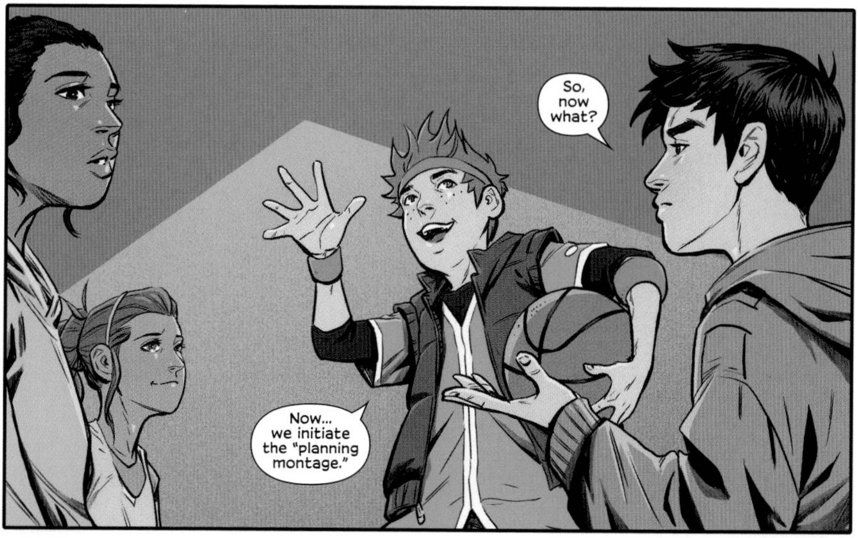
So, now what?
Now... we initiate the "planning montage."

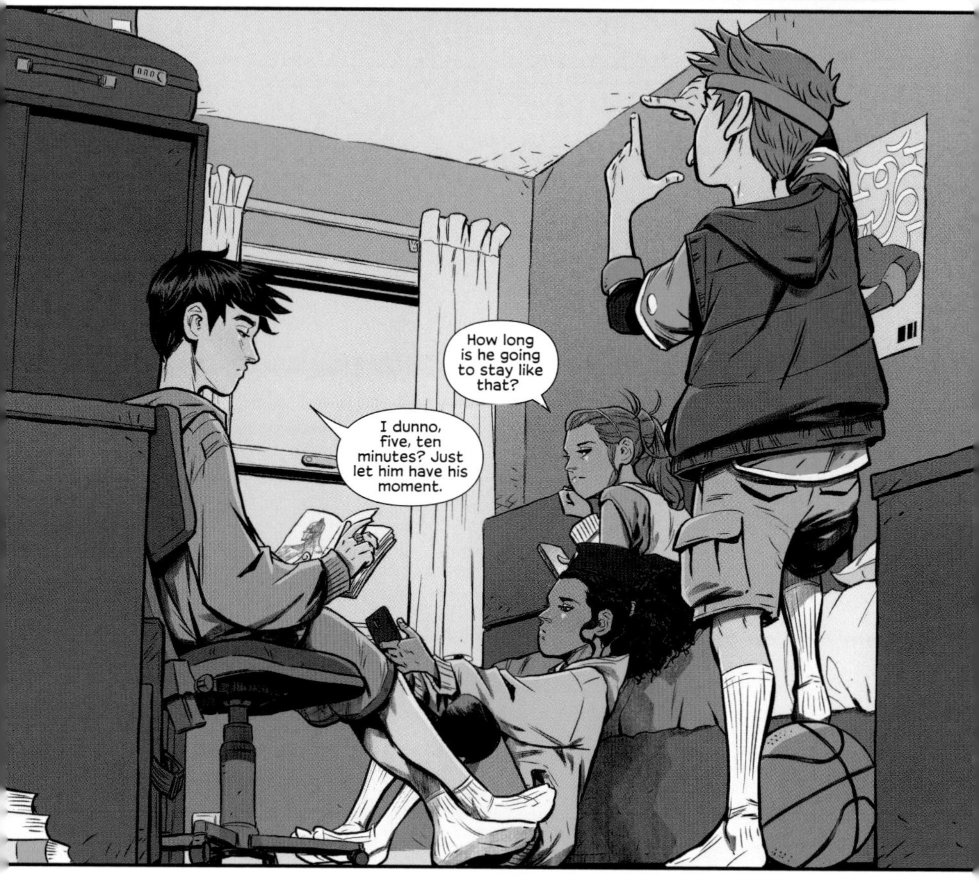
How long is he going to stay like that?
I dunno, five, ten minutes? Just let him have his moment.

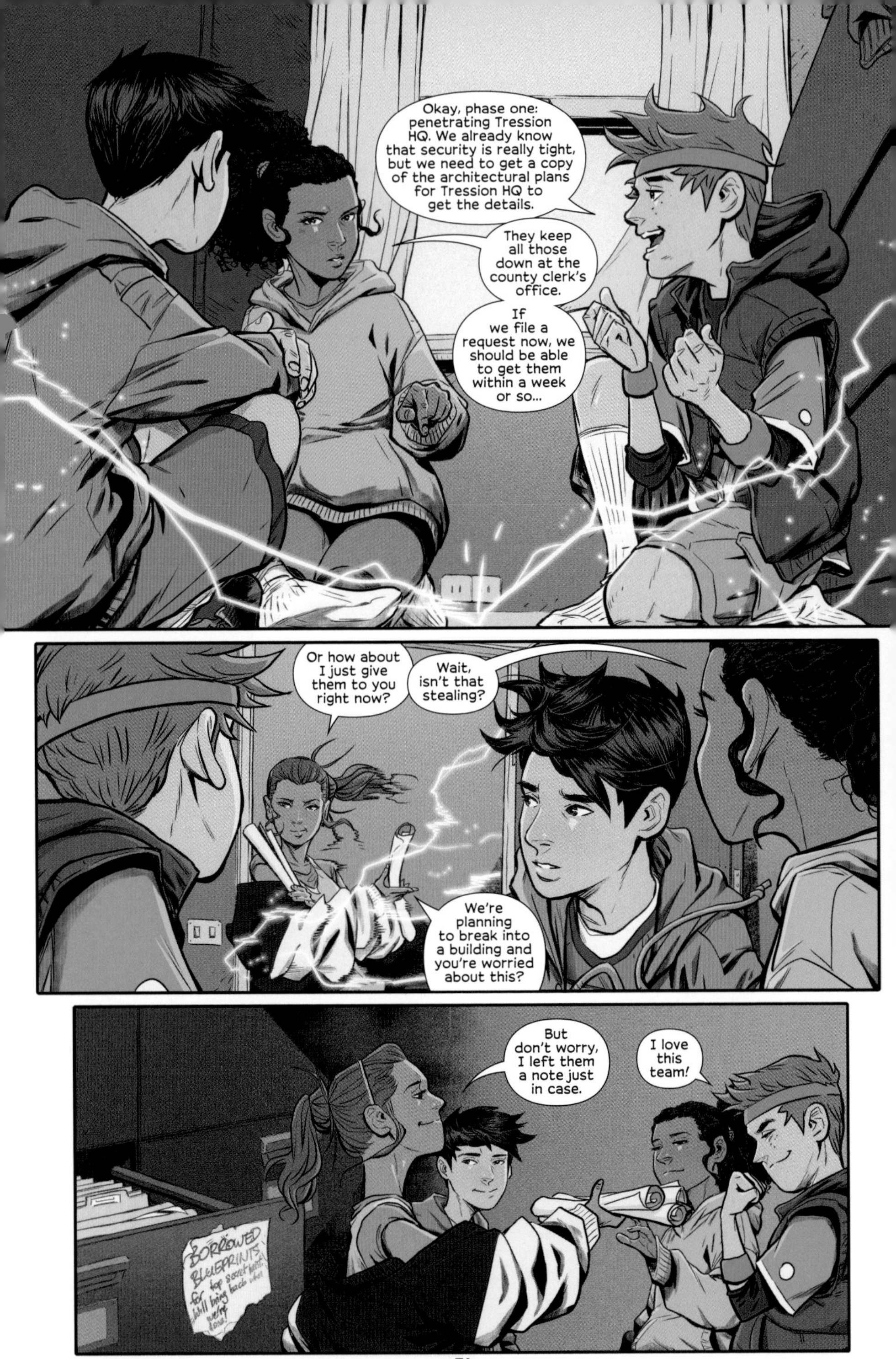
Okay, phase one: penetrating Tression HQ. We already know that security is really tight, but we need to get a copy of the architectural plans for Tression HQ to get the details.
They keep all those down at the county clerk's office.
If we file a request now, we should be able to get them within a week or so...
Or how about I just give them to you right now?
Wait, isn't that stealing?
We're planning to break into a building and you're worried about this?
But don't worry, I left them a note just in case.
I love this team!
BORROWED BLUEPRINTS

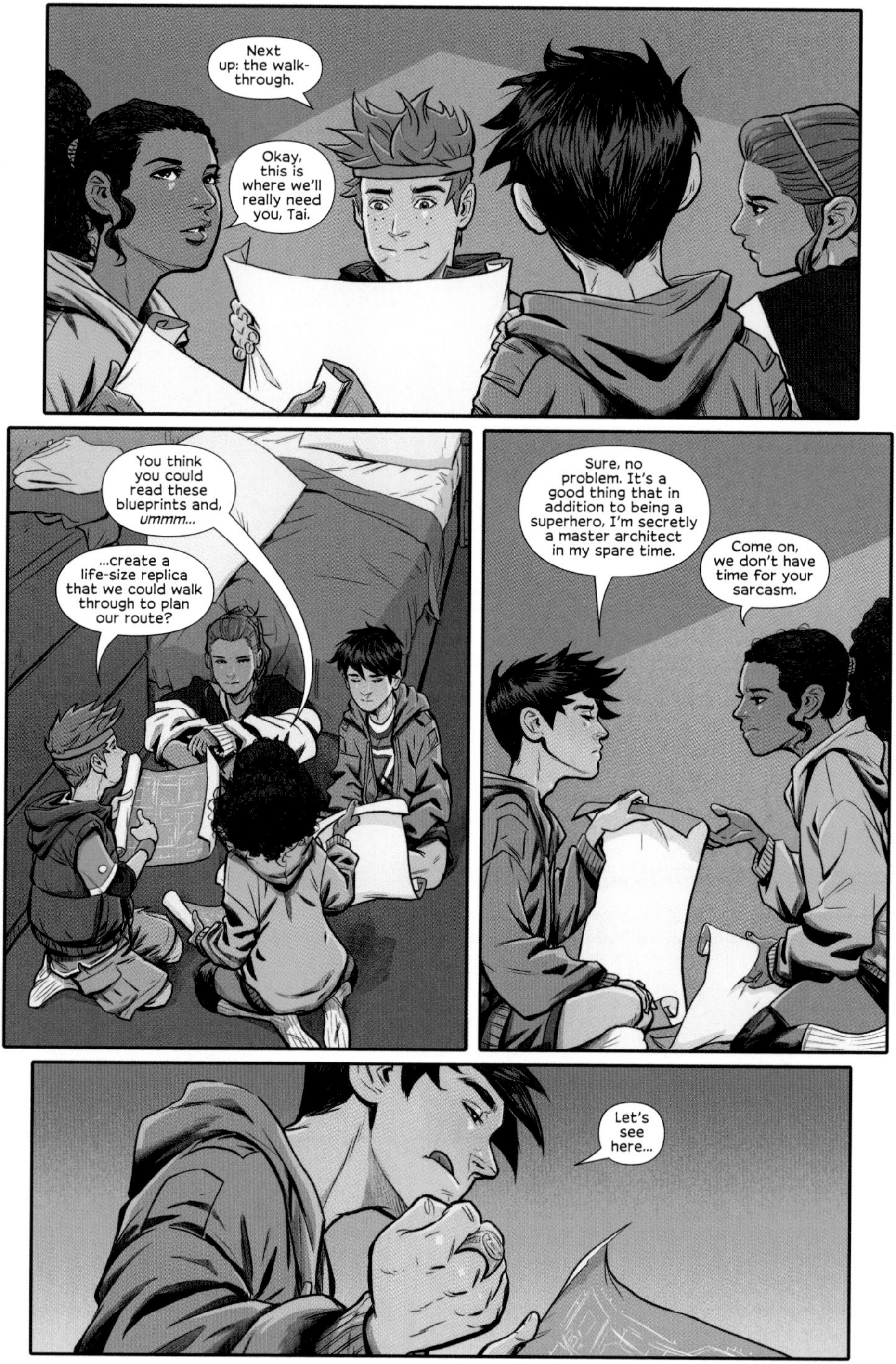
Next up: the walk-through.
Okay, this is where we'll really need you, Tai.
You think you could read these blueprints and, *ummm...*
...create a life-size replica that we could walk through to plan our route?
Sure, no problem. It's a good thing that in addition to being a superhero, I'm secretly a master architect in my spare time.
Come on, we don't have time for your sarcasm.
Let's see here...

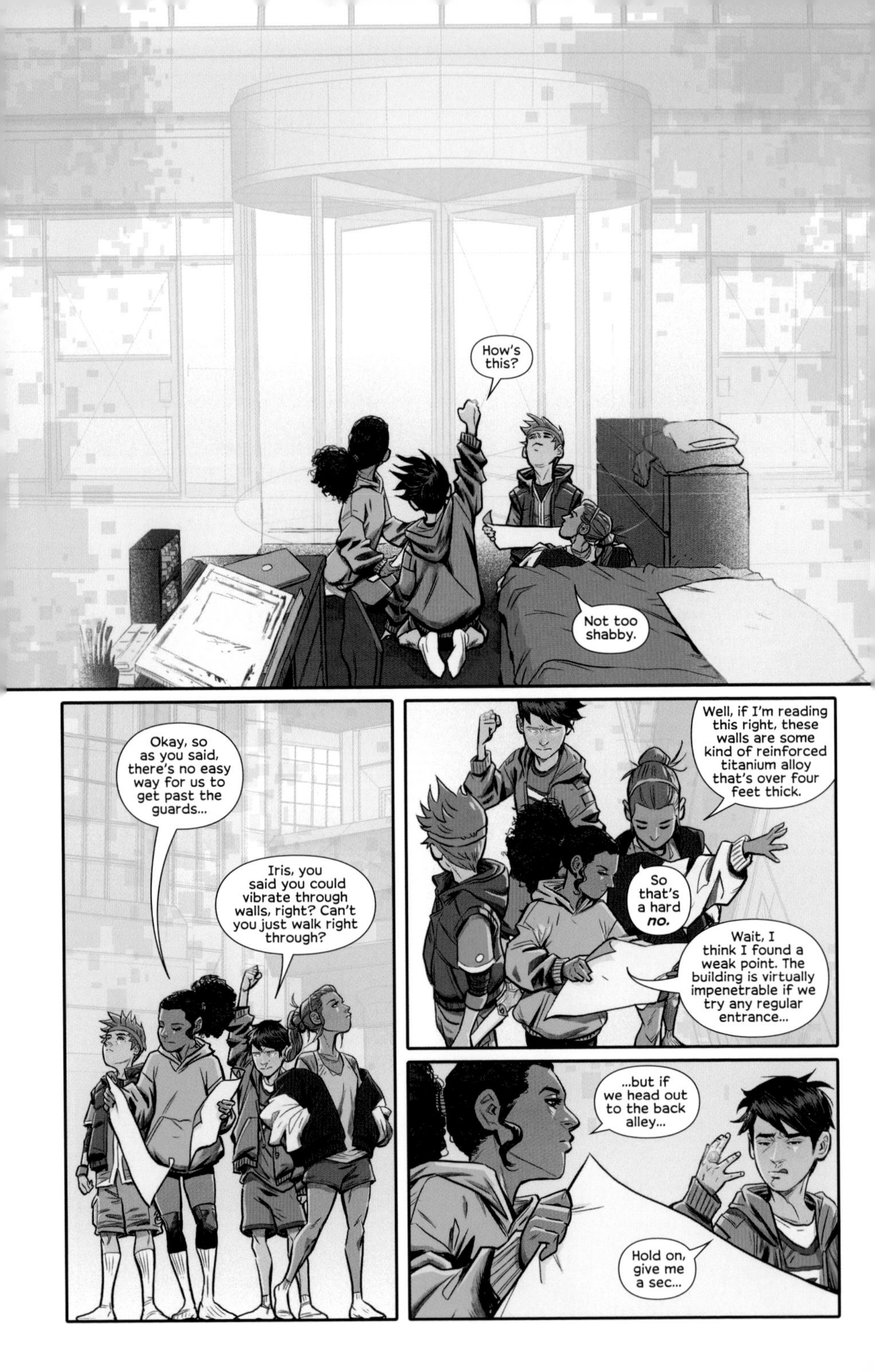
How's this?
Not too shabby.
Okay, so as you said, there's no easy way for us to get past the guards...
Iris, you said you could vibrate through walls, right? Can't you just walk right through?
Well, if I'm reading this right, these walls are some kind of reinforced titanium alloy that's over four feet thick.
So that's a hard *no.*
Wait, I think I found a weak point. The building is virtually impenetrable if we try any regular entrance...
...but if we head out to the back alley...
Hold on, give me a sec...

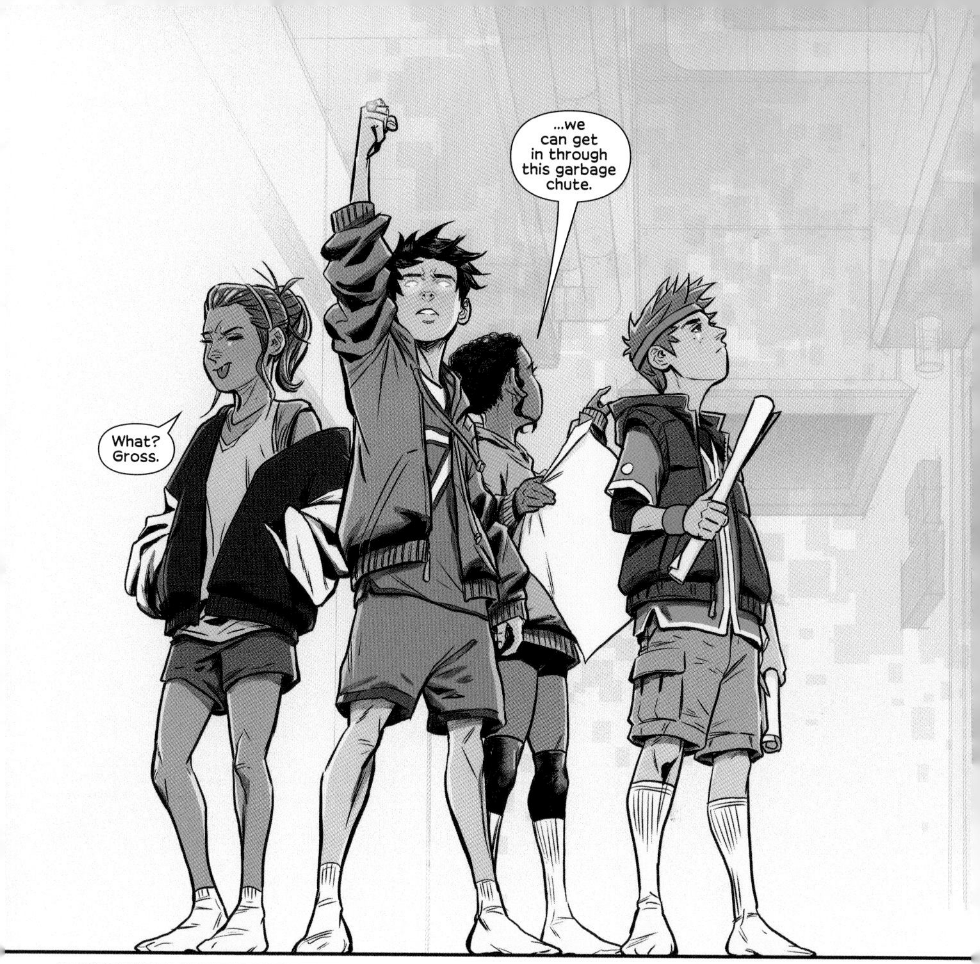
...we can get in through this garbage chute.
What? Gross.

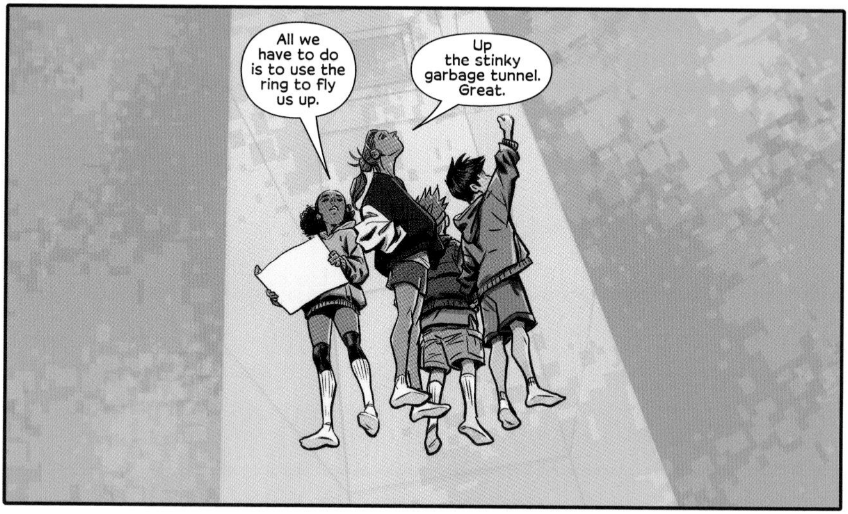
All we have to do is to use the ring to fly us up.
Up the stinky garbage tunnel. Great.

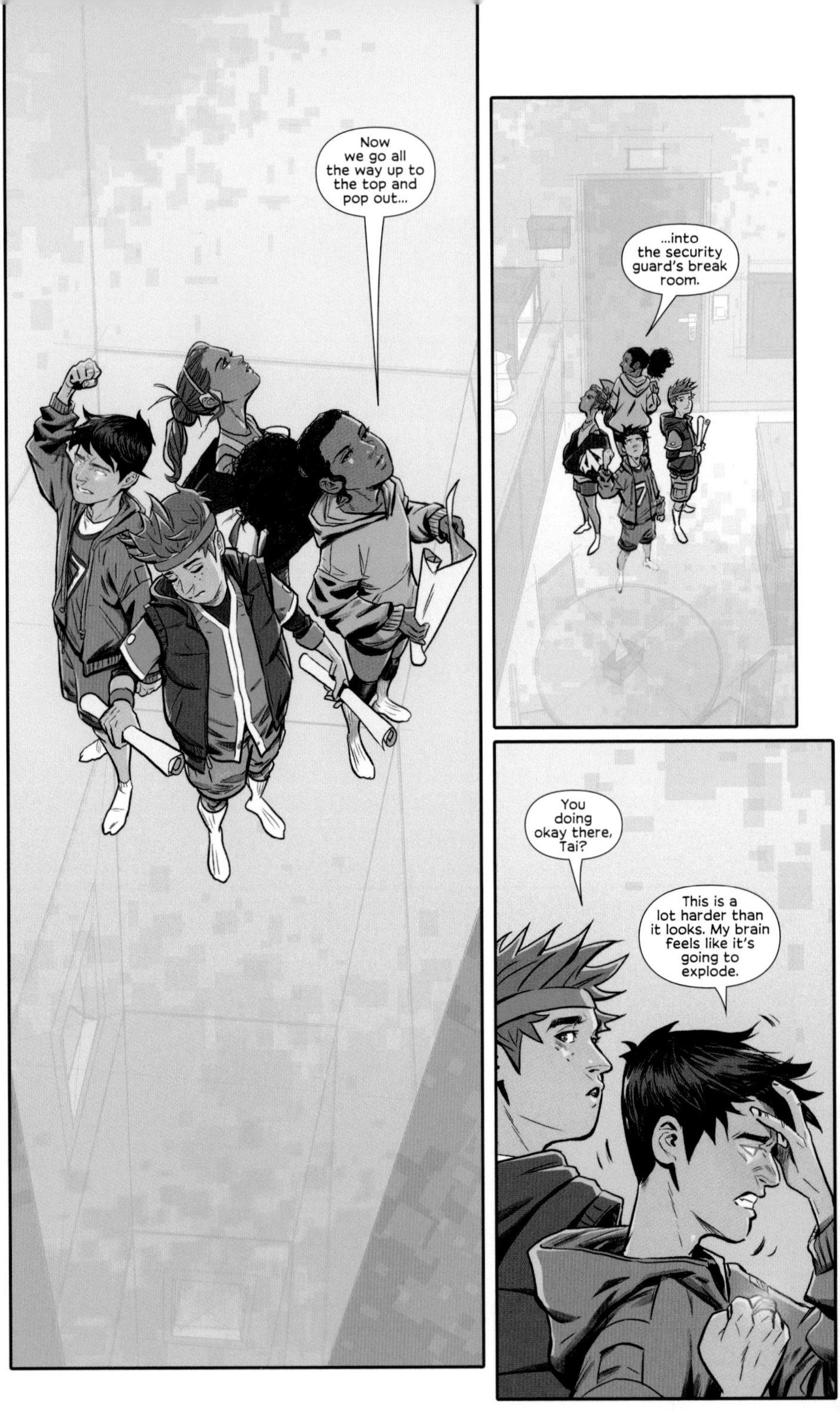
Now we go all the way up to the top and pop out...
...into the security guard's break room.
You doing okay there, Tai?
This is a lot harder than it looks. My brain feels like it's going to explode.

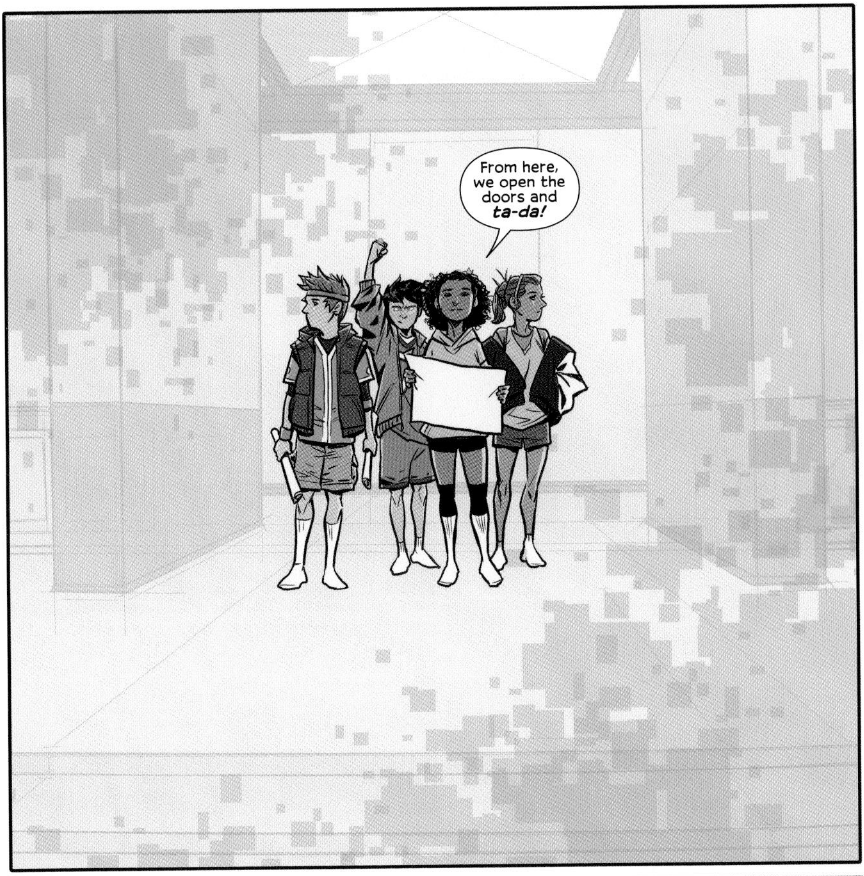
From here, we open the doors and *ta-da!*

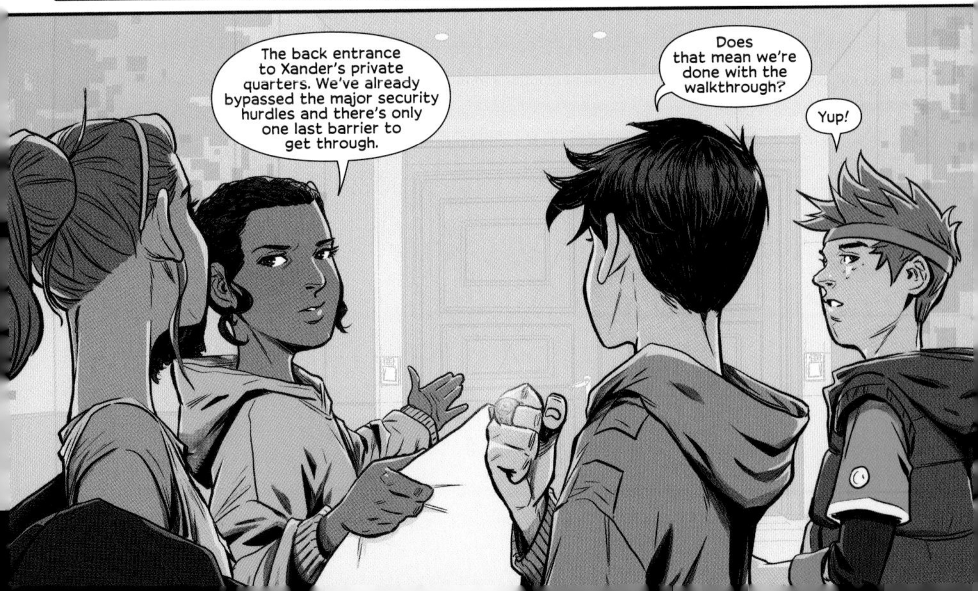
The back entrance to Xander's private quarters. We've already bypassed the major security hurdles and there's only one last barrier to get through.
Does that mean we're done with the walkthrough?
Yup!

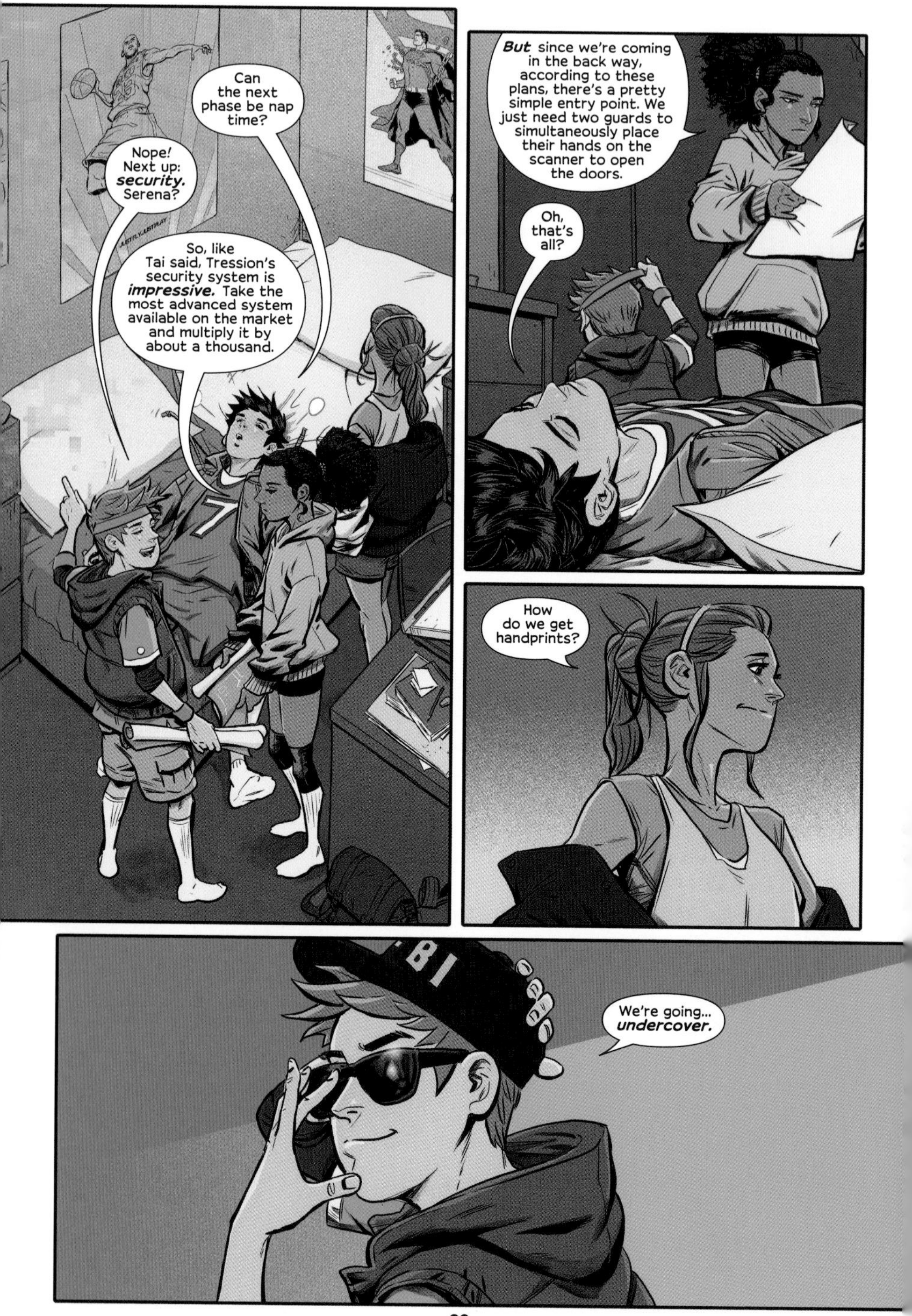

Can the next phase be nap time?
Nope! Next up: ***security.*** Serena?
So, like Tai said, Tression's security system is ***impressive.*** Take the most advanced system available on the market and multiply it by about a thousand.
But since we're coming in the back way, according to these plans, there's a pretty simple entry point. We just need two guards to simultaneously place their hands on the scanner to open the doors.
Oh, that's all?
How do we get handprints?
We're going... ***undercover.***

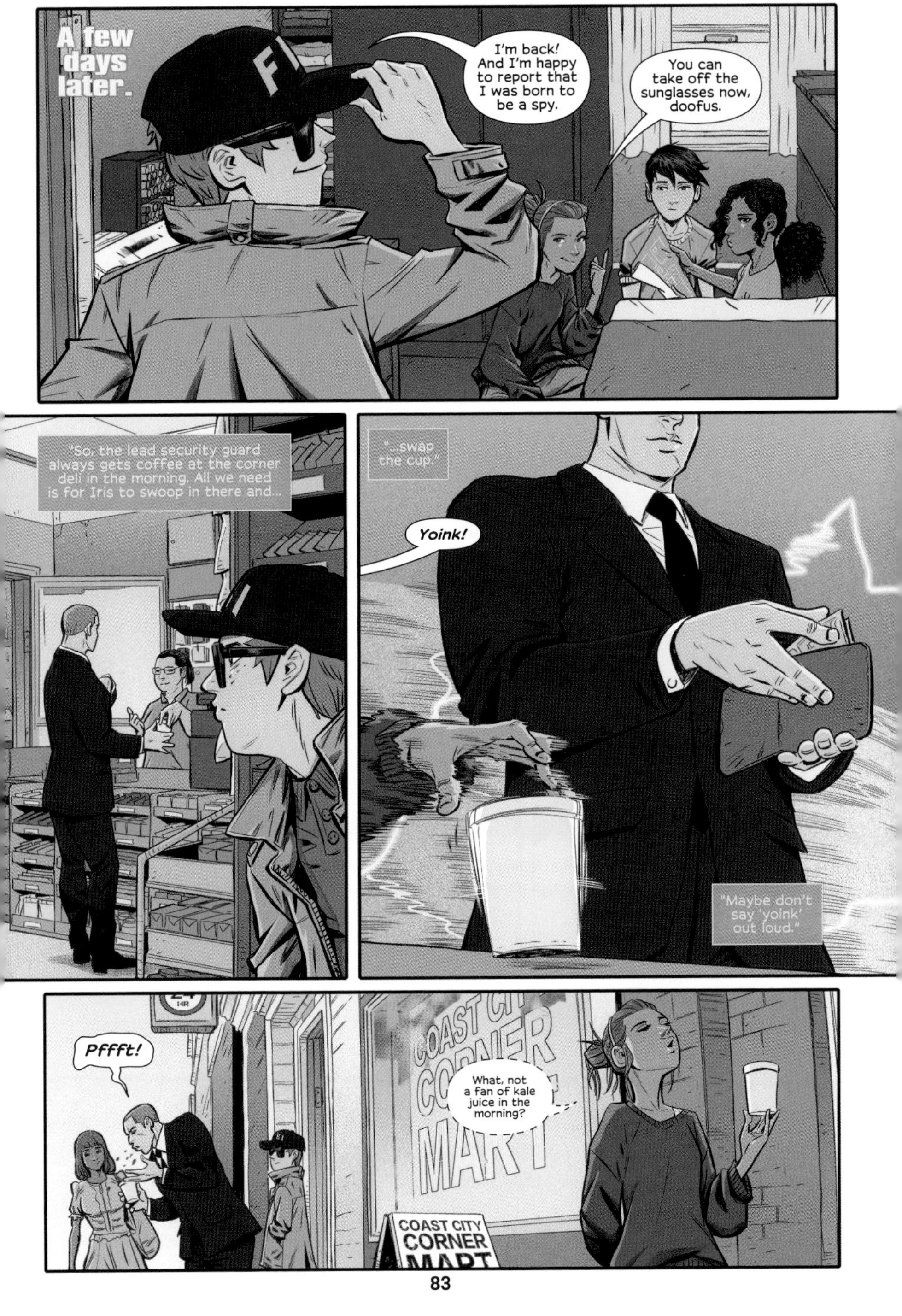
A few days later.
I'm back! And I'm happy to report that I was born to be a spy.
You can take off the sunglasses now, doofus.
"So, the lead security guard always gets coffee at the corner deli in the morning. All we need is for Iris to swoop in there and...
"...swap the cup."
Yoink!
"Maybe don't say 'yoink' out loud."
Pffft!
What, not a fan of kale juice in the morning?
COAST CITY CORNER MART

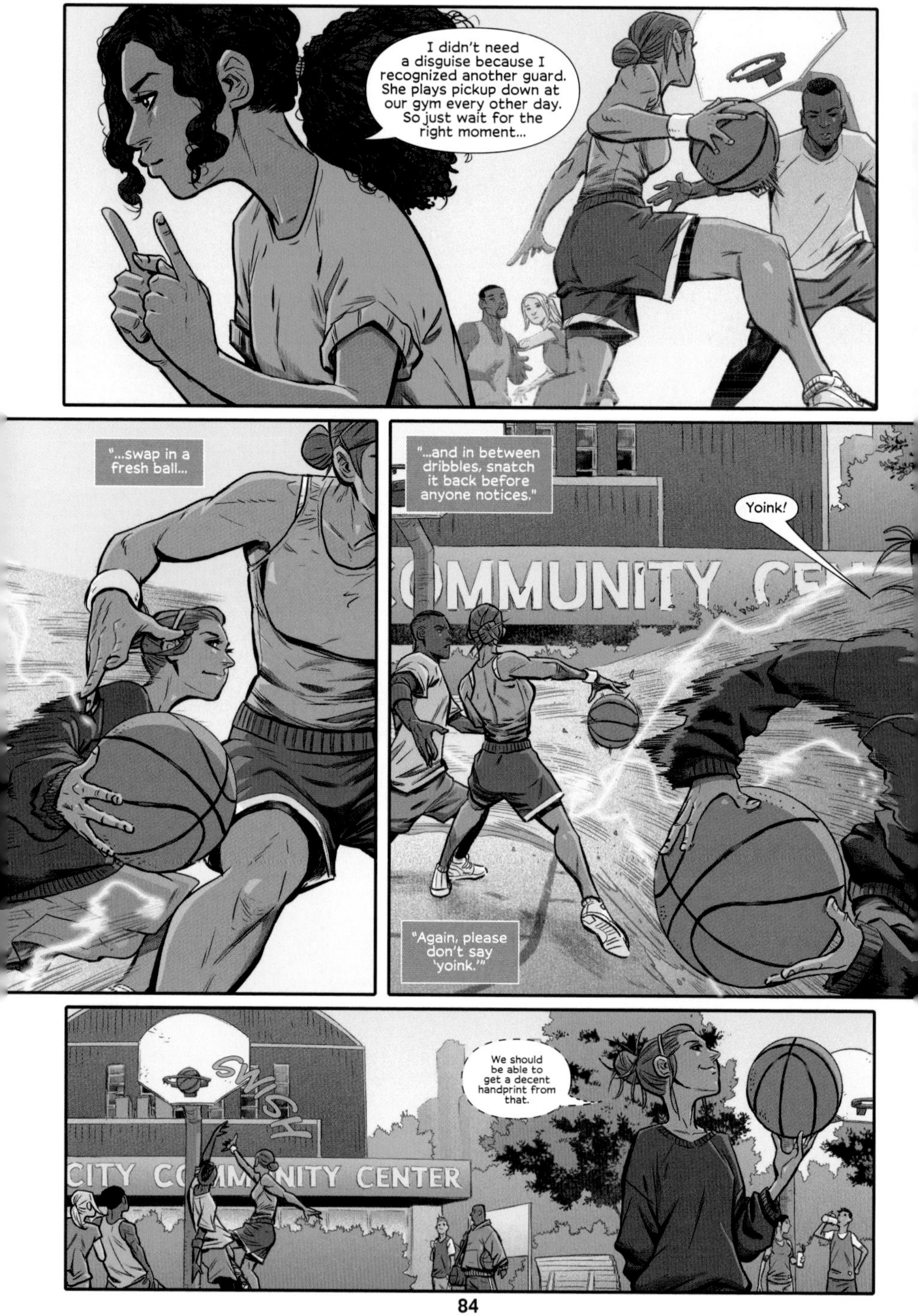
I didn't need a disguise because I recognized another guard. She plays pickup down at our gym every other day. So just wait for the right moment...
"...swap in a fresh ball...
"...and in between dribbles, snatch it back before anyone notices."
COMMUNITY CE
Yoink!
"Again, please don't say 'yoink.'"
SWISH
CITY COMMUNITY CENTER
We should be able to get a decent handprint from that.

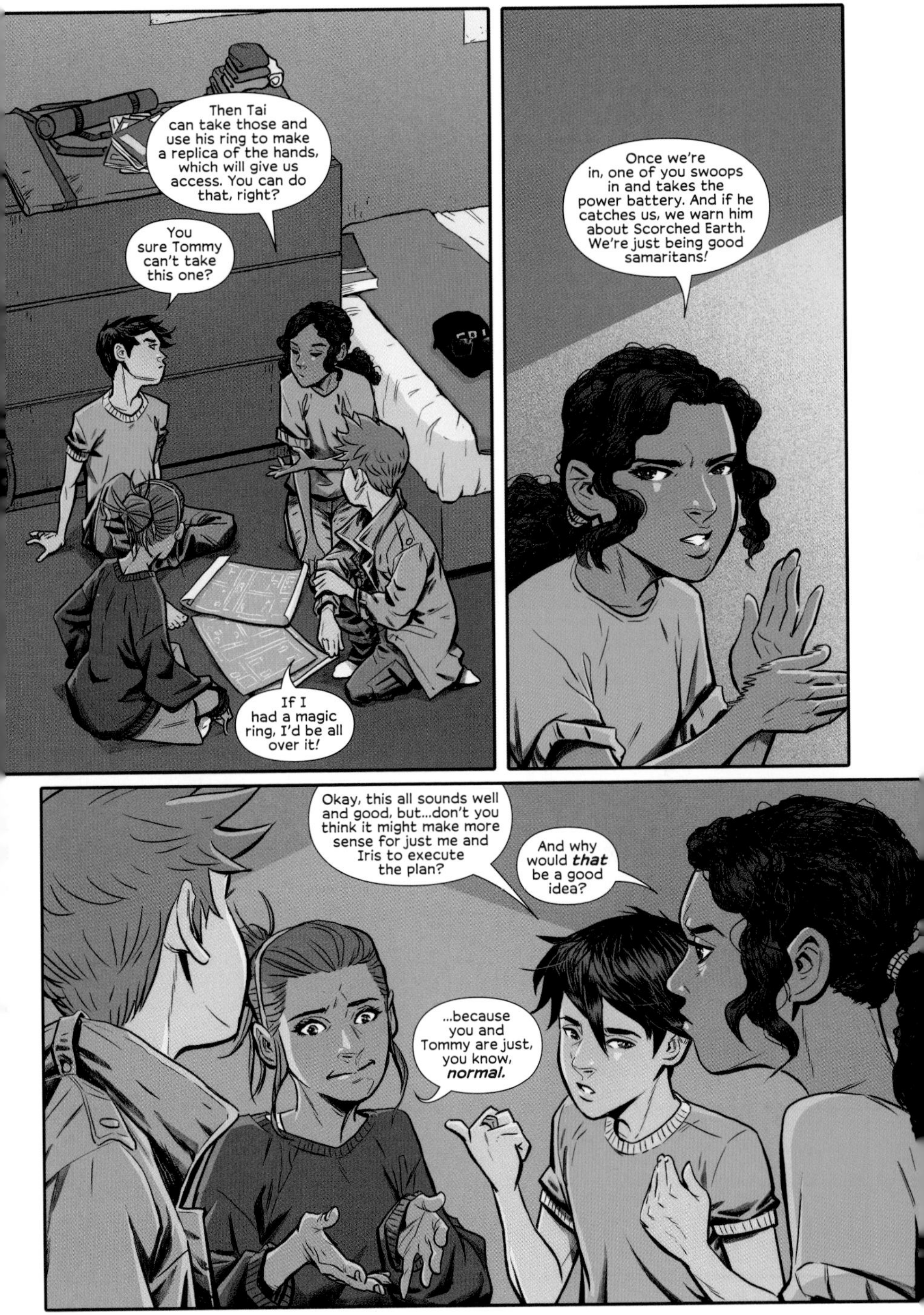
Then Tai can take those and use his ring to make a replica of the hands, which will give us access. You can do that, right?
You sure Tommy can't take this one?
If I had a magic ring, I'd be all over it!
Once we're in, one of you swoops in and takes the power battery. And if he catches us, we warn him about Scorched Earth. We're just being good samaritans!
Okay, this all sounds well and good, but...don't you think it might make more sense for just me and Iris to execute the plan?
And why would ***that*** be a good idea?
...because you and Tommy are just, you know, ***normal.***

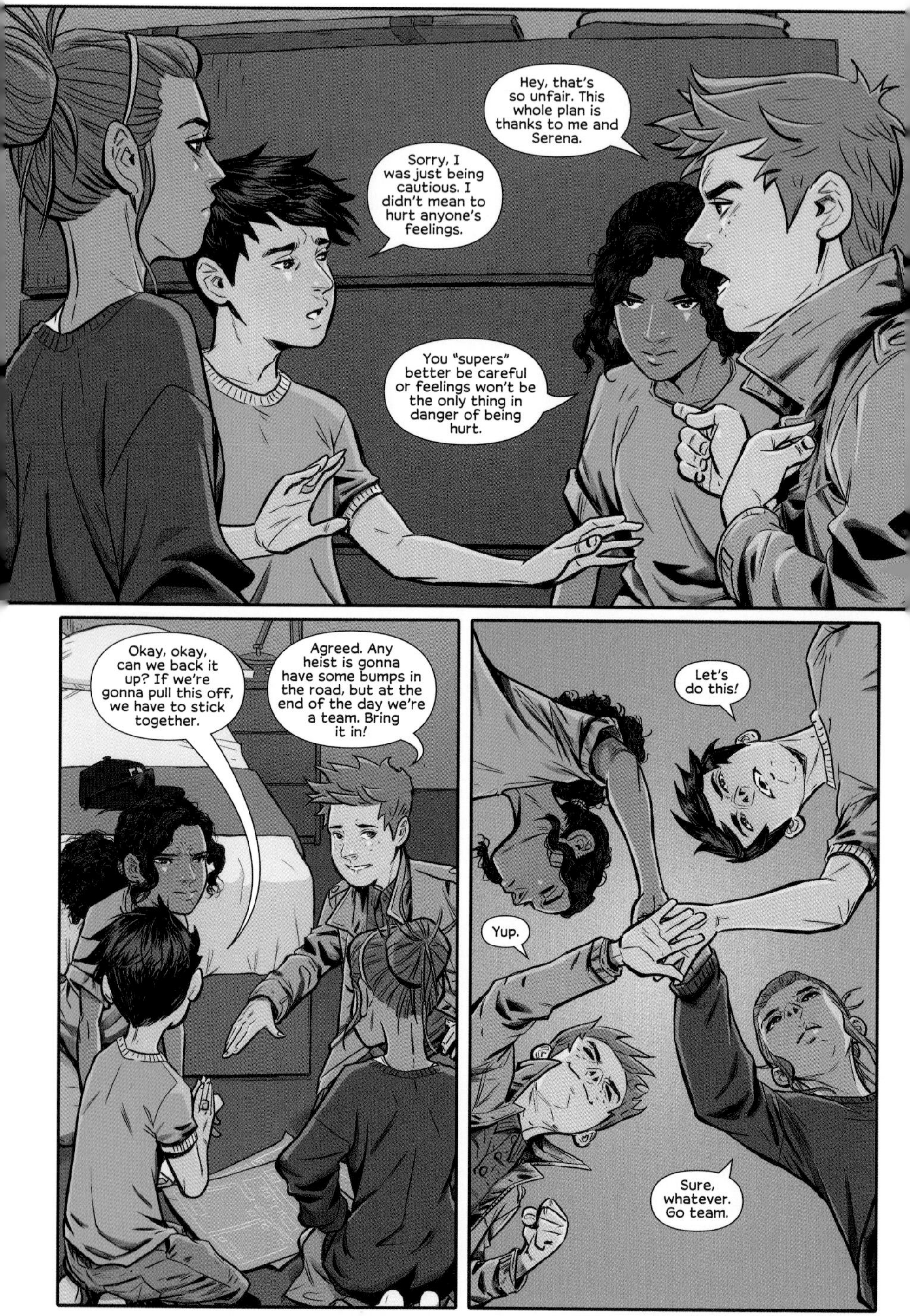
Hey, that's so unfair. This whole plan is thanks to me and Serena.
Sorry, I was just being cautious. I didn't mean to hurt anyone's feelings.
You "supers" better be careful or feelings won't be the only thing in danger of being hurt.
Okay, okay, can we back it up? If we're gonna pull this off, we have to stick together.
Agreed. Any heist is gonna have some bumps in the road, but at the end of the day we're a team. Bring it in!
Let's do this!
Yup.
Sure, whatever. Go team.

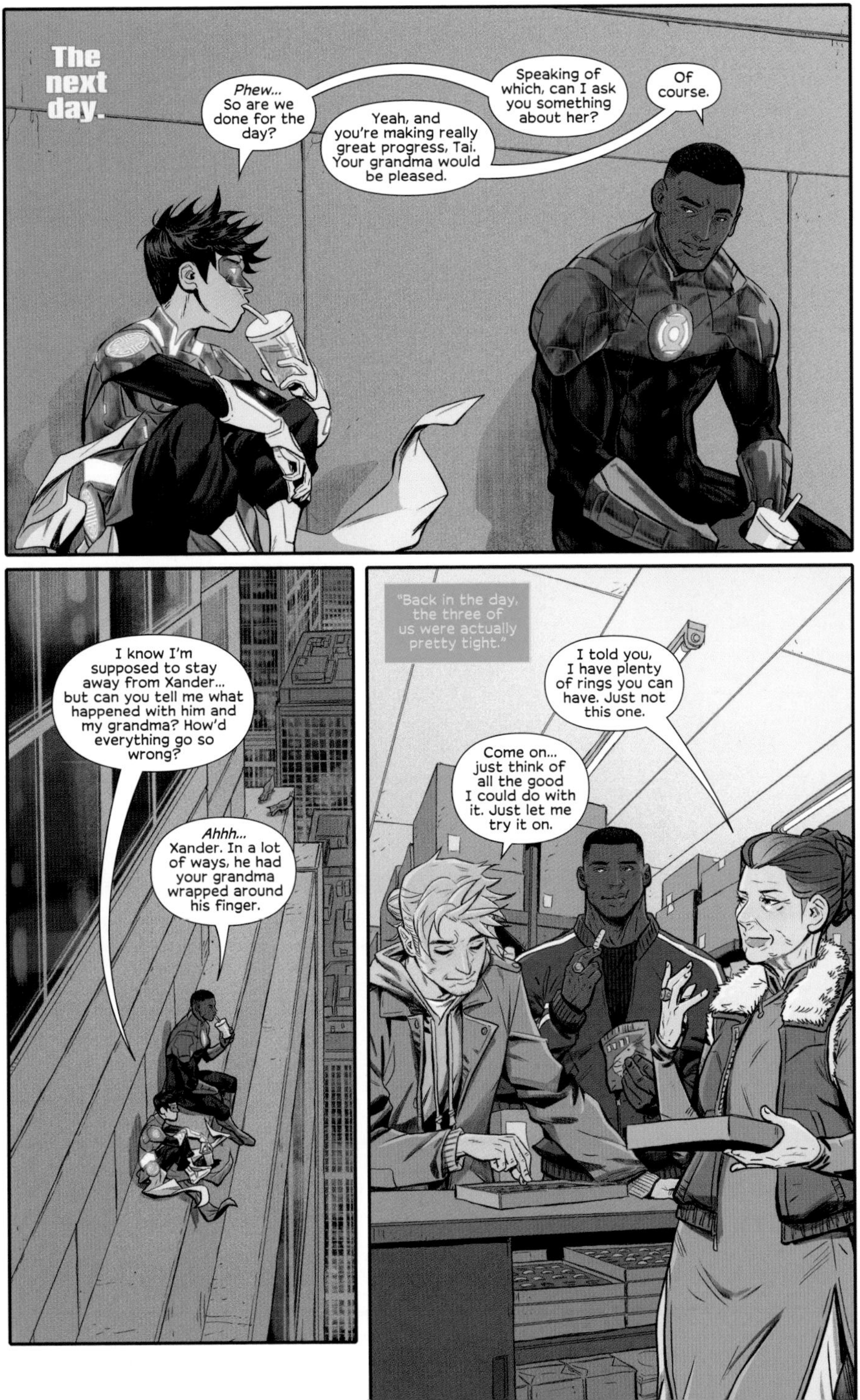
The next day.
Phew... So are we done for the day?
Yeah, and you're making really great progress, Tai. Your grandma would be pleased.
Speaking of which, can I ask you something about her?
Of course.
I know I'm supposed to stay away from Xander... but can you tell me what happened with him and my grandma? How'd everything go so wrong?
Ahhh... Xander. In a lot of ways, he had your grandma wrapped around his finger.
"Back in the day, the three of us were actually pretty tight."
I told you, I have plenty of rings you can have. Just not this one.
Come on... just think of all the good I could do with it. Just let me try it on.

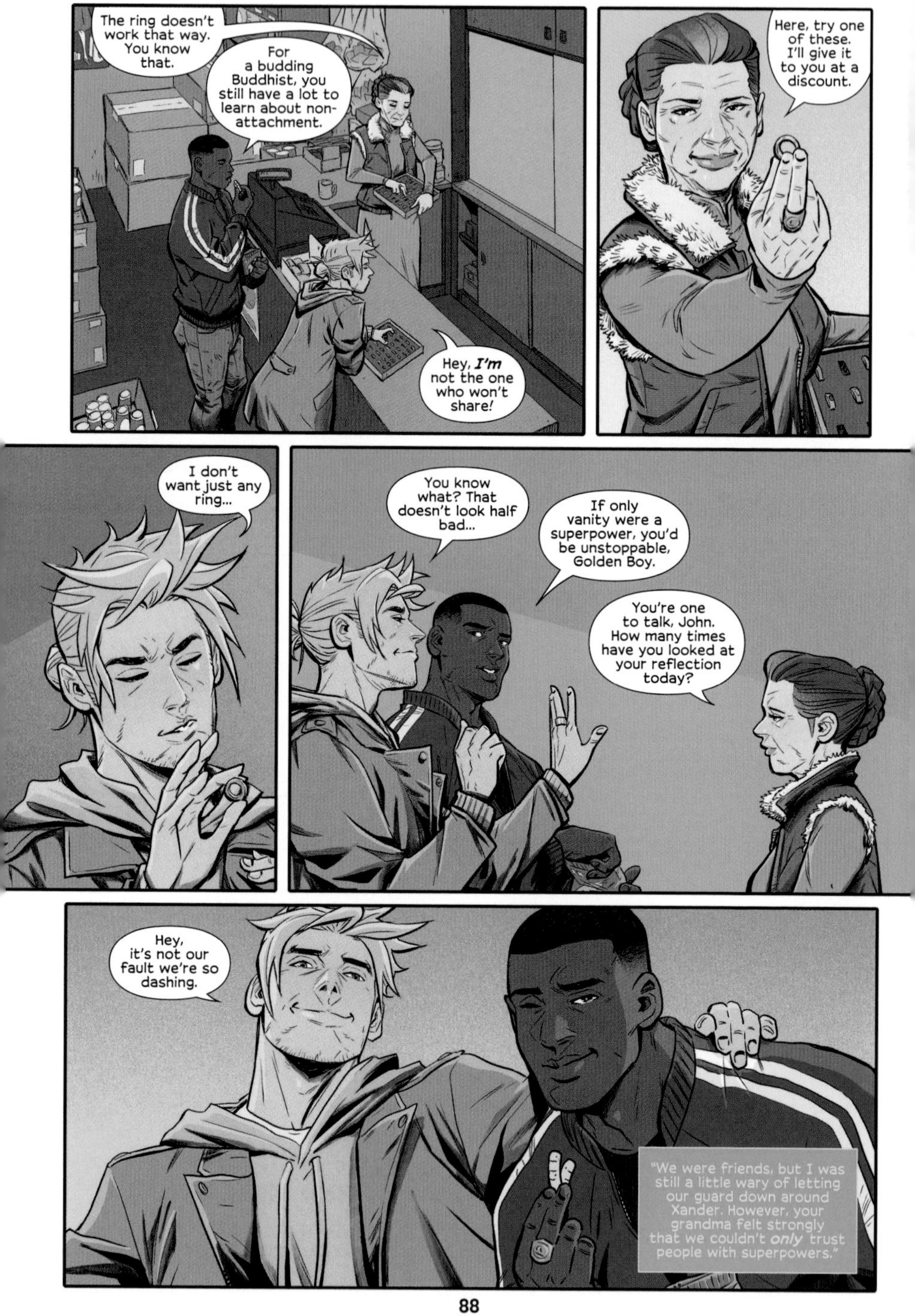
The ring doesn't work that way. You know that.
For a budding Buddhist, you still have a lot to learn about non-attachment.
Hey, *I'm* not the one who won't share!
Here, try one of these. I'll give it to you at a discount.
I don't want just any ring...
You know what? That doesn't look half bad...
If only vanity were a superpower, you'd be unstoppable, Golden Boy.
You're one to talk, John. How many times have you looked at your reflection today?
Hey, it's not our fault we're so dashing.
"We were friends, but I was still a little wary of letting our guard down around Xander. However, your grandma felt strongly that we couldn't *only* trust people with superpowers."

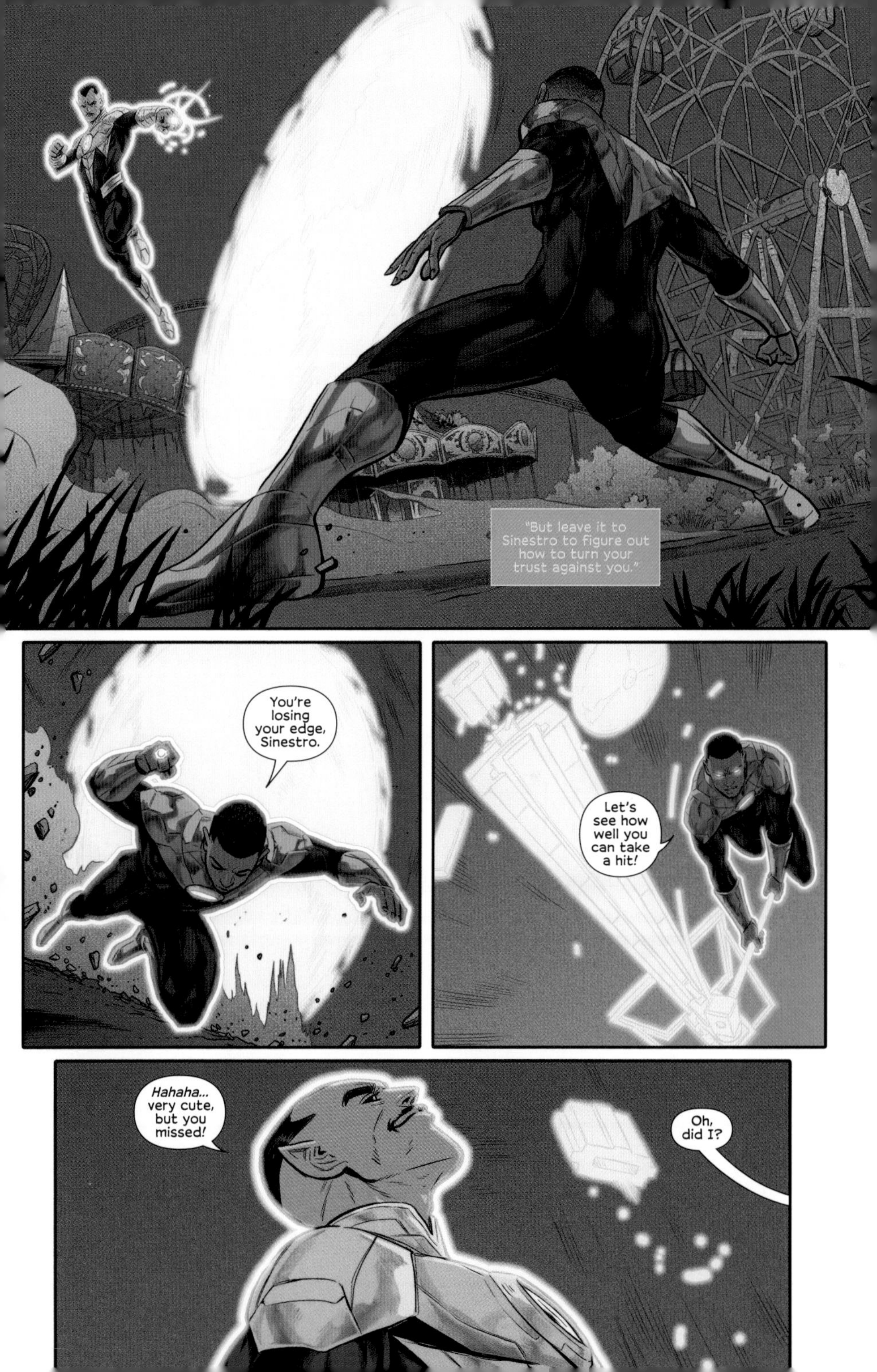
"But leave it to Sinestro to figure out how to turn your trust against you."
You're losing your edge, Sinestro.
Let's see how well you can take a hit!
Hahaha... very cute, but you missed!
Oh, did I?

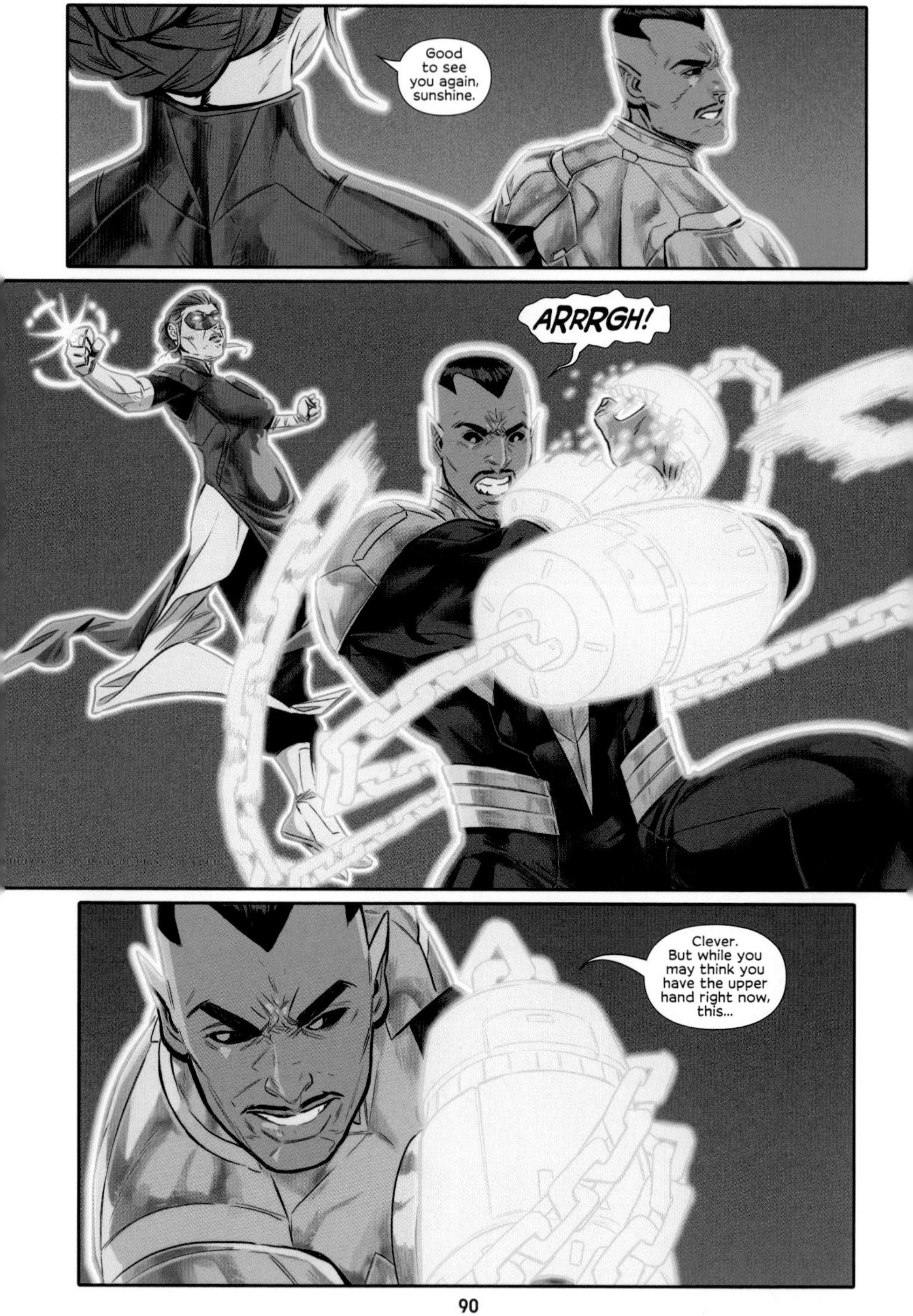
Good to see you again, sunshine.
ARRRGH!
Clever. But while you may think you have the upper hand right now, this...

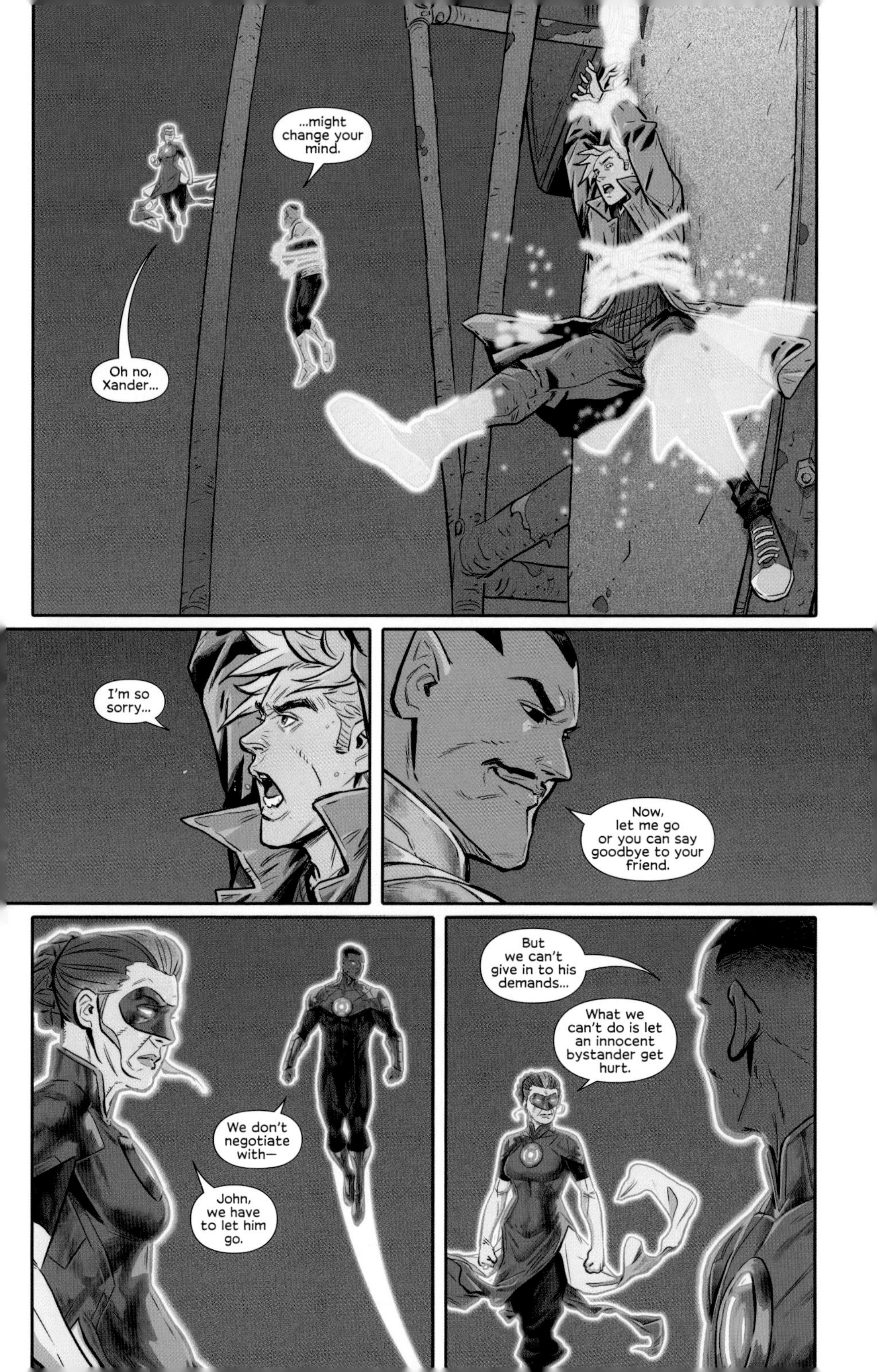
...might change your mind.
Oh no, Xander...
I'm so sorry...
Now, let me go or you can say goodbye to your friend.
We don't negotiate with—
John, we have to let him go.
But we can't give in to his demands...
What we can't do is let an innocent bystander get hurt.

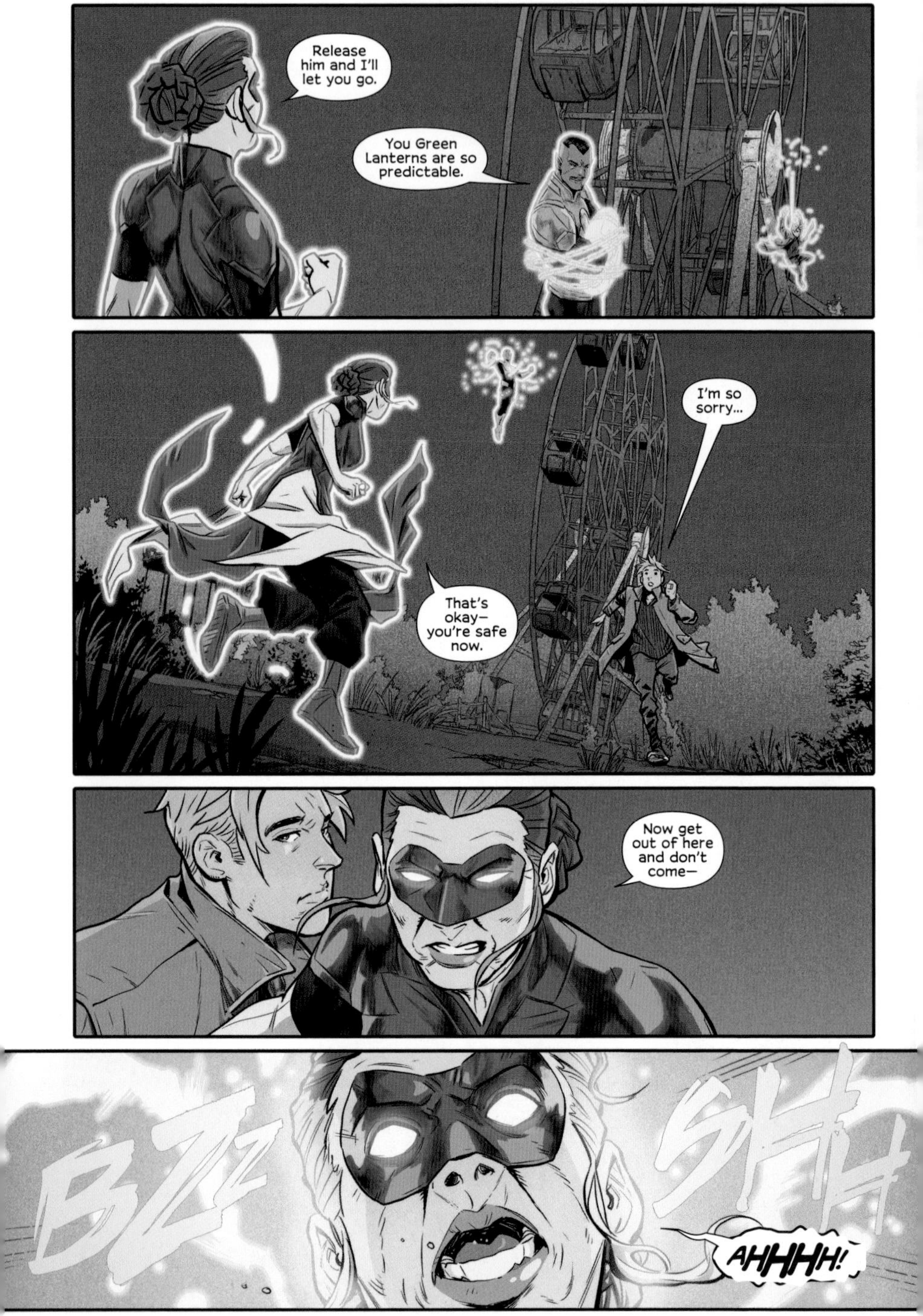

Release him and I'll let you go.
You Green Lanterns are so predictable.
I'm so sorry...
That's okay— you're safe now.
Now get out of here and don't come—
BZZ
SHH
AHHHH!

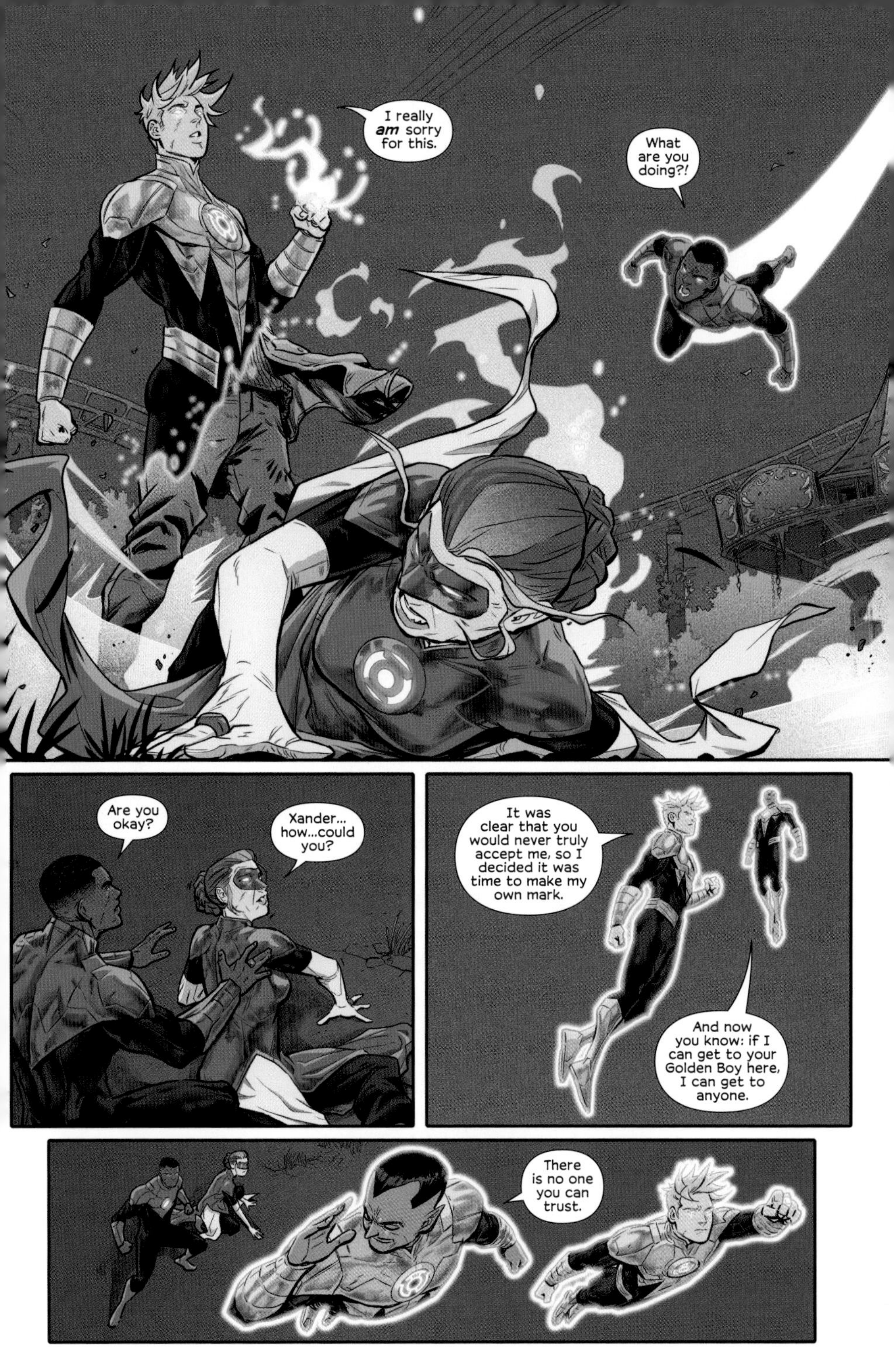
I really *am* sorry for this.
What are you doing?!
Are you okay?
Xander... how...could you?
It was clear that you would never truly accept me, so I decided it was time to make my own mark.
And now you know: if I can get to your Golden Boy here, I can get to anyone.
There is no one you can trust.

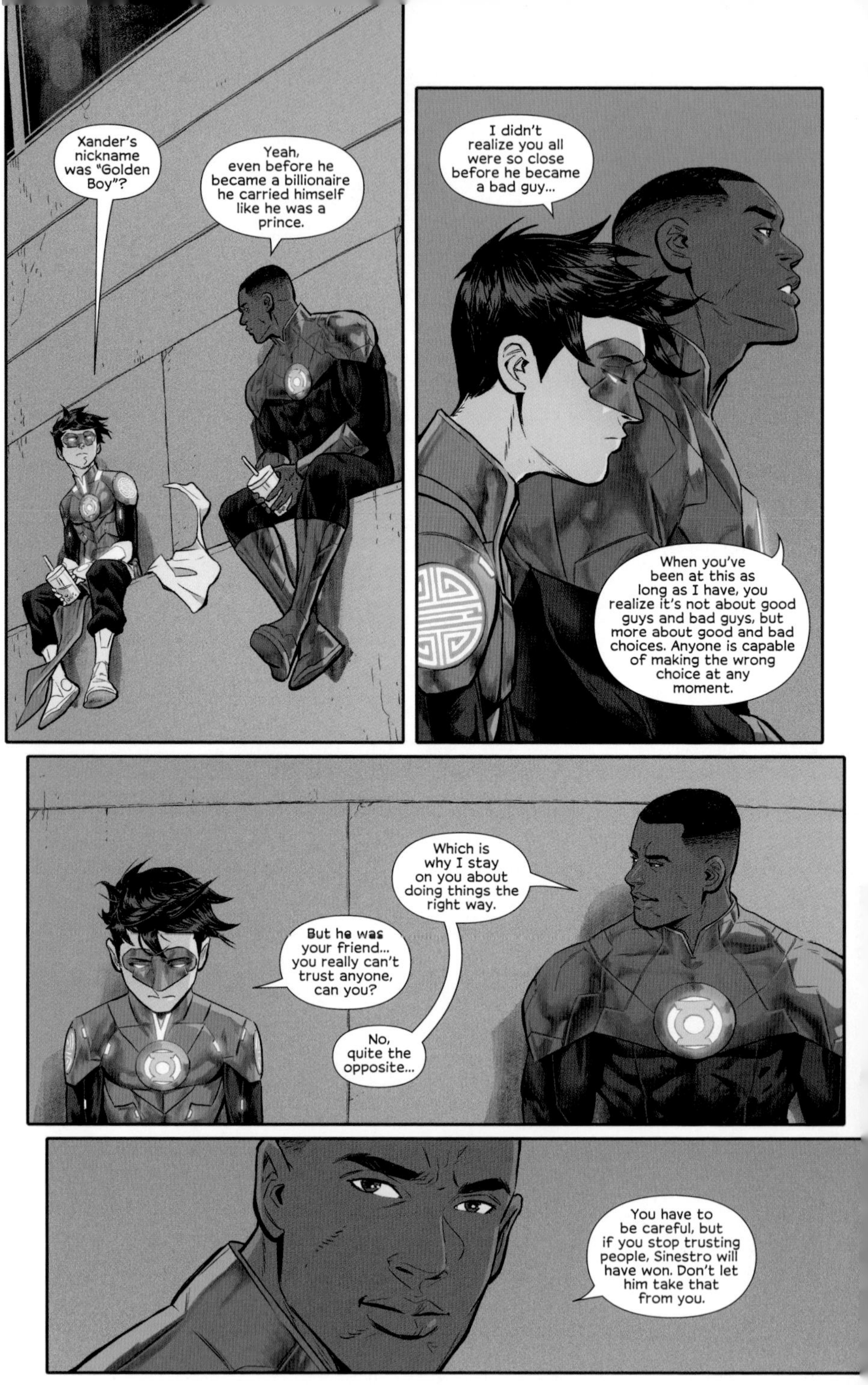
Xander's nickname was "Golden Boy"?
Yeah, even before he became a billionaire he carried himself like he was a prince.
I didn't realize you all were so close before he became a bad guy...
When you've been at this as long as I have, you realize it's not about good guys and bad guys, but more about good and bad choices. Anyone is capable of making the wrong choice at any moment.
Which is why I stay on you about doing things the right way.
But he was your friend... you really can't trust anyone, can you?
No, quite the opposite...
You have to be careful, but if you stop trusting people, Sinestro will have won. Don't let him take that from you.

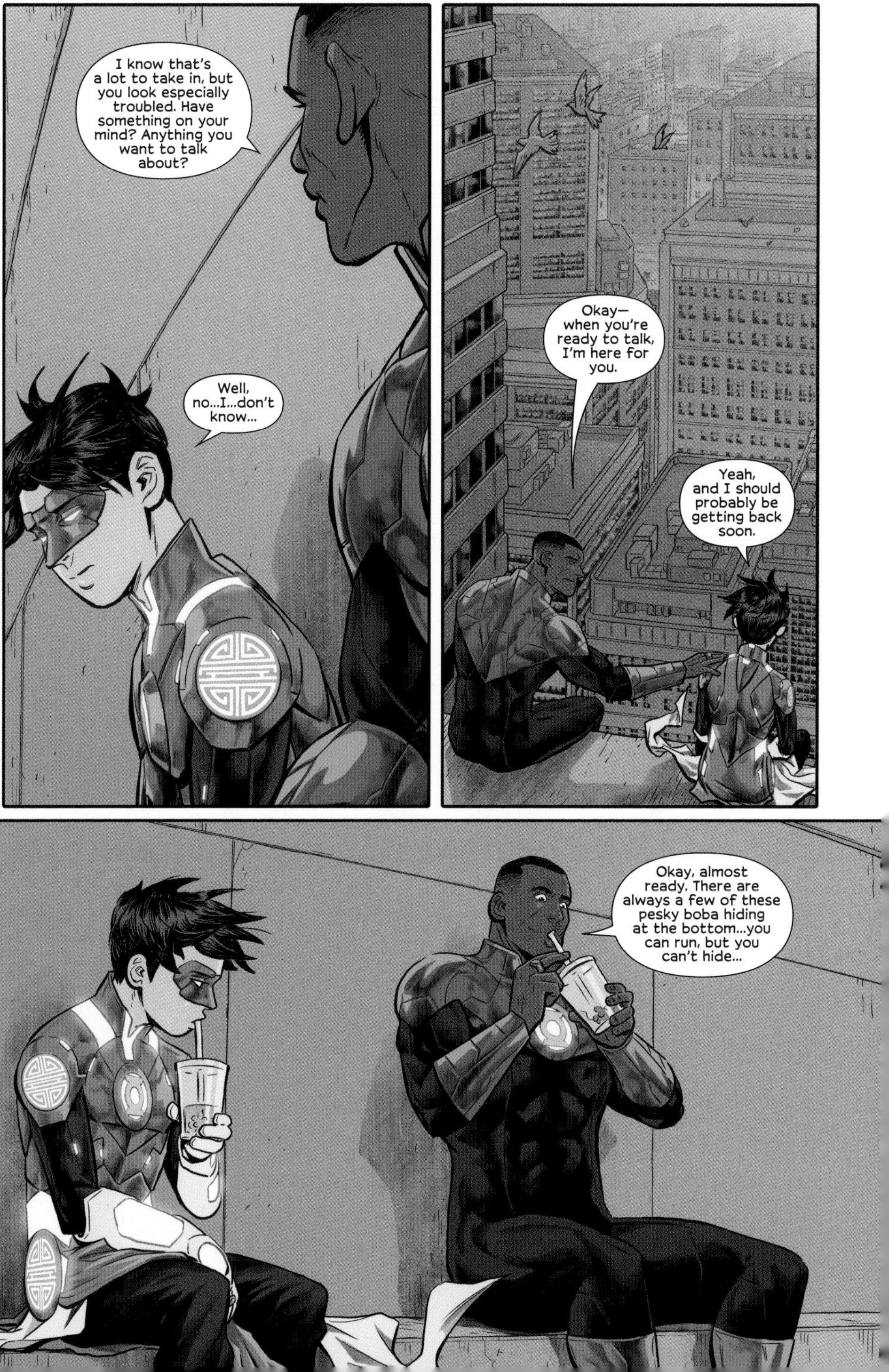
I know that's a lot to take in, but you look especially troubled. Have something on your mind? Anything you want to talk about?
Well, no...I...don't know...
Okay— when you're ready to talk, I'm here for you.
Yeah, and I should probably be getting back soon.
Okay, almost ready. There are always a few of these pesky boba hiding at the bottom...you can run, but you can't hide...

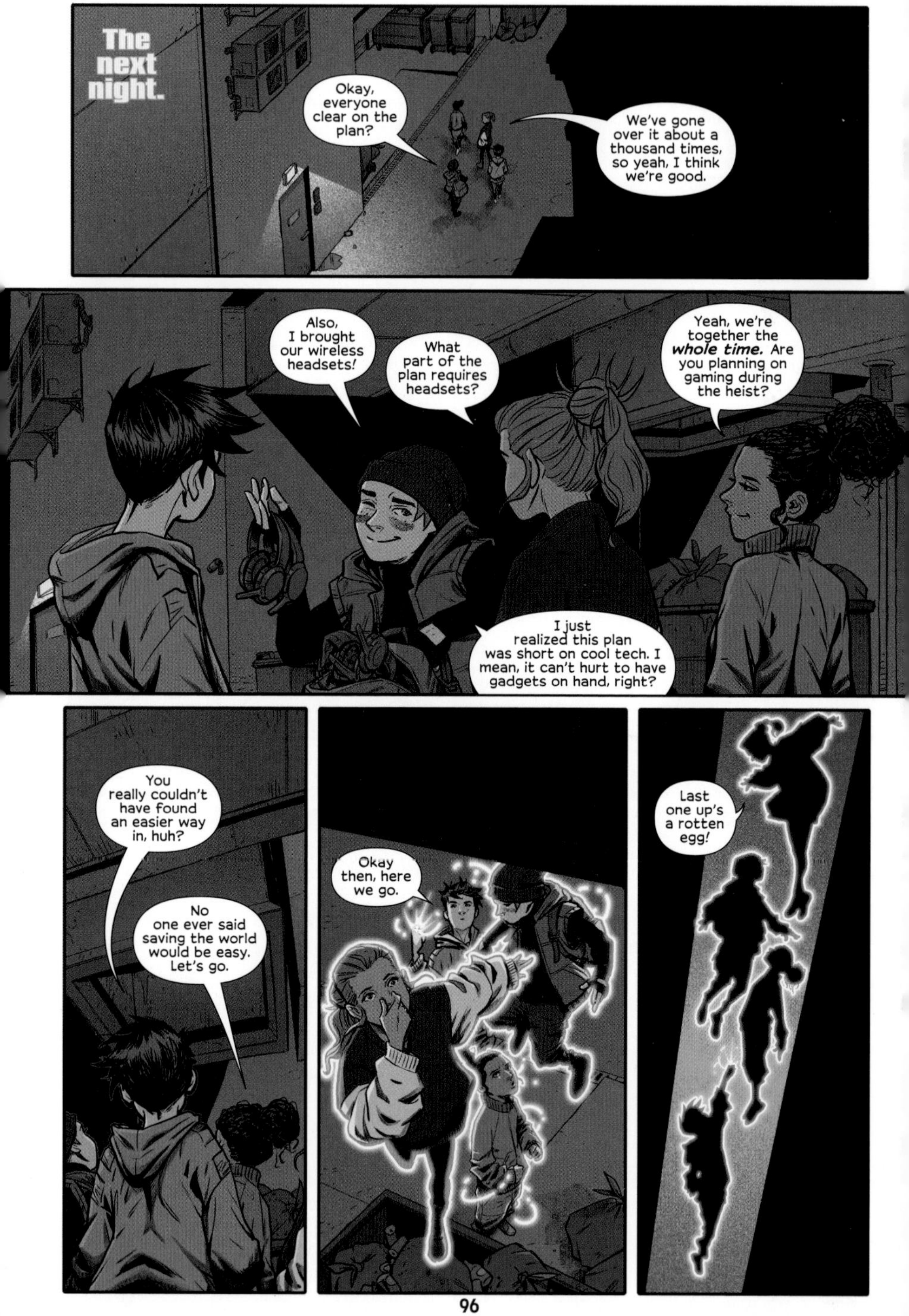
The next night.
Okay, everyone clear on the plan?
We've gone over it about a thousand times, so yeah, I think we're good.
Also, I brought our wireless headsets!
What part of the plan requires headsets?
Yeah, we're together the *whole time.* Are you planning on gaming during the heist?
I just realized this plan was short on cool tech. I mean, it can't hurt to have gadgets on hand, right?
You really couldn't have found an easier way in, huh?
No one ever said saving the world would be easy. Let's go.
Okay then, here we go.
Last one up's a rotten egg!

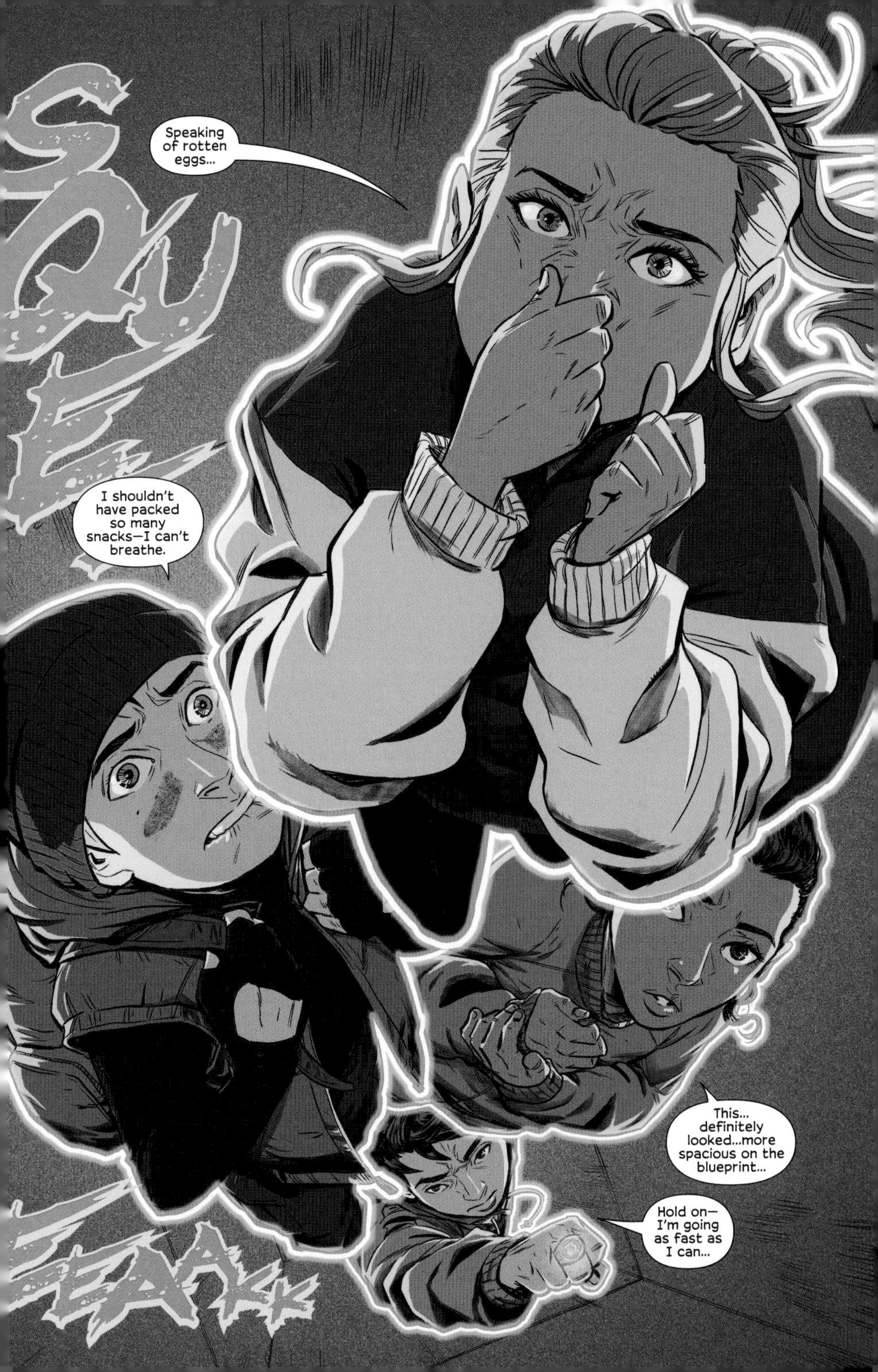
Speaking of rotten eggs...
I shouldn't have packed so many snacks—I can't breathe.
This... definitely looked...more spacious on the blueprint...
Hold on—I'm going as fast as I can...

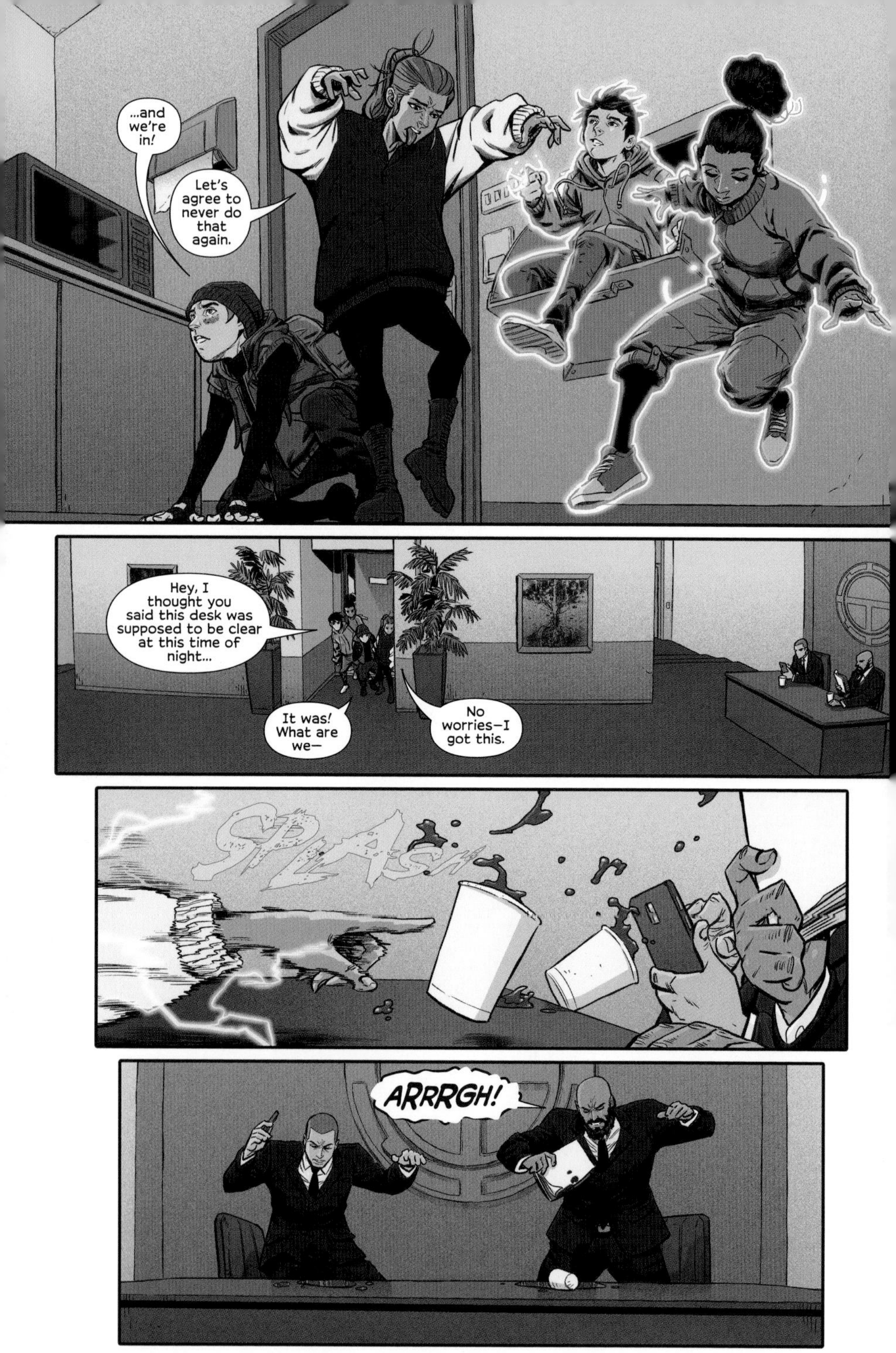
...and we're in!
Let's agree to never do that again.
Hey, I thought you said this desk was supposed to be clear at this time of night...
It was! What are we—
No worries—I got this.
SPLASH
ARRRGH!

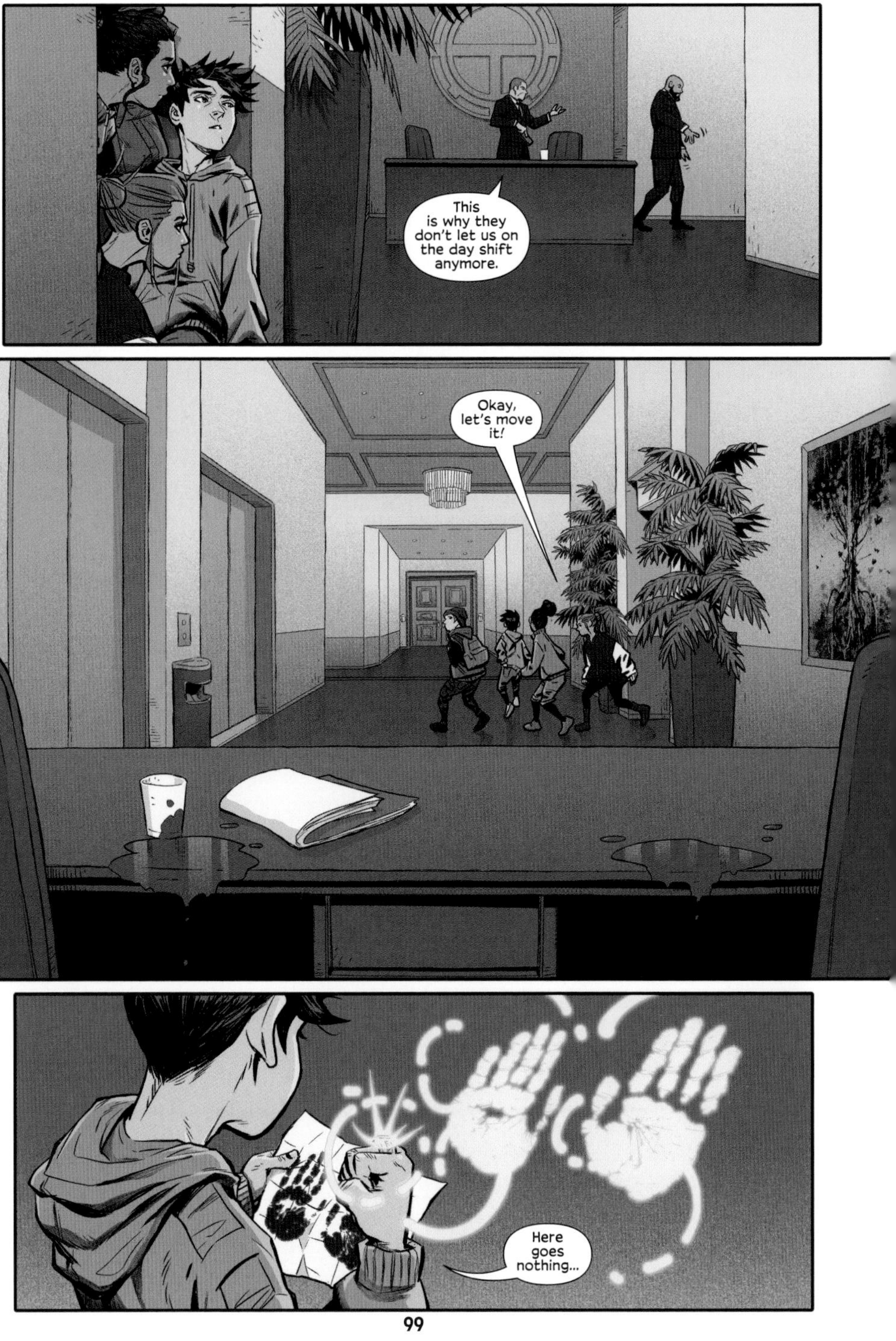
This is why they don't let us on the day shift anymore.
Okay, let's move it!
Here goes nothing...

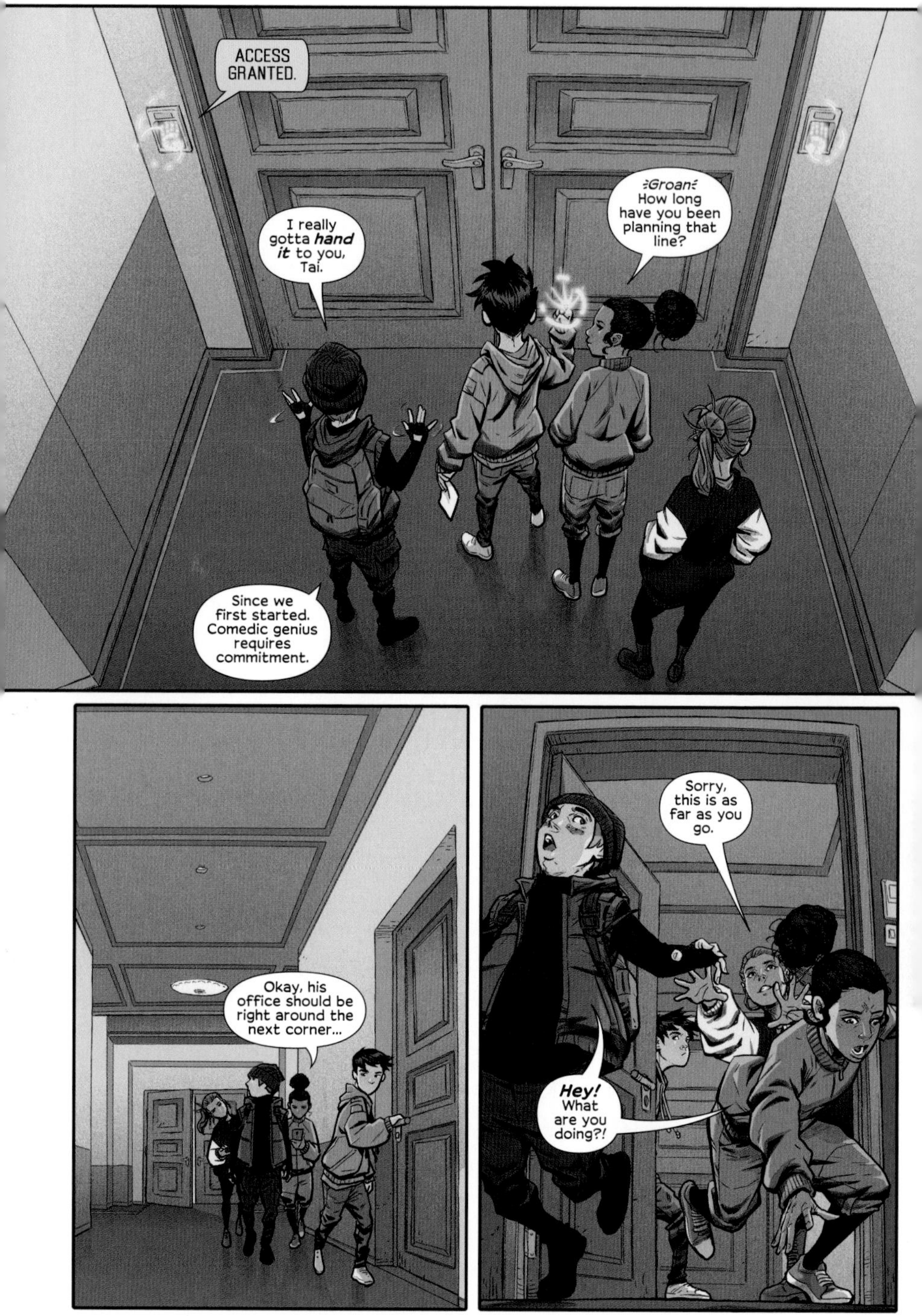
ACCESS GRANTED.
I really gotta ***hand it*** to you, Tai.
≈Groan≈ How long have you been planning that line?
Since we first started. Comedic genius requires commitment.
Okay, his office should be right around the next corner...
Sorry, this is as far as you go.
Hey! What are you doing?!

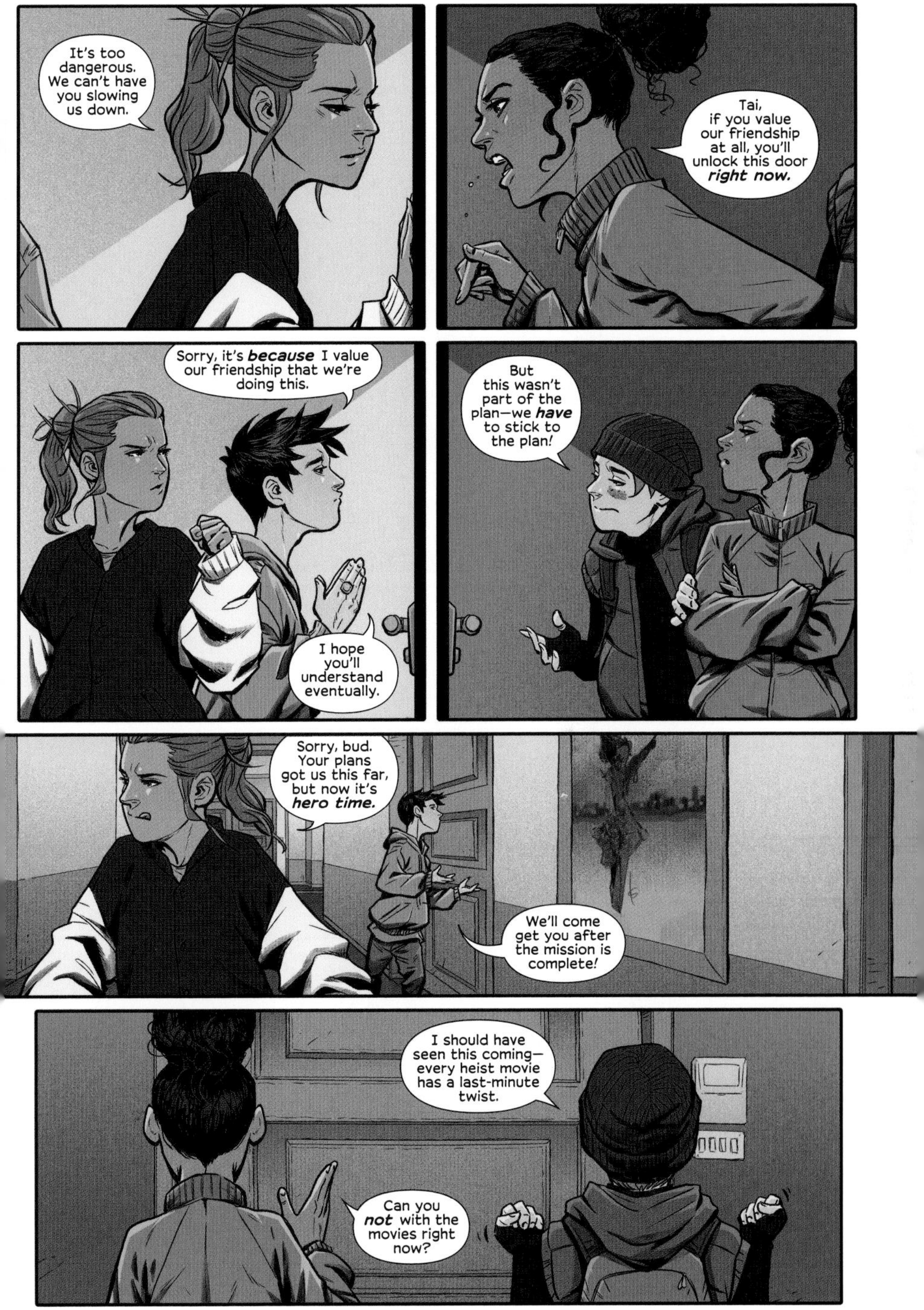
It's too dangerous. We can't have you slowing us down.
Tai, if you value our friendship at all, you'll unlock this door ***right now.***
Sorry, it's ***because*** I value our friendship that we're doing this.
I hope you'll understand eventually.
But this wasn't part of the plan—we ***have*** to stick to the plan!
Sorry, bud. Your plans got us this far, but now it's ***hero time.***
We'll come get you after the mission is complete!
I should have seen this coming—every heist movie has a last-minute twist.
Can you ***not*** with the movies right now?

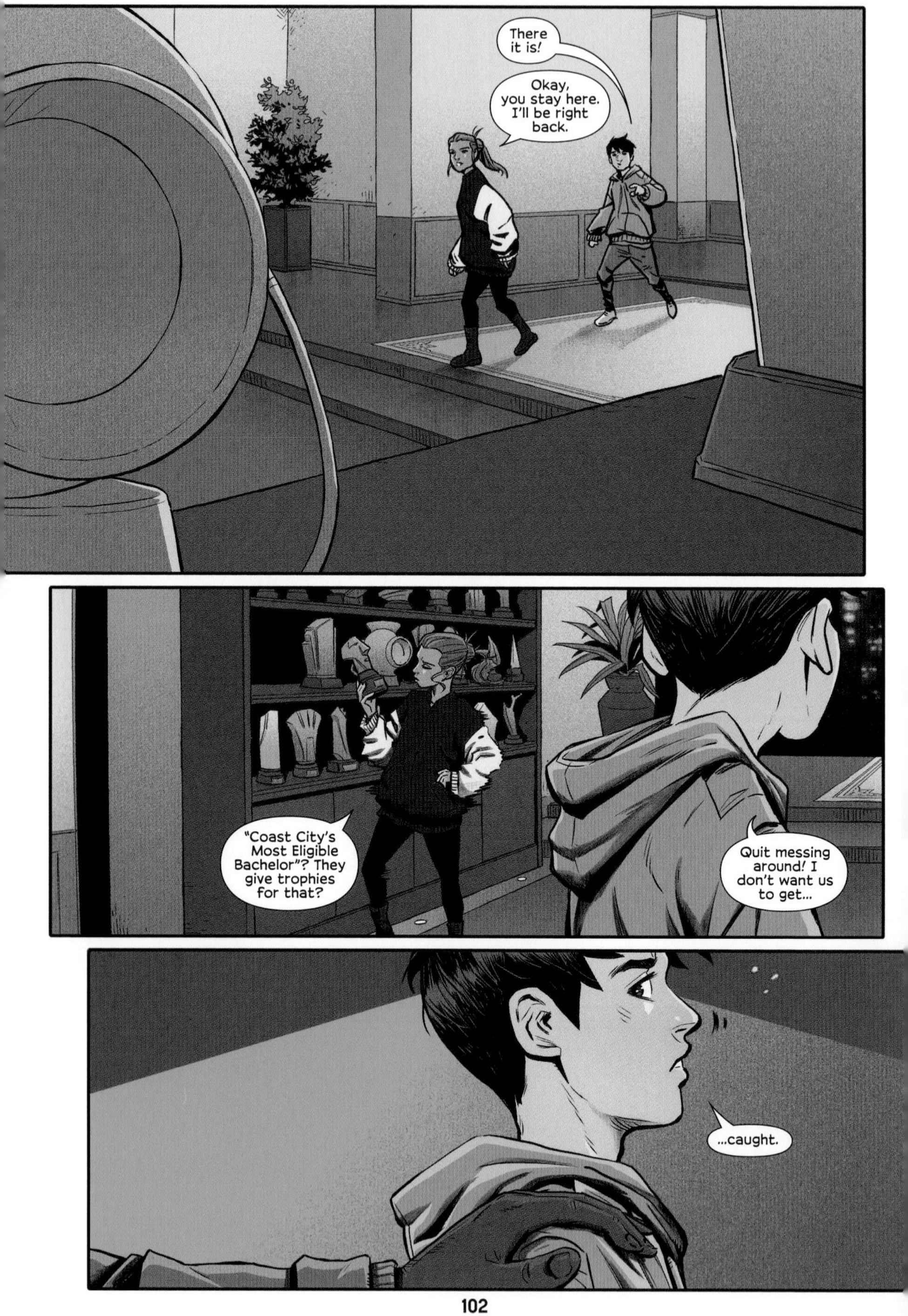
There it is!
Okay, you stay here. I'll be right back.
"Coast City's Most Eligible Bachelor"? They give trophies for that?
Quit messing around! I don't want us to get...
...caught.

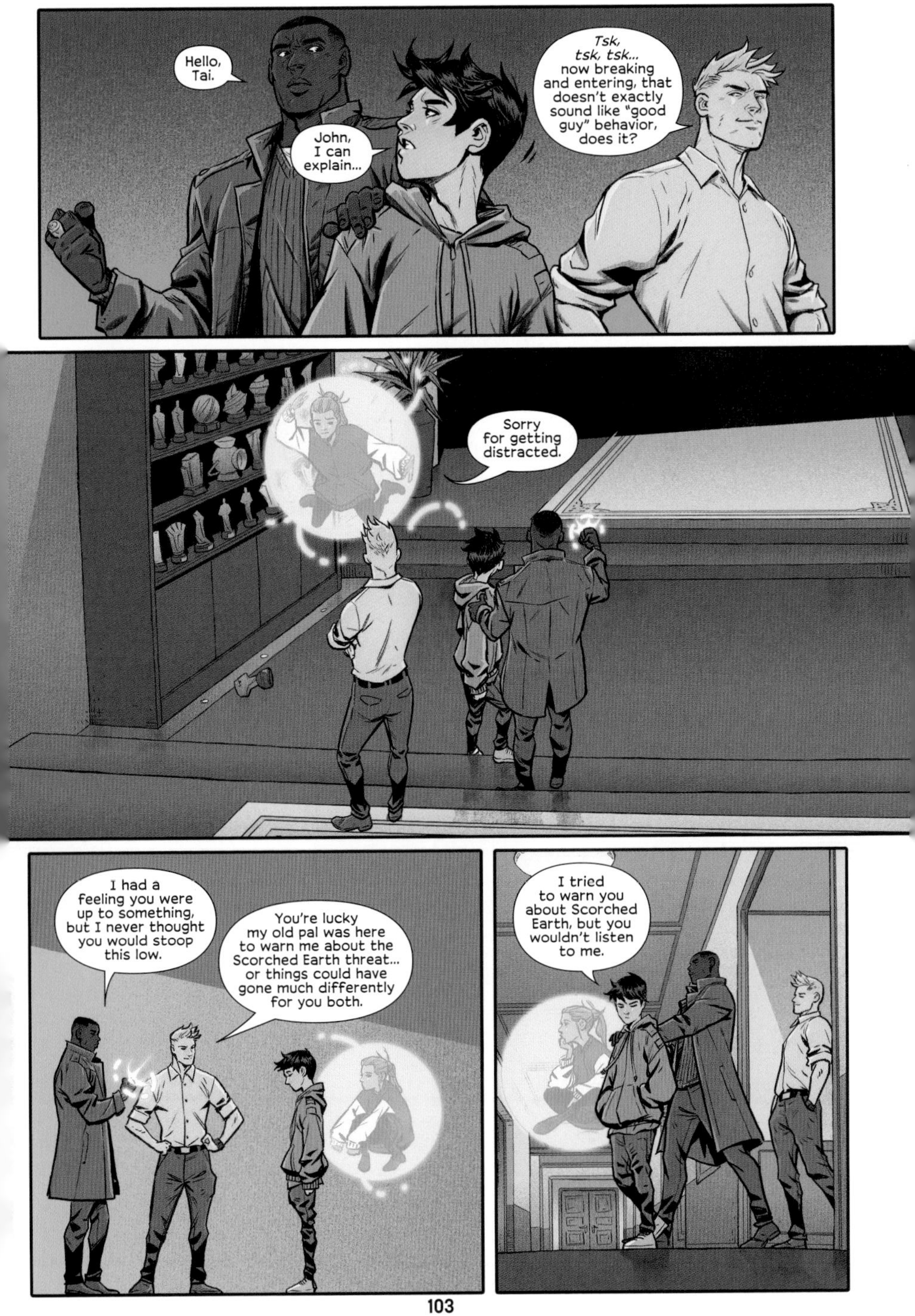
Hello, Tai.
John, I can explain...
Tsk, tsk, tsk... now breaking and entering, that doesn't exactly sound like "good guy" behavior, does it?
Sorry for getting distracted.
I had a feeling you were up to something, but I never thought you would stoop this low.
You're lucky my old pal was here to warn me about the Scorched Earth threat... or things could have gone much differently for you both.
I tried to warn you about Scorched Earth, but you wouldn't listen to me.

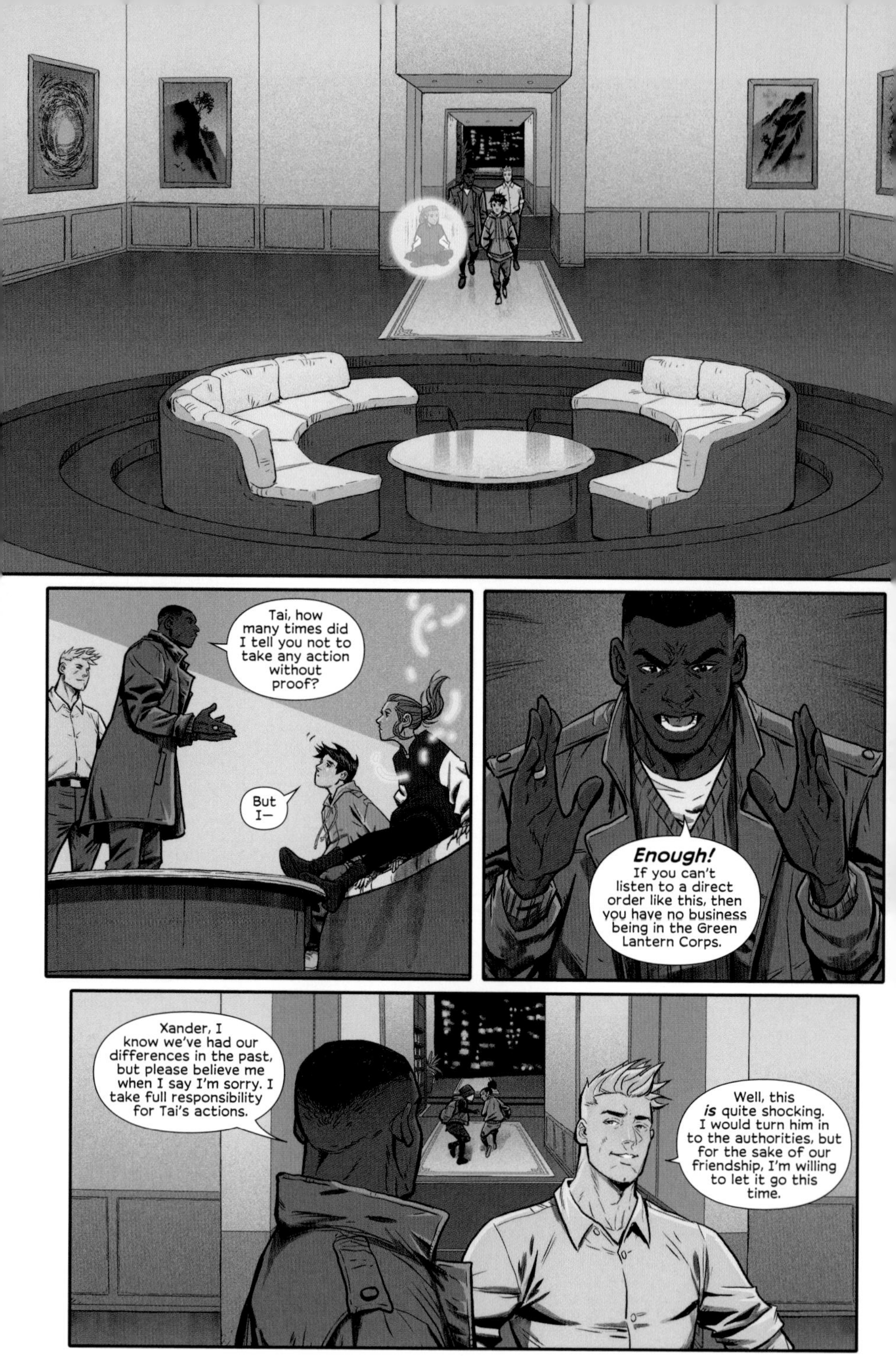
Tai, how many times did I tell you not to take any action without proof?
But I—
Enough! If you can't listen to a direct order like this, then you have no business being in the Green Lantern Corps.
Xander, I know we've had our differences in the past, but please believe me when I say I'm sorry. I take full responsibility for Tai's actions.
Well, this is quite shocking. I would turn him in to the authorities, but for the sake of our friendship, I'm willing to let it go this time.

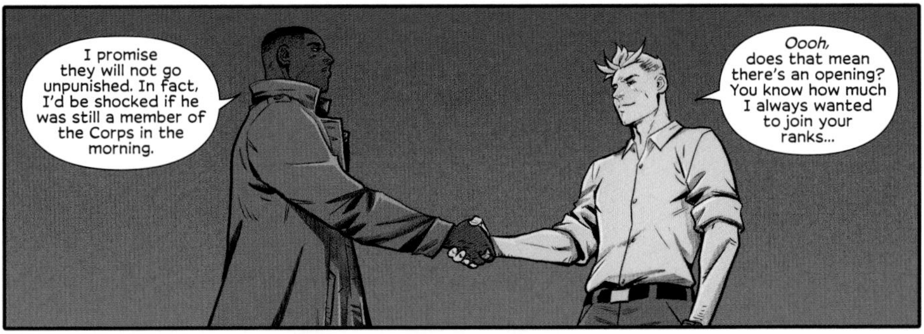
I promise they will not go unpunished. In fact, I'd be shocked if he was still a member of the Corps in the morning.
Oooh, does that mean there's an opening? You know how much I always wanted to join your ranks...

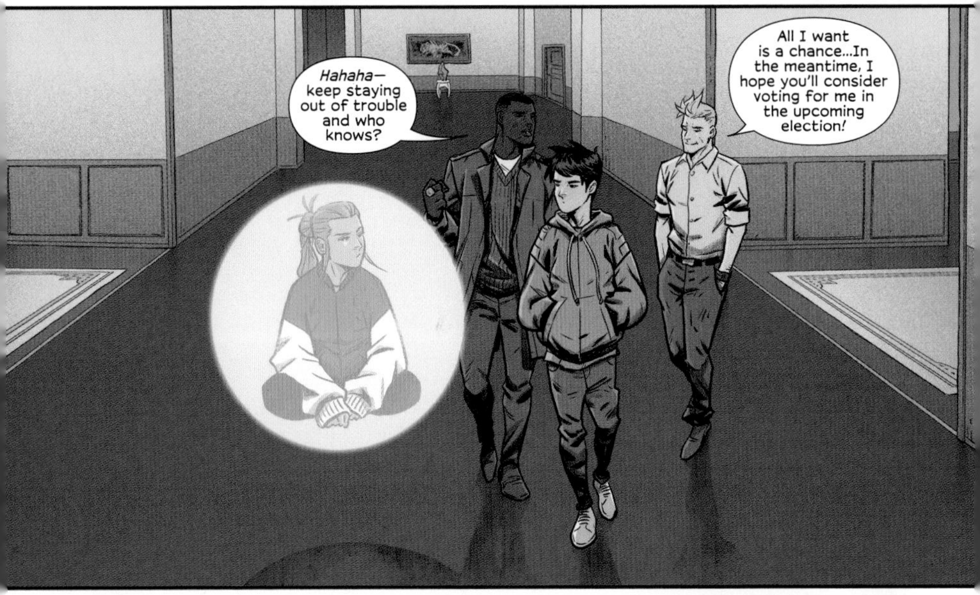
Hahaha— keep staying out of trouble and who knows?
All I want is a chance...In the meantime, I hope you'll consider voting for me in the upcoming election!

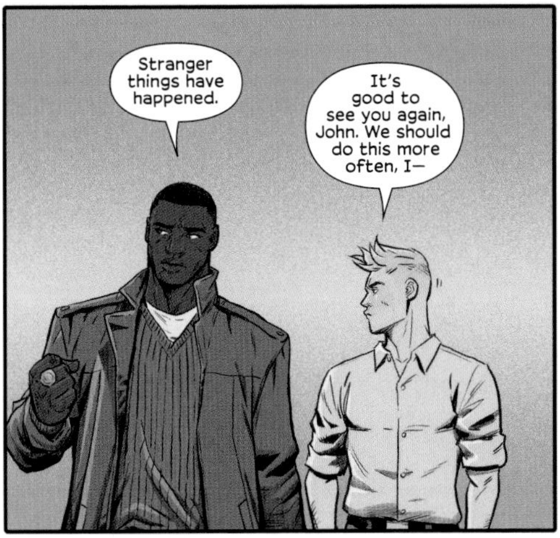
Stranger things have happened.
It's good to see you again, John. We should do this more often, I—

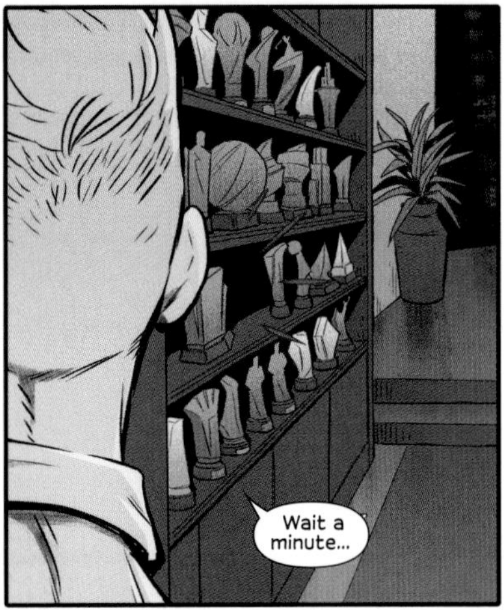
Wait a minute...

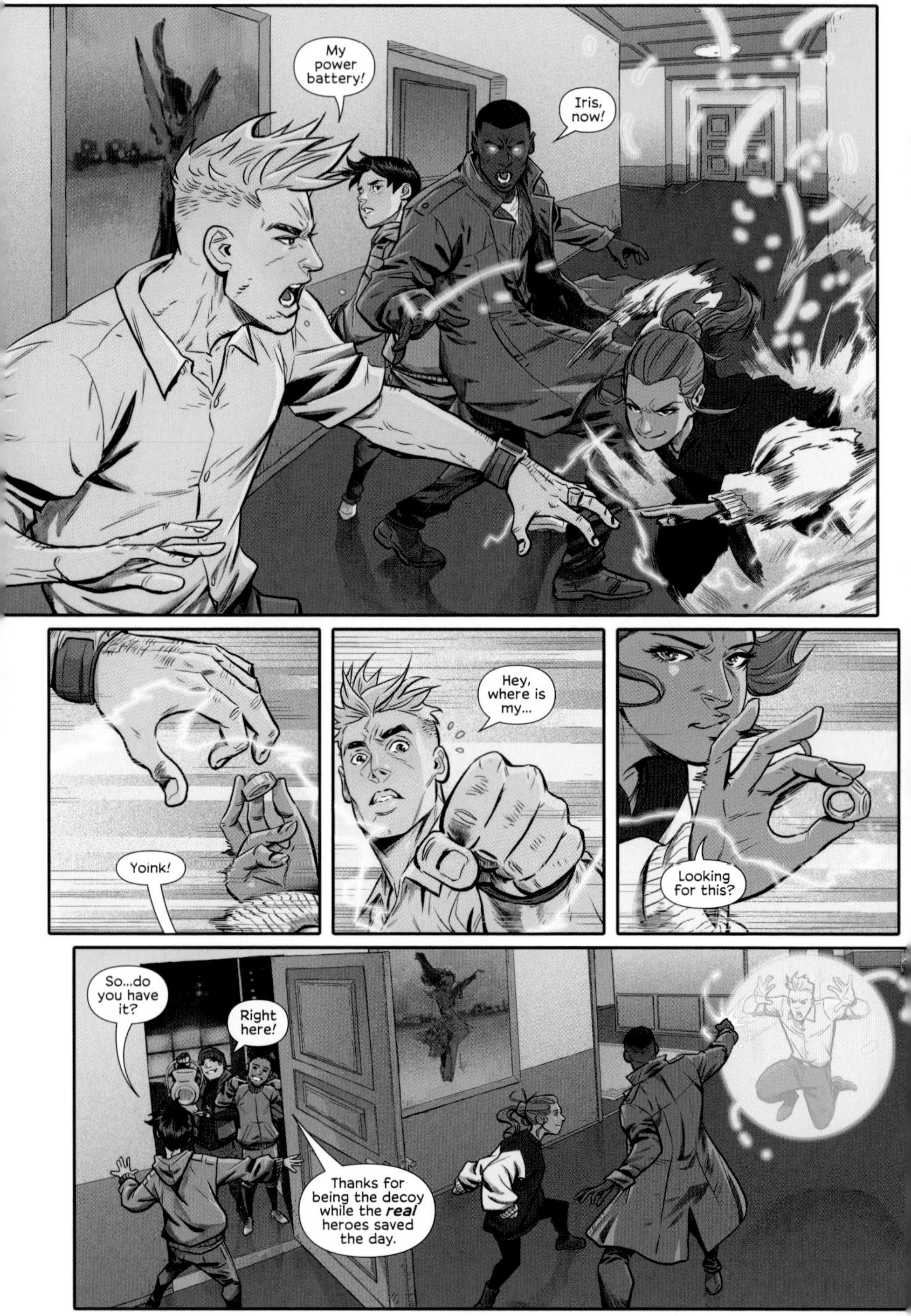
My power battery!
Iris, now!
Yoink!
Hey, where is my...
Looking for this?
So...do you have it?
Right here!
Thanks for being the decoy while the *real* heroes saved the day.

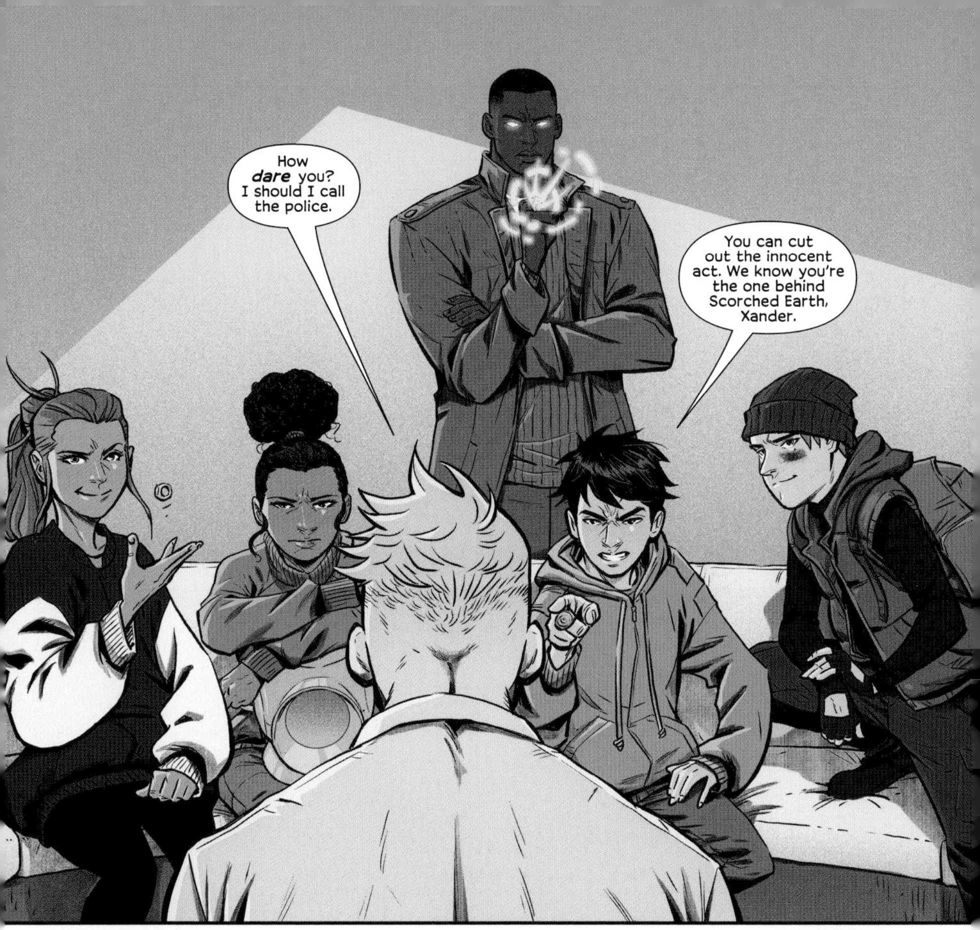
How *dare* you? I should I call the police.
You can cut out the innocent act. We know you're the one behind Scorched Earth, Xander.
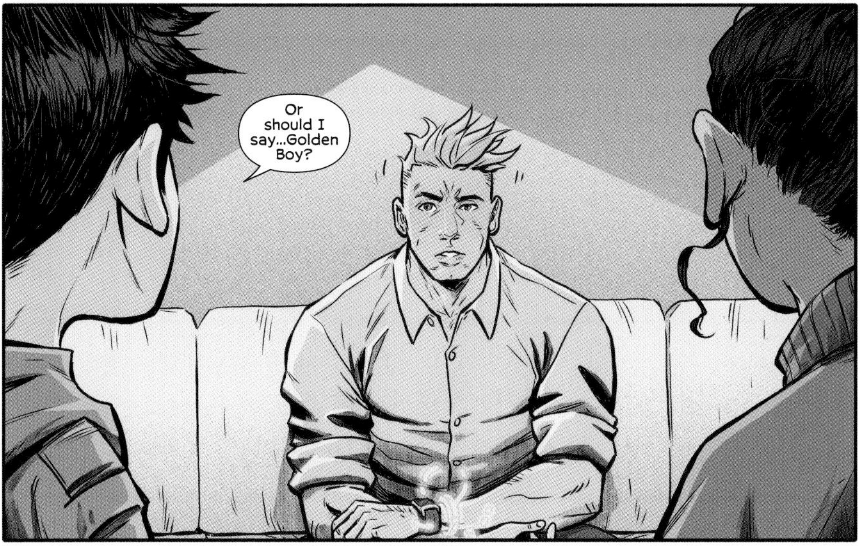
Or should I say...Golden Boy?

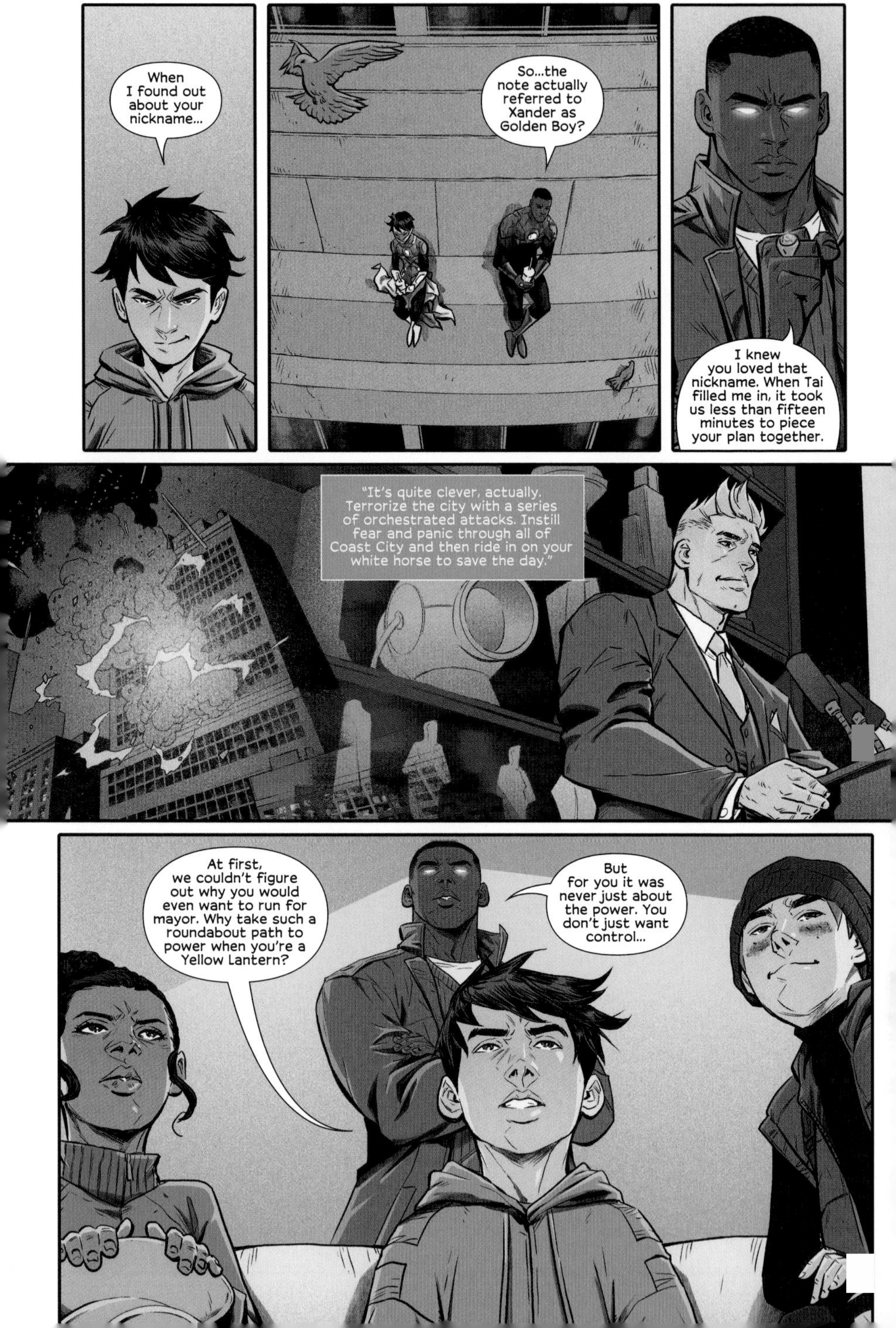
When I found out about your nickname...
So...the note actually referred to Xander as Golden Boy?
I knew you loved that nickname. When Tai filled me in, it took us less than fifteen minutes to piece your plan together.
"It's quite clever, actually. Terrorize the city with a series of orchestrated attacks. Instill fear and panic through all of Coast City and then ride in on your white horse to save the day."
At first, we couldn't figure out why you would even want to run for mayor. Why take such a roundabout path to power when you're a Yellow Lantern?
But for you it was never just about the power. You don't just want control...

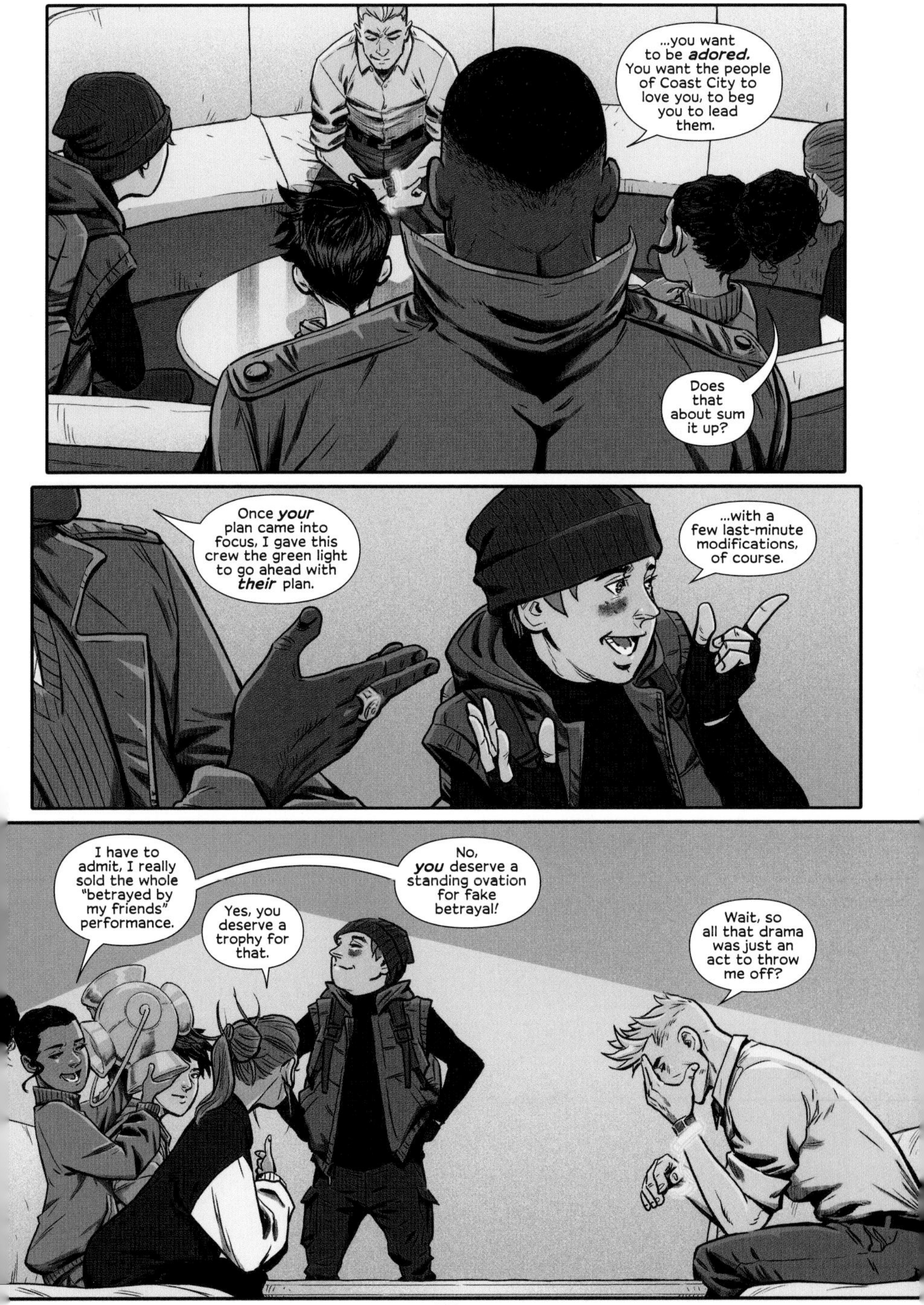
...you want to be *adored.* You want the people of Coast City to love you, to beg you to lead them.
Does that about sum it up?
Once *your* plan came into focus, I gave this crew the green light to go ahead with *their* plan.
...with a few last-minute modifications, of course.
I have to admit, I really sold the whole "betrayed by my friends" performance.
Yes, you deserve a trophy for that.
No, *you* deserve a standing ovation for fake betrayal!
Wait, so all that drama was just an act to throw me off?

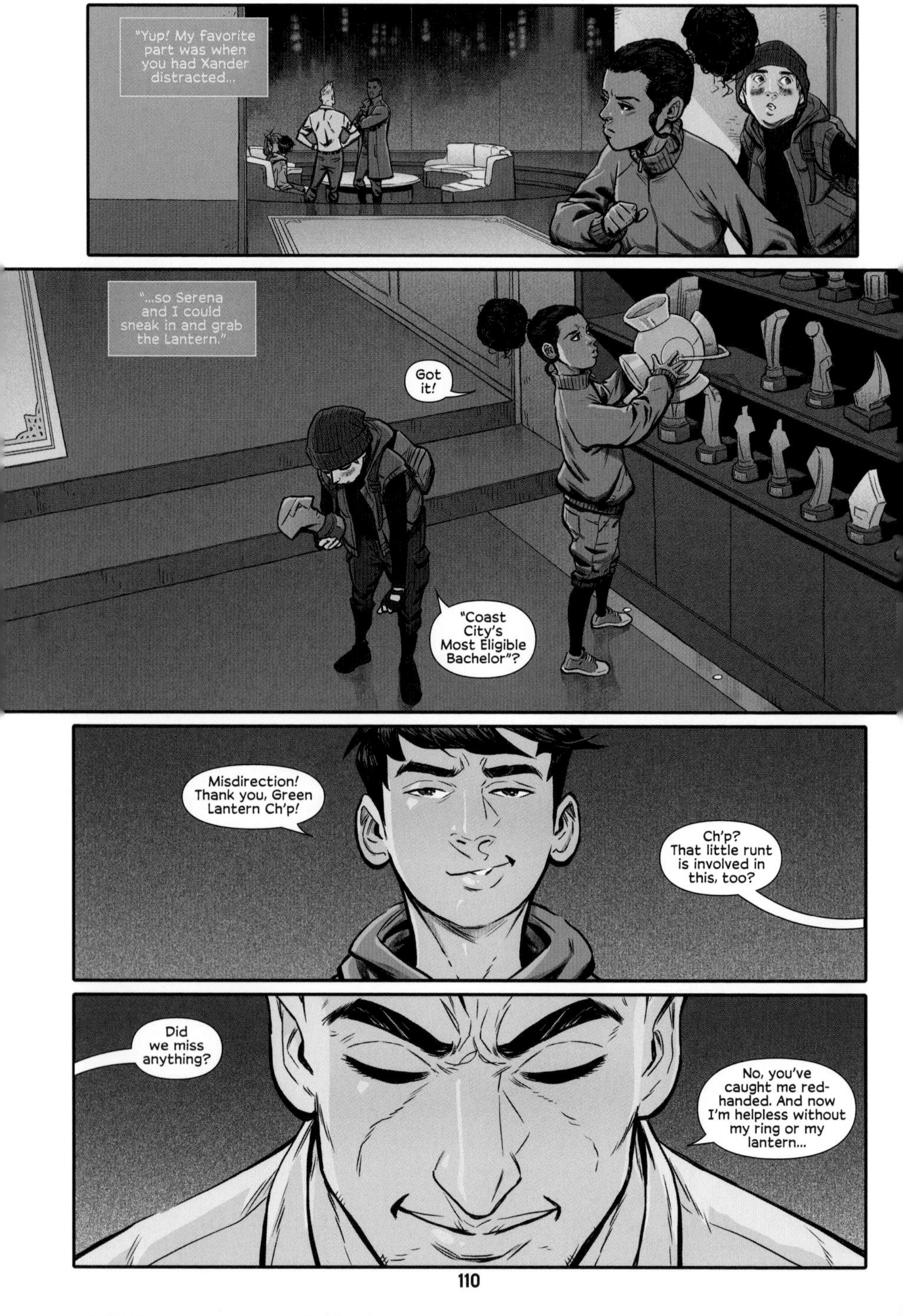
"Yup! My favorite part was when you had Xander distracted...
"...so Serena and I could sneak in and grab the Lantern."
Got it!
"Coast City's Most Eligible Bachelor"?
Misdirection! Thank you, Green Lantern Ch'p!
Ch'p? That little runt is involved in this, too?
Did we miss anything?
No, you've caught me red-handed. And now I'm helpless without my ring or my lantern...

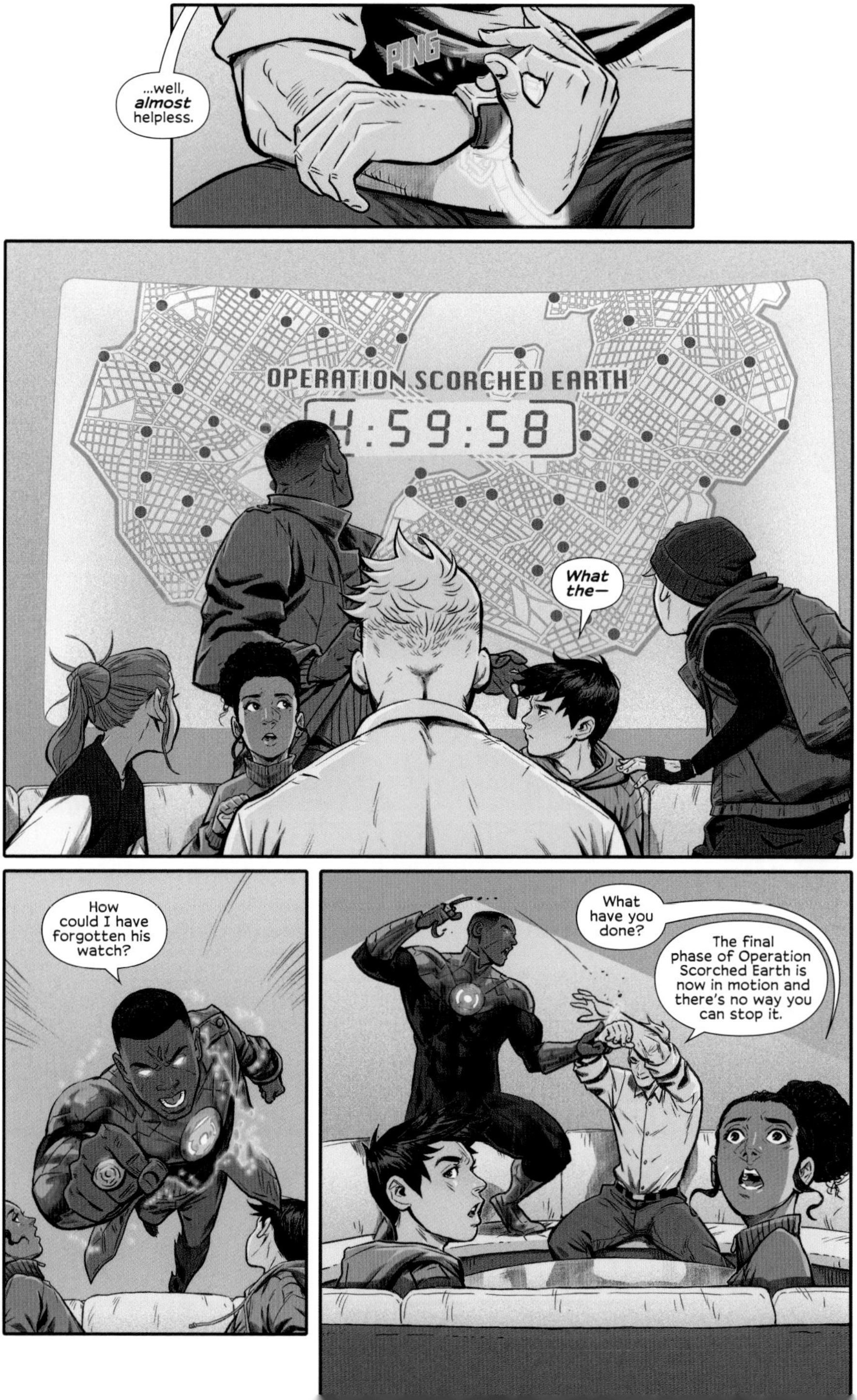
...well, almost helpless.
RING
OPERATION SCORCHED EARTH
4:59:58
What the—
How could I have forgotten his watch?
What have you done?
The final phase of Operation Scorched Earth is now in motion and there's no way you can stop it.

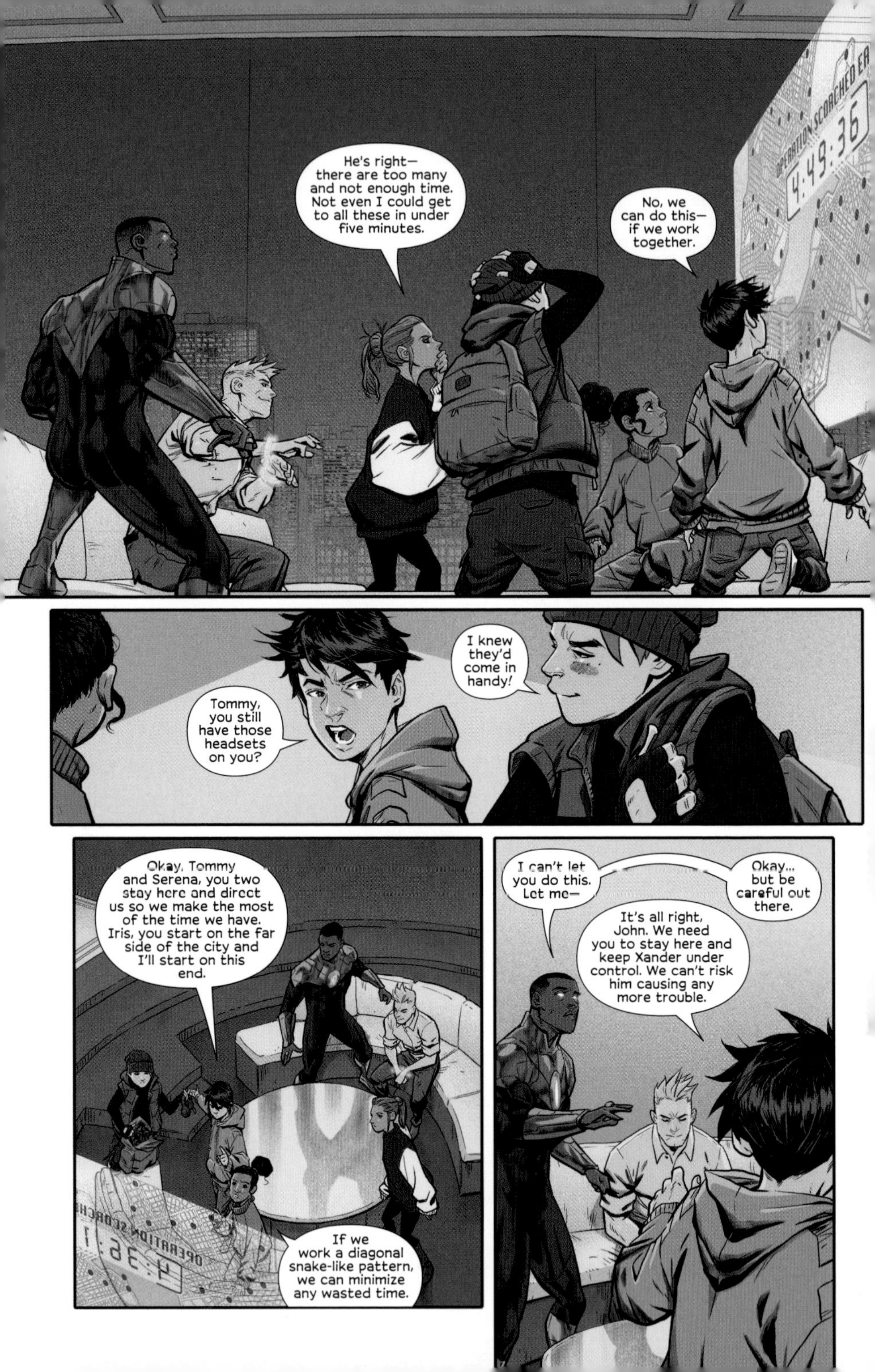
OPERATION SCORCHED EA
4:49:36
He's right— there are too many and not enough time. Not even I could get to all these in under five minutes.
No, we can do this— if we work together.
Tommy, you still have those headsets on you?
I knew they'd come in handy!
Okay, Tommy and Serena, you two stay here and direct us so we make the most of the time we have. Iris, you start on the far side of the city and I'll start on this end.
If we work a diagonal snake-like pattern, we can minimize any wasted time.
I can't let you do this. Let me—
Okay... but be careful out there.
It's all right, John. We need you to stay here and keep Xander under control. We can't risk him causing any more trouble.

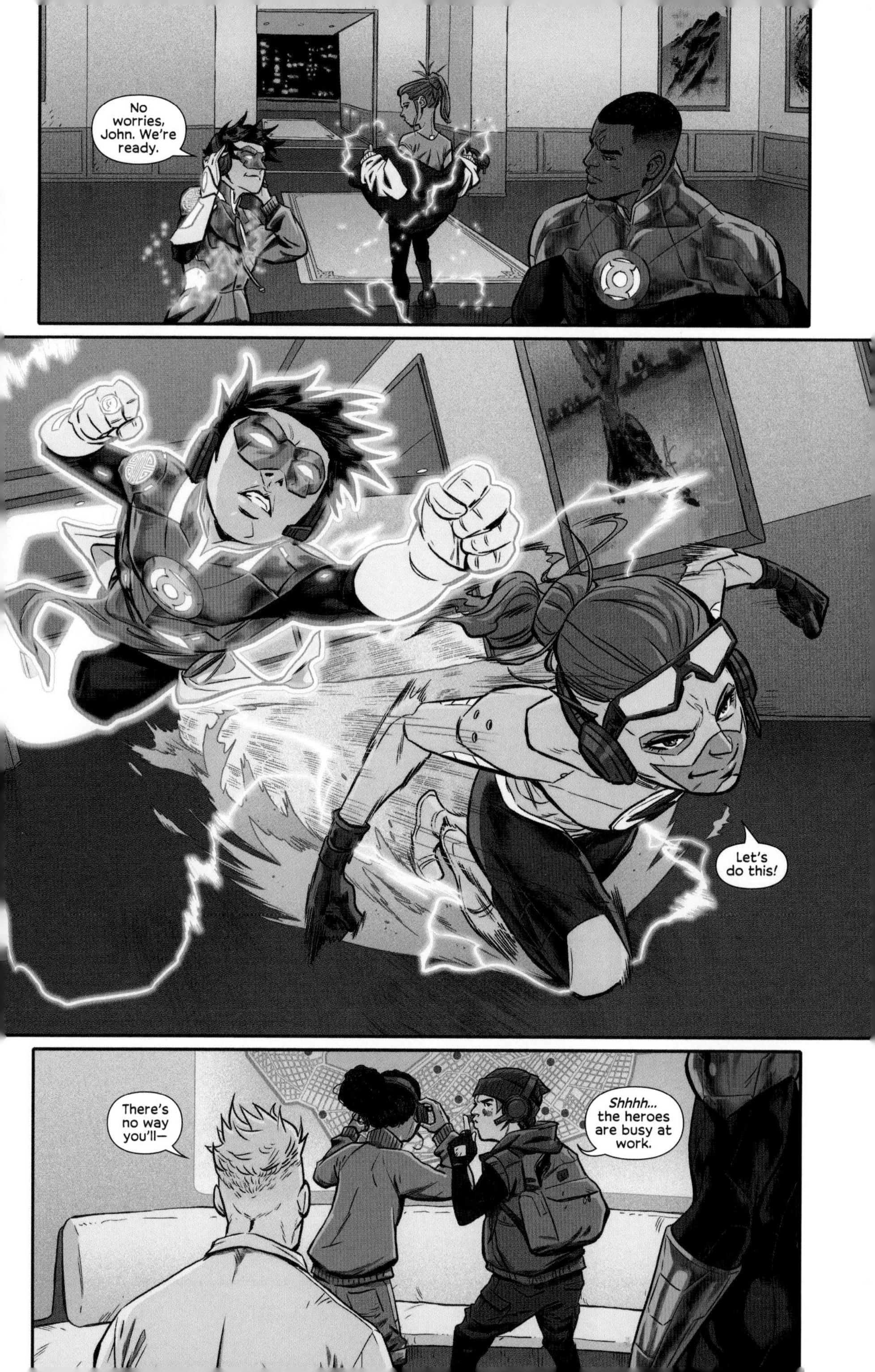
No worries, John. We're ready.
Let's do this!
There's no way you'll—
Shhhh... the heroes are busy at work.

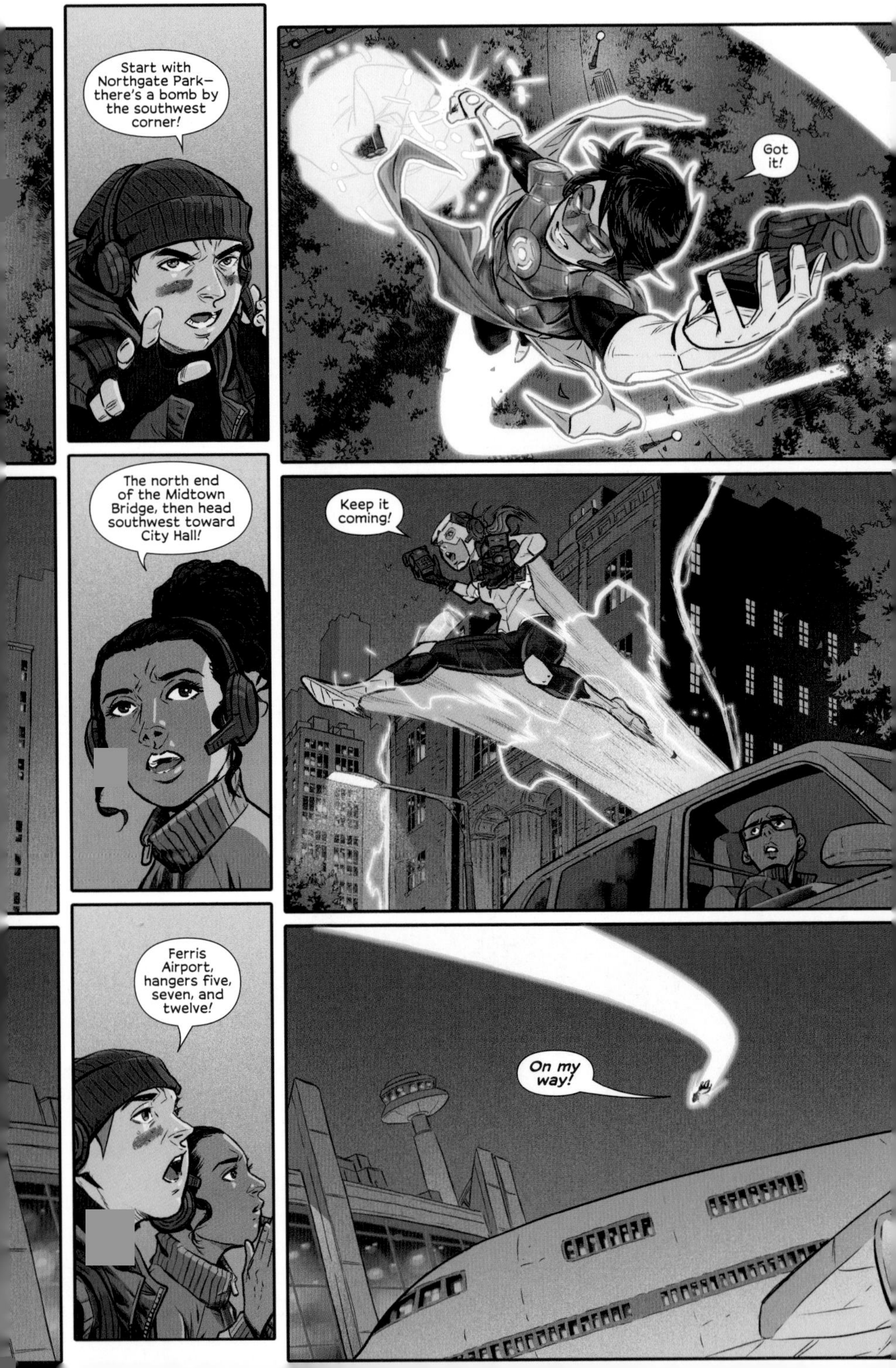
Start with Northgate Park—there's a bomb by the southwest corner!
Got it!
The north end of the Midtown Bridge, then head southwest toward City Hall!
Keep it coming!
Ferris Airport, hangers five, seven, and twelve!
On my way!

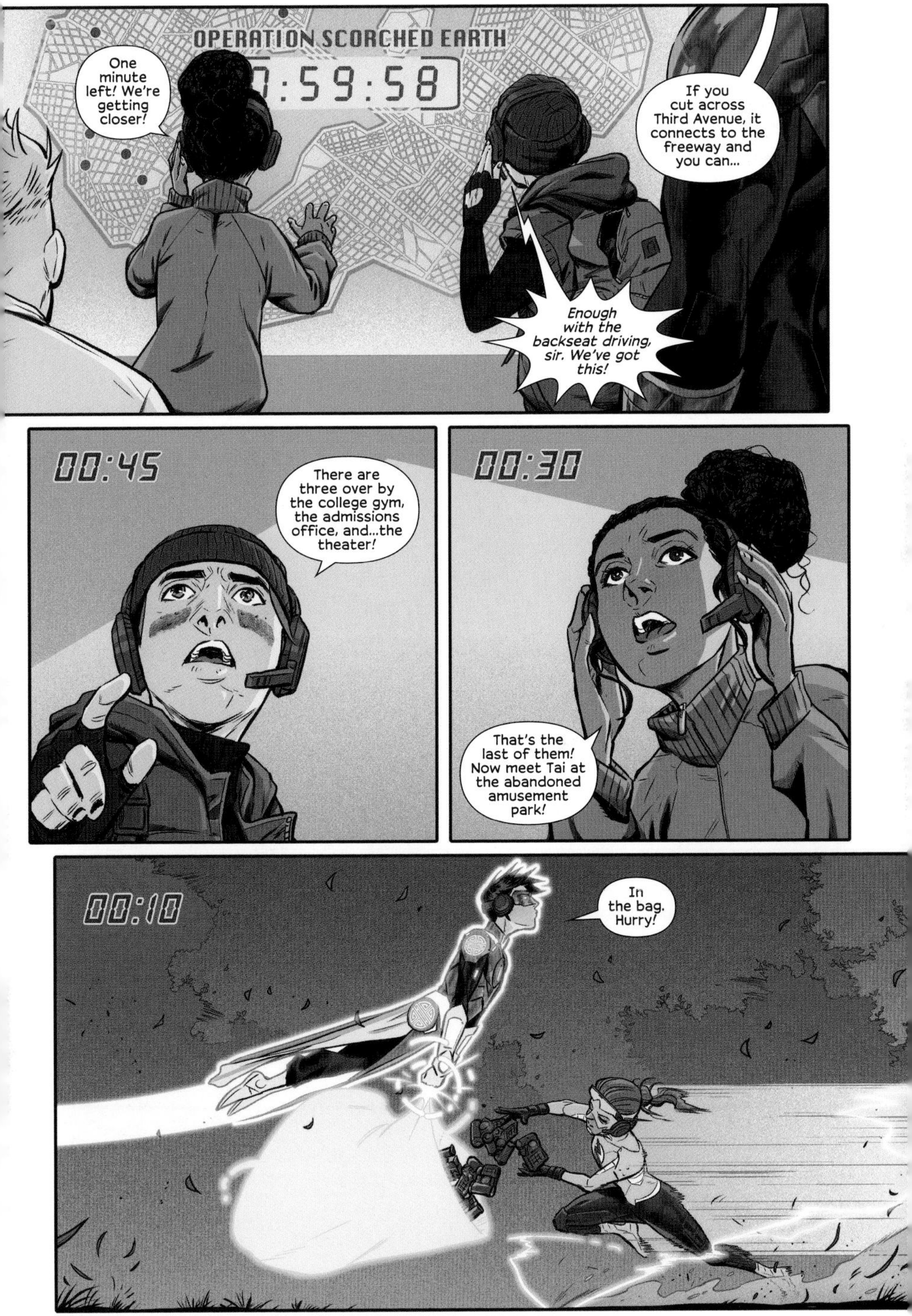
OPERATION SCORCHED EARTH
0:59:58
One minute left! We're getting closer!
If you cut across Third Avenue, it connects to the freeway and you can...
Enough with the backseat driving, sir. We've got this!
00:45
There are three over by the college gym, the admissions office, and...the theater!
00:30
That's the last of them! Now meet Tai at the abandoned amusement park!
00:10
In the bag. Hurry!

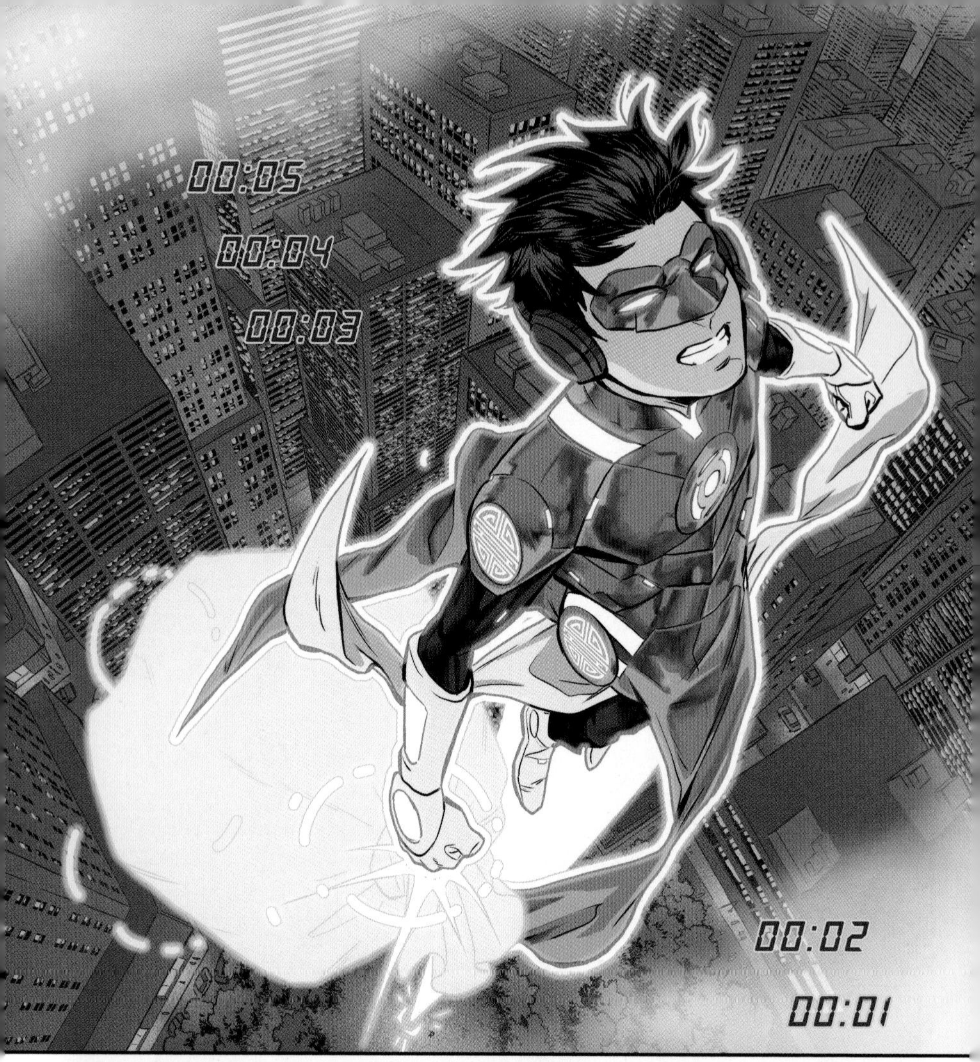
00:05
00:04
00:03
00:02
00:01

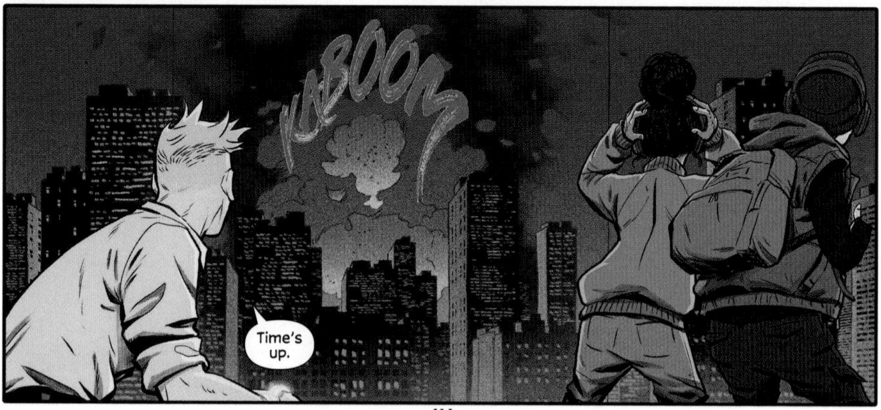
KABOOM
Time's up.

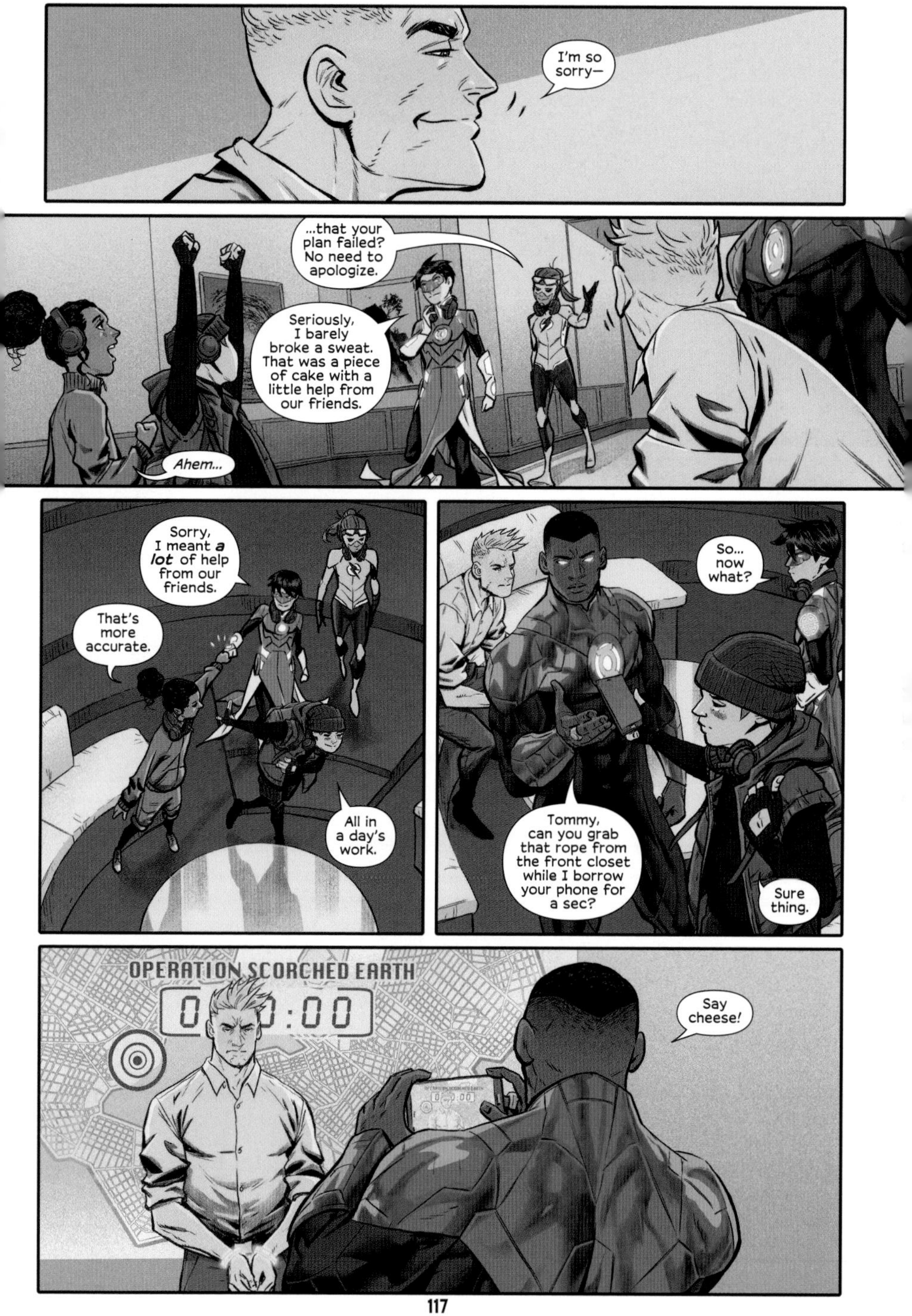
I'm so sorry—
...that your plan failed? No need to apologize.
Seriously, I barely broke a sweat. That was a piece of cake with a little help from our friends.
Ahem...
Sorry, I meant ***a lot*** of help from our friends.
That's more accurate.
All in a day's work.
So... now what?
Tommy, can you grab that rope from the front closet while I borrow your phone for a sec?
Sure thing.
OPERATION SCORCHED EARTH
Say cheese!

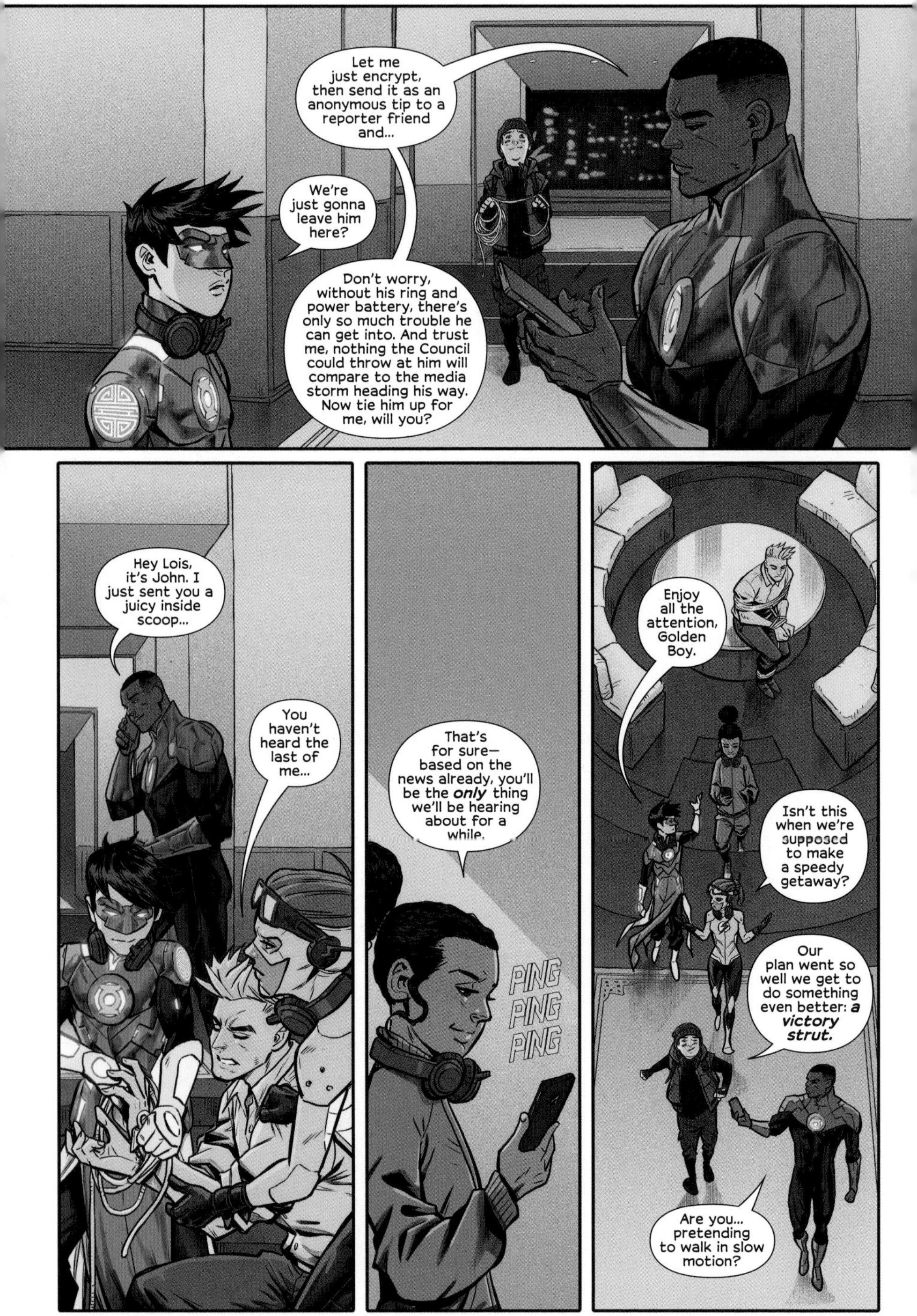
Let me just encrypt, then send it as an anonymous tip to a reporter friend and...
We're just gonna leave him here?
Don't worry, without his ring and power battery, there's only so much trouble he can get into. And trust me, nothing the Council could throw at him will compare to the media storm heading his way. Now tie him up for me, will you?
Hey Lois, it's John. I just sent you a juicy inside scoop...
You haven't heard the last of me...
That's for sure—based on the news already, you'll be the *only* thing we'll be hearing about for a while.
PING PING PING
Enjoy all the attention, Golden Boy.
Isn't this when we're supposed to make a speedy getaway?
Our plan went so well we get to do something even better: ***a victory strut.***
Are you... pretending to walk in slow motion?

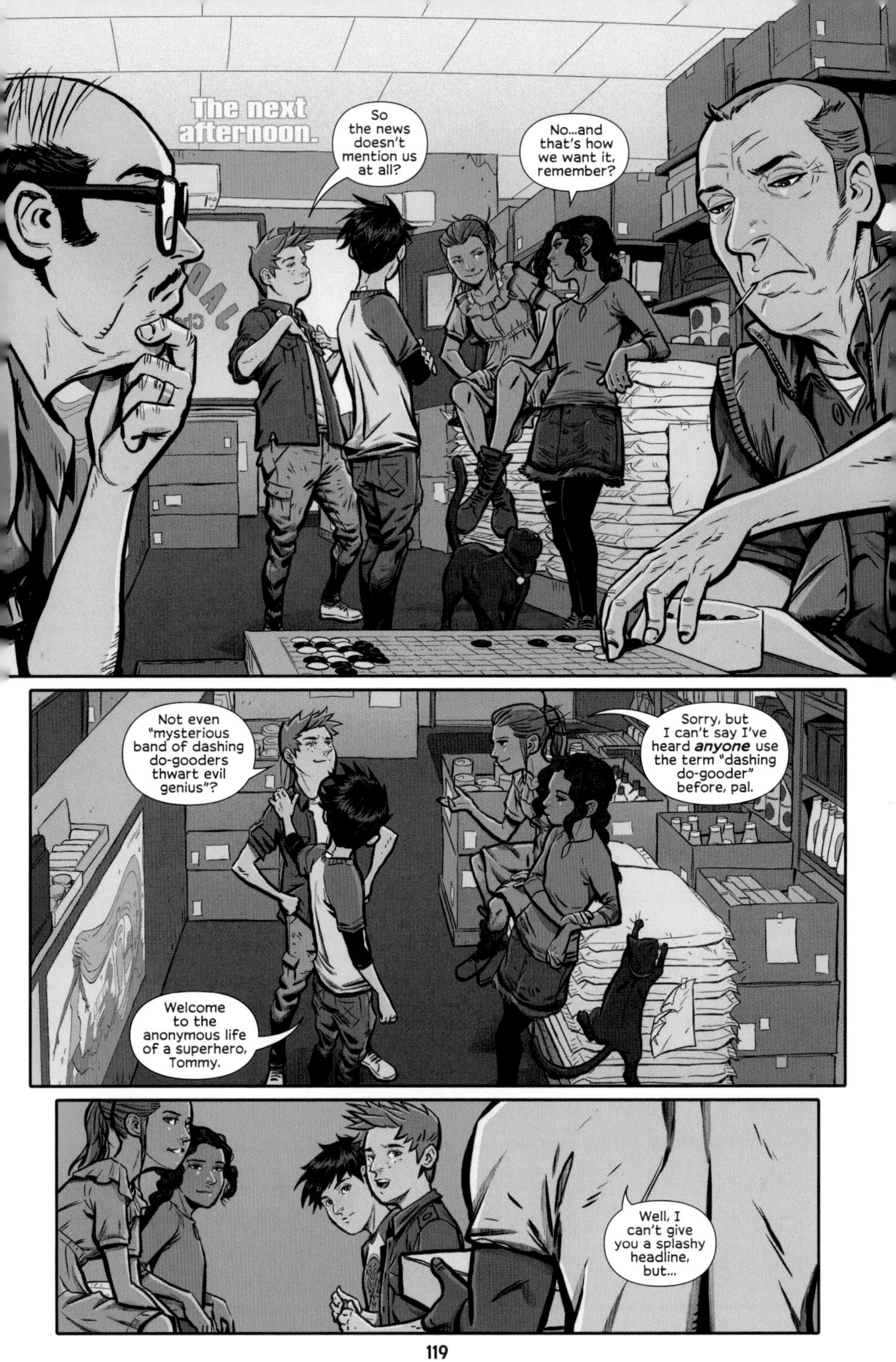
The next afternoon.
So the news doesn't mention us at all?
No...and that's how we want it, remember?
Not even "mysterious band of dashing do-gooders thwart evil genius"?
Sorry, but I can't say I've heard *anyone* use the term "dashing do-gooder" before, pal.
Welcome to the anonymous life of a superhero, Tommy.
Well, I can't give you a splashy headline, but...

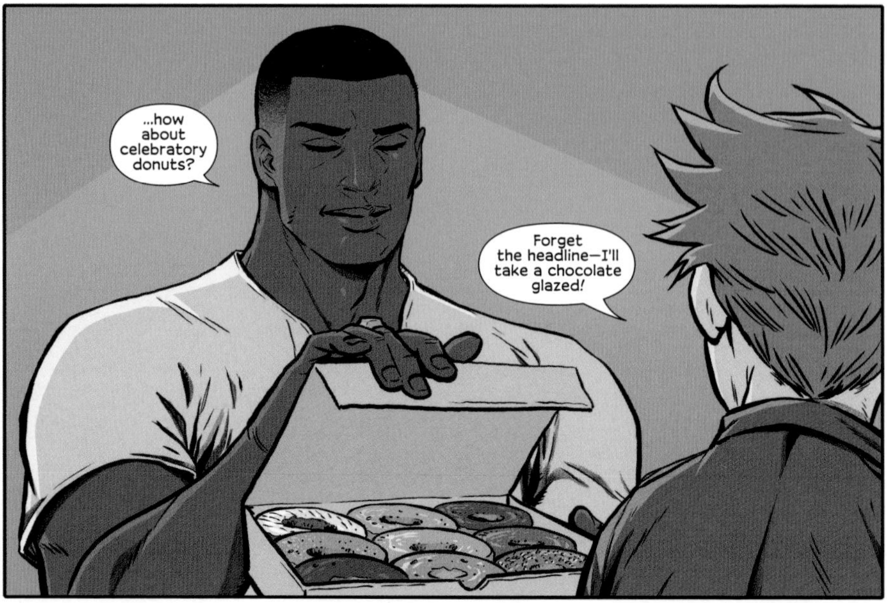
...how about celebratory donuts?
Forget the headline—I'll take a chocolate glazed!
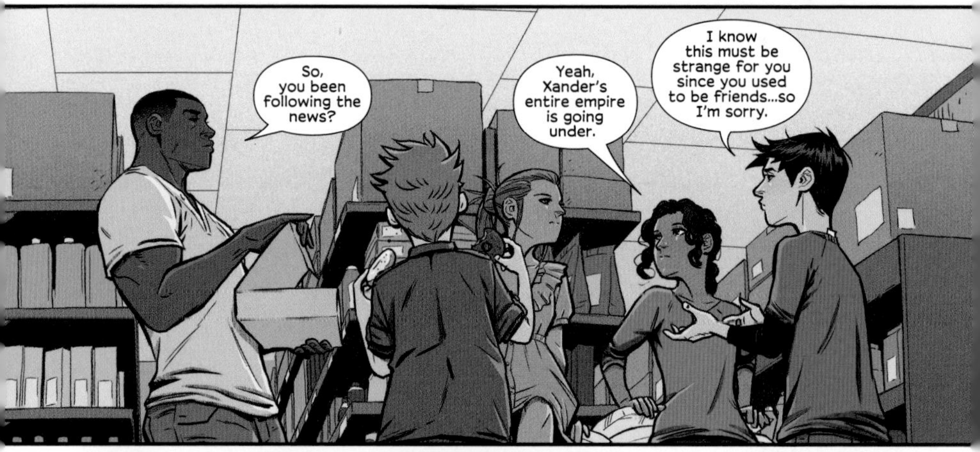
So, you been following the news?
Yeah, Xander's entire empire is going under.
I know this must be strange for you since you used to be friends...so I'm sorry.
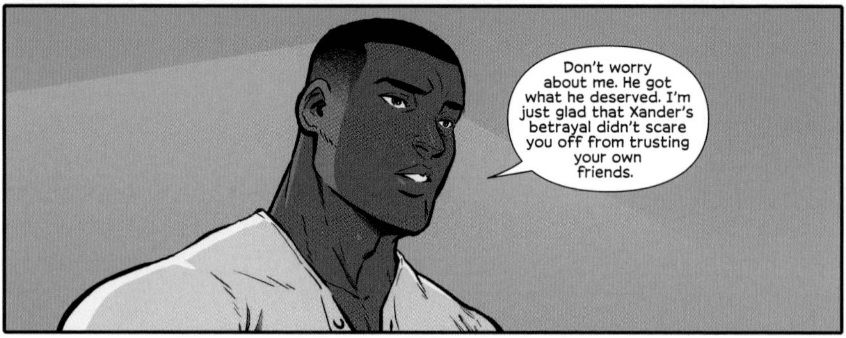
Don't worry about me. He got what he deserved. I'm just glad that Xander's betrayal didn't scare you off from trusting your own friends.

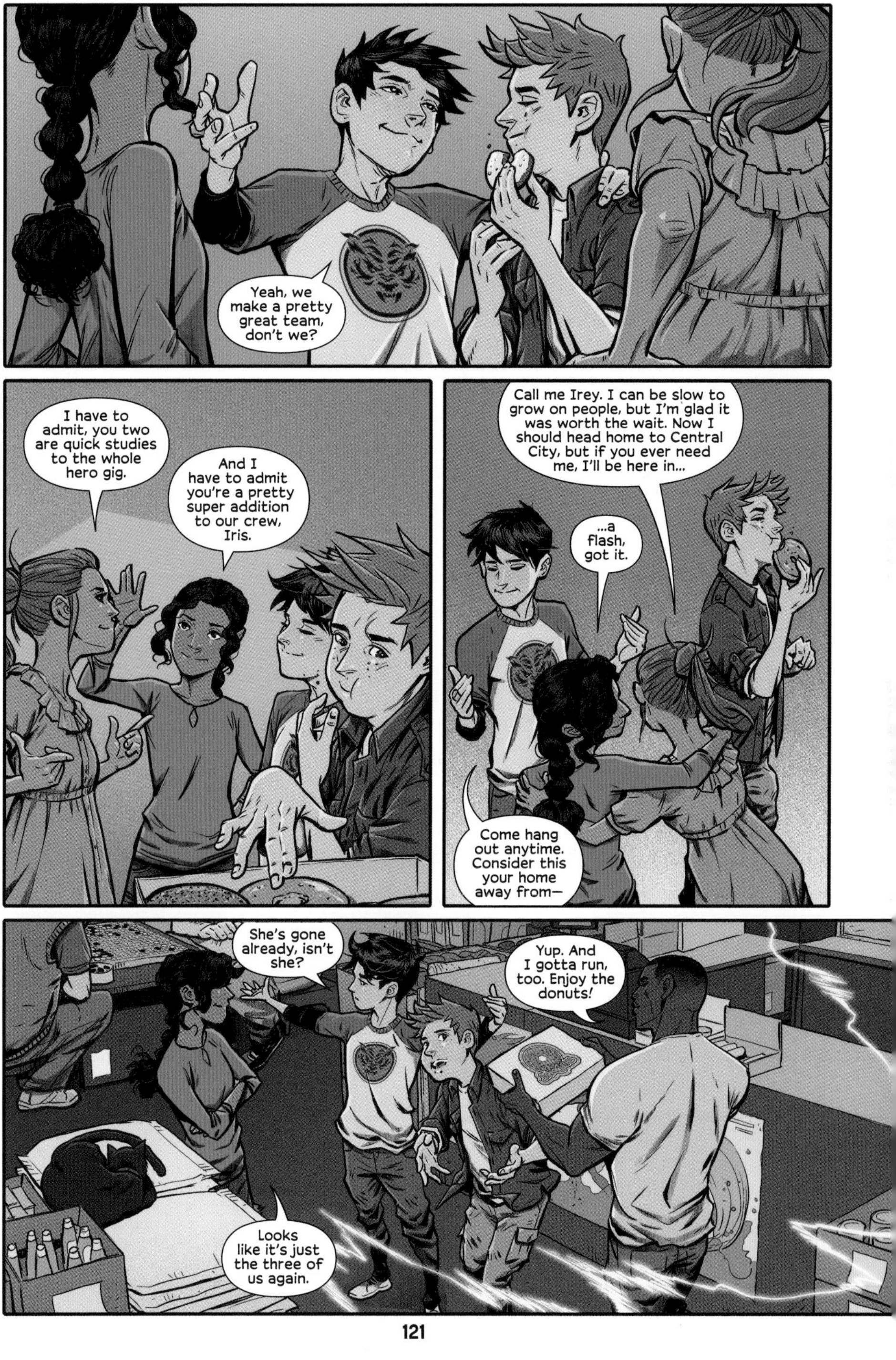
Yeah, we make a pretty great team, don't we?
I have to admit, you two are quick studies to the whole hero gig.
And I have to admit you're a pretty super addition to our crew, Iris.
Call me Irey. I can be slow to grow on people, but I'm glad it was worth the wait. Now I should head home to Central City, but if you ever need me, I'll be here in...
...a flash, got it.
Come hang out anytime. Consider this your home away from—
She's gone already, isn't she?
Yup. And I gotta run, too. Enjoy the donuts!
Looks like it's just the three of us again.

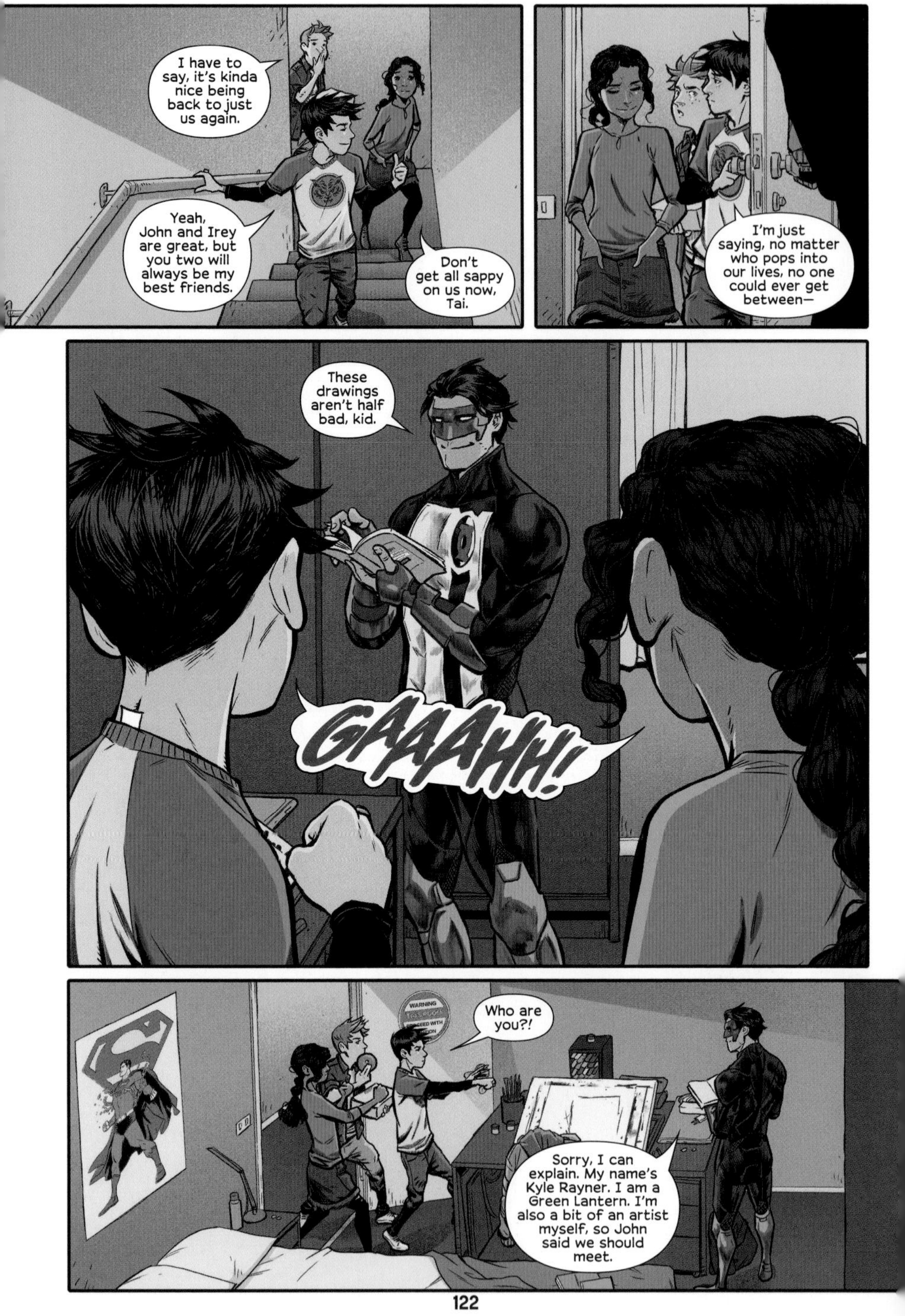
I have to say, it's kinda nice being back to just us again.
Yeah, John and Irey are great, but you two will always be my best friends.
Don't get all sappy on us now, Tai.
I'm just saying, no matter who pops into our lives, no one could ever get between—
These drawings aren't half bad, kid.
GAAAHH!
Who are you?!
Sorry, I can explain. My name's Kyle Rayner. I am a Green Lantern. I'm also a bit of an artist myself, so John said we should meet.

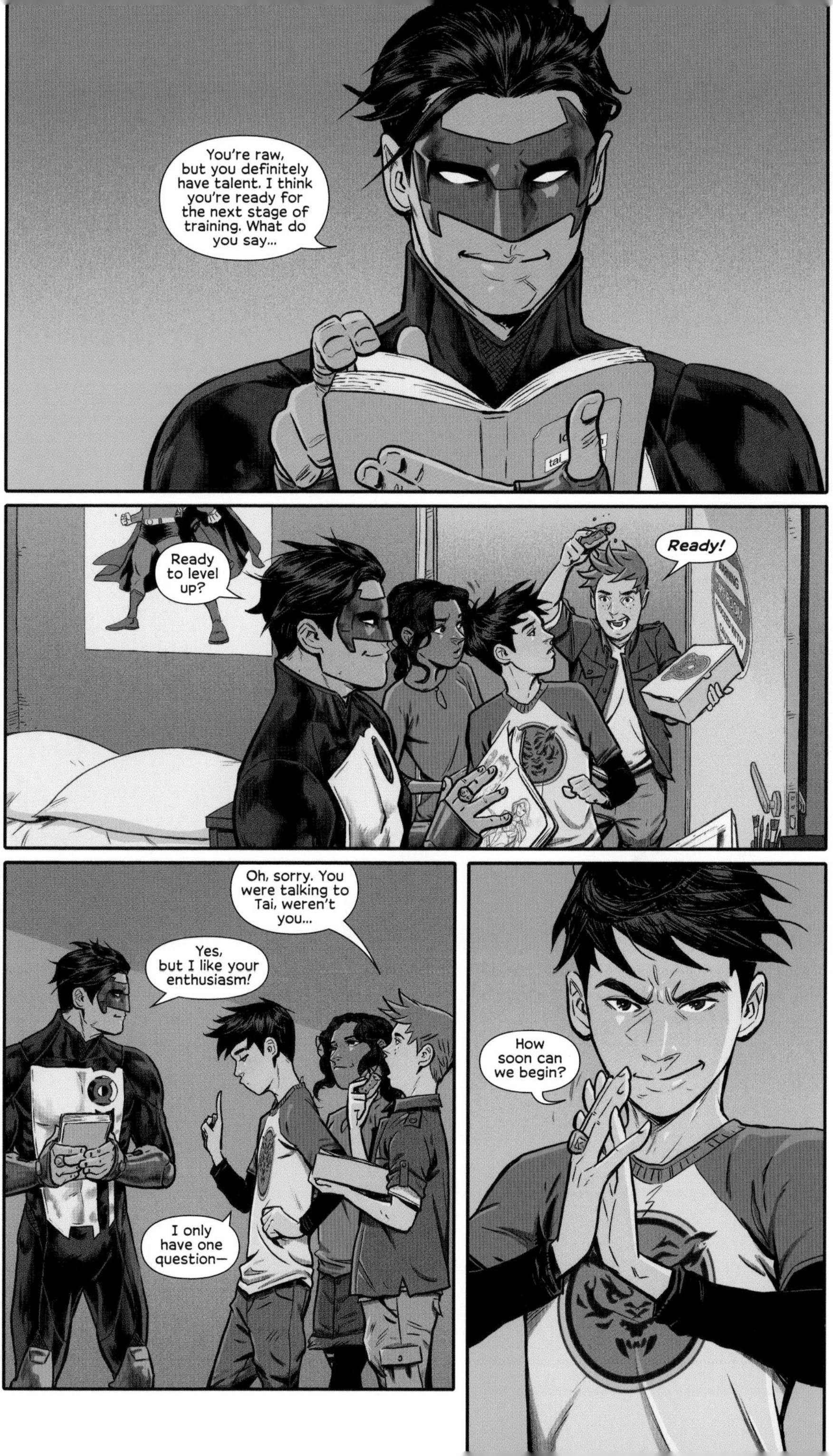
You're raw, but you definitely have talent. I think you're ready for the next stage of training. What do you say...
Ready to level up?
Ready!
Oh, sorry. You were talking to Tai, weren't you...
Yes, but I like your enthusiasm!
I only have one question—
How soon can we begin?

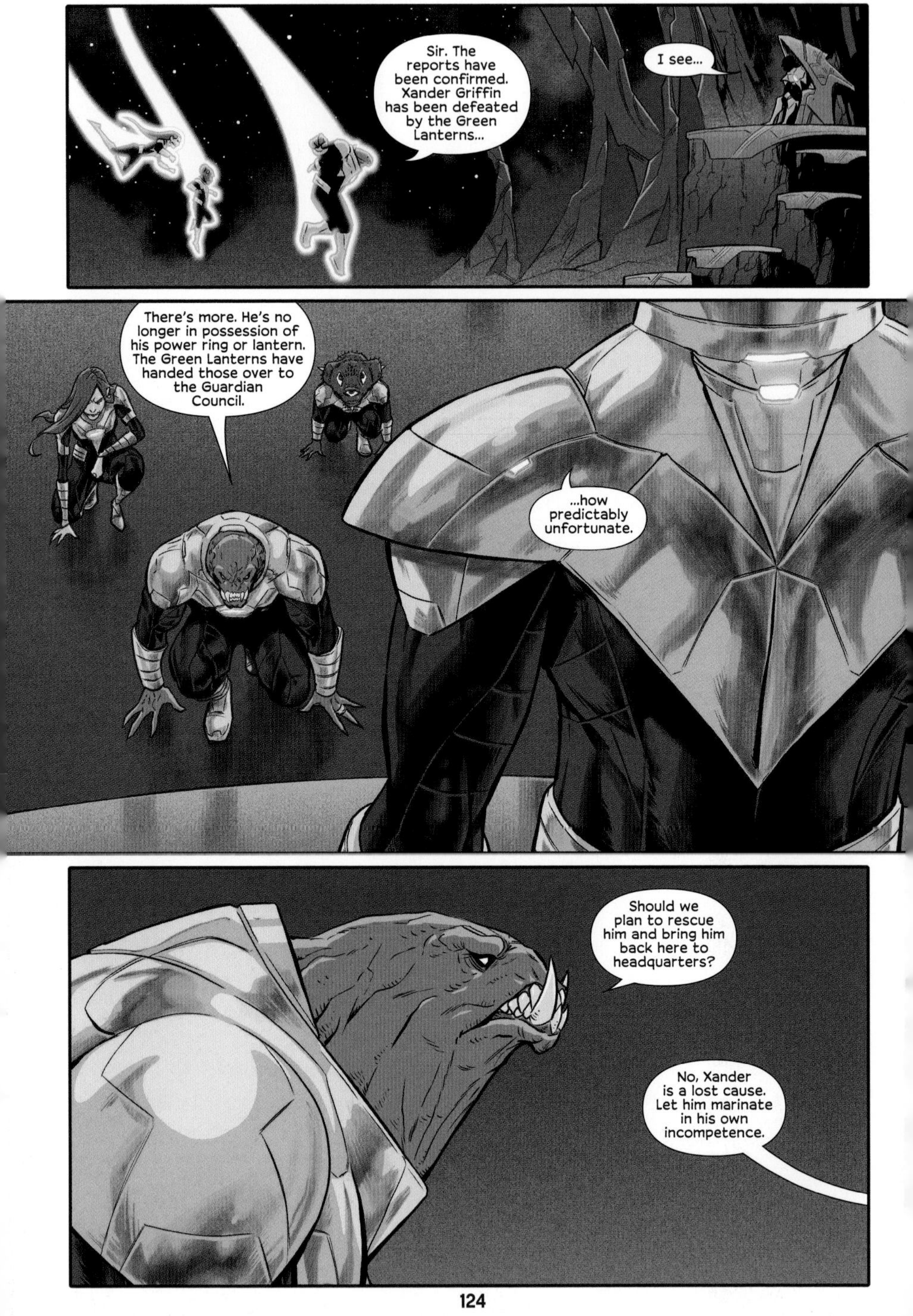
Sir. The reports have been confirmed. Xander Griffin has been defeated by the Green Lanterns...
I see...
There's more. He's no longer in possession of his power ring or lantern. The Green Lanterns have handed those over to the Guardian Council.
...how predictably unfortunate.
Should we plan to rescue him and bring him back here to headquarters?
No, Xander is a lost cause. Let him marinate in his own incompetence.

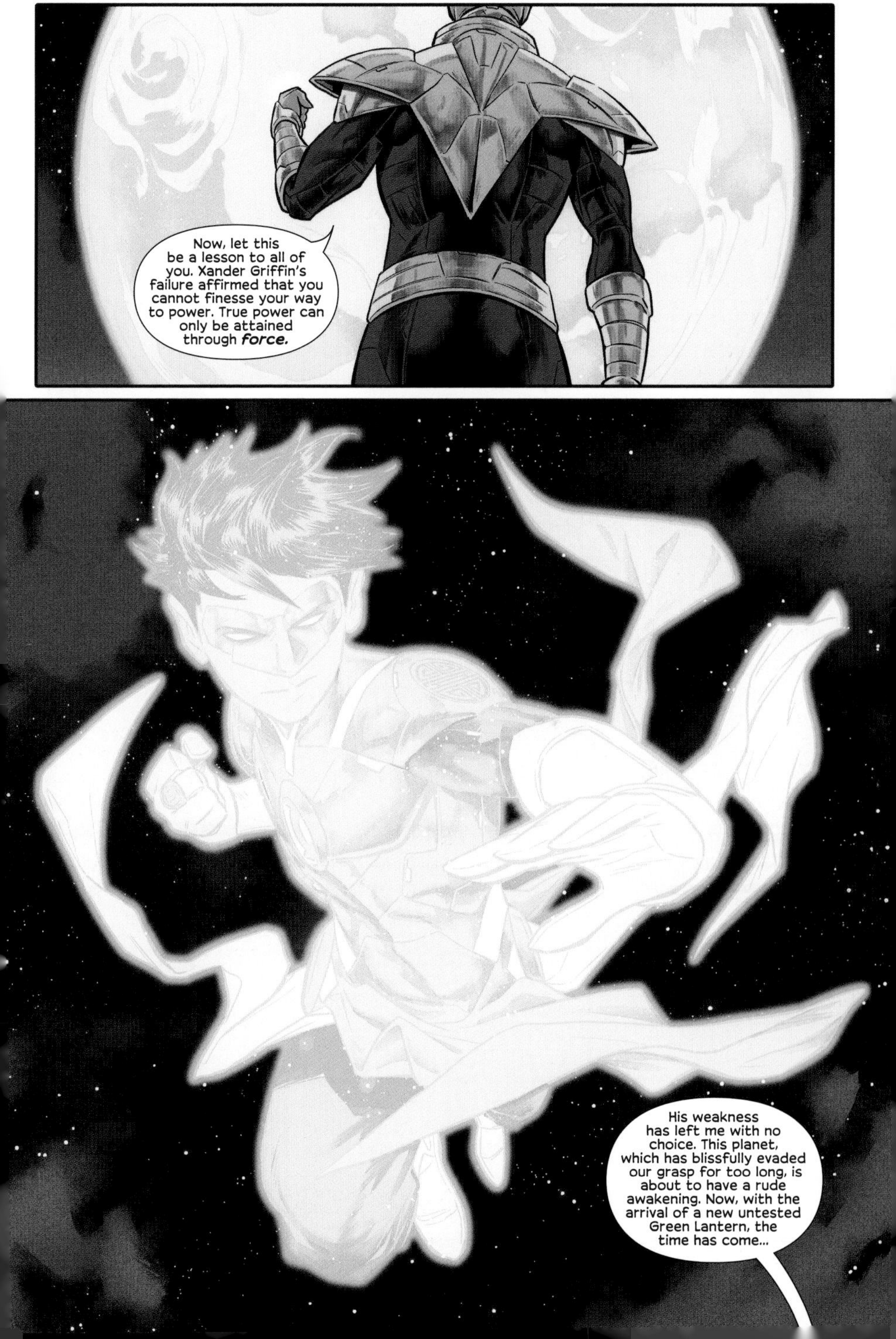
Now, let this be a lesson to all of you. Xander Griffin's failure affirmed that you cannot finesse your way to power. True power can only be attained through *force.*
His weakness has left me with no choice. This planet, which has blissfully evaded our grasp for too long, is about to have a rude awakening. Now, with the arrival of a new untested Green Lantern, the time has come...

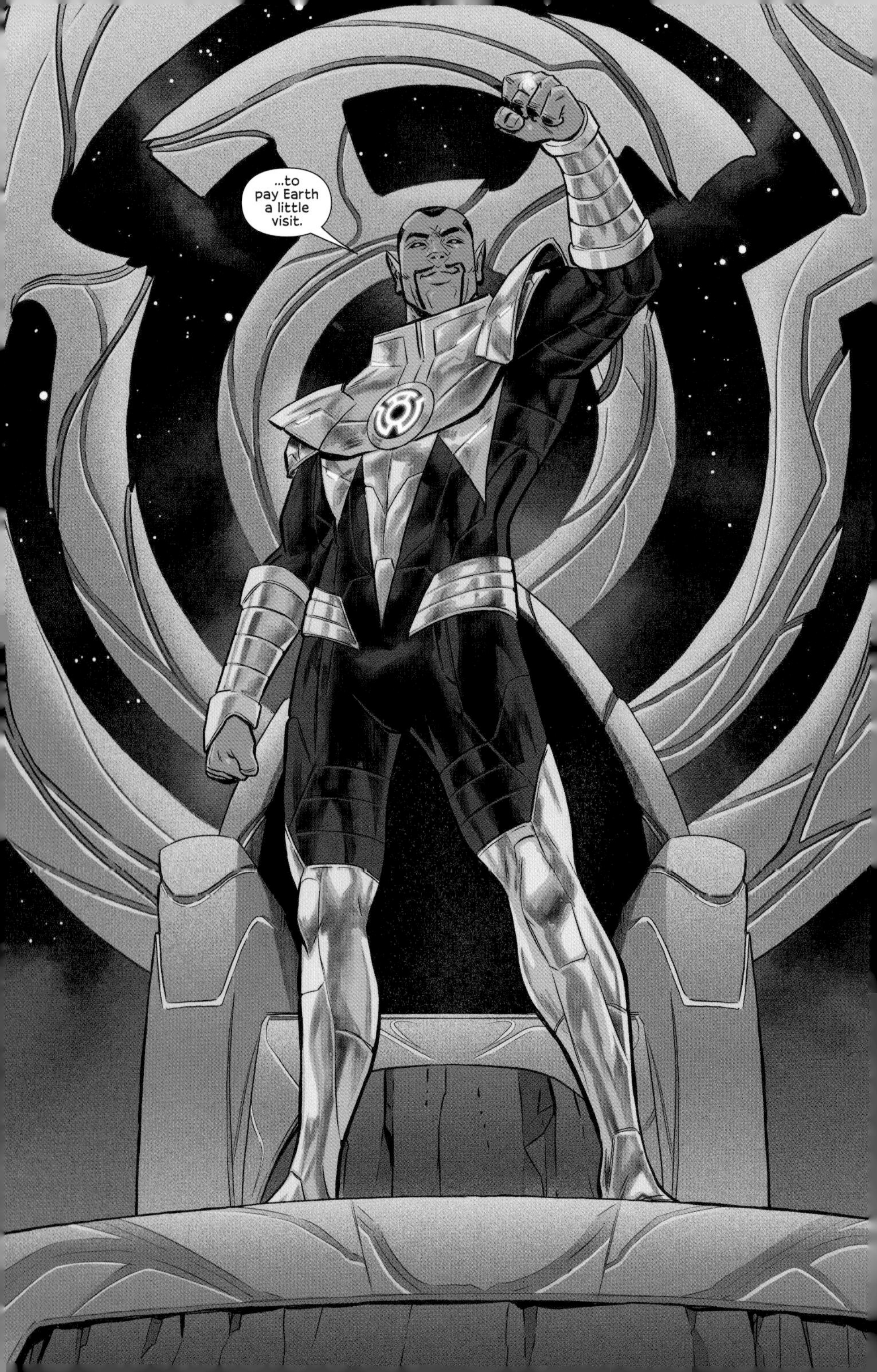
...to pay Earth a little visit.

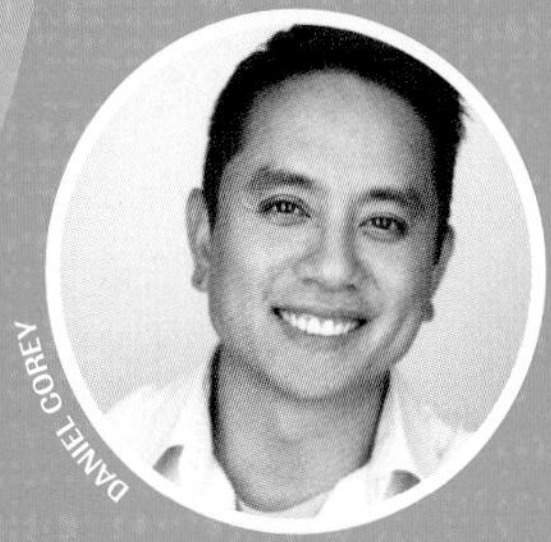
DANIEL COREY

Minh Lê is the author of the graphic novel *Green Lantern: Legacy* and picture books such as *The Blur*, the Eisner-nominated *Lift*, and *Drawn Together*, which was the winner of the 2019 Asian/Pacific American Award for Literature. In addition, he serves on the board of We Need Diverse Books, is on the faculty of the Hamline MFA in Writing for Children and Young Adults, and has written for a variety of national publications, including the Huffington Post, NPR, and the *New York Times*. Outside of spending time with his wonderful wife and children at their home in San Diego, his favorite place to be is in the middle of a good book.

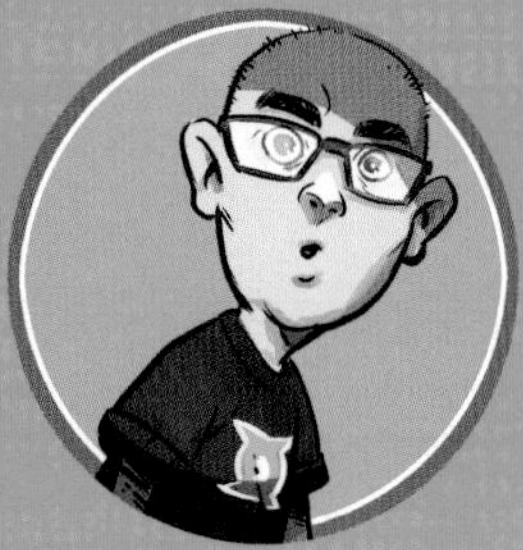

Andie Tong's past comic book and illustration experience includes titles such as *Green Lantern: Legacy*, *Spectacular Spider-Man* (UK), *The Batman Strikes!*, *Tron: Betrayal*, *Plants vs. Zombies*, *Star Wars*, *Tekken*, and Stan Lee's *The Zodiac Legacy*. Andie has also illustrated children's books for HarperCollins for more than 10 years and has had the opportunity to work on multiple books with Stan Lee. Malaysian-born, Andie migrated to Australia at a young age, and then moved to London in 2005. In 2012 he journeyed back to Asia and currently resides in Singapore with his wife and two children.

It's hard enough being in middle school, but it's even worse when you're the only kid at your school who doesn't have superpowers.

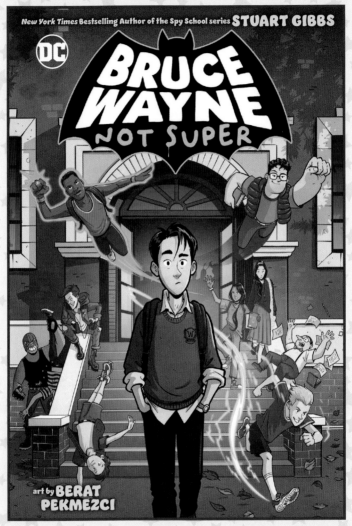

That's the case for poor 13-year-old Bruce Wayne at the Gotham Preparatory School for the Really, Really Gifted, where the struggles of being a non-super are made worse by the presence of so many exceptionally gifted students. He has no hope of winning a race against the future Flash, or a swim meet against the future Aquaman, and he always gets picked last for dodgeball. And when it comes to winning the attention of the most popular girls at school—Diana Prince and Selina Kyle—he figures he stands no chance at all.

Bruce does have a goal though: he wants to make a difference in the world. But how can he do that when he doesn't have any powers?

#1 *New York Times* bestselling author **Stuart Gibbs** (*Spy School*) and artist **Berat Pekmezci** bring readers a fresh and funny twist on the Batman origin story.

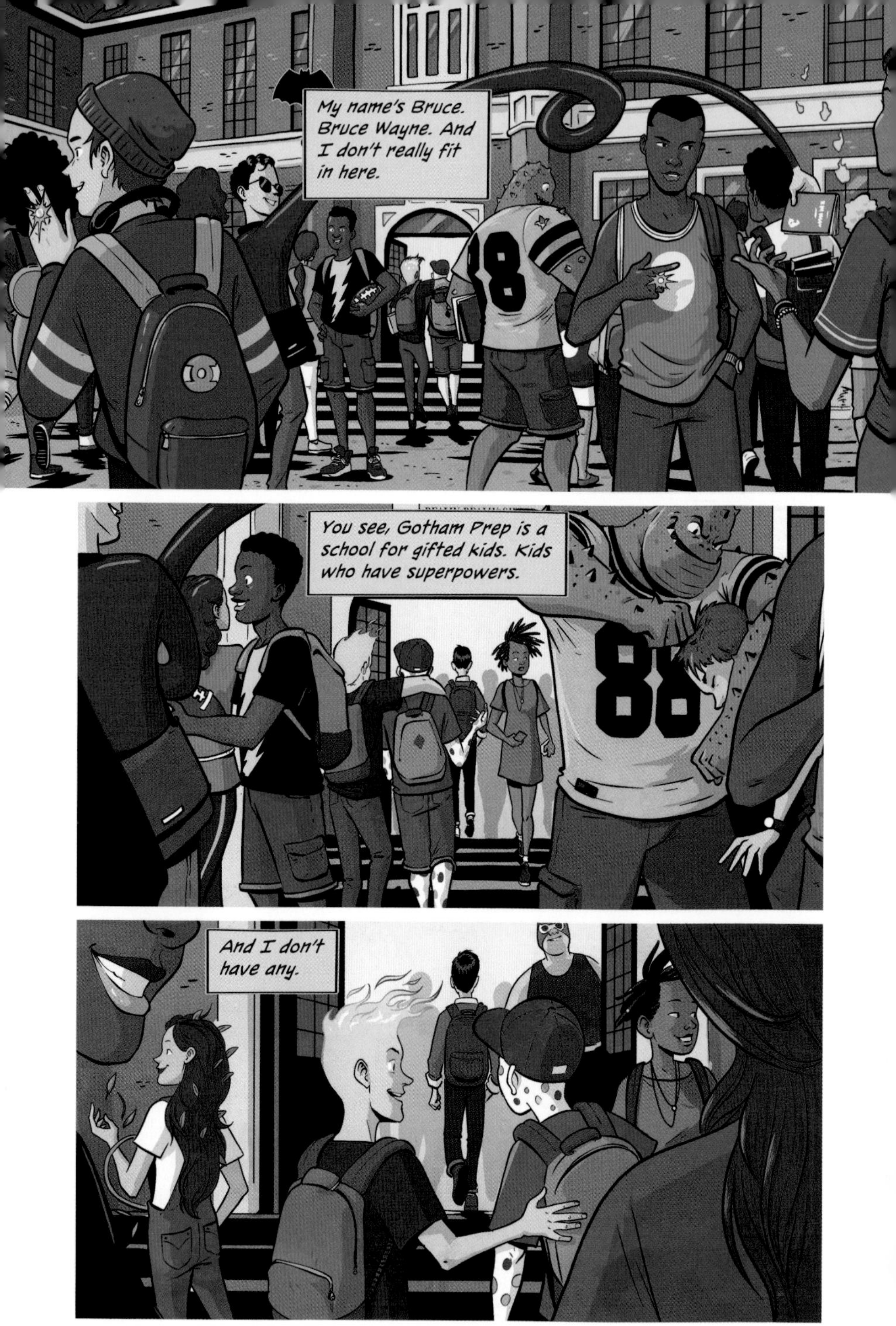
My name's Bruce. Bruce Wayne. And I don't really fit in here.
You see, Gotham Prep is a school for gifted kids. Kids who have superpowers.
And I don't have any.

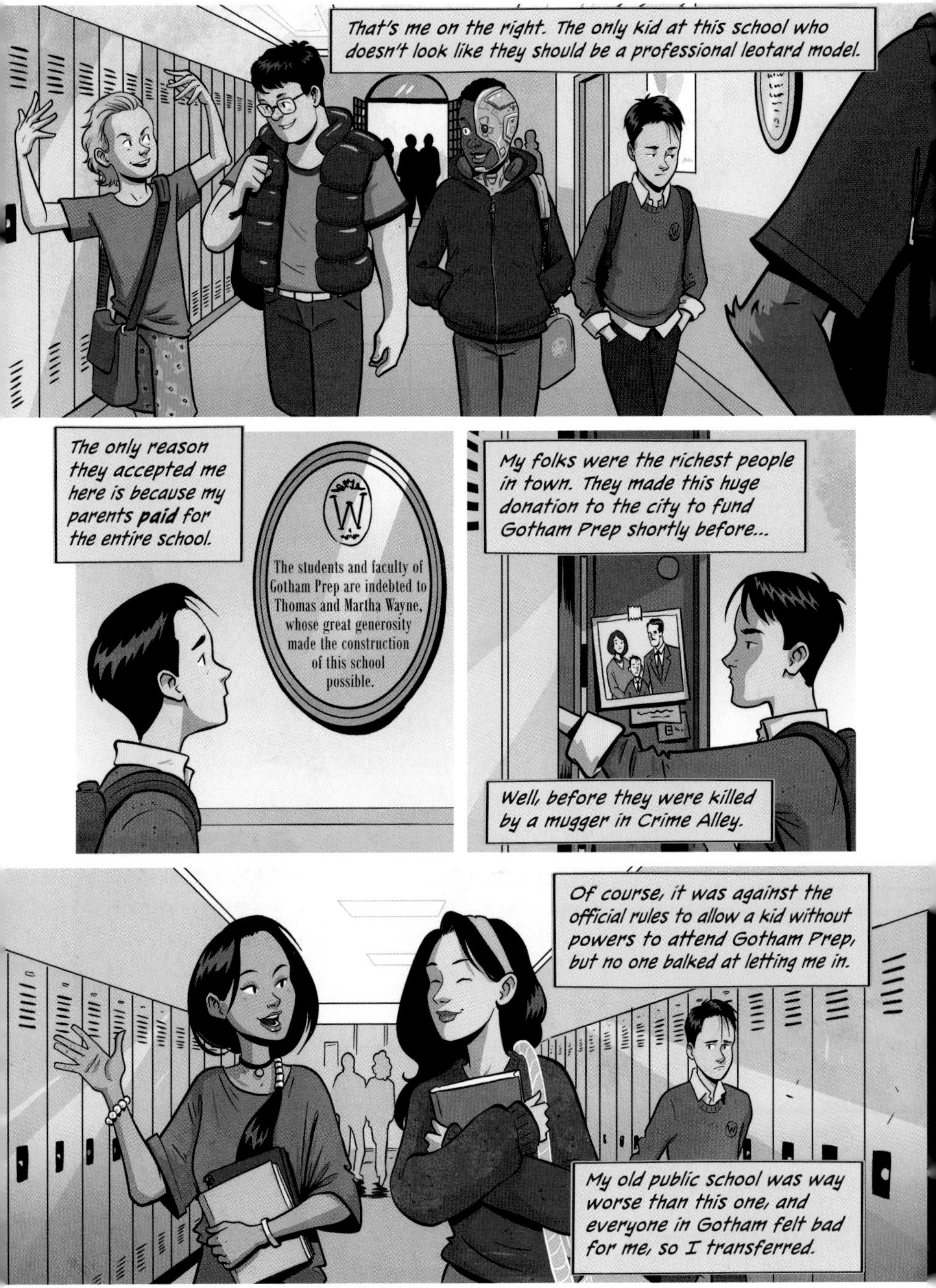
That's me on the right. The only kid at this school who doesn't look like they should be a professional leotard model.
The only reason they accepted me here is because my parents **paid** for the entire school.
The students and faculty of Gotham Prep are indebted to Thomas and Martha Wayne, whose great generosity made the construction of this school possible.
My folks were the richest people in town. They made this huge donation to the city to fund Gotham Prep shortly before...
Well, before they were killed by a mugger in Crime Alley.
Of course, it was against the official rules to allow a kid without powers to attend Gotham Prep, but no one balked at letting me in.
My old public school was way worse than this one, and everyone in Gotham felt bad for me, so I transferred.

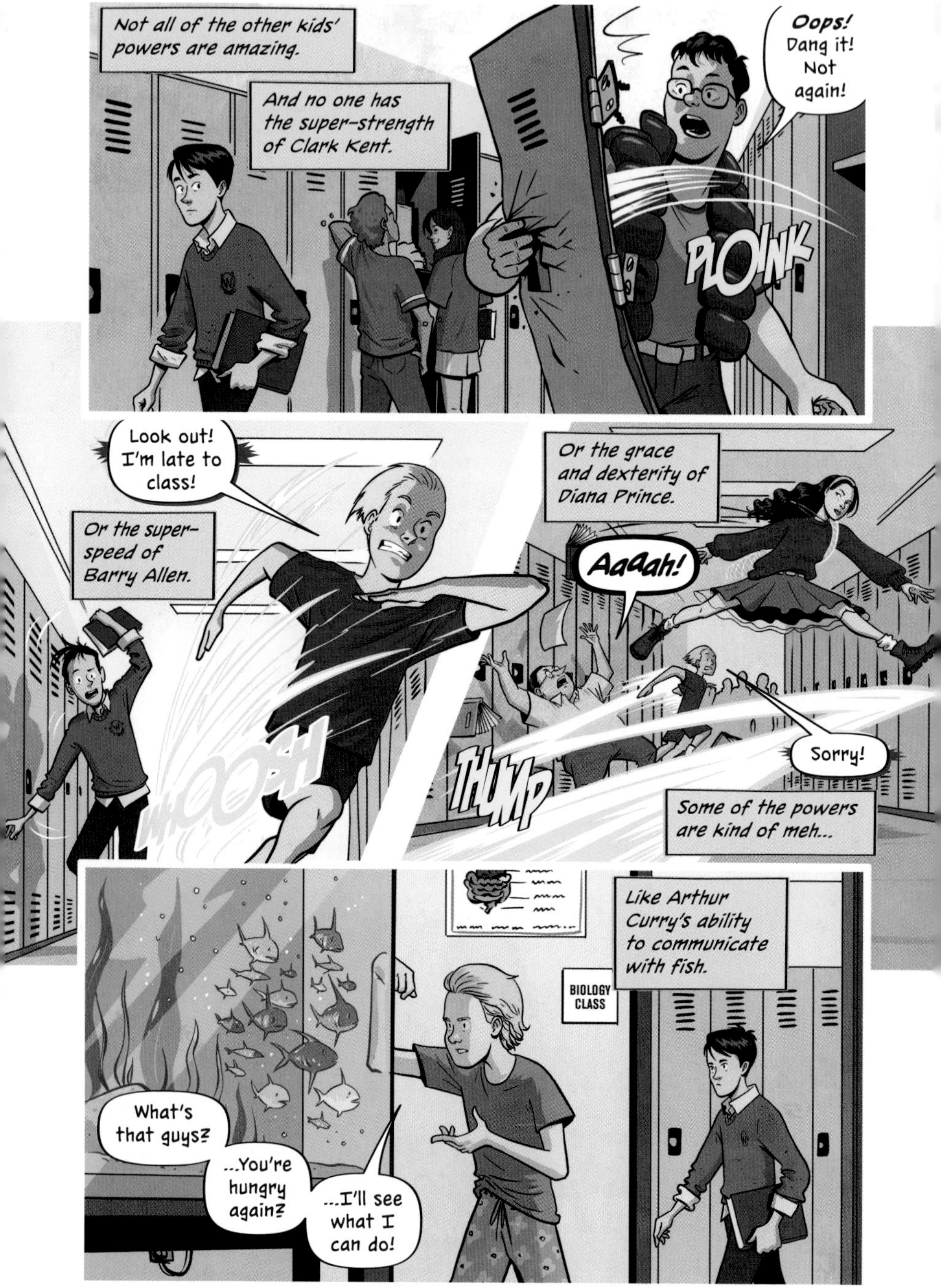
Not all of the other kids' powers are amazing.
And no one has the super-strength of Clark Kent.
Oops! Dang it! Not again!
PLOINK
Look out! I'm late to class!
Or the super-speed of Barry Allen.
WHOOSH
Or the grace and dexterity of Diana Prince.
Aaaah!
THUMP
Sorry!
Some of the powers are kind of meh...
Like Arthur Curry's ability to communicate with fish.
BIOLOGY CLASS
What's that guys?
...You're hungry again?
...I'll see what I can do!

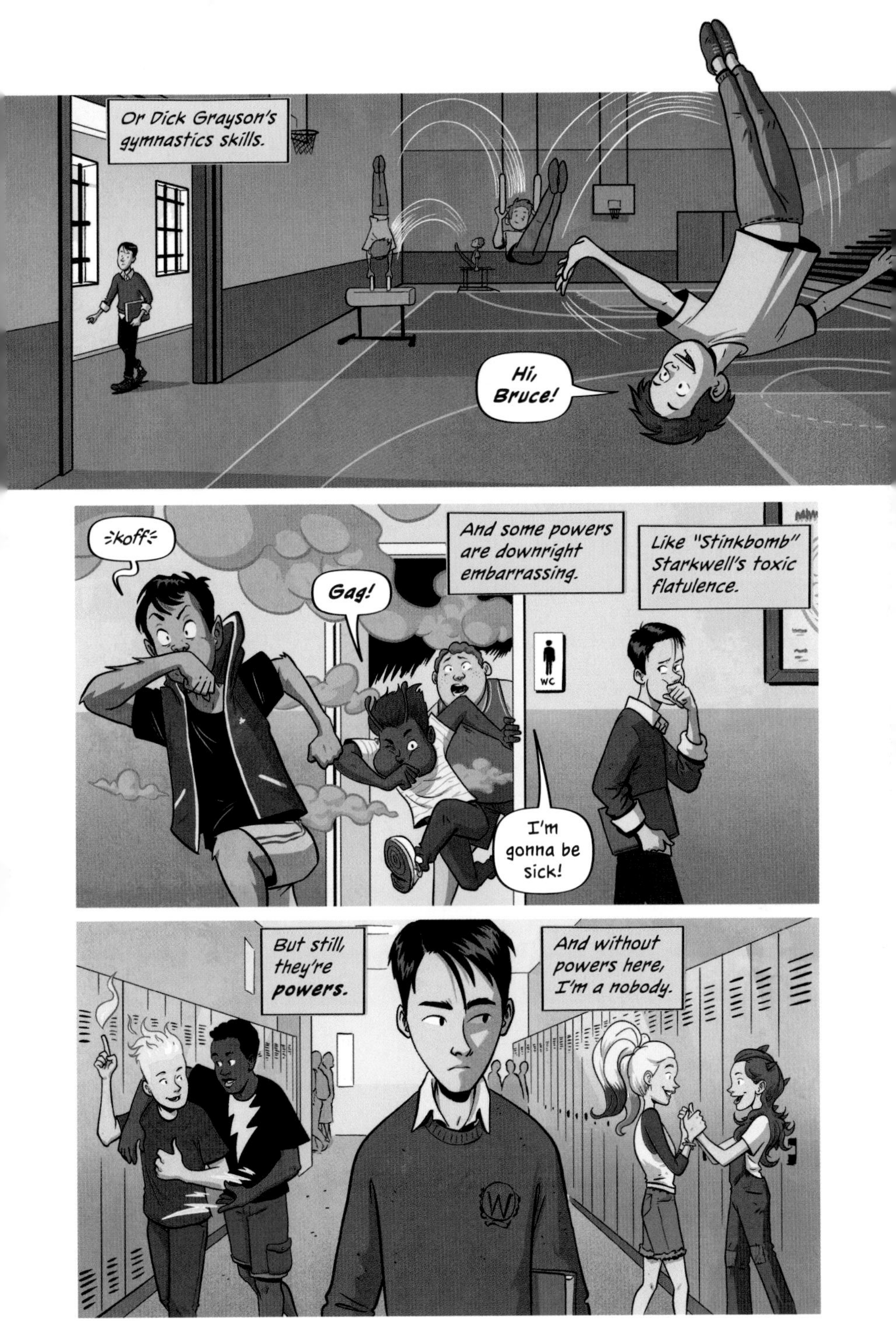
Or Dick Grayson's gymnastics skills.
Hi, Bruce!
koff
And some powers are downright embarrassing.
Like "Stinkbomb" Starkwell's toxic flatulence.
Gag!
WC
I'm gonna be sick!
But still, they're powers.
And without powers here, I'm a nobody.

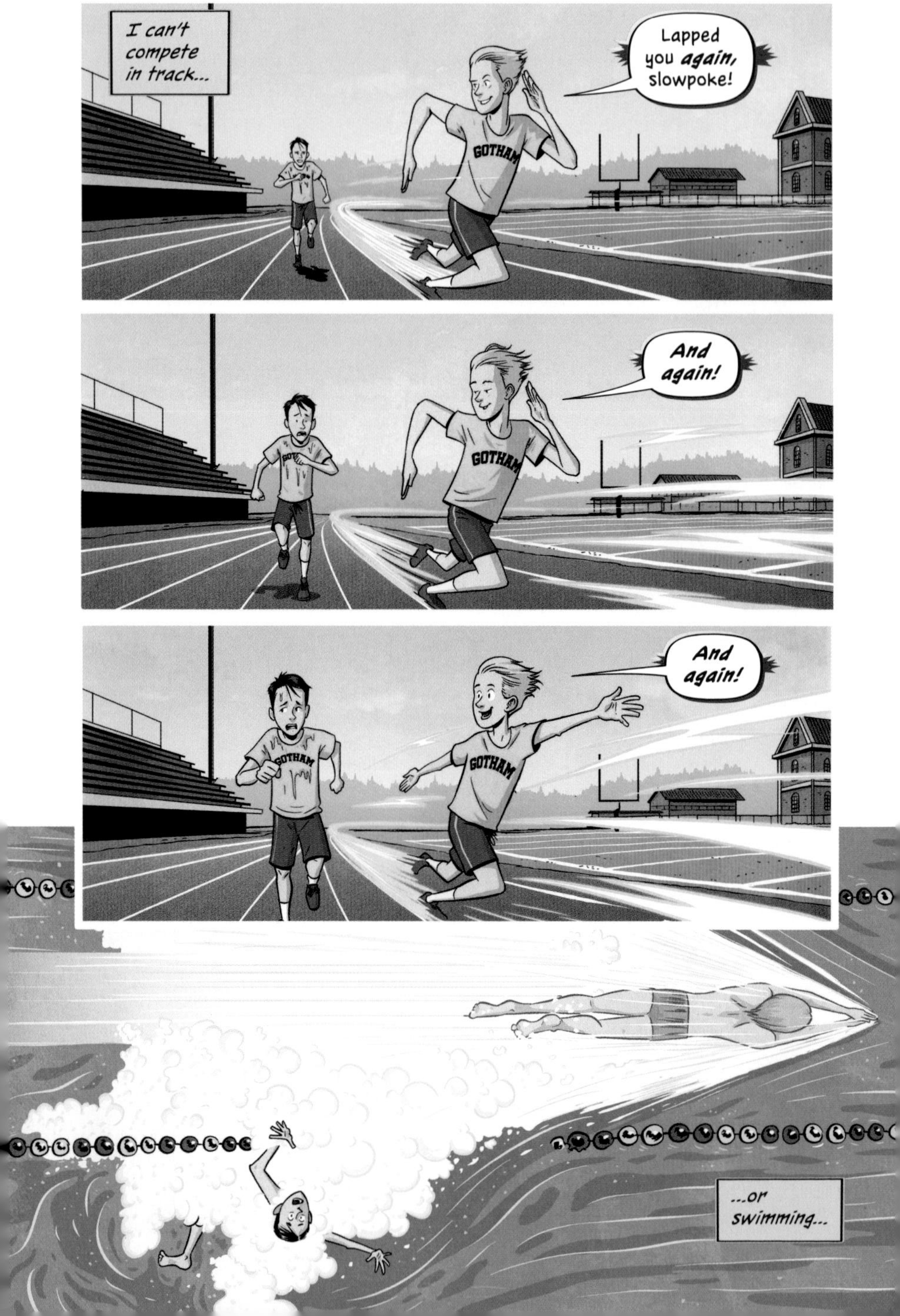

I can't compete in track...
Lapped you *again,* slowpoke!
GOTHAM
And again!
GOTHAM
And again!
GOTHAM
...or swimming...

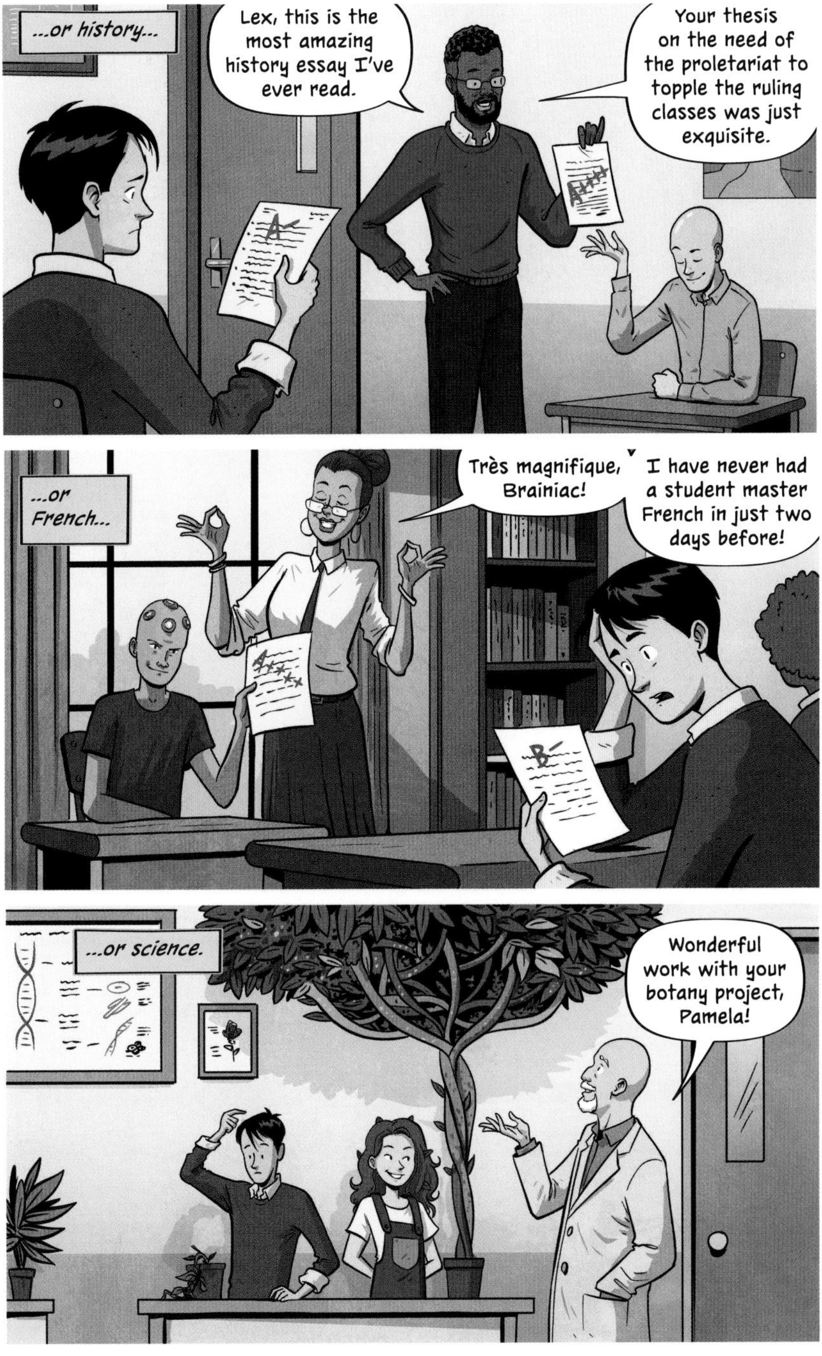
...or history...
Lex, this is the most amazing history essay I've ever read.
Your thesis on the need of the proletariat to topple the ruling classes was just exquisite.
...or French...
Très magnifique, Brainiac!
I have never had a student master French in just two days before!
...or science.
Wonderful work with your botany project, Pamela!

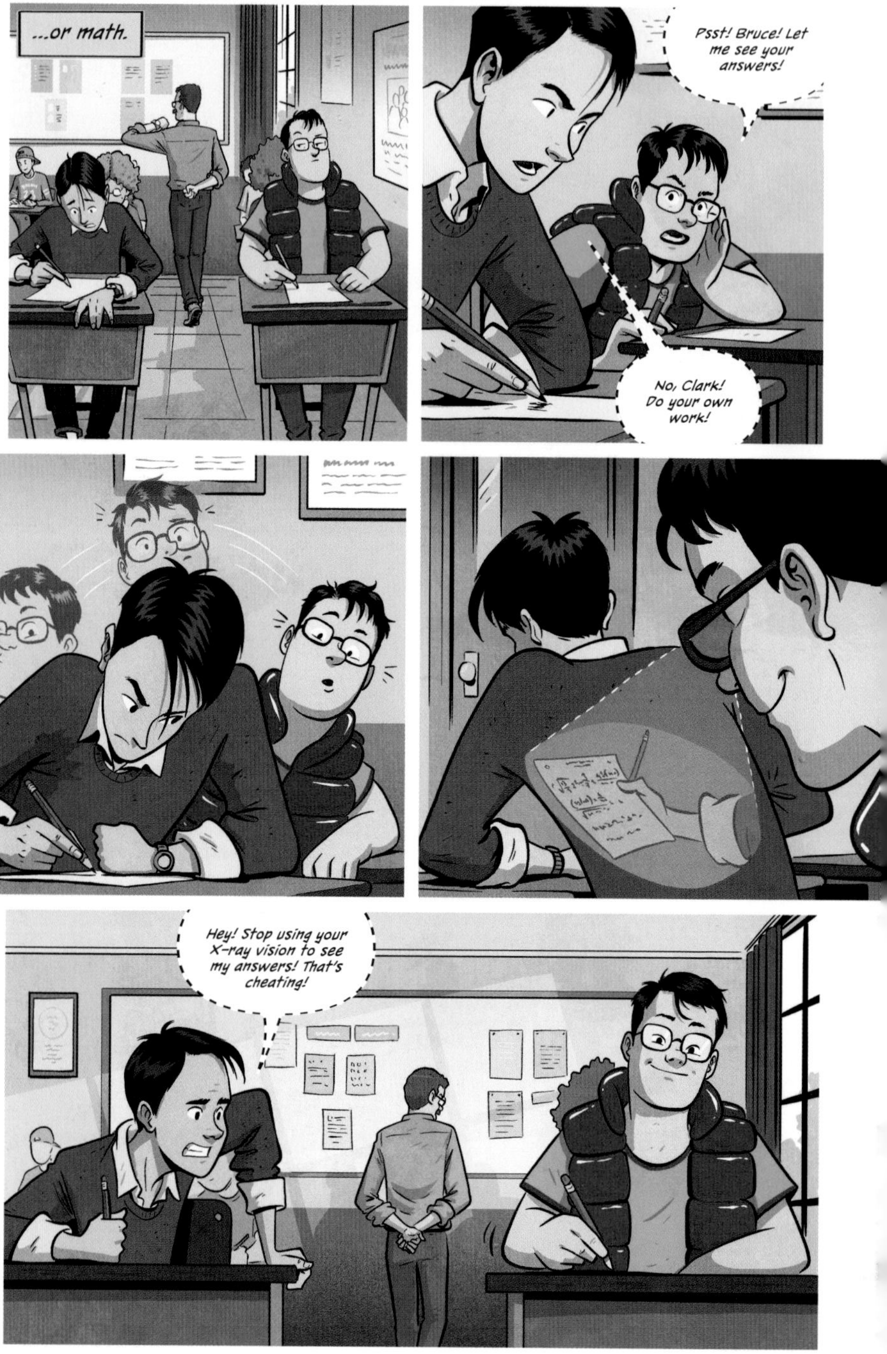
...or math.
Psst! Bruce! Let me see your answers!
No, Clark! Do your own work!
Hey! Stop using your X-ray vision to see my answers! That's cheating!

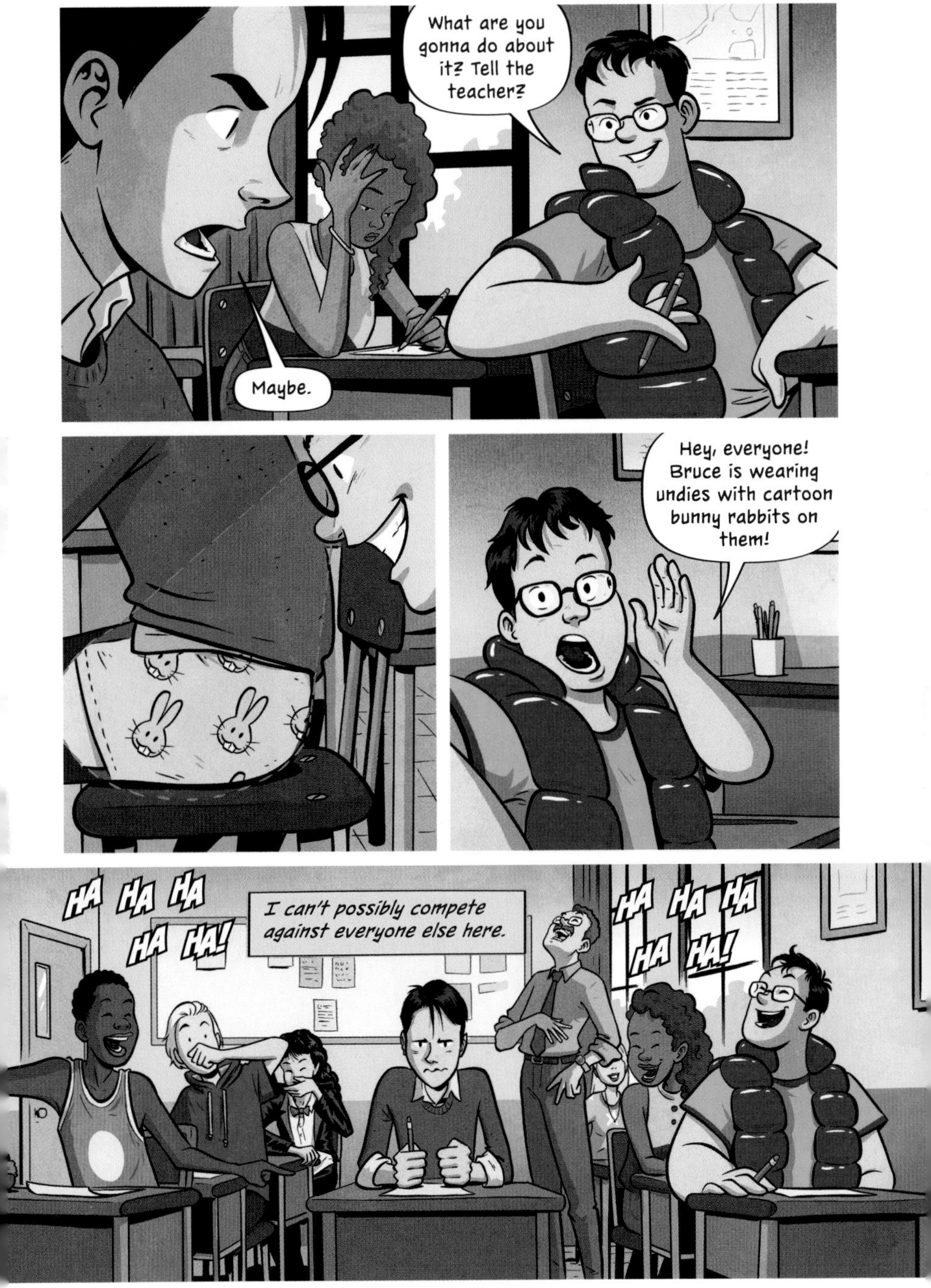
What are you gonna do about it? Tell the teacher?
Maybe.
Hey, everyone! Bruce is wearing undies with cartoon bunny rabbits on them!
HA HA HA HA HA!
I can't possibly compete against everyone else here.
HA HA HA HA HA!

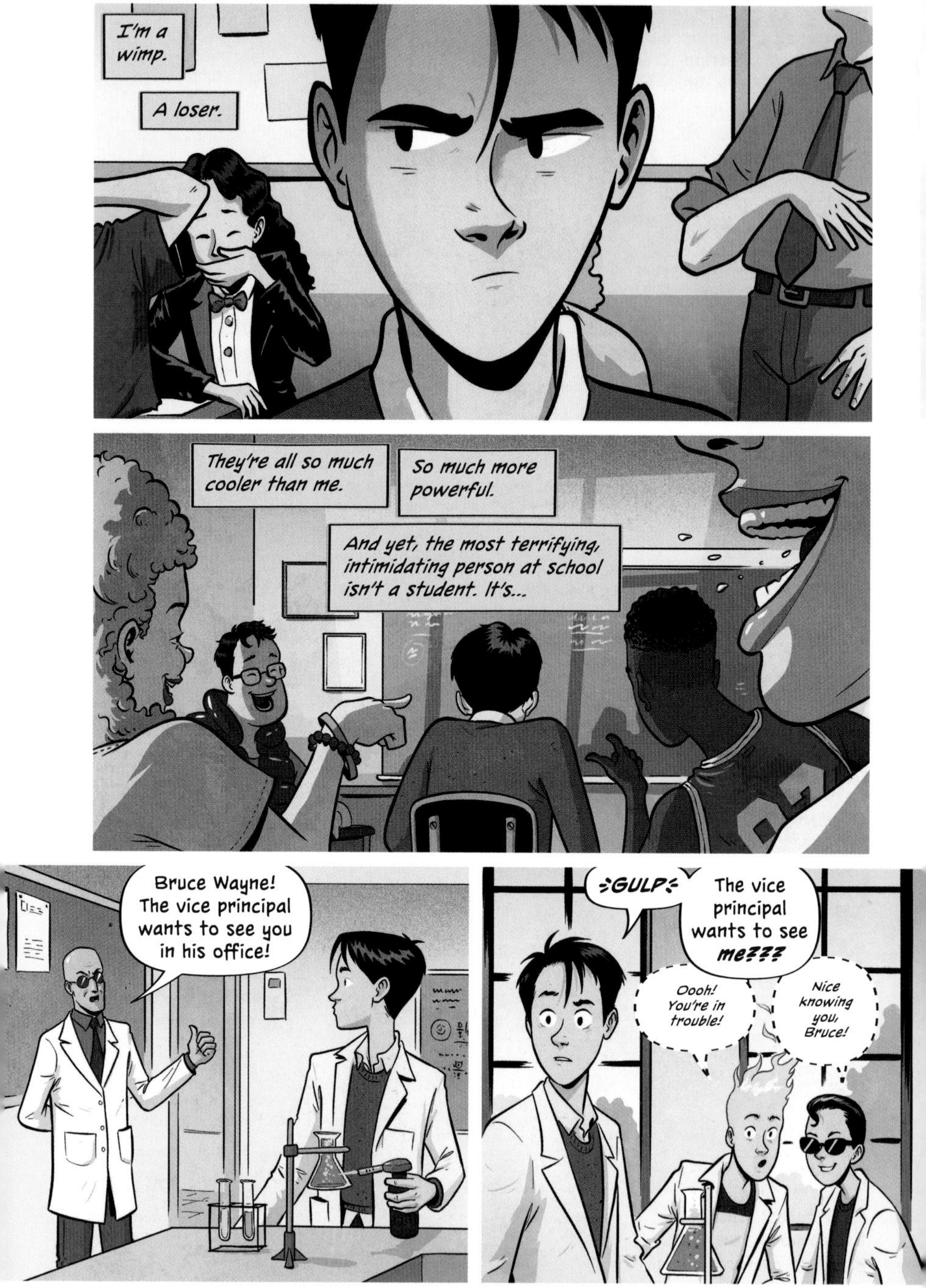
I'm a wimp.
A loser.
They're all so much cooler than me.
So much more powerful.
And yet, the most terrifying, intimidating person at school isn't a student. It's...
Bruce Wayne! The vice principal wants to see you in his office!
GULP
The vice principal wants to see me???
Oooh! You're in trouble!
Nice knowing you, Bruce!

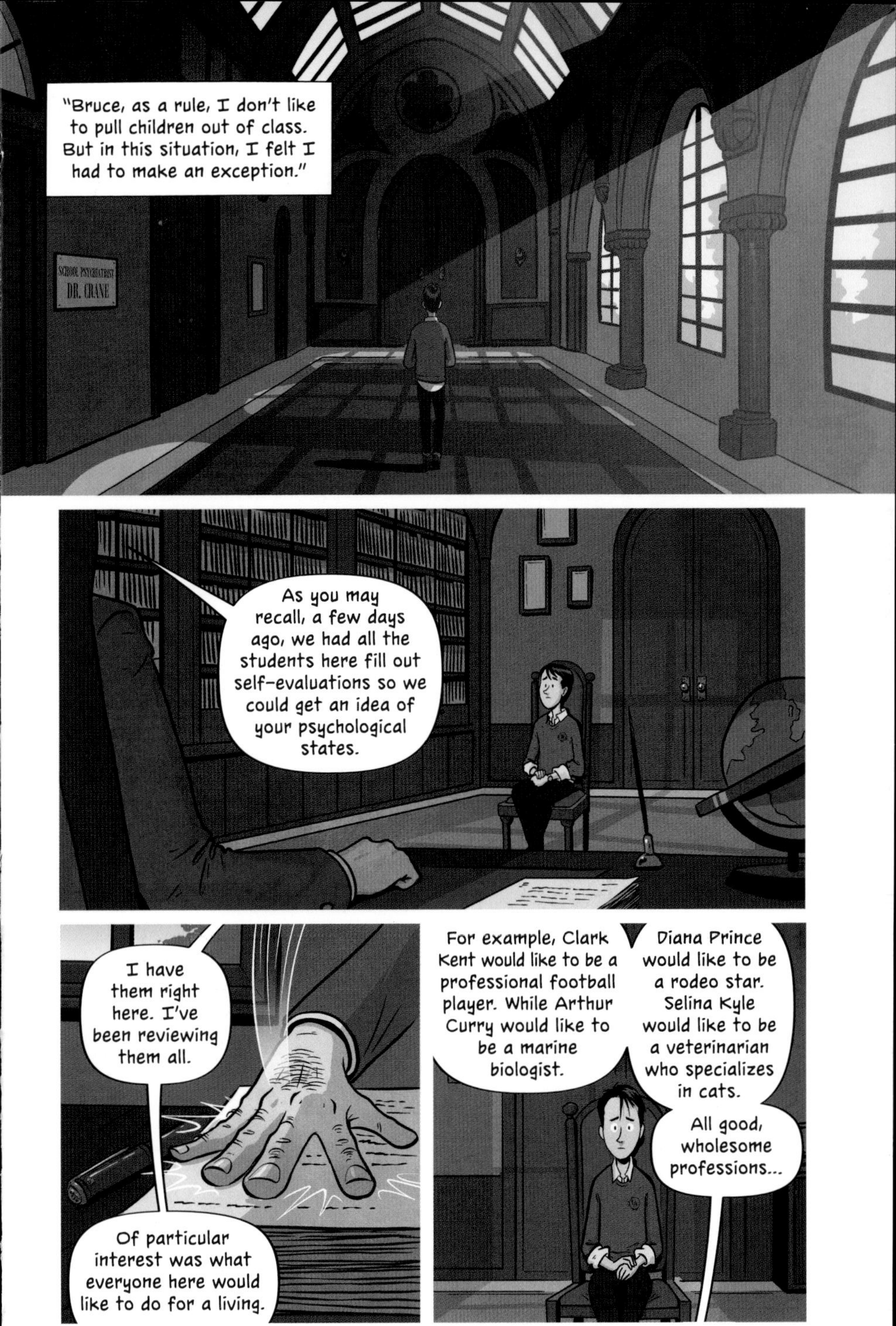
"Bruce, as a rule, I don't like to pull children out of class. But in this situation, I felt I had to make an exception."
SCHOOL PSYCHIATRIST DR. CRANE
As you may recall, a few days ago, we had all the students here fill out self-evaluations so we could get an idea of your psychological states.
I have them right here. I've been reviewing them all.
Of particular interest was what everyone here would like to do for a living.
For example, Clark Kent would like to be a professional football player. While Arthur Curry would like to be a marine biologist.
Diana Prince would like to be a rodeo star. Selina Kyle would like to be a veterinarian who specializes in cats.
All good, wholesome professions...

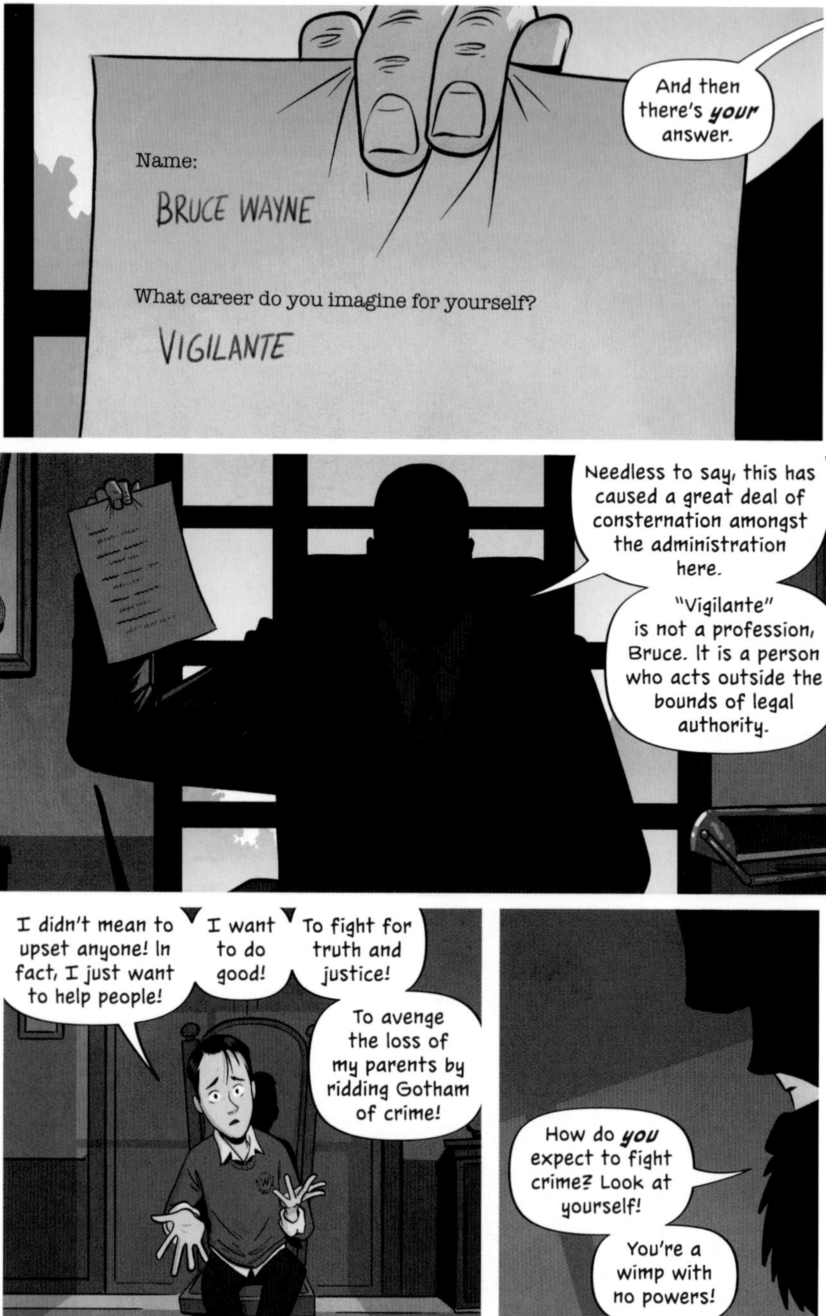
And then there's *your* answer.
Name:
BRUCE WAYNE
What career do you imagine for yourself?
VIGILANTE
Needless to say, this has caused a great deal of consternation amongst the administration here.
"Vigilante" is not a profession, Bruce. It is a person who acts outside the bounds of legal authority.
I didn't mean to upset anyone! In fact, I just want to help people!
I want to do good!
To fight for truth and justice!
To avenge the loss of my parents by ridding Gotham of crime!
How do *you* expect to fight crime? Look at yourself!
You're a wimp with no powers!

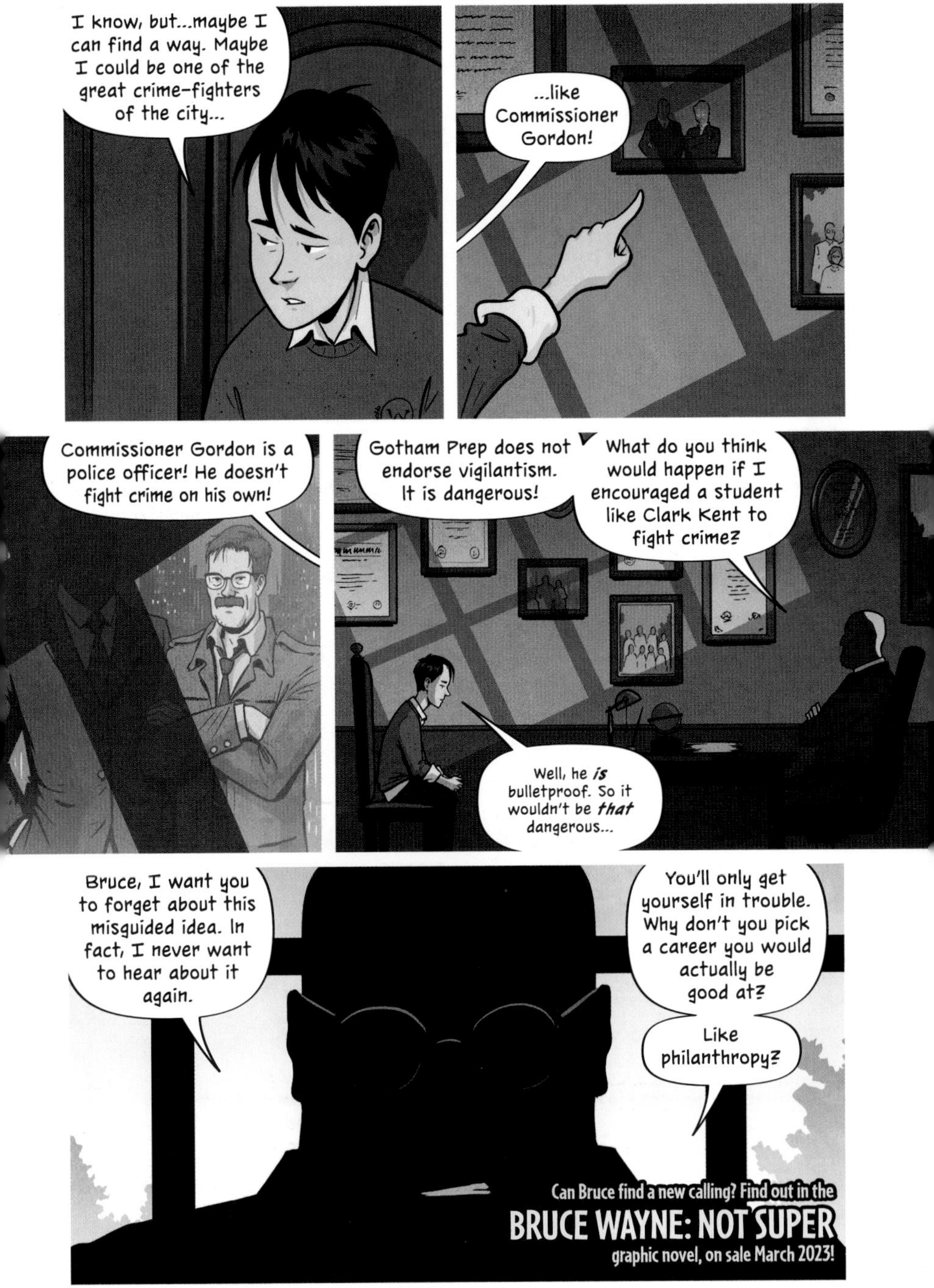
I know, but...maybe I can find a way. Maybe I could be one of the great crime-fighters of the city...
...like Commissioner Gordon!
Commissioner Gordon is a police officer! He doesn't fight crime on his own!
Gotham Prep does not endorse vigilantism. It is dangerous!
What do you think would happen if I encouraged a student like Clark Kent to fight crime?
Well, he *is* bulletproof. So it wouldn't be *that* dangerous...
Bruce, I want you to forget about this misguided idea. In fact, I never want to hear about it again.
You'll only get yourself in trouble. Why don't you pick a career you would actually be good at?
Like philanthropy?
Can Bruce find a new calling? Find out in the
BRUCE WAYNE: NOT SUPER
graphic novel, on sale March 2023!

CHECK OUT THESE STORIES FROM DC BOOKS FOR YOUNG READERS!

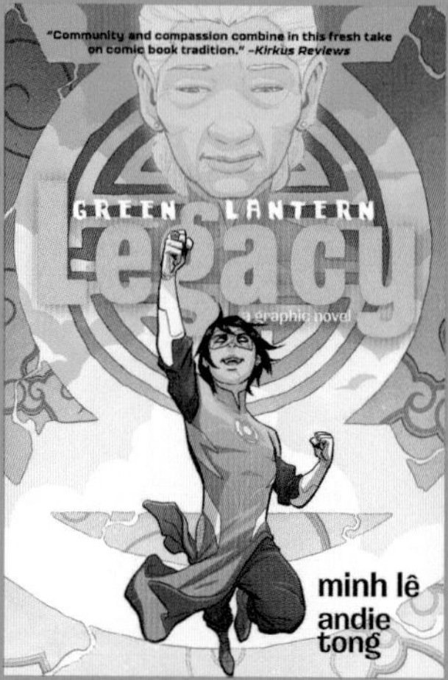
"Community and compassion combine in this fresh take on comic book tradition." –Kirkus Reviews
GREEN LANTERN
Legacy
a graphic novel
minh lê
andie tong

GREEN LANTERN: LEGACY

Minh Lê, Andie Tong

Tai Pham is the Corps' newest Green Lantern and soon learns that being a superhero takes more than just a ring.

ISBN: 978-1-4012-8355-1

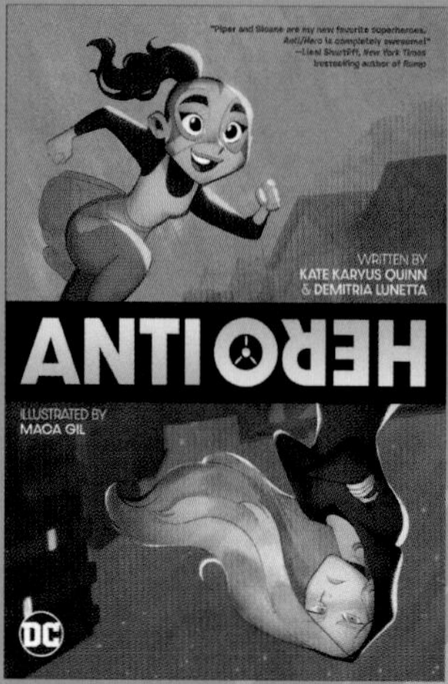
WRITTEN BY
KATE KARYUS QUINN
& DEMITRIA LUNETTA
ANTI HERO
ILLUSTRATED BY
MACA GIL
DC

ANTI/HERO

Kate Karyus Quinn, Demitria Lunetta, Maca Gil

A mission to steal an experimental technological device brings two polar-opposite new supers face to face and switches their bodies! Now they must live in each other's shoes as they figure out a way to switch back.

ISBN: 978-1-4012-9325-3

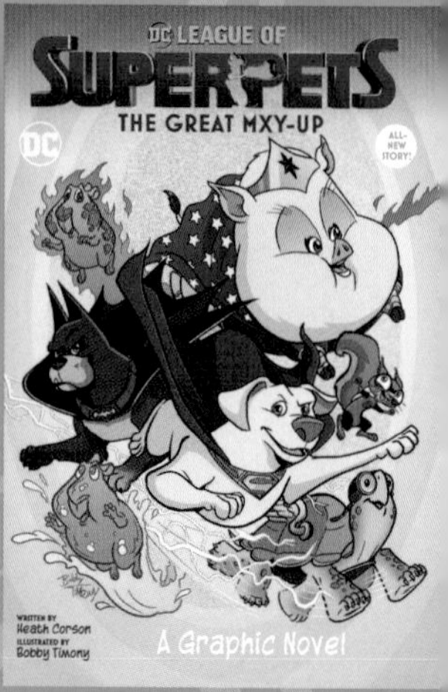
DC LEAGUE OF
SUPER-PETS
THE GREAT MXY-UP
DC
ALL-NEW STORY!
WRITTEN BY Heath Corson
ILLUSTRATED BY Bobby Timony
A Graphic Novel

DC LEAGUE OF SUPER-PETS: THE GREAT MXY-UP

Heath Corson, Bobby Timony

When Mr. Mxyzptlk arrives in Metropolis with a plan to wreak a little chaos and destruction, the Super-Pets will need a plan to prevent Mxy's mischief from destroying the city—while somehow trying to rescue their human counterparts in the process.

ISBN: 978-1-77950-992-5

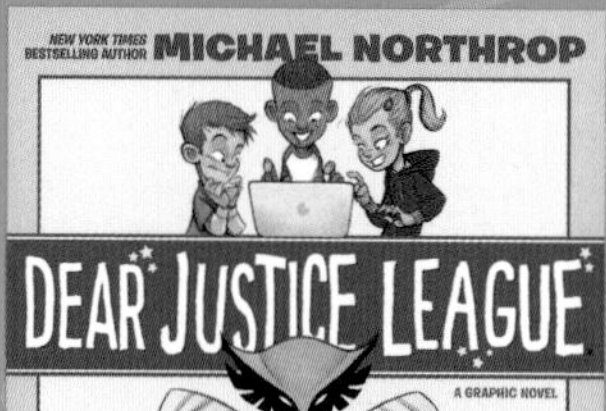
NEW YORK TIMES BESTSELLING AUTHOR MICHAEL NORTHROP
DEAR JUSTICE LEAGUE
A GRAPHIC NOVEL
ILLUSTRATED BY GUSTAVO DUARTE
"Prepare to see superheroes in a whole new way... or, in the case of Aquaman, SMELL them in a whole new way."
—TOM ANGLEBERGER, AUTHOR OF THE ORIGAMI YODA SERIES

DEAR JUSTICE LEAGUE

Michael Northrop, Gustavo Duarte

The greatest heroes in the DC Comics Universe, the Justice League, answer mail from their biggest fans—kids!

ISBN-13: 978-1-4012-8413-8

DEAR DC SUPER-VILLAINS

Michael Northrop, Gustavo Duarte

Peek inside the lives of DC's infamous rogues gallery in the sequel to *Dear Justice League*, where curious kids write to notorious scoundrels about life on the dark side.

ISBN: 978-1-4012-8413-8

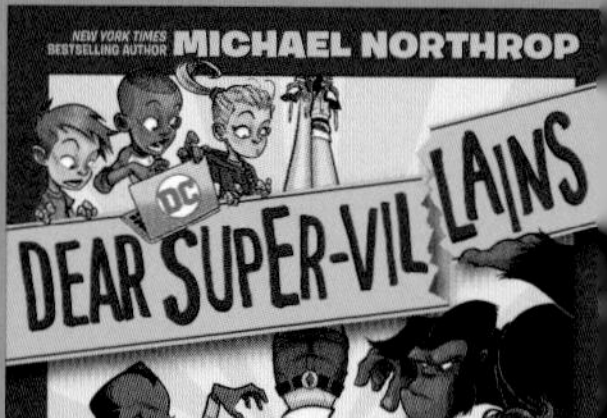
NEW YORK TIMES BESTSELLING AUTHOR MICHAEL NORTHROP
DC
DEAR SUPER-VILLAINS
ILLUSTRATED BY GUSTAVO DUARTE
"Fiendishly funny and wildly entertaining. Being bad has never been so good."
–Jerry Craft, 2020 Newbery Medal-winning author of New Kid